# Everybody Left Behind

## 4 minutes to chaos

bv

D0880281

LEARNED & HERSHAL
PUBLISHING

Copyright © 2015 by Time O. Day

ISBN 978-1-933151-02-1

Printed in the United States of America


Published by Learned and Hershal Publishing
U.S.A.

To that Jewish Carpenter,
who saw me as more than a tile man.

# Contents

# The Wrong End

Have you ever been inside a room and felt as if some-one was peering through a window, watching you? This apprehension crept in while I was eating supper one night with my wife Priscilla. Halfway into my meal, I was tempted to get up and flush out this bogeyman. What held me back was the enticement of a well-cooked piece of elk and fresh vegetables from our garden. But it was strange how strong a presence I sensed on the other side of the sun-room's darkened glass. It was even stranger that someone would peek in our window when we lived out in the woods, some thirteen miles from Charby, Montana.

Savoring a caramelized piece of onion, I asked Priscilla, "Did you see anyone in your travels that might have followed you?"

"No. Why do you ask?"

"I just have this sense that someone's looking at us right now."

She lifted her head to take in the kitchen window opposite her. "It could be Eli," she said hopefully.

Eli was our 24-year-old adopted son.

"You'd think he'd be in here eating supper with us. He loves elk." I chewed away, going along with her dreamy wish that he'd somehow appear, somehow come back into our lives. "It'd be nice to see him." Then disappointment led. "Who are we fooling? ... That boy's a ghost." Those prying suspicions returned and I had to stop myself from looking toward the sunroom. "I'd like to do something to catch this sneaky peek, if in fact he's real."

"Do what?"

"What do you think about going over and do something, say, by the fireplace?" I pushed my glasses up. "In the meantime, I'll go around the house and flush him out."

She looked perplexed, rubbing her fingers over her neck. "Do something?"

"Do something kind of flirty so the Peeping Tom's attention will be fixed on you. In the meantime, he won't notice me sneaking up behind."

"It doesn't sound proper." Concerned, she drew her sweater in.

"Can't you wave your hair about? Act real …"

Looking for the right word, I put a dab of butter on my cornbread, blankly stared at the butter melting in and considered my 59-year-old wife doing something showy. She's not one who can be tricked into something, at least not easily, but in imagining this I started to grin.

She flared, "I'm not doing a thing."

"Goodness." I tried to shut my big mouth.

Indignant, she shook her head. "Forget it."

"I'm sorry I even mentioned it, but there's someone looking in our window. I can feel him there …" I was tempted to look at that window "… now."

"Which one?" She turned toward the sunroom window.

"Priscilla, can you not look?" Thankfully she turned her head back to her plate. "I'd like to catch him." I pitched my chin toward the kitchen counter. "What if you get the coffee can of cash and set it on the kitchen counter, then start pulling out the cash?"

She frowned. "Why should we be showing everybody where our money is?"

"While he's watching you, I'll go around the house and whack him good enough that he won't know what money is." I arose. "Can you help?"

I think she thought this whole thing was kind of a skit or a school play because, after she got the coffee can out and placed it on the kitchen counter, she palmed it like a cat, clicking her fingernails across it, simply going through the motions to appease me. I was just the opposite, under a cloak of seriousness, near the back door, in an area shielded from the Peeping Tom, holding a club in one hand and gathering up a short-barreled shotgun in the other.

"Could you take the money out of the can slow enough to give me time to get around the house? And do it maybe with kind of flair."

"Flair?"

I rolled my eyes, thinking it was no use trying to inspire my lovely wife, who is one straight arrow and even looked like the town's librarian. But she surprised me with an artful toss of her shoulder-length silvery hair, ending with a playful smile. Awestruck, I returned her fun with an awkward lift of the club, giving her a thumbs-up before I snuck out the back door.

The shotgun I carried wasn't the type you'd want to be on the wrong end of. The first round was a slug, and the following was buckshot. This gun had an extended tube that held extra rounds, and a light at the end of the barrel that was activated by a squeeze switch. But the light switch dangled haphazardly, as I hadn't found a way to secure it because of the pump action.

As I crept around a bush, I felt the coolness of October, letting my bald head know of winter's approach. I'm not too bad in sneak mode, though far from perfect; this is especially true of my shooting abilities. The previous fall I used no end of ammo shooting at elk and deer, only to have them run off scot-free. I did have the good fortune, however, to get a quarter of an elk from our neighbor, Paul, who we allowed to hunt on our land.

This particular evening I had good balance and my slippers were quiet. By the glow of the house lights, I moved slowly, carefully stepping over rocks, tiptoeing around sage bushes toward the sunroom window. I reached the southeast corner of the house and waited, giving Priscilla time to add some flair to the cash in our coffee can. I can't speak for the bogeyman, but I still get aroused by her; she still has a nice figure, even after having three kids.

Most of my suspicions end up nothing but suspicions, so much so that they are humorous. But as I slowly moved my head around the corner of the house, my breath caught at the silhouette of a husky man. His presence was so shocking that my arm muscles began to twitch and tremble. A jolt of nervous protective instinct coursed through me. I wanted to club this dirty sneak. It didn't matter that he was ten years younger, stronger, and towered above the planter box that was two feet above the ground.

My peripheral vision caught something to my left, but a quick glance dismissed it. My focus snapped back to the big man. He was having my wife as he touched himself. My blood boiled at the sight of that pervert.

Any clarity of mind I had in attacking a brute who outweighed me by at least 100 pounds was overshadowed by the territorial bulldog inside me that wouldn't put up with anyone messing with my gal. I fisted the club tightly and took a step toward him. I didn't care if I broke his leg or bashed his head; as far as I was concerned, anyone who was foolhardy enough to sneak into a 160-acre property with No Trespassing, Keep Out signs and peek in a window at my wife, needed to be clubbed!

While I crept toward him, I wasn't thinking of what would happen if things went south, or of any consequences whatsoever. I inched forward step by step, intensely conscious of the slightest sound. The concrete planter box ran the length of the sunroom. His backside towered above it. The two-foot club in my right hand was raised and ready; the shotgun in my left hand was hot.

Six feet from him I lunged and swung the club at his leg. It struck with a wallop just above his knee. There was no snapping sound but the events that unfolded were like a tower crumpling so fast that I actually ended up breaking his fall.

Coming out of unconsciousness, I blinked, feeling a heavy weight pressing into me. I didn't know where I was, but I saw an upside-down view of windows. I didn't even know whose house the windows were attached to; my eyes registered a tiny glow in the distance, then returned to the windows. In an instant my mind cleared, and fear set my heart racing.

I felt like I was at the bottom of a rugby scrum, struck by a cattle prod. Above me a scramble ensued—the dark, shadowy movement of legs. I heard a painful gasp and glimpsed the reflection of a metal object. A knife?

I started to sit up but something hit my face with such force it numbed my nose, knocked my glasses off and sent me into the dirt. The world again turned fuzzy. Something warm sprayed my hand.

Fearing for my life, I gasped, "Hit him, Stan!"

Though my brother, Stan, lived some 700 miles away, I needed the lug to think there were others around. Confused, I saw movement in front of me, yet heard something behind. As I rolled over, a sharp pain seared through my lower back. I patted about in the dirt for my gun and heard the clatter of rocks down the hill.

At last I found the weapon. From there, it was a race to activate its light. Goodness, that darn cord wasn't leaping into my palm. Finally, I found the light switch. Light glowed.

I bent toward a reflected gleam in the dirt, hoping it was my glasses. Snagging them, I was disappointed that one side was broken off. As I rose to my feet, I noticed blood on my hand and sweatshirt. I checked myself over and felt my nose; it was bloodied, too.

In the distance I heard more clatter of rocks. The pervert was farther down the hill. Hot anger flashed anew as I thought of him slobbering over MY WIFE—my legs took off after him, the rest of me followed. I held my broken glasses up against my face with one hand and the gun in the other hand. This was awkward. Pain jolted my back but fueled my blazing fury.

The moon wasn't out yet, and I constantly flashed the gun's light to find my way, as there were many fallen trees from a previous forest fire. This was awkward too because I had to let go my glasses to squeeze the light switch. I pressed on downhill, trailing after the sound, but even with the light, I couldn't see him.

"Stop, you!" I yelled. The gun's light glowed over the land-scape. Though he was nowhere to be seen, I still called, "I see you there!" I let the shotgun howl. Its short barrel kicked like a mule and again I found myself searching for my fallen glasses. Without the light, I doubt I'd have found them.

I stumbled on. How I wished I didn't have to use one hand to hold my glasses; it was difficult enough to squeeze that dan-gling light switch on the gun with one hand. Seeing the light wane, I was even more disturbed as parts of the landscape were steep, with no end of rocks and fallen trees to stumble over. I shook the gun to brighten the light but that didn't help. The challenge was to catch the pervert before the light died.

The sound of falling rocks, fifty yards or so down the hill, grew louder. At times I could hear his wheezing. I figured he was taking his lumps too. As I closed in on him, a thrill swept … maybe, just maybe. I came over a rise and shone the dim light forward. Ahead was our wrought iron gate. I glimpsed his head bobbing as he ran toward a stand of trees.

"Halt or I'll shoot!" I shouted.

He didn't stop.

Quite apprehensive of the shotgun's kick, I held it tightly, wishing I had one more hand to hold my broken glasses. Aiming twenty feet beyond him, I pulled the trigger. The weapon resounded. Sure as lightning, my glasses fell again and the shotgun's light died. I shook the weapon, hoping to inspire the last of the batteries ... nothing. I listened for him as I rapidly patted the ground, searching for my glasses. At last I found them.

I stumbled up and pressed on, one hand on my glasses, the other on the weapon. It was so dark that if my hand hadn't been in front of my face, angled outward to assist my glasses, I wouldn't have felt pine needles and would've walked squarely into a tree.

Ahead, I heard the shaking of metal wire but didn't register what it was. Again I tried to sound bigger than I felt: "If you don't stop ..."

Then I heard a thump. Thinking I had come to an open grassy area, I closed in, moving toward the direction of the noise. He wasn't far ahead of me, crashing through sagebrush.

"If you don't stop ..." When I hit a barbed wire fence, my momentum carried me straight over it. I'm not sure if the shotgun caught on something or if my pants caught on the barbed wire, but the weapon resounded with a spray of buckshot. My head and shoulder plowed into the ground. I lay there, my legs hanging in the wire.

With much effort I rolled my legs off, my pants ripping away from the barbed wire. I saw stars while looking at the dirt and wondered if this was going to be a chiropractor thing or a hospital thing.

Examining myself, I touched the area where my pants exposed my knee and thigh to see if I was bleeding. I was. But from what I could feel, the barbed wire slashes weren't life-threatening. Crawling on all fours, I felt around, secured the gun and continued to pat about for my glasses and my other house slipper. I gritted my teeth as dirt got into the cut in my knee.

One thing for sure, the chase was over. No doubt he was long gone. Another point to be made: if someone was handing out awards for being the most awkward, clumsy, all-thumbs pursuer of bad guys that cold October night, I'd have been a strong candidate.

As I got up, I felt so dizzy and woozy, I let my head hang. Finally, I looked toward my destination, the wrought iron gate. Though I couldn't see it, I felt good knowing the road offered an easier way back, especially with one slipper on and one slipper off. My knee started to sting and I bent down to finger through the rip in my pants.

I heard an agonizing moan … a startling moan.

The sound lifted me straight out of my wounds. Rapidly raising the shotgun, I pumped the slide, reloading, aiming at the phantom. Listening, I gazed intently into the dark, expecting an attack.

"Help me." His gasp was weak.

I cautiously stepped forward, listening, listening, wondering if he had fallen and lost his wind. As I drew closer, I heard a weird gurgling sound. It dawned on me that he might have been struck by the shot when I blindly tumbled over the fence. This revelation made my face hot.

"You better stay down. I've got buckshot here!" I crept forward.

He didn't sound good. Still, my gun was aimed, as who knew what was up his sleeve. The foul smell of blood and guts met my nostrils, cut my suspicions and dropped my heart to the dirt.

I shifted the weapon to my other hand, then cautiously stepped forward and knelt. Reaching out, I patted about and found his leg, then his chest. My fingers touched something wet and warm. It could have been blood or body fluid. He was worse off than I imagined; most of his chest was damp.

I'd dealt with enough dying animals to realize his fate. There'd be no life-flight for this man.

He tried to say something, but only gasped.

I was overwhelmed. Something inside me wanted to say, "Get right with God, man, get right with God." This urge came with expediency—strange, as it wasn't as if I was right with God. And what good would it be coming from the man who'd shot him?

For a minute I was silent and then I couldn't help but say, "I'm sorry this happened." I touched his face, his whiskers, his forehead. "I'm sorry about this." Placing my hand on his forehead was bizarre, but I thought it might give him comfort. The only thing that wasn't surreal was his smell.

Time ticked ever so slowly as I listened to him struggle to breathe. It seemed an eternity. All was darkness, and again he tried to say something, but it was a whisper that I couldn't make out.

"What?" I leaned down to listen.

His breath was foul.

I waited.

He spoke again. His words weren't about repentance or loving last words, but I clearly understood them. "Lucifer … curse … you."

His breath vanished.

The night hung dark and silent. My hand still rested on his brow when a cloud of guilt came to call. What heaviness, to be cursed by a dying man. I needed relief, freedom, a way to blink and wake up from this nightmare, a way to push the rewind button. His body let out gas, startling me.

I found the shotgun and rose. Again his wretched smell filled my nostrils. I stumbled away from him, fighting the urge to puke.

With one slipper on, I rounded the gate, heading up the road, stumbling from right to left. As I limped along, darkness and depression slammed in. My thoughts were hopping all over the place at a fantastic speed; accusing voices had me standing before a judge, the iron doors of a prison, lawyers wrangling over the house, Priscilla homeless. The consequences were too weighty.

I clearly heard a voice intone, "You're a murdering man now."

"It was an accident." I spoke with wet-eyed desperation and wracked my mind about what to do with that corpse.

This voice was almost inaudible but may as well have been a shout. "Remember that fellow who ended up serving a sentence for a crime he didn't commit ... his wife ended up losing their home ... he was innocent ... not like you."

A picture of Priscilla flashed before me; she was dragging a dirty blanket down a city street. There was no way I was going to submit myself to the law. I had to shovel and shut up. I had to force myself to concentrate on getting rid of that horrid corpse.

In the midst of the barrage of accusations, again came the accusing voice, this time with rhyme. "When you're a murdering man, you think one way ... but saaay ... is it really that way?"

I tried to block this idea and count how many shots I had fired. It was the only thing that had announced his death. I was confused; was it three, four, or five? Looking back, it would have been easy to check how many bullets were left in the shotgun, but my reasoning was so confused, I never thought of it then.

Regardless, when this man showed up missing, the noise of my shotgun would draw curiosity. Sounds are strange in this area; sometimes I can barely hear a neighbor target-practicing just down the hill, other times I can clearly hear shots a half-mile away. Furthermore, Montanans liked to shoot and liked to hunt and it was legal to hunt critters at night. I grasped at the fact that a person could legally hunt critters at night. This could help my alibi, my escape.

There were two options regarding the corpse—either bury him on our property in a hole that a backhoe had dug years before, or drive him to the other side of the valley and bury him there.

The problem with driving him away was Priscilla. If I took the truck, she'd know something was up. Furthermore, if I ended up on the other side of the valley, it would be no small task to dig a hole deep enough to bury a big man, especially with the proliferation of animals that could easily dig him up, namely wolves and grizzlies. As I tried to reason this out, the barrage of accusing voices continued. Though I didn't want his corpse on my property, I was in no shape to dig a grave.

The cold nipped at me. I should have worn something to cover my bald head. Somewhere along the way, I felt my energy fade. This wasn't the case for the coyotes; they were calling, announcing a kill or the excitement of a new night. They carried on as if it were a family reunion. Silence fell until a lone wolf howled, echoing out of a south ravine.

Down by the garden, I heard the whinny of one of our horses.

Cold kept invading and I felt my age; my back stiffened as I limped up that road. I stopped near the garden as I considered using one of the horses to carry the corpse. But I could easily see that skittish animal bolting, running off, hauling that dead man straight down to the Sheriff's. No, no, I couldn't use the horses. It wouldn't be wise; they were just too jumpy.

I found the Y in the road and headed toward the barn, stumbling so much it's a wonder I didn't lose the other slipper. When I arrived at the barn, the big door creaked as it opened. Habit showed me the light switch. The four-wheel quad sat in the middle of the heavy wood-beamed structure. That machine had proved itself carrying game. It was going to be a different thing to have a corpse tied to its rails.

I looked about for a rope. It should have been on a hanger by the door. I glanced toward a cot that Eli used to sleep in. Did he take my rope?

# Eli

In our early years of marriage, we couldn't have children, so we signed up as foster parents. Eli arrived the day after Christmas. What a sight! You'd never know he was a 4-year-old; he looked not a day over two. My heart went out to him when I took off his shirt to put on his pajamas. His skin was covered with cigarette burns, cuts and purple bruises. The terribly bony boy just stood there, trembling, staring at my shirt. I imagined he thought he was going to get hit again and something rose up in me so strongly that I wanted to destroy whoever had done this to him.

The sight of him made me immediately want to be his dad. Right off I told the agency I wanted to adopt him. But a year-and-a-half passed before we were able to do that.

Eli was always on the move, reminding me of an amped-up scarecrow. His bones were good, as he tested them constantly, running into everything. And he fell so much that we got him a little hockey helmet to protect his precious head. It was a wonder that this kid didn't just fall apart, because he ate like a bird but was forever on the move and stumbling ... falling.

I always thought he'd step out of his quiet nature and take on our speech, but his sixth birthday came without his saying a word, then his seventh birthday, and still nothing. In those early years we first took him to an ear specialist, who confirmed that he could hear, then to more than one doctor and educator who said he'd never be able to communicate properly. I wasn't disturbed by the doctor's reports, as there was something about Eli—I reasoned that someday he'd just pop out of it and start talking.

During that time, the Charby public school didn't have a program for a mute boy, our town's population was only 750, so Priscilla took on the daunting task of home schooling. In the beginning, Eli showed very little progress with sign language, though Priscilla and I learned it.

Priscilla was relentless in working with him and praying for him, but sometimes this was discouraging. Who knew if he'd stumble into the kitchen for breakfast with his shirt or pants on backwards?

My wife worked with him on the piano as well. Interesting, for a long time he tinkered around with the keyboard, sometimes in a pounding fashion, and then one day, something clicked. It was as if he could hear a tune somewhere under the keyboard. He would work on it, over and over, to bring it out, and little by little, it appeared. It was surprising, the melodies he'd come up with; some were profound and reminded me of the outdoors.

Unpredictably, about a year after he arrived, we had our own first child, Raela. By the time she was two, you couldn't shut her up. Same with our second child, Bethany, born a year after Raela and our last child, Jerold, born a year after Bethany. But Eli, though he was a sweet brother, never said a word. It was disheartening to see his three younger siblings talking away while Eli sat there, mute.

He could learn tasks, however, not easily. If I wasn't out working on a job, he was my sidekick at home. I taught him how to look after the pets and the chickens, and he did his chores meticulously. He seemed to have a way with animals. Deer weren't afraid of him.

When Eli hit nine, Priscilla realized it didn't matter how much praying she did or how much blowing on her ram's horn shofar, to call out to the heavens, God wasn't going to be swayed to teach Eli how to read.

Eli's world had little to do with books or what went on inside the house. In fact, the confines of a room disturbed him. Sometimes I wondered if he had been locked up in a closet or room for a long, long time. Who knows?

One thing there was no mystery about: the outdoors was where Eli found his freedom, his friend, his world. Since our property bordered state land, he had a lot of room to roam. And roam he did.

I told him I didn't like him going beyond a certain point in the forest. But he'd go to said point, and take a long look back at the house, then as soon as we were out of eyesight he'd disappear into the woods. This stretching of the boundaries got under my skin.

I'd get up close and personal with him. "Look, buster, you need to know that there are animals out here that would like to chew on you." Sometimes I was quite loud, moving my lips about like an animated mule, other times I walked him to said point, by then a half a mile from the house, and pointed at the ground, instructing, "We can't have you go beyond here!"

When I lectured to him about this he had a studied look and when I finished, he'd give me a shake of his head or a nod, sometimes both, sometimes backward to what I was communicating, then a jolly pat, as if to say, "Good talking, daddy." And in no time he was past my line in the dirt.

I was at a loss at what got into that kid's head. Maybe there was a streak of rebellion in him, but I refused to beat him. I could see he'd gotten plenty of that from someone else before he was even four years old.

On returning from a hard day's work, Priscilla always reminded me of his absence. In the beginning, I'd drag his siblings out to look for him and sometimes the chase was fun. It was almost like playing hide and seek, "Eli … Eli." But he made a game out of it and, as soon as we knew we were being gamed, the game grew old. In the end, I saw my inflexibility on his absence was doing nothing to change the mute boy, and why should I be the next one to steal his childhood? My instructions shifted to, "Just be home by supper." And for my peace of mind, to protect him from predators, I made him a little spear.

Somewhere around age ten, he threw himself into fishing and trapping. After that, more often than not, he didn't even make it home for supper. This bothered us all. I wasn't going to reward his absence with a cold plate. But the loss of that meal didn't faze him a bit. If anything, he had more energy. It was then I realized he was eating the animals he trapped or fished. His leather pouch that he carried marbles in was now carrying meat. Thankfully it was cooked meat, but sometimes the sight of it was unsettling.

Eli was clever enough with his traps to catch muskrat, raccoon, coyote and bobcat. He carried his furs around like trophies, tucked into his belt or slung over his shoulder. One time he tried to come in the house with a skunk, which was skinned and dangling at his side. But I caught wind of it long before he hit the steps.

"From now on, I don't want you to bring any of those furs in the house. They might carry bugs, and bugs and humans aren't good. We can't have bugs crawling in our ears at night."

I tried to show him the importance of being sanitary, but I was at a loss without a microscope. Sometimes he'd drag himself in the house, sicker than sick, and I imagined the microscopic bugs in his little meat pouch had something to do with that.

"I've been praying you'd come back and stay around the house. See how good the Lord is?" Priscilla said as she dosed him with activated charcoal, then smeared a poultice of the black goo over his stomach. "He wants you to be healthy, eat more vegetables and live a long, long time." I helped her cover the charcoal with plastic wrap. We rolled it around his little frame as Priscilla finished with a soft touch. "Now this will draw the poison out."

To save his innards, I burned that meat pouch. Priscilla sewed him canvas bags and washed them often.

The girls showed little interest in Eli's world as they were too squeamish with dead animals. Eli wasn't squeamish about a thing, often appearing at the back door with dried blood on his hands.

One autumn day I was hanging around the barn when I noticed Jerold follow Eli into the woods. Right away a fatherly fear pushed me to correct that situation. This may seem inconsequential to those who grew up with brothers and I came from a family of four boys. We had no trouble playing in the woods, hammering on them while we hammered on each other. But Jerold was only five and it was one thing to have a ten-year- old mute son, head off to play in the woods, disappear in the woods, not obey me when it came to the woods, yet it was an entirely different scenario to see our youngest follow him. My correction of this ended with Jerold crying and Eli giving me a long look.

*   *   *

The first time I saw Eli looking at a book upside down, I knew he wasn't going to be a professor. I once showed him how to make a box, as I figured he was destined for the trades. He took to hammering nails and sawing wood with ease. This told me all I needed to know.

By the time our high-energy boy turned thirteen, he started really pushing his boundaries. The first time he didn't come home by 9 p.m., I got nervous. It didn't matter how much I searched, hollered, or waved my flashlight around; he didn't appear. Somewhere in my stumbling about the woods I heard the distinct sound of Priscilla's ram's horn. The reverberant sound went up toward the timber. I headed for the house because I thought Eli had returned. Oh, what frustration to find he wasn't there. Finally, I called Search and Rescue.

Somewhere around 2 a.m., a rescue worker found Eli, down by the river, working his trap line. When he came home, he seemed none the worse for wear, his shirt on backwards, happily displaying that night's catch, three muskrats.

I admonished him for being out after dark. I also determined to get him involved with more work about the place, something to keep him busy. This was challenging, as with four kids we pretty much had the chores covered. Priscilla also had him play the piano half an hour longer and extended his sign language lessons, but the second his opening came he was gone into his forest, his woods.

About two weeks later, he took Jerold into the woods and they didn't make it back till after supper. I couldn't have this spreading, and disciplined Jerold, then gave Eli a bit of a shaking over it. That was the first time I'd ever shook him and it really bothered me, but I was disturbed. I couldn't have Jerold fall into that world of no boundaries. No, no.

His behavior was hard on Priscilla as well. And hard on the kind folks at Search and Rescue. It came to a head during a time when construction work in the Yokino Valley was tough to find. I needed a change, something, anything. At that time, my brother, a contractor in the Bay Area, was begging for carpenters. Additionally, the Golden State had an educational system in sign language that was more geared for Eli than what Charby offered. Priscilla and I discussed moving to California and it wasn't a long discussion, as I needed work. We determined to keep our Montana property and rent a place in California.

Along with everybody, I didn't like leaving our home. When I held the car door open for Eli and watched him get in, I was hopeful about the changes coming his way.

But I didn't realize how poorly he'd handle them. Eli's world came to such an abrupt end when we moved to Concord, California, that he fell into a funk and showed no interest in learning anything. With his outdoor world gone, he even lost his rhythm on the piano. Maybe it was the summertime heat, maybe it was the throbbing metropolis, whatever it was, he went about confused and disillusioned. No matter what he did, it didn't turn out; on an innocent school field trip, he came back with poison oak so bad we thought twice about sending him back to school.

No doubt his heart was in Montana, and, after the umpteenth time the police, Sheriff or CHP picked him up heading northeast, I started planning our move back to Montana. This wasn't a snap-of-the-finger move, as I had taken on too much debt and not long after I arrived, my brother, Stan, handed his contracts over to me and took off for Washington state, so I was buried with work. I told Eli that we were going to move back to Montana, which settled him down a bit. But I didn't tell him when.

The longer this plan went on without materializing, the more distant he grew. He became more and more depressed.

He didn't like the confines of school, of buildings, of rooms. He was so much on edge with confined spaces that he slept in the backyard with our dog Curly. Rain or frost, it didn't matter to him. I was thankful we had a deck that he could get under on stormy nights.

Jerold saw Eli was having a rough go and regularly slept outside with him. It was different to see the younger brother take the older brother down to the park. I'd hear him often encouraging him. "Come on, Eli, you can't be sitting around

here all day, let's go see what the Canadian Geese are up to."
And Jerold habitually spelled out various words in sign language to him. Jerold was a good brother.

When the CHP picked Eli up on a freeway onramp in Sacramento, I had another row with him. It was then that he signed Montana, pointed at me and signed, You said we'd move back, vehemently moving his fingers as if adding an exclamation mark.

"I'm sorry. It's just taking longer than I thought."

But this display stunned me, as he'd never shown any indication whatsoever that he had learned sign language. From the speed he fingered out Montana, I figured he'd been stuffing sign language down a squirrel hole for quite some time. So I removed my recalcitrant 16-year-old son from school and took him to work with me. Whether it was legal or not, I did it anyway. I told everyone he was eighteen, though he didn't look a day over fourteen. If I hadn't done this, we would have lost him.

He was a good, hard worker and understood my instructions. In no time his grin returned, especially when I was up close explaining something, my lips animatedly moving.

After he got his second paycheck and embraced the money thing, he bought himself a warm sleeping bag, winter coat, tent, hiking boots, backpack, bow and arrows, flashlight and map of the western states. Later that evening, I noticed him leaning over the backyard table, his flashlight shining on the map.

I called out from my bedroom window, "What you got in mind with that map?"

His face broke into a great grin.

"You know when your paradise isn't fun any longer?"

He shook his head.

"When the food runs out."

\* \* \*

A few months passed and Eli kept purchasing more and more items for his adventure, even a cowboy hat. In his spare time he practiced with that bow in the backyard. Robin Hood had nothing on him.

One Saturday morning I walked past the kitchen table and noticed a hand-drawn outline of Montana. When I saw an X mark on Charby, a sense of emptiness came over me. Anxiety bled. I knew right then my son was on the way to Montana.

As his sisters stared at the map, they became teary-eyed.

Jerold said, "At least he left a note."

Part of me wanted to search all the freeway onramps and get Eli back, but I knew I couldn't rope in his spirit. I had to let him chase his dreams.

That afternoon I called Dewey, my neighbor back in Montana who looked after our house, and asked if he'd keep an eye out for Eli.

Dewey said, in a rather carefree manner, "That boy's going to make a good Montanan. He couldn't have picked a better time of year to come. Spring is just a-budding. You should get out here before California falls into the ocean."

A day later, Dewey called to say he'd seen Eli heading up toward our house, carrying a bow, lugging a backpack, cowboy hat and all. He'd caught up with him and told him he could always get a free meal at his place.

I thanked him dearly. It was good to know Dewey. He was older and old-school, lived by the Golden Rule. I couldn't ask for a better neighbor.

Priscilla wanted to go after Eli, but that rubbed me wrong. I had to let him live his life. Yes, he was a few years short of being a legal adult, but if I'd brought him back, wouldn't I have killed his dream?

*    *    *

As spring warmed to summer, I kept in touch with Dewey. He said Eli wasn't hanging around the homestead much and sighting him was like seeing a rare mountain goat. Much of my anxiety depended on my weekly conversations with Dewey. And much of my working day's thoughts and worries were about that kid. Would he be safe from predators? Was his food supply holding out? Was he eating right? Did he get lost in the mountains? How was his stomach? Would he clean that meat pouch? On and on.

Priscilla just prayed and prayed and prayed for that boy. I found myself praying for him too, and I wasn't even a praying man.

Fall faded into winter and my worries increased. Was he warm enough? Was his tent waterproof? Were his boots warm enough? Did he have enough socks and underwear? Did he wash his socks and underwear? Why didn't he eat at Dewey's? My mind reeled.

Though I was overwhelmed with work, we finally got away just after Christmas. No words can express how excited we were at the prospect of seeing Eli. After driving the thousand-plus miles I checked in with Dewey, but he said he hadn't seen him for some time. We all got busy looking for him, sure that we'd cut his trail. Jerold and I put on snowshoes and made it up into the tree line, while Priscilla and the girls went to lower elevations, searching, searching. But we couldn't even find a footprint in the snow, nothing.

Discouraged and exhausted, I wanted to call Search and Rescue, but I had called them so many times in the past, I figured I'd first search beyond the tree line. The next morning, early, Jerold and I did just that. With snowshoes we plodded up into the high country and burned no end of calories as we plowed through the snow, shouting and blowing our whistles. Again, there was no sign of Eli.

That evening, when we got back, I called Search and Rescue. When they heard it was Eli, and how long he'd been absent, they mentioned starting to look the next morning. I can only assume they thought he was dead.

As the sun set, Priscilla went out on the porch and blew her shofar. It was as loud as I'd ever heard, resounding as if it came from the bottom of her toes, and certainly from her heart. The sound went out across the snow-covered landscape toward the timber.

I thought, if Eli was alive, he'd hear that horn. But it wasn't long before those dark thoughts returned. Was Priscilla calling to a frozen corpse? Were the same critters that he had trapped and eaten now eating him? My hope started to die and a real sense of guilt came over me.

Before going to bed, I felt like a broken man. Priscilla was just as spent. She kneeled, praying. Her lips looked as if she was begging God for the life of her son.

I couldn't sleep. Despair followed me down the stairs to the kitchen. The kitchen light was still on. I stared blankly at the window, this question echoing in my mind, "So this is how it will end?"

At last I turned out the light. The darkness led to more bleakness. The kitchen felt so empty. I stood gazing at the black window, my eyes slowly adjusting to the dark, my legs fatigued and twitchy from all the hiking. I was just about to turn to go when I thought I saw movement outside.

I focused on the glass, waited, but was unwilling to let my hopes rise. It was terribly quiet. Strange, the more I stared, the more I had this feeling that someone was watching me. Drawn toward the window, I bumped into a chair. I extended my hand to feel the glass. So cold. As I palmed it, my eyes pleaded to see him. Outside, the blackness offered nothing. I tapped the glass. Tap, tap, tap.

How I wished he'd tap back. With silence came more heavy thoughts. To protect my aching heart, I turned away, forced my hopes back into a box, and locked them there.

My head hung low as I walked toward the hallway.

Tap, tap, tap.

I about melted. "Priscilla!" I shouted, "He's here!"

My fingers smashed into the wall as I flipped on the light. "Eli?" I hurried toward the door. Behind me I could hear Priscilla's footsteps thumping down the stairs. "Eli?" In my socks, I stumbled over my own feet, hurried out the door and into the snow.

Eli came out of the darkness. I lunged for him, grabbed him and hugged him tightly. His smoky, woodsy smell was so good, so wholesome. In a big bear hug, I carried him back to the porch, never wanting to let him go.

The porch light suddenly glowed. With a bang and a clang of the glass storm door, our family pressed in to touch him.

"Eli … Eli," called the girls' high-pitched voices. Jerold was chuckling.

As blunt as a construction worker, I bumped into everyone as I powered him into the house. We were all pressed in together, hugging him with laughter and tears.

I stepped back to remove my wet socks while gazing up at Eli, then blurted, "You are some Christmas gift!"

Jerold said to him, "You can stay in my room."

Eli grinned, slapping a fur mitten on his brother's shoulder.

He didn't know he was handsome, though his sisters surely must have thought he was. They were comical in helping him take off his coat, with one on each side, giggling, getting the most out of the tug-of-war and patting him like a new pet, without any break in the action.

"Wait, wait, it's stuck," Raela said with a serious face, letting go of the cuff. She stepped in front of Eli, then rammed her hand into his stomach, "Skkkkk." He folded inward in hilarity, as if zapped by electricity. Bethany moved into him, tickling him. Eli was helpless, bent over, laughing so hard he lost strength to push his sisters off.

Raela was darn near as tall as him and probably outweighed him, as the 12-year-old had gone through a growth spurt and had no problem powering in with her fingers to get at his midsection. "Skkkkkkk!"

His hilarity was so great, his eyes pleaded for relief.

"Raela, back off, we can't have him croak," I said. "Eli, find yourself a seat ..." I shoved the chuckler into a chair. "... and tell us your story."

He tried to head off his laughter by clearing his throat, over and over, while keeping a wary eye on his circling sisters.

I could see that his winter coat and the raccoon mitts had done him well.

Jerold picked up the mittens and stuffed his hands into them. "Where'd you get these, Eli?" He rubbed his cheek with one of them. "These are nice."

I could also see it would be difficult for the circling girls not to touch Eli. It was like having someone you thought lost, completely lost, suddenly reappear. He was such a novelty; it was like having a real, live 18th -century trapper sitting in our kitchen. And each time they touched this cour de bois, he'd go back into hilarity's prison. Concerned, I raised my hand. "Back off, you two." I leaned in to push Raela aside, but she was too light-footed, scurrying away in her teddy-bear pajamas.

"Eli, could you please tell us where you live?" I may as well have asked a tree stump, as he had his hands full with Bethany, who was behind him, feeling his cheeks.

"You are so cold." Bethany touched his shoulder-length hair and his neck. "Eli, are you okay?"

Jerold stepped toward his sisters. "Leave him be. He's okay." He waved at them to stop.

The girls were unfazed. Raela appeared on the other side of her sister, her hands doing a bit of examining. "Mom, he's so cold."

"If you came in from outside, you would be cold, too," Priscilla said.

I turned to view their damp-eyed mother, who was near the stove, looking toward the ceiling, mouthing what I assumed were thankful words. She lowered her head, picked up a lid and placed it on a pot of soup.

Eli's eyes had a doleful look, just cresting hilarity's mountain, but his sisters worked their magic and he was down the slope again, laughing so much I thought his cheeks would crack.

"You two ..." Priscilla broke away from putting a place setting on the table to give the girls a backhanded wave. "... get!" Her robe flowed back as she closed in on them.

Raela had more fear of her mother than me and ended up scurrying into the hallway.

"You don't have to be hanging all over him." Priscilla put her hand on Eli's forehead, looking as if she were checking his temperature, getting her touches, too, before returning to the stove.

Raela fidgeted, looking quite upset. "I don't know what the big deal is." She targeted her frustration toward her mother. "He's not from my bloodline. I wouldn't even have to change my name if he married me."

Rolling her eyes, Priscilla moaned, "Please, Lord Jesus," and glanced upward.

I tried to counter this by waving to Eli, then signing Montana.

"Eli, come on over." Priscilla poured soup into a bowl.

I got up from my chair, giving in to the urge to touch him as well, scooped him up under his arms, feeling how much muscle he had in his forearms. No doubt he could go the distance, but he was too slight for my comfort.

He continued to clear his throat, half-looking at the back door and then his sisters as I ushered him forward.

I delivered him to a steaming bowl of chicken noodle soup without even inquiring if he was hungry. "Help yourself; we've already eaten."

Again he glanced at the back door. I knew he felt confined. It was strange to see the same eyes of the 4-year-old who had come into our lives a day after Christmas so many years ago. His siblings didn't know how much they owed him, as for some strange reason we weren't able to have children until after he arrived.

\* \* \*

That night as I lay in bed thinking about the evening, I was very thankful and couldn't sleep. Angling my head toward Priscilla, I quietly said, "Are you awake?"

"Yes," she replied. "Isn't God good?"

"He is at that." I nodded, staring up at the dark ceiling. "He is at that."

\* \* \*

Before we left Montana we gave Eli his Christmas gifts: t-shirts, underwear, wool socks, and some canvas overalls. Our other kids might have thought that we loved them less when I gave Eli a Smith and Wesson .38 revolver and a bunch of ammo but I think they understood that he needed protection.

I felt somewhat relieved when I watched him shoot it, as I knew he would now be safe from predators. But there was also a measure of consternation; this firepower would make his paradise more livable, which didn't bode well with me as I had been worried enough over him and now desired him out of the woods.

I knew he wouldn't return to California so when I handed him the boxes of ammo, I said, "Don't ask me for any more ammo. If you need some, you're going to have to get back to civilization and get a job." With that, I gave him a telling nod.

# Hellacious Struggle

When we finally moved back to Montana, our three younger kids were either in college or chasing their dreams in California. And now, with the cold of October arriving, it was rare to see Eli, as he was trapping.

The night I shot the pervert I stood in the barn, staring at the empty spot where there should have been a rope. Had Eli taken it? This really irked me. I needed that rope to secure the corpse to the quad.

The single light bulb that hung off the rafter didn't offer much light, especially since I was without my glasses. With only one slipper on, I limped about, bending down, looking under the workbench, while mumbling dissatisfactions that don't need repeating.

At last I found a scrap of rope just long enough to be useful. I started the quad, backed it up, then dismounted to turn out the barn's light.

Not long after, I was puttering down our road toward the garden. The road T's at the garden and goes left, up toward the house, or right, toward the gate. The quad's lights illuminated the eyes of our two horses, their yellow-green glow just beyond our garden. I angled right, toward the gate. I'd always liked that area, as our dirt road follows a dry creek bed, but the ominous task ahead deterred any pleasant thoughts.

Our old military 6 x 6 truck came into focus. We had placed it fifty feet back from our gate, along with a POW flag, to subtly tell others that we had military experience, which wasn't actually the case.

The gate and the back of our Keep Out, No Trespassing signs came into view. I motored past the barbed wire fence, then steered down an embankment, into sagebrush. The quad's lights revealed the man's legs, then the rest of his body. The blood-covered corpse was distressing. My arm trembled. I wasn't sure if it was because of the cold or the corpse's stillness.

I backed up and turned the handlebars toward the barbed wire to light the section of ground where I figured my glasses and house slipper were. Dismounting, I limped in front of the headlamps. In the distance were a few house lights. With my pants backlit, I was quite conscious that I might be on life's stage. This lit a fire under the search for my glasses, which I luckily discovered at the base of a sagebrush; my house slipper was hanging on the barbed wire fence.

I backed the quad up to the corpse. Behind me the glow of a rising half-moon brightened the ridges of the Sapphire Mountains. The moon offered enough light so I could turn off the machine.

I found myself behind the corpse, bending down to get a grip on the back of his shoulders. Rigor mortis had begun its stiffening work and if he was a big lug before, he certainly was dead weight now. I strained to get him up, but couldn't get a good grip. When I tried to lift him, if I wasn't slipping backward, his legs were sliding forward.

Some of the buckshot had gone straight through him, so there was no getting away from his bodily fluid. What a putrid, nasty smell. My broken glasses kept falling forward and I had to continually press them back onto my nose.

In the battle to get him on-board the quad, I heard a scratching, clawing sound from a tree just up the dry creek bed. I reasoned it was a porcupine. The wife and I loathed porcupines, as they had killed no end of pines and here we were, already short on pines from the fire. For now, this porky's life was spared only because the light on my gun had died.

I continued the arduous task of trying to get the heavy corpse onto the quad with my hands locked under his arms. I'm not so sure he wasn't a 300-pounder, especially when his legs slid forward. I felt a sting and wondered if I'd torn my groin muscle.

After an exhausting, useless effort, I went for his ankles, as I was determined to halt his sliding legs. I ended up tying his ankles to one side of the back of the quad, then went down on my knees to get a good grip around his shoulders. I tried to lift him with all my might, but I couldn't get him up. When my slippers slipped, he dropped. I had to press my glasses back on with wet fingers from his ghastly blood and fluid. Somewhere in this I realized I was trying to get him on the quad back-ass-backwards. Some of this is embarrassing to write.

I've smelled my share of dead deer, elk, even wild pigs, but they were nothing to this pervert's horrid smell. He must have lived on anchovy pizza. His stench reached into the upper levels of my nostrils; gagging turned into losing my supper. Regardless of how much pain I was in, I knew I had to get him on that quad.

While I gathered my breath I went for his wallet. I'd never stolen a person's wallet before, but I had to know who he was. Turning on the quad's light, I afforded myself a look inside his wallet. His driver's license was in view—his name, Richard W. Wartal.

I hadn't a clue who he was and was quick to turn off the quad's light, lest it draw unwelcome attention. Before I started I actually felt sorry for him, but after more pain in my back and groin, I swore at Big Dick. He deserved to die!

Then I got angry at a lot of things, including those darn horses; and that porcupine needed some buckshot too. Kill my pine tree, would he? We'll see about that.

After a Herculean effort, panting, panting, panting, re-gripping the flopper, I just about had his midsection to the back of the quad, when on cue, the wheels rolled. In an instant his body went down, his head banging off the metal rack. Angry at my lack of forethought, I set the quad's brake.

When I finally got him on the quad, his muck was on me thick. I grabbed the rope and cinched him down good.

Then I motored on to the garden, where I picked up a shovel. Usually the horses draw near, looking for handouts. But not that night. They must have smelled the corpse or seen it draped over the back of the quad, because they were whinnying at the other end of the corral. We should have named them Spooky and Powder Keg. The only reason I kept them around is that the wife thought the world would soon be coming to an end and, as she says, "Without gasoline, who'd plow the garden?"

I had conflict with her about this. Doesn't every generation think theirs will be the last? Didn't the Russians think Napoleon was the Anti-Christ when he marched on Moscow? Weren't they sure Hitler was the Anti-Christ when the Nazis marched on Moscow? Isn't history's road cluttered with failed Last Day predictions?

Those darn horses cost us $5. a day. And here those hay burners were at the other end of the corral while my back was hurting like blazes. When I thought of the return on our investment, those horses just weren't cutting it.

I angrily tied the shovel next to the corpse, and then drove the quad to the backhoe dig.

At the dig, I went down into the hole, shovel in hand, to make sure it was deep enough. I had no intention of lifting the pervert once I had dumped him. It was a good four feet deep and I figured that would do. I backed up the quad and made darn sure its brake was locked before I untied him. Crawling back onto the quad, I spun around and braced my slippers against him.

"Good riddance," I mumbled as I kicked the body off the quad.

The words were hardly out of my mouth when I felt something bite into my ankle. It vaulted me straight over the back end of the quad into the hole.

My ankle hurt so bad I wasn't sure if I still had my foot. Feeling about, my fingers found a deep rope mark burned into my skin. When I tried to stand up, I fell right back down. I found myself on the side of the dig, with the pervert's smell drifting up.

For some time I sat there, wondering if his curse was more than just idle words. Looking up, I gazed at the night sky. The vastness of the heavens generally made me feel small, but this time I felt as if I was being watched, found out. Remorse lay heavily upon me.

It was a struggle to bury him. My ankle stung terribly. At the end of the shoveling, everything, including my soul, was hurting.

I motored toward the house, my tired mind mulling over what logical explanation I could give Priscilla. My wife is a praying woman, far more spiritual than I, and truth is quite important to her. But that night, she wasn't going to get the truth. Maybe I was too tired and cold, or maybe I was blocked by the man's curse, but no logical explanation justified my long absence.

The cold had penetrated my damp sweatshirt. I was trembling badly. Somewhere along the road I had the good sense to turn off the quad's lights; I hoped Priscilla hadn't seen them. About fifty yards short of the house, I stopped and dismounted the quad. Staring at the light from our kitchen window, I rubbed my bald head and mumbled, "Think, think, think," then limped along the road to our garage.

I needed a flashlight, as it is quite rare to see or hear a porcupine, and they must be exterminated quickly before they kill another pine. It would also be prudent to use porky's guts to cover the pervert's blood. This helped my alibi. This had possibilities.

Shivering, I slipped into the garage and flipped on the light switch. In the work area, I took a good look at the rope burn on my ankle. It was reddish and bruised; some of the skin was burned. I found an old coat. Unwilling to contaminate it, I took off that stinking damp sweatshirt. I also grabbed a knife, and batteries for the gun's light.

From the garage I limped to the quad and drove it down to the gate. Twenty feet from where I'd shot the pervert, I turned off the quad. Sitting there, I listened, hoping to hear the porcupine. I pulled my arms over my chest in a vain attempt to halt my shaking and worked on a suitable alibi; if Curly, our hunting dog, was younger, I could tell Priscilla that he took me on some wild goose chase. But she knew Curly was too old for any more night hunts. Once that silvery hound went into his doghouse, he wasn't coming out till morning.

What was odd about all this reasoning was that Priscilla was a diehard survivalist. You should not have to come up with any cockamamie stories to cover your tracks when you are talking to your survivalist mate; certainly, when the hard times come, there will be a lot of people sneaking around at night, trying to get your grub, so what's the big deal about just saying, "I shot a man and buried him in the backhoe dig?"

As I mulled this over, I thought about how much more of a survivalist she was than I; she had no qualms about spending our retirement savings on preparation supplies. What was perplexing was, we'd spent a bunch of money on a security system and that pervert just snuck in without warning. Were the batteries in the motion detector dead, too?

My musing ate up a few minutes; then a sudden scratching sound startled me. It drew me off the quad's seat. It had to be the porcupine, eating the upper bark of a pine. I took the shotgun out of its cradle on the quad, gathered up its dangling light switch, pulled the flashlight out of my coat pocket and proceeded toward the tree.

The flashlight illuminated the upper branches. Generally the strong instinct of the hunt would give me some thrill but not that night; when the flashlight caught a reflection of porky's eyes, it was business as usual. It was somewhat odd to aim that short-handled shotgun up a tree. I made sure I pressed back those darn glasses onto my nose before shooting. From the resounding blast I anticipated him dropping, but he didn't. I don't know if it was my aim, as he was pretty high, or if he was just tough enough to take more lead. I gave him another round of buckshot. He still hung.

I reloaded, pushed those glasses back again and shot twice more. Still, he didn't drop. I was beginning to think I might have to cut the tree down. Finally, cracking branches announced his fall; then with a heavy thump, he hit the ground.

The glow of the light illuminated the upside-down porcupine. With all the buckshot he took, I was surprised that there wasn't more blood. In the distance a dog howled, and another dog responded. It was as if the dogs were calling, "Seize it!"

I grabbed the porcupine's thorny paw and dragged him toward the area where I'd accidentally shot the pervert. This porcupine was a good size. At the barbed wire fence I dragged him under; with the shape my ankle and back were in, he wasn't about to be heaved over.

Not far beyond the barbed wire fence the flashlight illuminated the man's blood pile. The possibility of the dead porcupine covering the man's crimson liquid gave me hope. For the first time that night I wasn't bothered by continually pushing back my glasses, the pervert's stench, my aching back or my throbbing ankle. I dropped the porcupine right at the blood pile and examined him by flashlight. With his quill coat, he was quite the creature.

I cautiously rolled him over with my slipper. Setting the flashlight in a bush, I angled it toward the porky; that gave me a free hand with the knife. I carefully worked the blade up his belly, exposing his intestines. Though I accidentally cut into one, I didn't notice any smell. I gutted him out and cut out his organs, spreading them around the same area where the man's blood was. Then I flipped the porcupine over and set him atop his own pile. I liked the look of him there; he signified a way out of the mess I was in.

Completing that task, I motored back to the barn. After I'd parked the quad in the barn, I headed down the road, eventually passing the corral where the horses were kind of mumbling. Their costly presence didn't bother me just then, as I was thinking about the porcupine's guts. His guts made me feel a bit better.

I pushed the glasses back on my nose and looked up toward the night sky; the starlight never had such a bright twinkle. Odd; whenever I see possibilities, my front teeth press forward. I'm sure if Priscilla saw me, she'd know I was up to something. I really needed to watch my teeth.

By the time I got back to the house, I was so numb I didn't feel the cold. I took off my coat and the rest of my clothes, leaving the stinking, blood-stained pile, along with the sweatshirt I had snagged from the garage, at the back entrance where we brought in firewood.

In my underwear, I stepped into the house, shoved the corpse's wallet into a stack of wood and quietly crept to the inner door. Opening it, I looked about for Priscilla. She wasn't visible so I stuck my head in and could see the fireplace was still aglow. Taking a step into the kitchen area I looked toward the formal dining room and spied Priscilla at the dining room table. Her back was to me as she played solitaire. This was good. Very conscious of the slightest sounds, I went back for my clothes. What a pain to bend down to snag the pile. I headed for the fireplace, fully aware that I was leaving a trail of stench. If only I could get them to the fireplace before being found out.

While passing the kitchen table, I glimpsed her again, moving cards about. I reached the fireplace, quickly opened the glass door and hurled in the clothes. The flames leap on them. Satisfied, I shut the fireplace door, shoved the bolt down and limped toward the stairwell. If only those flames could obliterate everything.

Priscilla inquired, "What have you been up to, Mr. Hershal?"

I halted by the stairwell. "I got sprayed by a skunk and ended up on a wild goose chase, going down the hill after him."

"It would've been nice if you could've told me what was going on." She sounded put-out. "Earlier, I spent some time fooling with our money."

"Sorry. It was just a mad dash, and I ended up hitting a barbed wire fence."

"Oh … no!"

I heard her walk across the slate floor toward me.

"Are you okay?"

"I hurt my ankle when I went over the fence."

She came around the corner, looked me over and frowned. "Your legs and your knee are cut. And what happened to your ankle?"

"That darn barbed wire fence. I didn't see it."

"Is your ankle going to be all right?"

"It sure is sore."

She stepped closer, caught a whiff, covered her mouth and nose and stepped back. "A skunk?"

"Yes." I pushed my glasses back and hugged my chest in another vain attempt to stop my trembling. "I didn't get him, but I got a porcupine." I nodded assuredly. "When that porcupine fell, he shot blood everywhere, on my clothes, everything."

"A porcupine … oh, good." She looked as if she didn't know whether to grin, laugh or something. At last, she said, "A hot shower will do you good."

I nodded and painfully limped up the stairwell.

"I'll get some tea ready."

\*     \*     \*

A hot shower and hot tea can sure turn a ship around. I found myself sitting at the kitchen table with an ice pack wrapped around my ankle, sipping tea with Priscilla. The chamomile tea was relaxing, had no trouble melting my tired mind. Perhaps that's why I had this strange urge to spill the beans and tell her what really happened.

Priscilla has a mind that can ride around the gate before the bull is out, so the sane part of me was trying to be careful with my words. Even still, the fight with the intruder at the planter box was most perplexing, and I would have liked her input on the possibility of a third person being involved.

"He was just …" I angled my arm back, pointing toward the sunroom, then caught myself.

She gave me a curious look. "He?"

I sipped my tea and told myself to shut my big mouth. This was worrisome. In my tired state, it was an effort to twist the story into just a critter run. I managed a chuckle. "Everything about that chase ... hunt ... was ... just ..." I left that incomplete thought and jumped to, "It sure was cold out there. Funny to think that just a few days ago, it was warm enough to be out in a t-shirt. Maybe we'll get a winter after all."

I glanced over at the fireplace and watched the dancing flames. "And here it all happened the first night we started a fire." I forced a grin. "Next time we should be careful." Again I thought of the struggle around the planter box. Strange that it seemed so long ago.

"You said he. Was there someone there?"

"I don't know. Did I say he?" I covered my mishap with a yawn. It was difficult to calculate my thoughts and words. "I must've meant the skunk."

\*   \*   \*

The following morning I felt worse than the night before. When I got out of bed, my body hurt so bad I was reminded of the intruder's curse. It was difficult just to get my pants and shirt on. With great effort, I headed down the hall. I wanted to snag the corpse's wallet from the woodpile and then deal with any footprints that displayed the fight around the planter box. But my ankle, back and entire being were in such pain that when I got to the bottom of the stairs, I limped about in a half-circle, ending up leaning on the wall, thankful that I hadn't fallen over. I was off-balance, beaten, cursed, in such a weak, sorry state that I staggered to the nearest chair and flopped into it.

Priscilla came out of the kitchen. "Are you all right?"

"I just hope I don't fall off this chair."

She closed, then knelt to take a closer look. "Your ankle is so puffy and purple. I wonder if it got a rusty barb. It looks infected." She frowned, touched the area where the rope had caught. "There's a spot that looks like the lines from the wire. You might need a doctor."

"We don't have that kind of money."

"Goodness, Hershal, we're going to have to get some charcoal on that."

"Can you help me back to bed?"

*     *     *

Priscilla spent the morning working me over with ice, homeopathic remedies, chicken soup and prayers.

Generally, I sidestepped spiritual matters, but I was feeling so bad, I welcomed her prayers. It wasn't as if I didn't believe in the Christ. I liked His style, especially His first miracle, turning water into wine. That told me He liked people to enjoy life, to enjoy a celebration. From what I'd read of the New Testament I knew He was true, but I figured I couldn't be true to Him if I couldn't set Him above my guns.

My step-dad had instilled this in me, teaching us kids not to fool ourselves about a walk with God. He was a diligent man who dragged us off to church on Sunday, to midweek service, to anything that might get the Gospel into us. And he made it clear that, even though demons believe in the Christ, they surely weren't going to heaven; so either you were in, following the Lord, or you were out, doing your own thing.

The biggest issue for me in crossing the line and serving God was my guns. I loved my guns. I had lots of them, some short-range, most long-range, from revolvers, semi-automatics and pumps to bolt-actions. Some were made in the U.S., some in Russia, Germany, Israel, Austria, Italy, Brazil. I taught Priscilla and my kids gun safety and how to use and maintain them. I slept with my guns and was calmed by their protection. I knew men that had guns and served Christ, but I just couldn't literally give up my guns to a higher power. No way.

When we lived in California, there was a time when I was at my wits' end with Eli and his never-ending quest to make it back to Montana, where I had actually started to go back to church, mainly to support Priscilla's efforts of getting Eli into a structure that he'd connect with. There, I really felt a tug to walk the aisle and get right with Christ. But not long after that, Eli was off to Montana for good and I was back to visiting hunting and sporting goods stores on Sunday mornings for good.

# The Dream

While I was lying in bed, I figured that no matter what shape I was in, I'd better deal with the wallet in the woodpile and the shoeprints near the sunroom window, lest Priscilla figure out that my skunk story had holes.

When she went to the mailboxes, half a mile away, I forced myself out of bed, agonizing ankle and all, then hobbled down the hallway and eased myself down those darn stairs. The pain was excruciating. After snagging the wallet from the woodpile, I got a rake from the garage. Every step I took was like walking on hot coals. At last, wearing only a t-shirt and underwear, I made it outside to the area below the planter box.

There were a number of splotches of dried blood in front of the planter box, way more than my bloody nose could have produced, and I don't remember wandering all over the place, like this map of crimson showed. I also noticed three different sets of shoe prints, and there might have been four. It made me wonder if Priscilla had been out and about.

I would have liked to study this more, but I heard her car coming up the road, so I did my best to destroy the evidence with a quick rake of the scene. Then it was a race to get that rake back to the garage and haul my unsteady body up those stairs. I was in a hot sweat and shaking badly when I finally flopped into bed.

It took a while for my pacing heart to settle; I ached all over, especially that throbbing ankle. Half an hour passed before I went through the wallet. Richard Wartal was 37. I liked him less, since his wallet was full of porn. After much pain and hobbling, I stuffed the wallet at the back corner of my gun safe.

In late afternoon, Priscilla brought another bag of ice into the bedroom. My mind had been churning about those tracks—did I need to rake more? Once again, I considered telling her what had really happened. Strange that guilt begs for release.

She seemed a little rough in pushing my covers about while she iced my ankle.

"Did you shoot at the skunk up here?"

"I shot at a skunk, but he got away."

She looked as if she was trying to piece the puzzle together. "But did you shoot at a skunk up here?"

"No, I don't think so. Did you hear a shot go off up here?"

"No, but you must've hit something." Her small hand tucked the ice pack onto my leg. I winced. "There's a lot of dried blood out there."

"You've seen it?"

She nodded.

"Somewhere in all that excitement I had a nosebleed."

"But Hershal, there's quite a lot of dried blood out there."

With that, she left the room. I knew her search to find the truth wasn't over, as she is one thorough woman.

Later I heard the front door close. Since I knew my wife was now on the detective path, I forced myself out of bed. With great difficulty and pain I made it over to a window, pulled back the blind and peeked out, gazing over the planter box area. It wasn't long before our dog Curly came into view. Priscilla was holding his leash.

When that dog got to the planter box, his tail shot up. From then on, his nose led him forward. As I observed Priscilla pause and suspiciously look over the area, I wished I hadn't raked anything out. Curly was pulling to take her on the blood trail, but she held him back, still studying the rake marks. This was troubling. Now I felt found-out.

It wasn't long before Curly tugged her down the hill. This was even more worrisome. Though that bloodhound was old, he still had the ancient instincts of the hunt. I just hoped he wouldn't end up at the backhoe dig.

Again, I was shaking when I made it back to bed. Lying there looking at the ceiling, I felt totally helpless. It didn't take much imagination to envision Priscilla digging. Somewhere amongst my worries I sent up a fervent prayer, one that ends with, "Lord, if you get me out of this, I'll be a missionary for you in the jungles of Africa."

My mind was really stretched when I finally dozed off. In my sleep a dream came, so clear that when I awoke, it was before me. I had walked downstairs into an underground room that was painted a soft hyacinth blue. Before me were five long tables, each with fourteen place settings. Everything was blue, the tablecloths, the ornately decorated blue plates, the blue concrete walls. The entire setting had the feel of a festive event. What I found strange was that each place setting had five stacked plates.

In the past, I've had certain dreams that somehow came to pass. I've no idea how this was possible, but they did, right down to the way light and shadows portrayed the events. So, for the most part, I trust my dreams. But this vision of the underground blue chamber stumped me. Although its vividness and clarity begged for an interpretation, I was at a loss to its meaning.

I wanted to tell Priscilla about it before I forgot it, so I struggled out of bed. Striking pain shot up my leg as I limped down the hall and I had to clench my teeth as I went down those darn stairs.

On the main floor, I flopped on the couch in front of the fireplace and shut my eyes in a vain attempt to block out the pain. Priscilla was making stew at the kitchen counter. I glanced her way.

"How's it going, hon?"

"I took Curly for a walk."

"How was it?"

"He caught the blood trail by the planters and pulled me down to the fence. I saw your porcupine."

"Quite the prickly creature."

"Yes." She stopped chopping a carrot, and looked my way. "I was wondering why there was blood all the way down the hill?"

"I don't know. Was it all the way?"

"Yes, all the way down the hill."

"That skunk must've had a lot of blood."

"No skunk has that much blood. Could you have shot an elk or something?"

"Shot? Well, maybe. Buckshot flies everywhere. I suppose I could've shot an elk."

Her smile was telling. "It would have to be a pretty light-footed elk. I didn't see any animal footprints, only men's."

I let out a long breath and again considered telling her the truth. But it was bizarre—I didn't know the full truth. What held me back was her belief that the truth will set you free, even if it involves the law. "I know that my nose was bleeding."

"Did you rake out those prints by the sunroom?"

"I'm afraid so."

"Why?"

Our eyes met. I shrugged wordlessly.

"From what I saw, something lost a lot of blood. You didn't shoot a two-legged skunk?"

Now I was scrambling. "Did you hear a gun go off up here?"

"No."

"I'm as perplexed as you about this blood trail." Gazing at the fire, I watched the upper part of a yellow-orange flame dance about. I realized I was looking at something that I'd previously seen but never really noticed; the bottom of the flame was darn near the same blue color as the walls in my dream. I watched the flame eat away at a log. "When I was asleep upstairs, I had the most interesting dream."

"Oh?"

I gave her the details, right down to the five plates stacked one atop the other.

Her response was quite matter-of-fact. "Five times fourteen is seventy, a very important number in the Bible. In Joseph's time, there were seventy direct family members who came into Egypt to avoid the famine, and there were five years left of the famine." She looked thoughtful. "I wonder if God wants us to provide for seventy people for five years." She said this in such a definite way that there was no question of its validity.

"Are you kidding me? Seventy? There are towns in Montana that don't have seventy people, and we're supposed to provide for seventy people for five years?"

"If we start, God will provide."

I was taken aback. She took this seriously.

"To build an underground facility like that would cost thousands." I shook my head. "I mean thousands, and that's not including food."

"You're a builder; you can do it."

I was stunned at her quick reply, her stark interpretation, how fast this dream had snagged her attention. What had happened to the blood trail and the two-legged skunk? "Wait, wait … your interpretation would clean out our retirement account, and then some."

"If we're living in the Last Days, who's to say there'll be any retirement?"

I frowned at the enormity of it all. "No, no, that dream was probably because I ate pizza the other night."

"Do you really think so?"

I was afraid to answer. The vision was so clear, the foretelling type, and if I admitted the truth, I knew she'd be gung-ho to start stockpiling.

"You know …" She continued, now chopping away on a potato, "… I've been praying for a vision for us. What's fascinating," she looked contemplative, "it's like a Noah's Ark for seventy people."

"I suppose God would have to get me on His ship first."

"He always leaves that up to you."

"Sometimes I wonder if you married the wrong fellow. Maybe you should've married more of a church-going man." I could see this disturbed her, as she was vigorous in her chopping of the potato.

"Wasn't it your vision?"

"I suppose. It's just that, without a job or money coming in, such a wild adventure would zap everything we have left. It would be different if we were rich."

She had an acute look. "I think that vision was from God."

"I don't possess the same passion you have for saving everybody. Nor am I a socialist. My first thought is, what's in it for me? How would we ever get paid back for putting seventy folks up for five years?"

"Don't you think the Lord would pay you back?"

I struggled to get up, as her questions were hitting too close to the bone. "It isn't hard to see that a number of nations are having financial problems. I can see that without glasses, but who's to say it will get so bad that seventy folks will need food for five years? Isn't this is the land of plenty?"

"The Bible says the Last Days will be like the days of Lot and Noah. To me, that means events will occur unexpectedly. The book of Revelations speaks of wars, scarcity. We are going to need food, lots of food."

I made my way toward the stairway.

"God will pay us back for looking after them. He pays good. The Bible says this is one of the first things Christ does when He returns."

I felt defensive as I neared the stairway door. My voice rose. "Who knows when He'll return?" I shook my head in defiance. "I'm not cashing in our silver."

"We can't eat silver. Revelations says during that time, a man will work all day for a quart of wheat. Think of it as a transfer of wealth from silver to food." She raised a potato. "Food, wheat, will have great value ..."

I thought something was amiss; why would God give a murdering man, a cursed man, a vision to save seventy people through the Last Days? This was wildly crazy. I called out, "I think that vision was from the Devil."

"Do you think the Devil is into saving people?"

I didn't want to hear anymore and limped up the stairs.

*   *   *

That evening I stewed over all the money we had taken from our retirement to spend on preparation goods; we'd increased our diesel fuel tank capacity to 2,000 gallons, adding a 1,000-gallon propane tank, put a rock wall around the tanks to stop stray bullets, added water storage tanks, 1,550 and 2,400-gallon tanks for the garden and a 300-gallon tank for the house, set up a command post, built a bunker and a root cellar, installed motion lights, purchased no end of barbed wire, buried caches in case we had to bug out quickly, buried guns as well, changed the electric stove to propane so we could cook if the grid went down, laid in a three-year supply of seed, increased our food storage far past the point of being hoarders, not to mention my thirst for guns and ammo and her insistence on a security system, and the purchase of that 6 x 6 military truck and those fat horses. The more I thought about it, the more off-balance I knew we'd become.

Furthermore, what good was all this stuff when a pervert just sneaks in without warning? Why didn't those Vicious Dog signs or the old military truck scare him off? And here Priscilla had locked onto this vision of providing for seventy people?

Embarrassing.

\*   \*   \*

The second morning after the unfortunate event, Priscilla was up early. I would have liked to be moving around, but I was still stiff, hurting and laid out in bed.

On a mission, she came into the bedroom, looked me over like a schoolteacher with a student who needs motivation, then began, "I want to put some lavender oil on your ankle."

Before I knew it, she anointed my head with the remains of the oil, then prayed for Jesus to heal me.

"How do you feel now?" She had that expectant look, as if I was going to leap straight out of bed.

I tried to stretch out my leg and got a quick jab of pain. "Like I've been beaten up."

"We're going to need you back in shape. Roll over and I'll massage your back."

In great pain, I rolled over.

She began massaging my leg and back. "Oh Lord, how are we going to proceed with this vision when his leg is this way?"

My eyes rolled at my wife's expectations.

"Lord? With seventy people and all, we're going to need lots of electricity." She bent her head toward my ear. "It'd be prudent to press ahead"—when she said press, she massaged my back harder—"with a solar and wind generator, especially for our well. We'll need lots of water."

"I'm not sure a wind generator is a good idea. Why? Because if the stuff really hit the fan, the tower a windmill sits on is quite tall, like a beacon to the ones without food. If it were up here someone could see it from the highway. Regardless, the cost of all that stuff would definitely clean out our retirement funds." I raised my voice. "And I'm not cashing in any more of our retirement funds to get ready for the supposed big bata-boom."

"Someday you'll be thankful we have our supplies. Money spent on preparation goods is money well-spent." She pressed her hand hard into my back. "Hershal, you are so tight."

"I've no argument with you if we spent it on guns and ammo, but why buy horses that can't do anything but eat up our money?"

"When we can't buy gas, they'll come in handy to plow the garden."

"They're good for nothing right now, and who's to say they'll be any good at plowing?"

"We just have to train them."

"And why do we need an old military truck that doesn't scare off anybody?"

"It will still run after an EMP knocks out all the computers."

"If we can't get gas for it, what use is it?"

She was silent.

"And what do we need so much food for? Goodness, we got enough for two lifetimes."

"We have to look after our kids."

"We do, do we? Aren't they all grown up? Didn't we teach them to be independent?"

"But how will they survive after things fall apart?"

"That's their problem. I've spent enough retirement money on this big bata-boom thing, and now you're talking about looking after seventy?"

"Let me remind you, we started into this build-up because of your dream of the world's financial ship rolling and sinking."

The decision to stockpile seemed such a long time ago that I had forgotten how we got started. But in recalling this, I knew she was right. Still I wasn't going to tell her that. "Regardless, we got no business cashing in our retirement fund for any more of this stuff."

"Who's to say there's going to be a retirement for anybody?"

"You've said that a number of times." I only hoped my stern voice would get through to her. "Here lately I've been wondering a lot about these darn dreams and visions, and I think that blue room one was kooky for sure." Frustrated, I shook my head. "And when I think about the one with the world's financial ship rolling, it didn't make sense; it's nutty too. How can the world's economy ever roll when American women are at the helm? They are the ultimate shoppers; they will always stick a fork in it, they will always get-her-done."

"I believe that dream was from God. Something will destroy our dollar and slow the ladies down."

"I've got more faith in our American women keeping the ship afloat; even if the big bata-boom was nuclear."

She pressed into my back muscles as if I needed to be brought into line. In pain, I dropped my head to the sheet and heard her say, "Please, Lord, empower us to be faithful to Your great vision of looking after the seventy."

Her prayer really got under my skin.

She went on rebuking every devil that ever thought of coming our way … my way … the highway. After her rebuking, she stopped working her fingers into me.

I rolled over and saw her at the base of the bed, lifting her shofar.

I suppose you'd have to go back a few thousand years to see one of these ram's horns used in battle. One thing for sure, I wouldn't want to be a devil when she was on the warpath.

She took in a deep breath, then delivered. The sound of that shofar was so loud, the sheets on the bed would've bolted had I not been holding onto them. It came across with such an exclamation mark that when I got out of bed I was smarting, flustered.

"I'm not cashing in nothing for that seventy." I gave her a mean look. "Nothing!"

"Wasn't it your vision?"

I used the wall for support. "This is too kooky."

"I don't feel kooky."

"I don't care what you feel. From now on, if you're going to blow that thing, do it outside."

She came alongside me, placing her hand on my back, looking up at me with the most tender eyes. "Hershal, I'm just trying to be a support here. That's all."

"Well, I'll tell you what, if God drops the two hundred thousand-plus dollars it takes to do such a crazy build-up, then wake me up; otherwise, it's best to forget about it."

She looked as if she had gotten a revelation, and her hand rose toward the ceiling. "Lord, you heard him."

\*　　\*　　\*

Why I had such a headstrong woman was perplexing. But she was a bulldog when it came to spiritual things. If I have anything to be thankful for, once she makes her request known, she usually won't badger me directly again. Even still, she is a vixen at working it out indirectly, and petitioning the heavens. Not long after her morning coffee, regardless of rain, frost or snow, she'd be out on the front doorstep and I could hear that forlorn sound of the ram's horn. Thank goodness it happened only once a day.

One morning I was watching a herd of elk pass. The lead bull roved about, anxious to work his masculinity upon a cow elk, calling out to her in his impatient whine. Seconds followed before Priscilla cut loose on that shofar. The entire herd stopped in its tracks and looked straight up at her. The lead bull seemed threatened by this bigger, phantom bull on our front doorstep. He angled wide and trotted away from the cow elk as if to say, "You can have her."

But regardless of how loud my wife's petitions were, I wasn't about to cash in on anything when at any moment, the Sheriff could be hauling me away for murder.

# So the Skunk Got Away?

Five days later, I found myself with the folks who lived in our area at our yearly road maintenance meeting. It was uneventful until Toby, a neighbor, asked, "Did you hear about the guy down the road who disappeared?" He thumbed north.

"No. Who was he?" I tried to look naïve, my mouth hanging open, wondering why he had asked me instead of someone else.

"Richard Wartal."

One of the ladies added, "Wasn't he on the pedophile list?"

"I think he lives with his brothers and a woman who just had a baby."

Another neighbor asked, "Didn't he work at Sam's Appliances?"

It all came together when he mentioned Sam's Appliances. We had purchased a new propane dryer at Sam's, and Wartal must have been part of the delivery team. If he was, he certainly could have scoped out our place and realized Curly was nothing like our Vicious Dog signs portrayed.

Another neighbor asked, "Where'd he live?"

"About a half a mile that way." Toby pointed. "Just down Mountain View."

"One of his brothers said he never came back from a walk."

"When was that?"

"About a week ago. He went for a walk after supper and never came back."

The same lady who'd identified him as a pedophile gave a smarty frown. "Who goes for a walk after dark?"

"Maybe a wolf got him." Toby had such a straight face I thought he was joking, but I kept my mouth shut.

"Ya think we're safe?" a heavyset rancher joked.

"Someone said they heard shooting up near your place." Toby's eyes met mine.

Sometimes when I get nervous I get giddy, which I don't understand, so I joked, "Well … if I'm not shooting at my wife, she's shooting at me." I shrugged. "She always wins, though."

There were some chuckles and the rancher went on to tell a joke about husbands and wives. Since the meeting was over, I started to move away.

I was limping toward my truck when Dewey, our closest neighbor, called out, "Hershal, why are you walking with such a gait?"

I half-turned. "Would you think any less of me if I said I fell off a ladder?"

On the way home, I stopped at our gate to check on the porcupine. The prickly creature was upside down. A predator had eaten his innards. The ground around was disturbed enough for me to flip him over and drag him back to the remains of Wartal's blood pile. Gazing up at the gathering clouds, I hoped there would be rain or snow to wash the blood away.

That night my hopes came to pass; the silent covering laid a three-inch blanket of white fluff over everything. I was confident it would erase the man's blood when it melted. But you know how it is when things go too well.

The following day I heard the motion detector sound off around 11 a.m. It was good to know it worked, as I had replaced the batteries in the unit down by the gate. At the time, I was balancing the checkbook and not in the best of moods. When I saw a black SUV with Sheriff's markings on the side doors plowing through the snow and heading up our road, my heart skipped a number of beats.

I was in a sweat to get to him before Priscilla did, as she can put two and two together faster than a hawk pouncing on a rabbit. I couldn't get my boots and coat on fast enough. With my limping gait, I must've looked like the Hunchback of Notre Dame.

The wind caught my unbuttoned coat as I busted out the front door. Priscilla was shoveling snow off the steps that led down to our driveway so I turned and headed back inside, shutting the door behind me. A fright of indecision drove me toward the telephone. I took the phone off its cradle, set it on the kitchen countertop, hurried across the floor, down the basement stairs and to the door that leads to the garage.

Hastily I entered the garage and heard the vehicle, as the garage door was open. I tried to calm myself. This was difficult, especially when the SUV cruised by; it possessed such a heavy presence.

The SUV curved to the right, into our parking area.

I exited the garage, limping toward Priscilla. "There you are, there's a phone call for you." She started to go up the stairs. "I'll take your shovel."

She handed it to me. "I wonder what the Sheriff wants?"

"We'll see."

Killing time, I nervously worked the shovel around the snow while chiding myself for not making more effort to camouflage the area around the backhoe dig. And why hadn't I filled in that hole completely? Two officers were coming my way so I placed the shovel against the wall and limped toward them. I knew Dave, as he had always been the Sheriff; he helped look for Eli back in the day. I hadn't a clue who his sidekick was.

"Hershal."

"Dave."

We shook hands.

He thumbed toward the young officer. "This is my new Deputy, Justin."

I shook his hand as well; he had a real firm handshake. I could best describe him as medium height, clean-cut and wiry.

"He's our up-and-coming," Dave joked, then asked, "How's the family?"

"Fine, fine." I tried to look as casual as possible. I was sure my front teeth showed. "How's yours?"

"Good; what's Eli up to?"

"He's out there … somewhere." I pitched my chin toward the Sapphire Mountain Range. "Trapping. He likes this time of year."

"Yes. So do I."

"How's your family?" Nerves made me repeat this question. Perhaps it was the piercing eyes of his Deputy. I was quick to grin. "What can I do for you?"

"Have you heard of Richard Wartal, your neighbor?"

"There was talk of him at the road maintenance meeting. Did he finally show up?"

"No. I'm just following up leads. Someone said they heard shooting up this way the night he went missing."

"What night was that?" The wind was cold and if I was a kinder man, I'd have invited them in but I could ill afford casual information over a hot cup of coffee.

"A Friday night, a week ago yesterday."

I did my best to look thoughtful. "What was I doing Friday? I wonder if that was the night I got a porcupine?" I shrugged. "I'm not sure."

"Do you hunt much at night?"

I pushed back my glasses. "No. It's just I stepped out and caught whiff of a skunk and it took me on this wild goose chase. I ended up down by the gate. That's where I heard this porcupine up in a tree. He wasn't as lucky as that skunk."

"So the skunk got away?"

I nodded.

"And here I thought you were a dead-eye?"

"Well, in the midst of the chase I fell and broke my glasses." I took off my taped-up glasses to show him. "I was having to constantly deal with them." Again I shrugged, and gave him a forced grin. "Who's to say I'm a good shot, anyway?"

Dave gave me a studied look, one that darn near looked clear through me. I'm not sure what he saw, except my bald head, which in my panic I forgot to cover. It was a relief to hear him finally say, "A porcupine … The Natives like those for their costume vests and such. Do you still have him?"

"I think so."

"Do you mind if I snag him? I harvest their quills."

"I can show you where he's at, at least where he was." I thumbed back. "He's down by the gate."

"I can give you a ride down."

"That's okay. I've got to feed the horses anyway."

As we went to our respective vehicles, I felt stiff, awkward and cold.

When I pulled out of the driveway, I saw that Priscilla had returned to shoveling snow off the stairs. I must confess, even though I grew up with the Golden Rule and knew the rights and wrongs of the Ten Commandments, while I drove down the road, I was disturbed at how calculated I had become. I didn't like it and wished I would've submitted myself to the law, straight-up. But why was it my fault for accidentally shooting someone who blatantly snuck onto our land and was peeping in our window? When I considered this, I realized the buckshot had struck him just off our land, which borders state property; that gave me even more reason to play the game.

At our gate, I stopped behind the SUV and got out. The Sheriff and Deputy were already waiting. As my boots crunched across the snow toward them, everything seemed surreal. Not far off was our WWII military truck.

There was a freshness to the first snow of the year, a cleanness, a brilliant clarity of white. Conversely, I was shrouded, doing my act and forcing another grin. "Isn't it something to be part of the first snow?"

"Maybe this year will be a good year for snow pack."

"A good snow pack would put a hit on those summer fires." I passed them, pointing. "It's right over here."

They followed. "Do you remember if you saw anyone?"

"When?"

"The night you got the porcupine."

I shook my head. "No."

"Was there anything unusual about that night?"

I wanted to say a lot of things, but said, "Not off-hand."

We walked past the gate. Their tire marks left a clear imprint in the snow.

"Did you hear any other shots?" This was the first question from the Deputy.

I casually touched the top of the barbed wire to knock off the snowflakes. "I might have. I seem to remember something about coyote hunters. So maybe I heard some shots."

"Where?" asked the Deputy.

My hand angled back. "They probably came from the south, the state lands."

"Where exactly?"

"I don't know. Last week seems like a long time ago."

"I know what you mean," the Sheriff agreed. "I'm finding, as I get older, the weeks are speeding by in a blur."

Relieved to see a lump protruding from the snow, I limped through the sage. "Here he is." My breath rose like steam. I nudged the porcupine with my boot.

"Good, you gutted him," the Sheriff said with pleasure. "Were you thinking of keeping him?"

"Yes, but after getting poked by a number of his quills, I gave up."

Again he looked thoughtful. "Somebody said they saw lights flashing about this area."

"Oh, yes, I had to be lighting up the world."

"They said maybe it was a quad."

This remark really made me wonder if Wartal was running with someone else. "Well, somewhere in that night's adventure, my flashlight died and I ended up going head-first over that barbed wire." I pushed my glasses up on my nose. "I lost my glasses, so I went back to get the quad because it's got a strong light. That's when I heard the porcupine, scratching in that tree there." I pointed to the tall pine.

"I see." The Sheriff looked content. "That explains it." He reached down and snatched the porcupine by the paw, holding it up like a trophy, admiring its quills. "Yep, I can sell these quills or trade them with the Natives at their yearly Pow-Wow. Have you ever been up to Arlee to see the Flatheads dance?" He rambled on while we walked toward the vehicles.

When we got to his vehicle, he slung the carcass in the back. Then there were the goodbyes and the handshakes.

They left with the trophy, but I was left with uncertainty.

\*     \*     \*

After feeding those good-for-nothing horses, I drove toward the house, thinking about what lies I'd tell Priscilla.

All my calculated answers came swirling about when I pulled in and saw her still shoveling snow. I parked, got out of the truck and paced toward the garage, hoping to avoid an encounter. But my wife took the appropriate steps to nip that hope in the bud.

"What did the Sheriff want?"

I halted just short of the garage. "Evidently a neighbor went missing."

"Who?"

"Some fellow."

"From around here?"

"Yes, one of the Wartals."

"What day did he go missing?"

"Last Friday."

"Wasn't that the night you got the porcupine?"

I nodded. "I ended up giving it to him."

"Giving what?"

"The porcupine." Careful to keep up my act, I shut my big mouth.

"Was he … was the Sheriff satisfied with your answers?"

"I don't know." I gazed down at some ice, considering. "He seemed to be."

My eyes met hers.

It was evident that she was disappointed. After 35 years of marriage, your spouse can sometimes read you without the headlines.

I limped away.

*　　*　　*

In the days that followed, I was quite conscious of that curse. I'm a builder who survives on good-quality work with a competitive bid, but during those days and weeks, I couldn't buy a job. It could've simply been a sign of the times, the recession, or my quotes, but I guessed it was that damning Wartal curse.

Sometimes I thought if I dug up the corpse and moved it off our property, I'd rid myself of the ever-hovering cloud of misfortune, but when I considered his smell, and his heft, there was no way I was going to touch him. Coyotes and wolves are good at digging up the dead when starvation beckons, yet I never did spot an animal track near that grave.

*   *   *

Charby was so struck by this recession that the elementary school lost one-quarter of its students, as parents had to move due to lack of work. Many headed east to the oil fields in North Dakota. I thought that was where I'd end up, though at 58, swinging a hammer in the cold winds of North Dakota wasn't appealing. Yet, appealing or not, spending retirement funds on survivalist stuff had consequences, and as I watched our savings dwindle, even the oil fields began to look good.

Priscilla had written down the vision of the blue room and knew it better than I. She had a home economics major and had no trouble figuring out how much it took, food-wise, to sustain oneself for a year. Totals were crunched for five years for seventy people, for wheats, from kamut to hard red for bread making, to a variety of beans, rice and other grains, right down to providing the oils the body needs through flax seeds. I longed for her to give up her quest, but every morning she diligently called out to the heavens with her shofar.

I think she believed, if she started stockpiling for the seventy, God would miraculously provide the funds to complete this unattainable vision. I first noticed this when she came home from her once-a-month shopping adventure in Missoula with an extra bag of rice and beans. This was disturbing because we already had enough rice and beans for two lifetimes. I told her to stop.

She did stop the extra stockpiling, but wouldn't stop working other angles. At times she'd try to scare me by pointing out faults with the present administration. "Did you read about the law that empowers the President to send any citizen to a foreign prison without trial or due process and keep them there indefinitely for simply suspecting they are supporting terrorism?"

I was adding wood to the fireplace while she kneaded bread dough.

"It reads, 'by simply suspecting!'" She pressed the dough hard to make it behave. "Can you believe how complacent Americans have become? Allowing this President to get rid of habeas corpus in exchange for a feeling of security." She looked at me in stunned disbelief. "And Congress drafted it!"

She raised her arm in an exasperated manner. "I wonder what Congress would do to protect their fat pensions, their private medical care, if George Washington and Thomas Jefferson showed up and started talking about how much lead was needed to bring real change to this nation. No doubt Congress would send those two off to a foreign prison ... indefinitely." She rolled the dough with force, looking like she was ready to lead a revolution. "I tell you, Hershal, we want to be ready when the system unravels." She plowed into that bread dough as if it were the enemy. "America has lost its fear of God."

The next night, she worked away, tenderizing a cut of meat. "Did you hear the latest on the new U.S. Army training document?"

I was sitting on the couch in front of the fire, trying to read a magazine.

"It declares that anyone frustrated with mainstream ideologies is a terrorist." She pounded away on some meat. "Can you believe that?"

I knew this had more to do with stockpiling for the seventy than the entire U.S. Army.

She raised the meat mallet in a pointy manner. "They say you are an extreme right-wing terrorist just because you are suspicious of centralized federal authority." She banged away at the meat. It didn't stand a chance. "Both of us fall into that category!" She looked indignant. "If you are a Christian, then you are classed as an extremist. And presently, our military is removing Christian men in leadership, from the top down." She continued, "And how many years will they keep that Congressional investigation on the last attack on the US hidden from the public?" She shook her head. "There's something scary behind those concealed doors especially when those senators say they were shocked to read those twenty-eight pages." Her voice rose over her clubbing of the helpless meat. "The Bible speaks of intrigue in the Last Days." At last she stopped hammering. "It is here." She guardedly looked about. "Hershal, did you ever wonder if they are going to orchestrate the big bata-boom?"

I know when she gets like this, it's best to be quiet.

"This nation is no different than a Peeping Tom." With venom, she pointed at the sunroom window. "It uses lasers to look inside buildings and prides itself on drones as well as on cracking codes, but it's really nothing but a perverted Peeping Tom that snoops on e-mails and listens to phone conversations." She looked like she wanted to smack somebody in the mouth. "You know this nation has over 900 military bases in over 140 countries. Imagine those forces in the Devil's hands … Think how worthless our money will be after they orchestrate the big bata-boom." She gazed directly at me. "Right now, solar panels are cheap."

Though I believed alternate energy was important, especially when it came to a 496-foot well, I still couldn't spend the last of our retirement funds on that. Furthermore, the area we lived in didn't receive a whole lot of sun in winter, so solar wasn't the best answer. I wondered if the doom-and-gloom my wife felt had more to do with a lack of sun. For sure, she needed to get outside more, as I've heard that helps encourage optimism.

*   *   *

The next day, any optimism I possessed vanished when I got a call from the Deputy Sheriff.

After the cordials, his questions began. "Hershal, we're just following up on that night. You say you heard shooting south of you?"

"What night?"

"The night Wartal disappeared."

"Okay, so what was your question?"

"You said you heard shooting south of you?"

"Did I?"

"Yes."

"Okay."

"Who did you say you thought it was from?"

"Don't know, who could know; maybe coyote hunters?"

"Why do you think that?"

"I just heard coyotes howling and thought they needed to get shot. There's so many of them. I didn't see one fawn last year. Do you have too many coyotes in your area?" I rambled on. "Sound is funny in our neck of the woods, sometimes I don't hear fellas doing target practice just around the corner …"

When I finally shut up and hung up, heat came to my face. Goodness, much of what I'd said could come back to haunt me.

That night, a winter Chinook blew up from the south. The November temperature rose to 62 degrees F. This melted the snows and left a hanging humidity.

The next day, Priscilla came in from a walk, her face covered with concern. "There's something near that backhoe dig that really smells."

I quickly sat up. "I don't know if I told you, but I shot a coyote that was near as big as a wolf and buried him there."

"It really stinks. You'd better do something to cover that smell; otherwise the Fish and Wildlife officers will smell it from Missoula."

"Good idea."

This was frightening, and I got on it right away, putting lots of lime, air freshener, and charcoal down that hole, mixing it with soil and mounding it up.

At the end of my workings, though I couldn't smell Wartal, I could still sense his curse.

# Montana Livestock Business

With our savings dwindling, I felt the tug of oil country, but my limp and back spasms helped me fight the urge. I was really racking my brain, looking for something other than the cold winds of North Dakota to generate income.

One area of work I've always liked was agriculture, yet of our 160 acres of rocks, there were maybe twenty tillable acres. So the concept of making a living off the land was far-fetched at best, until a salesperson down at a pellet mill told me about a pheasant operation that had grown to where they were sending thousands of chicks across the States. We had a few game birds, mainly partridge, doves and grouse, but it really didn't click until one cold morning in late December, when I noticed the rock rabbits.

"Rock rabbits," as our neighbor Dewey called them, were less than half the size of domestic rabbits. The pellet mill salesman told me, pound per pound, you got more out of rabbits than any farm animal.

So while I waited for spring, when I figured I'd be heading to oil country, I took a gamble and bought a couple of bags of rabbit feed. I really didn't put a whole lot of hope in it.

I didn't know if it was legal to propagate these animals, as they might be wild, so I called Montana Fish and Wildlife and described the bunnies to the receptionist. The hind legs were short, the hind feet were comparatively broad and heavily haired, the ears were short, rounded and small, and the color was a mixture of cinnamon to gray.

She asked where we lived, then said it was probably a domestic rabbit that had gone wild. If so, Fish and Wildlife had no jurisdiction over that type of rabbit.

Previously, these rock rabbits were a bugger to keep out of our irrigation boxes, so I decided to give them the shelter they were seeking. On the far side of the woodpile we set up a number of these boxes. We became consistent in providing water and pellets for them.

For fun, Priscilla brought the irrigation boxes in and painted pictures on them. I don't know if it was the long winter, but it was comical how many rabbits hung around the box that had a rabbit with a sombrero on it. Bugs Bunny wasn't far behind. Then there was Elvis with rabbit ears, and the farmer and his wife with rabbit ears.

About a month after we started providing food, the bunny population exploded. They were everywhere around the house. There wasn't a spot in the snow that didn't have a rabbit track or droppings. Despite not having a market, once we saw how much their population increased, we leaped right into the rabbit business.

I figured a dog would be a good investment to keep predators at bay. We had Curly, but he was well past his prime, hard of hearing, no longer a protector of anything but his sleeping blanket. This decision coincided with an e-mail from a member of our preparedness group who had to give up his dogs, as he was moving. One of them was a wolfhound.

I was quick to call. While heading over there, I told myself not to get a dog older than four; what good were two dogs past their prime? But this Irish Wolfhound was such a stunner, the top of this head was just over four feet and though he was pushing 150 pounds he was very fleet-footed and even though he was past six, I had to have him. His name was Cane, as in hurricane.

Shortly after getting Cane, I took him on a run around the property. I was on the quad and clocked him going 23 mph; he looked like he was just loping. We traveled the boundary line and on finishing I told him to protect the property from coyotes, wolves and bad boys. I don't know if he understood, but predators certainly did.

Cane was a fascinating dog. At times he didn't like to be petted; he had a side to him that you wouldn't want to cross. Toward evening, he moved into the doghouse with Curly and our cat Clyde. How they all fit in there was a wonder. At first the bunnies were scared of Cane, but about a month after, they ran about as if they owned him.

There came a time when the land around the house was inundated with bunnies. They were everywhere. And with the cost of rabbit food and dog food, we needed to harvest them before they harvested our savings. That forced me to become a salesman. I've never been much of a salesman, nor has Priscilla.

I suppose both of us looked as if we were selling our brothers and sisters when we carried a few little cuties into a pet store in Missoula.

The clerk petted one fluff ball in awe-like wonder. "I've never seen such an interesting rabbit. They almost look wild." She examined its feet. "Strange. They look webbed. What species?"

Priscilla said, "Everybody just calls them rock rabbits."

"I'm sure they will be a hit."

Boy, when she said that, hope flowed. "How many would you like?"

She mentioned some encouraging numbers but what really stuck was when she finished, "I'll need your permit number to proceed."

I didn't have a clue what permit she was talking about, and thought it best to back-off rather than look too hillbilly-ish. "Yes, well, I'm afraid I left that back at the warehouse." As if I had a warehouse!

We didn't know if the permit was going to be a six-month process and cost thousands of dollars or was an over-the-counter deal. When I got back home, I called a friend, who said it might either be an agricultural permit or something like a dog license. He finished with, "You might have to get a vet up there to inoculate the rabbits; that way you can protect the public from any strange diseases. If that's the case, you can bet you need to start paying into Medicare for them rabbits, because the government wants everyone on it."

I knew he was being sarcastic, but when I hung up I wondered, What's next, a marriage license for the bunnies?

In the meantime, I called a hunting operation down in Texas and asked the manager if they were interested in purchasing any rock rabbits.

"Are they fast?"

"Sure, they're fast. They'll run like the dickens." I knew they weren't jackrabbit-fast, but I was in sales now and was learning how to stretch it.

"How much do you want for them?"

"How many would you consider taking?"

"We get our pheasants in lots of fifty. Maybe a hundred or so, if the price is right. What's your discount structure?" His deep Texas drawl immediately pumped life right into my pocketbook.

We wanted to sell them for $9 each but … if we could sell fifty at a time! I was scrambling, with no clue as to the price. "Yes, we sure do have a fifty-or-more discount. Yes." There was a long pause. I was still rambling, scrambling.

"Well, what is it?" he asked, as blunt as the end of a shot-gun barrel.

"Six." I didn't know where that number came from.

"Do you send to other hunting clubs?"

"Oh, yes." I figured lying was fair game in sales. "We've got six clubs presently." There was that number six again.

"Okay, you can send one hundred of them down to the Dodge airport and if it works out, and hunters like shooting them, you'll be getting an order from us every month."

If my mind was trying to find second gear before, now it had jumped past second and slammed into fourth.

When I got off the phone, I was sure we'd broken the curse. But not half an hour later the phone rang, and Priscilla came down the stairs to tell me, "It's the Sheriff's Deputy."

With dread, I headed toward the phone. I attempted to sound lighthearted, but what a struggle. "Hi, Justin."

He was just as blithe. It wasn't long before he got to his real purpose. "Hershal, I was talking to the Wartals, who say they're pretty sure Richard headed south, toward your place, the night he was shot."

"Shot?"

"I mean, disappeared."

"Wartals?"

"Yes, the brothers of Richard Wartal, who live in the house in your area."

"Okay."

"So you think he came south, too? You saw him up there?"

"Did what?"

"Did you see him up there?"

"Noooo. I thought I went over all that with the Sheriff."

Soon our conversation ended. The Deputy's leading ques-tions were disturbing. He made me wonder, even fear, that somewhere in that night a third person was involved.

That evening Priscilla asked me a number of questions. "What are we going to put the bunnies in to ship them to Texas? Will the bunnies be able to survive the flight?"

Her other questions were just as pertinent, but my worries were on that Deputy. His entrapment was fixed. What did he know from this third person?

# Canes

Around noon the next day, I was setting the kitchen table when the motion detector ding-dong went off for the front door. Because of our growing rabbit population, I didn't pay much attention. Ding-dong. Ding-dong. What got me moving was a knock on the door. Strange that our motion detector down by the road hadn't picked up any vehicle. Were the batteries out again?

Opening the door, to my surprise, there was Eli. He looked tired and windblown.

"Well, look at you."

He had this ancient long mink collar coat that looked as if it had come out of Grandma's closet. Below it were the same pants he had on last month, with the knees torn.

"Where'd you get that coat?"

He didn't respond.

"Are you okay?" I talked louder, as I didn't know what got into his head. "Don't make me come out there to get you," I jokingly said while going through the storm door. "Are you going to tell me how you are?"

He looked so distant that I wasn't sure if he even heard the question.

It was then I noticed his spear that sat atop the snow. "I haven't seen you with that spear in a long time. What happened to that gun I gave you?"

He nodded.

"You got it on you?"

He shook his head.

"Sometimes I just don't get you. If you got a gun, you should have it on you." Scooping his arm, I felt for strength, then leaned toward his ear, and softly stated, "It can't protect you if you don't got it."

Generally, when I'm up close and personal, his humor will show but that wasn't the case now. He looked grim.

I guided him toward the door. "You need to put on some weight." The storm door wang-banged as we went through.

Just inside the doorway, I let him go, then gave him a playful, instructive finger. "It's not good to eat just meat, meat, meat."

He grinned but it was a sad grin.

"Boy, do you ever look as if you've lost a battle." I glanced toward the kitchen, wondering why Priscilla hadn't showed. "Priscilla?" Again, I took him by his arm, and escorted him toward the kitchen table. "Priscilla, you'll never guess what the cat dragged in." At the table I gave him an insistent look. "You will have lunch with us."

Priscilla came out of the bathroom, rounding the corner into the kitchen and about shrieked when she spotted him. "Oh, Lord Jesus." She closed on us. "What a beautiful day to see my son." As she neared, her arms invitingly opened. She hugged him in.

Eli looked as if he needed lots and lots of hugs. I gave his back a rub, my fingers roving over his coat's black mohair which was swirled into tight balls. It was cold.

After all our goopy welcoming, the haggard kid flopped down at our kitchen table. I helped ready some bowls, then sat next to him. Across from us was the kitchen window.

With the overcast sky the view wasn't that cheerful, so I was doing my best to liven things up, grinning. "So what have you been doing with yourself lately? Have you got a job? Have you met any interesting gals?"

He gave a disappointed shake of the head and the way he extended this spoke of a hermit drawing in. This was concerning.

"What do you think about hanging out here for a while?" I patted his shoulder. "That way you could get your legs back. Eating right will get you some muscle. It's not good to eat just meat, you have to be balanced. Your body really needs those enzymes from vegetables. That's very important."

His head was down and he looked as if he was contemplating.

Priscilla added, "He does like chicken noodle soup."

"Who doesn't like your chicken noodle soup?"

I stared at the side of his face. Eli appeared to be mentally battling with something.

"He's always liked my whole wheat buns."

"Who wouldn't like your buns? Especially when they come out the oven." I gave him a nudge. "With butter."

It was good to see his head come up. The window was now in his view, but all wasn't rosy. Across the outside of the glass came the sight of something that made him jerk back in fear. It was Cane's large head. A smaller dog wouldn't have been seen from that window, as it was three and a half feet off the floor. I imagined Eli's first view of the wolfhound would be like seeing an imposing dinosaur. Moreover, Cane's jaw hung, exposing his impressive teeth that looked freshly cut and sharpened. If that wasn't intimidating enough, underneath Cane's shaggy forehead was a brown eye that was fixed on Eli.

"Nothing to be afraid of, Cane's our newest addition."

As Cane walked along the window frame, his total focus was on Eli. Halting, he looked as if he were peering straight into the trapper's soul.

"He's big but he's tender." I arose. "Come on, Eli." I slipped my hand under his arm to help him up. "Let's go meet him."

He was a bit tentative.

"Come on, he's only a dog. A big dog, yes, but he won't harm you."

When we exited the house, Cane was waiting, ten feet or so away, his eyes taking in our visitor.

"Cane, come present yourself to Eli."

Half looking back, I noticed Eli eying his spear, then my pet. Cane plowed through the snow toward us. I stepped aside. He passed me and put his big head right in Eli's chest. Awestruck, Eli stepped back. No doubt Cane's noble appearance was arresting.

"He is a bit imposing, isn't he?"

Just as Eli's hand came up to touch him, Cane veered off as if to say, Ah, ah, ah.

"He has a side of him that you wouldn't want to cross. They were bred to kill wolves and take men off their horses."

Cane came to me and I rubbed his neck. Eli stepped up to touch his side. Cane pulled away, meandered in a long half-circle, then turned and stood. Again his focus was on Eli. As abruptly as he'd left, he returned and once more put his head straight into Eli's chest.

"I think he likes you."

It was good to see Eli grin.

Eli ended up staying the night. I'm not so sure he would've stayed if it wasn't for Cane, as he went outside a number of times to visit him. And when I say stayed, he didn't sleep in the house but on a cot inside the barn with the barn door open.

We sure wanted him to stay longer, though we knew he didn't care for the confines of our house and there was something about him that had to be on the move. Still, he did take a shower, which must've felt good along with a change of clothes, which Priscilla had patched from a former visit.

But that was it, the next morning the barn door was shut, the cot put away and the sleeping bag rolled up and sitting on the quad. When I grabbed the bag, I recalled a conversation with him at the supper table that was a bit perplexing.

I had asked him, "How's it going out there?" pointing toward the darkened window.

He shook his head, and signed out, "Cane."

"He didn't bite you?"

He shook his head and signed out, "Canes," then flashed his fingers, his whole hand, twice.

"Cane's not ten, he's six." I gave Priscilla a look as I wasn't sure what he meant.

She arose, walked toward the kitchen cabinet, then looked back at Eli. "I bet you haven't had any vitamins in a long time."

I said to her, "I wonder if the loneliness of that old forest is getting to him." Then turned to him. "It's not good to be alone. That forest will make a stranger out of you."

Priscilla returned with the vitamins. "You're never alone if you have Jesus."

"You're never alone if you got a gun either. Maybe you need to get back to civilization and get a job. There are ranchers out here that are looking for a young buck like you. With all the money you'd be earning, you can get a good rifle. No need to be hauling that little spear around."

# Bunnies Unlimited

Priscilla's concern over shipping the bunnies to the hunting club in Texas was resolved with a trip down to Feed and Farm Supply. The manager was kind enough to give me a couple of cardboard crates that he received chicks in. They appeared strong enough, but Priscilla pointed out that bunnies weren't birdies and might be able to chew through the crates.

"You worry too much," was my response. "Sometimes I wonder, where's your God in all this?"

She finally brightened. "I was doing some figuring."

"Oh?"

"If we could get into these clubs, it really wouldn't take much to make $3,600. a week."

I gave her a studied look; it was good to see her swept up in this livestock business. She hadn't been this motivated since that darn vision of sheltering the seventy. And if I was really lucky, this might quench that silly seventy thing.

She said excitedly, "I've got a good name for it, too."

"What's that?"

"We can call it Bunnies Unlimited."

*　　*　　*

It was a cold March morning when we took 100 bunnies down to the Missoula Airport for their flight to the Texas hunting club. The airport personnel weren't shy about putting their fingers through the holes to pet the little critters. The boxes were stuffed tight, as bunnies are bigger than chicks.

Priscilla was constantly fidgeting and going over to talk to the freight handler. "Do you think the boxes are strong enough?"

"Not to worry," said the 20ish-looking fellow while lifting up a roll of duct tape. "We got everything."

I thought his demeanor was refreshing; them 20-year-olds don't worry about a thing.

On the way home, Priscilla was hopeful. "With God blessing us here, it won't be long before we can start the solar and wind generator."

I rolled my eyes at the thought of that. "Do you really think God is in this?"

"Absolutely, God wants to bless us," she exclaimed excitedly. "He's showing us a way. Can't you see His hand when you see how fast the rabbits started multiplying? And look at our man from Texas."

# When it Rains, it Pours

When we got home, I noticed the blinking light on the phone's recorder. I never realized that touching such a small button could start such an avalanche of events. BEEP! "Mr. Beecher, can you call Horizon Airline? We've had some trouble with your containers." BEEP! "Mr. Beecher, this is the Missoulian newspaper, can you …"

I came to find out that the chick boxes got perforated by some renegade bunnies as they sat on the tarmac. This happened while passengers were boarding the plane. Understand that the boarding area at Missoula Airport isn't enclosed, so the same tarmac the rock rabbits were bounding across was the same tarmac where the passengers were loading. Furthermore, the plane wasn't a jumbo, but only a 76-seater, so the theater for this event was watched by bleeding hearts, the Devil and real-time cell phones. Did I mention that Missoula has no shortage of environmentalists?

Some passengers tried to catch the little runners. For safety reasons, the plane's twin props were shut down. Somewhere in the midst of all the excitement, somebody noticed that the innocent bunnies weren't going off to a spa and golfing club in Texas, but to a hunting club. And just as suddenly, the owner of Bunnies Unlimited became a very evil man.

If that wasn't enough, the freight manager said something in a threatening voice about having called Fish and Wildlife. I must say, this rabbit adventure was like the quickest laxative ever.

I wasted no time in heading back to the airport to pick up my rabbits.

What a relief to finally get out of there as the manager of the operation kept looking at me as if I was a wicked, wicked man.

As I drove away, an emotion rose in me with great conviction; I was angered at what a bunch of environmentalists this state had turned into. Montana used to be the second-highest state in the country for jobs, but now, with this pervasive mindset, it was forty-eighth. Someone needed to stand up to the environmentalists!

*   *   *

The next day, guess what was on the front page of the Missoulian? The headline was: Rare Pygmy Rabbits illegally sold to Texas Hunting Club. Did I ever appear guilty! All day long I got hate calls from bleeding hearts and some weren't subtle about where to stick the pitchfork. I concluded that redneck Texans have nothing on those bunny huggers.

My bride could see my gloom and ended up calling some friends from what she called the Underground Church, which was just a neighborhood prayer group. Throughout the day I could hear the sound of that shofar.

I was about to go lock our gate when the phone rang again. I had come to the point of not picking it up, due to the continued abuse. After the recorder engaged, I heard the caller say, "I know your address. We're coming for you."

At that, I picked up the receiver. "I've got the Sheriff on the other end of the line. Is there something else you want to say to him?"

The line went silent.

What dread. I went straight down our road to lock our gate.

*   *   *

I had just fastened the lock when I saw our neighbor's rig come around the far corner. Dirt rose off the tires as Dewey's truck came to a stop.

Hardly out of his vehicle, he lifted a newspaper. "Have you read the paper?"

"No," I lied.

Though in his 70s, he paced quickly toward me. "There's a saying," he shoved the newspaper through the wrought iron openings, "you can get away with murder in Montana, but don't get caught doing something against wildlife." I took the offered paper. "The imbalance of justice is severe in this state toward certain offenses." He lifted his chin toward my house. "They'll throw the book at you."

My eyes returned to the paper. The first sentence began with, Bunny man. To say I looked at fault, with my teeth pressing near out the paper, was an understatement. "I didn't know they were wild. I thought they were a mix." I heard another vehicle. "Didn't you say they were rock rabbits?"

We both turned. A car came into view. A woman was behind the wheel.

I scowled. "I bet she's from some environmental group."

"I better move my truck," Dewey said.

"Could you wait a minute?"

The car came to a stop behind Dewey's truck.

In a flash, the woman pulled a leather bag from her vehicle and marched toward us.

My eyes met Dewey's. "She's serious about something."

When she reached into her leather bag, I cautiously stepped back.

"Do you know if this is 437 Eastbrook?" The question hit as a demand.

"Can I ask who you're with?"

"I'm with the Census Bureau and correcting some of our readings." She pulled out what looked like a handheld electronic unit. "We've found some of the addresses that don't line up with the GPS, and 437 Eastbrook is one of them."

Relieved that she hadn't pulled out a gun, I asked, "What's with this GPS stuff?"

She looked past me as if I wasn't there. "Is this 437 Eastbrook?"

I grew suspicious; maybe she was a bunny hugger and was using this as a ploy. Even if her story was true, why would I want the government to know my GPS coordinates? At the rate I was going, they'd be putting missiles down my smokestack.

"I don't know."

"Do you have a handicapped son living with you?"

Her question caught me off-guard, actually disturbed me. "You're with who?"

"The Census Bureau. Is this 437 Eastbrook?"

Dewey said, "Where's Eli these days?"

I gave him a firm look. "I'll call you later."

"I better move my truck." Dewey backed away.

"Is this 437 Eastbrook?"

I abruptly turned and headed for my vehicle. It isn't my way to leave someone standing there, but this was different. Even if she was legitimate, what business had the government with my handicapped son?

A pile of differing suspicions and scenarios played out in my mind as I slid into the truck, put it in gear and headed for the house. Was the world that small, that she had my GPS?

Motoring past our garden, I looked up the hill toward Wartal's grave. Were all these troubles because of his curse?

I stopped the truck outside the garage. I wanted to ask Priscilla if there was something about the Census form regarding the handicapped, and hustled up the outside stairs.

At the front porch, I abruptly halted. Just before me, on the middle of the slate, two wooden matches stuck out from underneath a rock. One was unlit, the tip of other was burned and I could smell smoke.

A note under the matches read, Kill rabbits, will you?

An intense feeling of vulnerability gripped me. I sent a searching glance across the hillside, then leaped off the porch and hurried around the sunroom, hoping to catch the culprit. Bunnies scattered.

I ended up at the back of the house, searching, searching, then hustled toward our concrete bunker. At the bunker I opened the door and peered in. It was empty.

From the house, I heard Priscilla call, "There's a fellow on the phone."

I feverishly looked about, desperate to catch the intruder before I headed her way.

"Hershal," she waved, "there's a fellow who wants to purchase all the bunnies."

She was still standing at the back door when I approached. I gave her a hard look. "Someone wants to burn us out."

"What?" she exclaimed.

"He's out here." I thumbed toward the landscape as I hurried up the stairs.

"Why would they do that?" She looked down the hill.

I passed her, went through the doorway, heading for the phone. Picking it up, I mumbled a hesitant, "Hello."

"Hi, I'm Fred Auburn from The Wildlife Foundation and I'm heading up the possibility of purchasing all your rabbits. Do you know how many rabbits you possess?"

I tried to calm my heavy breathing and stiffly replied, "I haven't taken a count lately."

"If we were to take all, what would you be willing to sell them for?"

Maybe, just maybe, this buyer could be my salvation. Maybe, just maybe, the whole ordeal would blow over if I sold them all to him. "We were getting nine dollars apiece. If you want them all, I can give you a deal … say, eight."

"Selling them elsewhere, do you mean the hunting clubs?"

"Well …"

"Those poor little innocents deserve a better life than getting shot at. Wouldn't you agree?"

I was about to hang up on him. "If you buy them, they will."

"This is Don from KNBO radio and we just did a … GOTCHA!"

In the background, I heard a pre-recorded can-laugh. I hung up, feeling like the laughingstock of Yokino County.

Priscilla looked expectantly at me.

"We need to gun-up." I pointed toward the front door, speaking quickly, "These people are nuts. We need every six-shooter and then some, if they surround the place."

"What?" Perplexed, she stepped toward the front door.

"They want to burn us out." I went straight after my weapons and barked, "Get gunned up!"

She bolted for the stairway.

Within minutes, I had my .38 special and 10 mm. in their holsters, my bandoliers across my chest and all the blackout blinds lowered.

The stairwell door opened and Priscilla entered the room, with six-shooters strapped to her sides.

"It might get real hot in a minute." Taking one of my bandoliers, I laid it across her shoulder. "You're going to need no end of ammo."

"We just need sombreros," she said dryly, touching my elbow.

"You always say that when we get holstered up."

"What did you say about burning us out?"

"Someone left a note and two matches under a rock on our front porch."

"Just now?"

"Yes." I pulled out the .38 and headed for the back door. "They think nothing of reducing the world's population by two-thirds so they can save something …"

"We have to be careful not to shoot anybody," she said, following.

"The heck we do! If these people need anything, it's lead!" With that, I yanked the back door open, stepped out, aimed my gun toward some fallen trees and fired. Blam! Blam!

From down the hill, I heard, "Hold on. Hold on. Don't shoot!"

"I see you there, get your hands up!" This was a lie, but adrenaline drove me and I glanced back at my bride. "What'd I tell you?"

She moved about me to look down the hill. A youngish, long-haired radical was raising his hands.

"Start walking this way or I'm going to …"

Priscilla blurted, "Don't say it. Don't say it."

To my surprise, the man stepped over a log and came our way. He wasn't wobbly-kneed in the least, but moved with confidence as he romped up the hill, moving as if we had been playing tag and he'd been found out. His buoyancy was irritating.

I glanced at Priscilla. "The first thing I'm going to do is kick him in his environmental …!"

"You can't do that. They'll sue us. Those people have big money, lots of money." She fidgeted nervously. "Can we get these off?" She started to lift the bandoliers. "They're too heavy." She looked flustered. "We should be careful. We don't want to hurt anybody. Lawsuits are no fun. They can take everything we have."

The phone rang. We both jumped, we were so on edge. She jabbed my arm, instructing, "Let's do right."

"When you're in there, call the Sheriff." Focused on the radical, I set my jaw, quite aware how fast the situation with Wartal had gotten out of hand.

As the young man approached the woodpile, I motioned with the end of the gun barrel, indicating the direction I wanted him to go. He obliged, coming round the rabbit boxes, then walking straight up the incline. He was as light-footed as a billy-goat.

The bunnies scattered before him.

"Sit right there." I pointed to the base of the stairs, just beyond the rose bushes.

He sat down, crossed his legs and looked quite comfortable. The bunnies that had bolted, now closed in on him to see if he had any treats. I wondered where Cane was in all this.

Priscilla appeared, looking pale. "It's a Sergeant with Montana Fish and Wildlife."

"What's he want?"

"He wants to see our operation."

My heart dropped. "When?"

"Why don't you talk to him?"

"Cover him, will you?" I gave her a wide-eyed look, whispering, "Get your gun out."

My wife pulled the gun out as if it were alive. I headed inside, wondering when she was going to take guns more seriously.

My hot attitude found humbler tones as I picked up the phone. "Hello?"

"Are you the man behind Bunnies Unlimited?"

"Well …"

"This is Sergeant Johnson with Montana Fish and Wildlife. I'd like to come up and look over your operation."

While trying to catch my breath, my mind raced over what I would do if these rabbits were indeed wild. It would take over an hour for an officer to get down here from Missoula. I could get rid of our make-shift irrigation huts. I'd just tell him I didn't know how all the rabbits showed up. All this went through my bean at the speed of light.

"I never shot a rabbit." I have no idea why I said this.

"News of your operation is spreading. It appears the species you are selling is wild."

"These are domestic rabbits."

"I need to verify that. We need to inspect your operation."

"I'm a bit busy right now. Maybe …" I paused, "… what do you think of coming next week some time?"

"Presently I'm at your gate."

The word gate froze me. "Yeah … well … okay. I'll be down shortly."

I hung up. My fingers trembled as I lifted the bandoliers over my head and draped them on a chair.

I felt lightheaded when I went outside, stepping toward Priscilla. "That was Fish and Wildlife."

"I know."

I motioned for her to come inside so we could talk. She stepped through the doorway.

I whispered, "They're at the gate."

She nodded.

"Do you want to go down and let them in, or cover this guy?"

She caught my eye, quietly saying, "I'll watch him."

I took a guarded glance upward. "I bet they're watching the house by satellite."

"Or drones … I'll pray."

My breath was heavy. "I should take my .45 just in case it's a trap."

"I'll pray." She laid her hand on my chest, mumbling a quiet prayer.

"I better go."

She gave me the type of hug that was meant for men who go off to war.

*　　*　　*

As I drove to the gate, Dewey's words rang in my ears—"You can get away with murder in this state; just don't do something against wildlife."

When I parked at the gate, I saw there wasn't just one Montana Fish and Wildlife officer, but three. They waited outside their SUV.

I slid the .45 under a coat on the truck's seat before getting out. Conscious of their glare, I heard the gravel crunch under my boots. My cheeks were warm. Every move I made, unlocking the gate, then opening it, seemed awkward, surreal.

Despite the dry country and cool weather, when I approached the Sergeant, sweat rolled down my neck. The big man was kind enough as he introduced the rabbit specialist, but she, a solid-set woman in her 50s, was cold as ice. Then there was an older man who I assumed was the head iceberg. He didn't say a word, just gave me a stoic nod.

I thumbed up the hill. "There's someone up there I want you to meet as well. Can you make arrests?"

"Oh, yes," the Sergeant boldly said, staring directly at me.

"Well, there's a fellow up there that we just caught. He left this note and a few matches on our front doorstep." I produced the note.

They looked it over.

"He's up there?" asked the Sergeant.

"Priscilla's got him covered."

"There's no need for that kind of nonsense."

From up the hill, I heard the long, foreboding sound of the shofar. I must've looked strange, eccentric, as I abruptly broke away from them and headed for my truck.

Overwhelming worries cluttered my mind as I powered my truck up the hill. Why had Priscilla blown the shofar when she should've been covering the intruder? And who was she calling to, me or God? What was perplexing with this avalanche of unfortunate events was her belief that God was in this rabbit business. Didn't she say He was? If so, where was He?

At the top of the hill, I pulled in and parked. Concerned over my wife's well-being, I wasted no time in hopping out and pacing toward the house. "Priscilla?" I loudly called, looking toward the back door. What a relief to see her at the back door.

Behind me, I heard the SUV pull in so I quickly headed back for the Fish and Wildlife folks, determined to show them better hospitality, since I had so abruptly left.

They were gathered at the back of the SUV. Curly drew near them, his tail wagging slowly, looking to be petted. They were too stingy to even give him one pat, so he flopped down on the ground.

As I approached them a darker cloud of dread came over me. "The radical is over here." I gave a gritty thumb toward the stairs before heading back.

Looking toward the back door, I again called, "Priscilla?" Where was she now? Everything had been such a hurry-up, and where was that sneaking environmentalist?

"Priscilla?" I hustled up the stairs. What a panic I was in when I rapidly entered the house.

Priscilla was next to the kitchen table, undoing her holster.

I hastily asked, "What's going on? Where is he?"

She tiredly said, "He walked away."

"You didn't shoot him?"

Her look was stark. "The Lord wouldn't have me shooting anybody, especially if they're walking away." With a clunk, the holster and gun hit the table.

"Where'd he go?"

"Down the hill."

"Did you call the Sheriff?"

"Yes."

Disturbed, I shook my head as I headed toward the porch. Before going through the back door, I saw the officers waiting at the bottom of the steps.

They looked expectantly up at me.

I addressed them, "He just took off." My gaze went out over the countryside. "You want to see if we can catch him?" I started down the stairs. "He's out there … somewhere."

"That's a lot of land to cover," said the Sergeant, skeptically.

I really hoped they'd help me catch him.

The Sergeant angled his palm toward the bunnies. "What if we finish here first?"

From that point on, everything went downhill. It didn't matter what I said about calling their receptionist before we got in the business or the fact that bunnies were using domestic irrigation boxes as their home, or all my other excuses; they were a waste of breath.

When I finally stopped pleading my case, the Sergeant solemnly began, "From what we can see, these are Rare Pygmy Rabbits. I'm going to write you up to cease your operation. It is illegal to sell or ship them in or out of state …"

He went on, speaking clearly, but I heard nothing. I was dealing with the dark cloud, a business failure, another gamble that had gone wrong. Bizarre that this whole deal came about from simply trying to make a living off livestock.

While he came to his conclusion, I stared across the landscape to where I'd buried Wartal and considered his curse.

# So Your Daddy's a Survivalist?

That weekend, the weightiness of the coming Fish and Wildlife penalty was like an anchor. Everything that morning seemed to irritate me as I worked away, cleaning up the barn.

Earlier I'd heard Priscilla blowing that darn shofar. That irked me too; why was she was calling out to God? And why was she still on that seventy thing when we were now facing a big penalty coming from Montana Fish and Wildlife? I didn't get that at all.

Adding to this was my frustration at not finding things. Where was my pitchfork? My only suspect was Eli. I suppose I was guilty of turning a blind eye to him taking certain items, but that morning, it irked me.

My nerves were so shot, the first sight of Eli standing by the barn door gave me a jolt. His stillness was like a ghost.

"You about scared me to death." I turned away, as I didn't want him to see how frazzled I was. My voice was downcast. "How's it going?" I continued to fiddle around, organizing the screwdrivers to see how many were left.

A minute passed before he gave me a jolly pat.

I turned and viewed him. He appeared windblown and still wore that ancient coat with those tight black mohair balls.

"I can't seem to find my pitchfork. Do you know what happened to the pitchfork?"

He was mute.

"If you see the guy who took it, tell him I need it back." I talked loud, straight to his face. "Okay?"

He nodded.

"You're going to have to start thinking about getting a job. That way you can buy your own stuff." I pointed toward the barn door, where a chicken was pecking. "As good as you are with chickens, you'd be good with cattle. Maybe one of those cattle ranches will take you."

I squeezed his arm to see if he still had muscle. To my disappointment, there wasn't much. "We just got to find out which cattle ranch wants you. At least, you'll be paying your own way." Still gruff, I pulled him toward myself, but the troll in me was softening. "You want to buy stuff at Wal-Mart, don't you?"

He gave me a broad grin.

"Your mother and I are going to the preparedness meeting today. You want to come?"

Considering, he gave me a long stare.

"Those are the meetings where everybody learns how to survive without electricity and out on their own, kind of like what you do. When you start talking, we'll have to get you up there teaching it."

He laughed.

"Anyway, I'd like to see you go with us. It'd be fun to share the afternoon. I haven't seen you for a while."

To my astonishment, he nodded.

"We'll have to get you into another coat." He'd outdo all the hicks if I brought him there wearing that coat. "You'll be too hot in it, anyway." It was surprising to see him wearing a heavy coat like that in the middle of March. But it was strange weather—a week earlier, most of the snow was gone in the lower elevations, yet last night it snowed. I was getting tired of winter.

\*　　\*　　\*

The cold bit when I stepped from the truck at Tex and Joan's place. A rust-bucket of a truck pulled in beside us, then backfired. An old, gray-bearded fellow stepped from his jalopy, gave me a nod and looked at Eli, saying, "You boys stay by the truck. I might need a push to get it started."

I grinned at his joke and watched him head for the shop. His jalopy matched some of the vehicles that were strewn about Tex's yard. I suppose if you didn't have a few broken-down vehicles in the Yokino Valley, you weren't a Yokinoer.

Priscilla and I must've looked as overcast as the sky when we entered Tex and Joan's shop. Eli tagged along, looking over Tex's welder, torches, paint sprayers, work benches, machine tools. And there was big Tex, sitting like a watchdog. You could hear lots of chatter beyond the next door. I gave Tex a nod.

"Welcome." His Southern accent was always warm. He angled his heavy hand toward the door, letting us pass. You don't get into such a meeting without someone knowing you, and I mean, really knowing you.

The rant was fat, with forty-plus people milling around. I noticed the noise level drop as we entered. I'm sure most knew whose face was on the front page of the Missoulian, and scuttlebutt is thick in a small community. As it quieted, I suppose my reddening face got redder. Some folks were kind enough to take the gab level up a notch, thank goodness.

I was maneuvering around a hefty teen when he asked, "How would you survive on the little ones?"

I gave him a perplexed look.

"There's no meat on them little bunnies. And no fat, either. Why didn't you grow the bigger ones?"

I probably looked like a rabbit in headlights.

"You ever hear about rabbit starvation?"

Speechless, I gave him a small shake of the head.

"Eating lean meat all the time will give you diarrhea."

It was one of those awkward moments where I just wanted to evaporate. I quietly said, "Diarrhea's no fun," still hoping to get by him. The predicament was resolved as Eli gave me a helpful push. I slid past him, did a quick jig around a pot-belly stove and flopped into a seat right next to one of our local doctors.

The speaker, our leader Tex, though slow in voice, didn't miss a beat. "Welcome." Half-joking, he continued, "We are here to prepare you now so we won't have to shoot you later." After the chuckling subsided, he went on, "You know our motto—it's better to prepare ten years too early than ten minutes too late."

He wore a John Deere baseball cap, and everything about him was big. "You can see how far off-track this administration has taken our nation in their quest to enhance the U.N. agenda." He casually moved a chair over, offering it to one of the ladies. "This valley is on Agenda 21 radar. Their plan is to eventually steal your land. They want to empty it of mankind and turn it back to wildlife."

I glanced about the quiet room. Most were farmer types, ages fifty on up, who were suspicious of both political parties.

Tex continued, "When things fall apart, the key is to be prepared spiritually, mentally and physically. You don't want to be saying to yourself, 'What could I have done that I didn't do? And why didn't I do it?'" He gazed straight at me. "Someone said, 'Life isn't about how you survive the storm, but how you dance in the rain.'" His Southern drawl drew out, "raaain."

He proceeded to go over the seven areas of preparation—information, shelter, water, food, protection, alternate energy, intentional community trade.

This group wasn't a militant group, as guns were fifth on their list. They were more of a producer group. Though I wished they had placed guns higher up. You can produce all you want, but if you don't have weapons to protect your stuff, what good is it?

Tex waved a dollar in the air. "These are frauds. They've been taken off the gold standard, long ago, and are only backed by thin air. They're doomed!"

I found his theatrics entertaining. It was good to get my mind off the forthcoming Fish and Wildlife penalty.

"These are Yokino Bucks." He lifted up a pink fluorescent dollar. "Ultimately they'll be backed by silver and when things go south, we could use them as the new currency."

When I saw that pink dollar, I don't know why, but I envisioned a Pygmy Rabbit as its symbol. For some reason when I get downcast, I get corny. I figured I'd end up paying thousands of those Yokino Bucks to the courts, and here I didn't even breed them bunnies, they bred themselves.

We had a good group of speakers, one on garden herbs, another showing off a sniper rifle, another teaching how to start fire with flints, and another talking about when we draw the line with government.

Though the meeting lasted over three hours, it went by in a flash. When it concluded, I sat staring blankly out the only window in the shop. Outside, the overcast sky and snowflakes were strange to see this time of year. I wanted to talk to Priscilla. Her charitable side troubled me; it could get us in the soup.

I rose and drifted toward the old bearded fellow who'd parked next to us. He grinned. "You know, my daddy moved us to this valley when he found out it was one of two in the US that could be blocked in, cut off from the outside world by its passes." We headed for the door.

"So your daddy's a survivalist?"

"Oh, goodness, yes. He always talked about the valley's precious water and it being the headwater."

"When did he move you to the valley?"

"Just after the Korean War."

Priscilla and Eli had already slipped out.

"So your dad thought the end of the world was going to happen way back then?"

He nodded.

"Is he still alive?"

"No, he's been gone a while." A cold breeze swayed the fellow's long beard as we exited the shop. "You hear how much volcanic activity is going on at Yellowstone?"

I shook my head.

"They say from this year to last, it has increased 100-fold." He went on to talk about the Evergreen Project.

Here I thought I was a doom-and-gloomer, but this old fellow had me by a mile. I looked down at the snowflakes atop my boots. At last I asked him, "Ya think we're getting closer to the end of the world?"

He grinned. "Sometimes it's hard to predict the end of the world." He sobered, glancing back at the shop. "Best thing we can do is get the stuff while the trucks are still rolling."

*   *   *

On the drive home, I was itching to talk to Priscilla about her charitable nature. This might be a thorn in our side after the big bata-boom. I half-glanced at her. "I think we need to decide where to draw the line as far as giving away food if things go south."

She said in a soft voice, "I think we should help anyone who comes to the door."

Her words upset me. "I don't think so. Are we the new social welfare program? Isn't that why the government is bankrupt?"

"Think of what a witness it will be. A lot of souls will come to know the Lord."

"And what will those good converts do after we run out of food?"

She didn't answer.

"I say they'll turn you into Deviled eggs."

"Oh, honey, don't you see it will be a great time for a harvest?"

"This isn't going to be some average power-goes-down type of time. You get the big bata-boom and fear and hunger are going to rule ... maybe cannibalism."

"God will look after us if we do what's right." She said this in such a simplistic manner, I gave her a double-take.

"They say you can't feed a person just once. They say that after three days without food, people will steal for it and after seven days, they'll kill for it."

"What do you propose, ward off everyone with a gun?"

With my hand on the wheel, I viewed the frost-covered farmland. "Funny you say that."

"Will you be like that man at the meeting who says he'll bury anyone crazy enough to enter his property?"

"He does have the right to protect his property."

"How will that man stand before God?"

"Food can disappear in a hurry if you have twenty-plus eaters. Why should we be storing up for them?"

"We have to look after your sisters and brothers if they come." She gave me an exasperated look. "They're your sisters and brothers."

"I'm not my brother's keeper. No way. They got jobs, good jobs … they can get their own." I glanced over at Eli. "What do you think about this survival stuff?"

He gazed out the window into the cold future. Finally, he gave a telling moan.

# Tie-dye

It was a strange, sad day when a number of federal vehicles pulled into our driveway. I found myself watching from a bedroom window. Some had come all the way from DC. Sergeant Johnson was there, along with the head iceberg and the rabbit specialist. Because of our attempt to sell the bunnies out of state, the core, 23 men and women, came out of federal vehicles, not Montana Fish and Wildlife. They appeared a formidable group.

The leader, a woman, a sure-footed, straight-haired, prideful-looking thing, surveyed the situation, walking near the irrigation boxes. The bunnies sensed something was wrong and swung clear. She then had a pow-wow with five others. They drew up their war plans. There was paperwork, maps drawn and more paperwork. Some of the rest of the group got tired of standing around and took off for who-knows-where in a stand of trees, one of the few stands that had missed an old forest fire.

Around 10 a.m. they were called back. Of course they had their break. A half- hour later they came out of their break and milled around some more. While the group of five thoroughly examined the Pygmies, walking completely around our house, I noticed others handing out ten-foot-long nets. Not long after, one of the five gave instructions on using these nets. A few questions from the grunts sent the five back to the drawing board. Again, some headed down to the treed area to do their thing. They were called back around lunchtime. Of course they all took a long lunch, as the stress of their work must have been intense. Somewhere in this, I realized I was going to pay for all this action or lack thereof, and I headed for the bathroom.

After lunch, the leader held a safety meeting, then pointed out instructions. Again the group gathered up the ten-foot-long nets. Finally, mid-afternoon, the troop took off after the Rare Pygmies. The bunnies dispersed in all directions.

With all their planning, I was surprised they didn't surround the area and close in on them. It was quite bizarre to see the entire group chasing the bunnies with those extended nets. They looked like they were after butterflies. The only thing these federal folk needed were tie-dyed t-shirts.

Though they were able to catch some unharmed, most of this hurried, robust capturing ended with wounded animals.

It reminded me of my granddad, who had experienced the Dust Bowl in the '30s and had participated in rabbit drives; if he saw these patty-cake people running around with their long nets, he'd roll over in his grave. And here we were, just trying to start a livestock business in Montana.

# You Need a Rifle

The night of April 1 it snowed again, about a foot. It might've been appropriate on April Fool's Day, but I wasn't smiling. When would winter ever get behind us?

Yesterday was the first morning I didn't hear Priscilla out on the front step with that shofar. She was under the weather. I'm not sure if it was the failed rabbit business, or the stalled seventy adventure, or the 1,000-page book that the Department of Agriculture sent us, with Subchapter A, Part 1-6, dealing with the Animal Welfare Act. Regardless, she went about with a long face.

That morning, I pushed through the fresh snow atop the driveway with a bowl of dog and cat food. My thoughts were on that Texas hunting club and the Department of Agriculture. Was I supposed to give them an emergency plan for the rabbits even though we were out of the rabbit business?

Usually Cane would hear me and appear at the doghouse doorway. He'd give a slow stretch, looking as if he was moving half-frozen flesh. Finally, he'd emerge. Then the cat would appear and do the same long stretch. Curly was past the age of early rising, but the three were smart enough to sleep together, though it sure must've been crammed in there.

For some reason, Cane didn't show himself. I called him while changing out his water and searched here and there, but to no avail. This was worrisome, as lately he'd just up and disappear, then, a day or so later, reappear. I wondered if he had the Devil in him. Clyde, our cat, was the only one to show his face and with it, the long stretch.

I shivered as I limped back across the snowy driveway and up the stairs. A breeze caught me at the porch. I saw movement down the hill and halted. It was a person, maybe Eli, coming up the road. Yes, it had to be him in that long black coat. Excitement embraced me.

I had planned to make pancakes, but that morning we were out of eggs so I got a can of beans and waited for Eli to see if he would like a bean burrito. It was exhilarating to hear the doorbell and good to see him standing in our entrance, a breeze ruffling his coat.

"Good morning, sunshine." How he didn't freeze was a wonder. I waved, motioning him to come in, but he motioned for me to come out. "It's cold out there." I looked past him, rather puzzled. "I can make a bean burrito for you if you like." Again, he waved for me to come with him.

"I'm not going anywhere till I get geared up. What's up?"

Then I realized how weary he looked, more haggard than I'd ever seen. "Are you coming in?"

He shook his head.

The cold breeze was too chilling to just stand there. "Please come in. I can fix you a bean burrito with avocado and salsa."

He shook his head.

I don't like shutting the door on anyone, but it was just too blasted cold. Inside, I geared up with a hood and mitts, as I thought he was taking me down to the barn.

Stepping out the door, I said, "Okay, I'm ready."

He rose from the porch steps, picked up his wooden spear, and led east. I had no idea where he was taking me, but from his downcast demeanor, I knew something was wrong.

When we hit the road, I swept my arm around him. "How you been?" I playfully powered him forward, trying to cheer him up. He was such a lightweight.

He shook his head, quite sorrowful, then shifted his spear to his other hand.

"When are you going to put on some weight?"

He didn't even smile at my joke, but looked distant … pitiful.

When we hit the field, it was easier to follow him than break a new trail in the snow. Trudging behind, I looked over the back of his black mohair coat. It had a strange rip. I found this odd, as those coats are pretty well-made. I do say he was quite a sight in that mink-collar black coat, tromping through the white crystals.

When we got onto state land, I wished I'd eaten breakfast because I ended up following him down a ravine, along the dried creek bed, then up toward the tree line, all through over a foot of snow. I burned no end of calories on that dreary, cold day. The whole time hunger knocked at my door. He pressed on, up and up and up in elevation.

Somewhere along the path we stopped for a rest. He was a few yards uphill. "Cane wasn't there this morning. You didn't happen to see him?"

His frown was sad, a sadness that made me ill at ease.

About an hour after we started, we were within the forest, his forest, tramping along a trail, his trail. The snow was deeper here. Had I previously known I was going to follow him to Timbuktu, I'd have brought food and a gun. Generally, I don't go out in the woods without a gun. And here he was, taking me deeper and deeper into the timber. I started to really wonder about my son. What kind of individual would live in this dark wilderness and feel at home?

We went over one ridge and down the other side. How I wished I'd eaten something before we got into this trek. About 2½ hours into the journey, in the belly of a saddleback we came upon a small opening in the timber. Then I realized I was in his camp. Off to the side, I noted a lean-to covered in snow. A rusty stove pipe rose from one end. I went to it, bent and gazed into the doorway. Inside was a worn, torn sleeping bag and a number of shabby blankets. Hides covered the floor and back wall, one was shiny black that I assumed was a bear. A small potbelly stove sat in the corner. I was curious where he had gotten it.

I righted myself and looked over his camp. Leaning against a tree were my pitchfork, rake and axe. Hanging from nails on a tree was an assortment of pots and pans that Priscilla was missing. I had mixed feelings about this and told him, "It's not right to just take our stuff. You either pay for it or ask for it."

He dropped his head.

I continued looking about; his one attempt at luxury came from a large stump that he had axed out into a seat, though it was snow-covered. Nearby was a creek that was half frozen-over. Some hides were stretched about trees—an elk, some deer. Interesting; this area of the state was a coveted hunting zone that few could get tags for, yet here my son was sticking a fork into whatever crossed the aim of his arrows.

It hit me that if I couldn't get him out of the woods, he'd end up a total recluse hermit. Considering how I could get him back to civilization, I stepped through the snow, my boot hitting a leg bone, probably an elk. Beneath another protrusion were ribs, antlers—bones, bones and more bones. Looking over his world, his home, nothing came to mind on how to get him back to civilization.

"I'm starving." The gurgle from the creek made me hungrier. "You got anything to eat?"

He went to a tree, untied a fishing line, then lowered it. Down from a tree branch came a satchel. He handed it to me.

The dried blood on the leather's surface reminded me of all the meat pouches he'd had. Apprehensively, I opened it. Some uncooked meat looked quite fresh. Taking a piece, I gave it a cautious sniff. "Deer?"

He shook his head.

"Elk?"

Again, he shook his head.

I took a bite and wondered what type of meat it was. It tasted gamier than deer but at that moment I didn't care. I was hungry.

"Can you warm some water?"

He disappeared into his lean-to.

Shortly, smoke poured from the smokestack. Eli exited the lean-to, this time carrying a pot. He swiftly strode toward the creek, moving like an energized scarecrow. How I wished he'd put on some weight.

"This meat's pretty gamy. What is it?"

He angled his chin toward the other side of the water before heading back into the lean-to. There, a haze of gray caught my eye, but I didn't think much of it at the time, as so many animal remains were scattered around and I was getting cold. I followed him to the lean-to.

The heat drew me in. I got on my knees to monkey along 'til I sat on his bed. The place was so small that I ended up next to him.

He fed the fire from his pile of kindling, stacked nicely in the corner. The heat was magnificent.

"What do you dream about out here?"

He shrugged.

I bit into another chunk of meat. Half-chewing, I spoke, "I'm proud of you, Eli; you put an exclamation mark on living in Montana! You are the ultimate survivalist." I shook my head in amazement. "Goodness, son ..." I gave his elbow a friendly thump. "... on the other hand, you worry me some." I studied his face. "I mean, you're way out here." His apprehensive sadness still hung. I thumped his elbow again. "Don't you get lonely?"

Though his abode was rough, it was cozy. I noticed remnants of tent fabric hanging from the ceiling and assumed it was the tent he'd bought in California. The door to the little stove was open and the reflection of the flames danced mystically.

Viewing Eli in his element, I treasured the moment.

The meat and the heat made me heavy-eyed. In no time, I fell asleep.

I awoke from a nightmarish view of a wolf towering above me. I had no clue where I was. Shadows covered the interior; a shaft of daylight from the doorway revealed the potbelly stove. Movement outside caught my eye. I sat up and saw pant legs moving by. At last I realized where I was.

Scuffling along, I made it out of the lean-to, stood up and rubbed my mitts. "You see any wolves out here?"

Eli appeared even more troubled as he gave a small nod.

I saw his bow hanging from a tree branch, but the way it hung looked odd. Taking a closer look, I noticed its bow string was busted. "How's that handgun I gave you?"

He gave another nod.

"Let's take a look at it."

He bounded toward the lean-to, then bent down into it. In no time he was back, offering the Smith and Wesson to me. Safety-wise, he knew enough how to pass it properly. I'd taught him that. But that was as far as he went when it came to the care of a gun. In spots the bluing was pitted with rust.

I was taken back at its condition. "Why would you ever let a gun get rusty?" I gave him an admonishing look. "I couldn't do that to a gun." I pointed at some rust. "This is horrid." My irritation rose. "Why would you do that to a Smith and Wesson?"

He tentatively stepped back.

"You could've covered it with oil … any oil. Goodness, Eli, this isn't right. Let me see the bullets. Have you kept them dry?"

He shook his head.

"What's with the shaking of your head business? Let's see them!"

He signed out, "No more."

"You're telling me that now????? Why didn't you tell me before?"

He shrugged.

"Sometimes you scare me. I couldn't live out in the woods without a gun." I looked about, my eyes resting on his wounded bow, its dead string lying against the bark. "And here you are fooling around with spears?" I adamantly shook that Smith and Wesson. "This isn't right. You need to get back home." I frowned and handed the useless gun back to him. "Why did you bring me all the way out here?"

With a sad countenance, he turned toward the creek, his hand angling to the far side.

I walked over to the creek and looked across. Gray fur scattered everywhere atop the snow marked a conflict. Dread rose in me when I realized whose fur it was. I leaped the creek, entering a ruthless arena. Red drops atop white snow. Wolf prints proved that it had been a fight to the death.

"Why'd you bring Cane here?"

With a sorrowful moan, Eli drifted backward. I could see tears forming, then flowing down his cheeks.

"He wasn't your dog to take," I murmured as I walked about, trying to dispel my anger.

At last, I asked," How many wolves were there?"

He flashed his hand twice.

"Ten?"

He gave a solemn nod.

Concerned for our safety, I leaped back over the creek and hurriedly went after the pitchfork. I picked it up and noticed that the tines were crimson. They had stained the snow. I carried it toward Eli. "Did you use this on a wolf?"

He nodded.

I jumped the creek again and began following the wolves' trail. It led into thicker timber. I led with the pitchfork. Eli followed, spear in hand. The trail of blood droplets led about thirty yards before I saw Cane's remains. It was a disturbing sight of entrails, bones and tendons. He'd been torn to shreds. He was their meal. Alarmed, I took a firmer hold on the pitchfork and warily looked about. Sprinkles of blood led into the darkened forest.

Even with the pitchfork, I felt vulnerable. My eyes scanned the bushes. Long shadows flowed back from the falling sun. I froze when I saw black. A wolf? It was silhouetted behind a tree and difficult to make out. The color was too dark against the white to be anything but an animal.

A tense moment passed; I jumped toward it. "Hey!"

It didn't budge.

I nervously glanced around for the pack. The deepening shadows weren't in my favor. I cautiously stepped forward. The black one appeared laid out, dead.

We closed in on the carcass. In the quiet stillness the crunch of snow under our boots was loud. The wolf lay sprawled in its fullness, jaws open, fangs revealed, tongue hanging.

I'd never touched a wolf and a long pause ensued as I warily looked about, pointing my pitchfork at a darkened area by a clump of trees. I bent, pulled off a mitt, and ran my finger over its impressive pads. Rigor mortis had set in. I noted four red holes where the pitchfork had entered. Fur had been torn off its hindquarters and a chunk of flesh was missing. Scanning the area, I considered the missing flesh, then glanced down at the carcass. Strange, it appeared cut, not torn by teeth, but cut out.

I glanced back at Eli. "Did you …" I paused, considering what I'd eaten, "… did you cut this meat off him?"

He nodded.

"You are something!" Setting my pitchfork down, I flipped the large beast over. It was heavy. I'm sure it weighed over 130 pounds before my resourceful son started working on it. He had also taken the meat from the opposite hind quarter. "Did you stick anymore?"

He pointed toward the blood trail.

I arose and guardedly followed the droplets of blood. We went another twenty yards. I became more apprehensive as I looked into the darkening forest. Maybe my unease was caused by the number of wolf prints, or the two carcasses or the waning winter sun casting long, ominous shadows through the trees. I couldn't imagine living by myself, let alone out here. This kid of mine, what kind of bloodline was he from?

Ahead, I made out something grayish and halted. Another wolf? I stabbed the pitchfork forward and gave a hardy, "Hey!"

Nothing moved. Droplets of blood drew me toward the body. I was taken aback when I noticed a radio collar. "Goodness!"

I gave the wolf a poke with the pitchfork. It was stiff. I figured the transmitter would broadcast a cold body and lead the authorities to it, so I removed it.

Facing Eli, I spoke clearly, "After you do what you do with these wolves, you might want to drag them away from here. You don't want the government men knowing about this. They might institutionalize you. Believe me when I say those are some walls you don't want to be in. They already got me pegged as the Bunny Man." I put my mitts on his chest. "Do you want to be the Wolf Man?"

He nodded, then shook his head.

I looked about the darkening forest. "You need a rifle and some ammo." A glance back revealed Eli's only protection, that spear. "I couldn't live out in the woods without ammo."

With pitchfork ready, I headed toward his camp. When we passed Cane's carcass, I stopped. A part of me wanted to strongly reprimand Eli for taking my dog, but I knew that wouldn't bode well in my effort to draw the hermit out of his den. Somehow I pulled my eyes away from Cane's sacrifice and faced the person he had saved.

"If I were you, I'd come back home and work for a rifle." It was tough to suppress my ill feelings; my mitts angled toward his lean-to. "This will always be here when you come back." I pitched my chin toward the dark forest, the area where the wolves' carcasses lay. "You need a rifle."

# Back to Civilization

I was relieved when Eli followed me out of his camp. On the way down the mountain, I tossed the wolf's radio collar in one of the deep holes left by the old miners.

When we trudged up the driveway, I was pretty much worn out. As I passed the doghouse, I noticed Curly, curled up just inside the doghouse doorway. There was a strong realization that Cane wasn't there and would never be there again.

I gave Eli a hard look. "Let me tell you something …" Part of me still wanted to reprimand him for taking Cane. He waited for me to say something as I ran my hand across my whiskers. If I scolded him, would he go back to the bush? "… You're welcome to sleep in the house or the barn or …" I raised my hand toward the sky, "… or under the stars. Either way, we've got elk, so please have supper with us, and we'll look after you."

Eli signed, "I'll look after you, too," and pointed toward the sunroom.

It was rare for him to communicate and later that evening, as I ate supper, I thought about his statement, then took a long look toward the sunroom window and wondered if there was more to the conflict around that window.

When Eli didn't show up for supper, I figured he must've felt bad about Cane. Then again, being alone in the mountains too long can make a stranger out of anyone. His mother ended up taking a plate down to him in the barn. She came back cold but cheerful, talking about praying for him and what plans the Lord had for him now.

\* \* \*

With one less dog in the doghouse, I added another blanket for Curly. What I should've done was put a 100-watt light bulb in the doghouse for warmth, but with our cat, Clyde, plus the coming of spring, I figured he'd be all right.

I had just returned from taking Eli to two cattle ranches and one sheep operation for possible employment. It was midday before I noticed that Curly wasn't around. I went to the doghouse and bent to look inside. The dog appeared asleep, his head tucked between his legs. But when I touched him, I knew. Tears filled my eyes as I dragged out his rigid body.

I ended up burying him just south of the house, our pet grave that we can see from the sunroom. With two dogs down, it was a sad week.

*　　*　　*

If there was any good news, it came from two of the three ranches that I had taken Eli to for employment. Both called to say they'd take him on. This was ironic; here I'd been looking for work for what seemed like forever, and my mute son got two possibilities to choose from the first week.

He took the sheep operation. I think because it was closer to his camp. Then again, it could've been the sheepherder's daughter, who, when Eli showed up, latched onto him like an old pal.

A week or so passed before I got in touch with the sheep man to see how Eli was doing. He was quite cheerful in talking about Eli, said he caught on quickly and had shot two coyotes. There was a bit of excitement about the man as he happily rattled on, saying with Eli around, his daughter had shown a lot more interest in the operations. What I remembered, she was a good-sized gal who could certainly club my son back to civilization, if need be.

I was really pleased and relieved that Eli had moved out of the mountains. On the home front, Priscilla was back blowing that darn shofar. I say "back," as she had stopped for a few weeks and went about heavy-hearted, perplexed about something. I hoped it wasn't that seventy thing. I'd hoped she'd given that up.

That morning, I sat at the table eating breakfast and watched her pull her shawl over her shoulder, pick up her shofar and head for the front door. I knew where she was going but asked anyway, "What are you up to?"

She slowed before the doorway, but didn't look back as she determinedly declared, "I'm going to give that Devil one more round."

This was concerning, especially since she'd started fasting for her quest and didn't weigh an ounce more than 110 pounds. I concluded if God liked food, He'd be listening to her.

Oftentimes I'd feel a slow conviction moving me to walk to the end of the doom-and-gloom plank, cash in the rest of our retirement and stockpile for the imagined seventy. I was diligent to suppress that conviction. Yet, I wondered about the future. What really bothered me was finding out that our government had purchased millions of hollow-point bullets. Internationally, these expansive bullets were outlawed in war. So was DC going to use them on their own citizens? Creepy.

# Noah?

It takes a bit to get psyched up to travel over 750 miles to the cold of North Dakota in pursuit of carpenter's work, especially when I was still limping about from the pain in my back. Occasionally, sudden spasms would bend me over. In those times I always thought of that curse from the last breath of the dying man. But I needed a job; there was no question about it. And with the looming penalty from the failed livestock business, there was no mystery about needing funds.

Sometime in late April, Lady Spring kicked out Old Man Winter, and I knew I had to travel. My plans were to leave on a Tuesday, but an interesting letter showed up the day before. It was from Priscilla's mother. In it was an early inheritance check, as well as a note that mentioned she'd get the house and ten acres.

Priscilla was elated. I heard no end of, "Praise the Lord. It's an answer to my prayers." She hopped around like Jiminy Cricket. "Oh, hallelujah. God is so faithful."

I was astounded at her good fortune. The property was in Saskatchewan, Canada, out in the country, surrounded by trees, four large granaries; you could grow anything in its black topsoil. If everything went south in the States, we could go north.

Of course, with her good fortune, I conveniently put off the trip to oil country, hoping this money would refurbish our already depleted retirement funds. Instead, I started thinking about a trip to Canada to get that house ready to rent, which would nicely shore up our financial situation. My back was feeling better just considering the possibilities.

That week I got more smackeroos from Priscilla than anything. I didn't know if spring was in the air or if it was my attractive bald spot or my pressing front teeth, but she had no end of affection for me. No doubt somewhere in my dopey countenance there's a very handsome man, but you might need rose-colored glasses to find him. Did I say I had a white goatee to cover up my lack of a strong manly chin? Regardless of how handsome I must've been, boy howdy, did I ever get some hugs that week and lots of encouragement too.

The only line that set me ill-at-ease was when she pulled me in close and said, "God wants you to be his Noah for the seventy."

Right then I saw the squirrel in the tree.

This all lasted five days and don't think for a minute she wasn't sitting by the calculator, crunching numbers. After she gathered all her figures, she approached me, looking mission-bound, and spoke with expectation.

"There's enough here to cover the cost of food for the seventy, with eighty thousand extra." Her happy hand jerked upward. "We can use it to build the underground facility, the solar and wind."

"Eighty thousand won't cover solar, a wind generator and the construction cost of an underground facility."

"We can sell the house and land in Canada."

My eyes widened at this one; this was a stunner. "Goodness, why would you sell your heritage, that's your heritage. What? To save seventy Americans?"

"This is the Lord's money and I know He wants to save the seventy." She touched my arm with deep sincerity. "Americans are my people now."

"I can tell you with a straight face that those seventy Americans are not in dire peril."

"I will add one word to your statement … yet." She took a few steps, considering, "Isn't it exciting that we received it five months after I started praying, to the day?"

My mouth hung open at her comment.

"Don't you see the importance of five?"

She was so sold on this, I wasn't sure if I could talk.

"He wants us to provide for the seventy for five years."

Amazed, I stared at my eccentric wife, then somehow shifted my gaze out the window. The valley was greening up nicely, the buds on the trees spoke of a new season, hope for the future; a robin flew past. It was such a contrary view of the doom-and-gloom world that would have to arise to shove us underground that my numbness held.

My eyes returned to the woman who was determined to spend her inherited funds on saving the imagined seventy. She had a hopeful, expectant glow about her that read, "Part of the puzzle has come together, Mr. Hershal; now it's your turn."

I knew enough to clamp my lips over my big mouth. I was afraid to speak.

*       *       *

That week I thought I was going to have to do some side-stepping on the subject of getting started, but there were no more promptings from her. She just moved about in a confident manner as if it was all looked after, somehow all in-the-bag. This bugged me. Somewhere in this quiet vigil, I wondered how a woman motivates a man to get started on some wild adventure, to save seventy people, which would cost thousands and thousands of dollars. My woman went silent, not silent about everyday life, just silent about the quest. At the same time, she was content, and I mean, happy as a mama bear that had her house in order, with heat in her stove. This bugged me as well.

In the midst of this, I wasn't sure if I should carry on with my plan to head east to the oil fields or talk to her again about renting the house in Canada. I sorely didn't want to go to the oil fields, but my pride level wasn't at ease in relying on my bride's inheritance. Even still, she didn't say a word about the house. This bugged me, too.

Six days after the letter arrived, I sat at the kitchen table, cuddling a morning coffee. Priscilla had just come in from the porch, having blown that darn shofar. I watched her set the horn atop the mantle.

I began, "We need to talk."

"Yes?"

"We need to talk about that house of yours in Canada."

"Okay."

"It doesn't make any sense to just have it sit there. I think we should rent it out."

"I'd rather sell it."

"For what?"

"For the build-up of the seventy."

"I … you know I'm not a practicing Christian nor a socialist, so I'm a bit perplexed on this seventy thing. Why would God drop that one on me?"

"God works in mysterious ways." Her eyes came up to meet mine. "Maybe He knows you."

"Maybe the angel that dropped the blue room vision had the wrong address. If I was looking after seventy people for five years, I'd want to get my money up-front." I shrugged. "Better yet, I want real silver. So, shouldn't that vision have ended up at a house where they had a bunch of compassion and where everybody was up to saving everybody?"

"God will pay us back. He pays good."

"That brings up another point." I considered telling her about being a murderer but held with, "I'm not a good man."

"We're human."

"Well, I'm sorry, but being unemployed, I wanted to hang onto those funds and rent that house out." My hand nervously rubbed my coffee cup. "For safety's sake, you know. It would shore up our financial situation. You're well aware how much we've spent on all those prep goods, darn near cleaned out our retirement fund. And let's not forget about that coming fine for the rabbit adventure."

"I think the Lord has something bigger in mind for us than just looking after our own needs."

"Priscilla, I can see that our country is bankrupt and we're going to have some challenges, but to store up for seventy people for five years is a pretty big vision." I shook my head. "I just don't have the faith for that. No doubt you do … I don't."

She had a forlorn sadness to her. "Without faith, the Bible says, it's impossible to please God." Her hand rested on a chair. "If you don't have the faith, you can always pray for it. He's faithful in …"

I cut her off, "This is the land of plenty. There's no end of food here." I shook my head. "I can't see it. I just can't see it."

"Hershal Ward Beecher, God will move on with His purpose, with or without you." She raised her index finger toward me, then caught herself and turned to walk away, heading toward the staircase.

I could see that the meeting was over, and felt I had stolen her joy. Still, I repeated, "I'm not a socialist or a Christian, why should I provide for seventy people for five years?"

She halted before the stairway. "That's fine. But remember this, if we don't do what He wants, in the future what you think is yours may be taken from you, and the money that you seek to hold, seek to save, will be worthless." With that pronouncement, she went upstairs.

Her comment stuck sourly in my being. I got up and loudly called out, "God doesn't give visions like that to murdering men."

Hearing the pitter-patter of her feet rapidly coming back downstairs, I sat down again. My fingers gathered around the coffee cup as if it were the rail of a ship, while I braced for a huge wave.

"What did you say?" She moved around the dried flower arrangement, steadfast and real.

"God doesn't give visions like that to murdering men."

"Who's … who's murdering men?"

"I am." I don't know why, but tears came to my eyes.

"What?"

I stared blankly at my coffee. "That night, back in the fall, one of the Wartals was peeking in the window." I thumbed toward the sunroom. "It was an accident. It really was. When I hit the barbed wire fence, the gun went off."

Strange how my emotions swept. "I told you it was a coyote in that stinking dig, but it was Wartal … That makes me a liar, too. Regardless, God don't give visions like that to murdering men."

She walked slowly toward me. At my side, she stood for a while.

I wished she hadn't touched my shoulder, as my eyes were already damp.

"So you're saying that God doesn't give visions to murdering men?"

I nodded.

"I believe, if there's one thing God is good at, it's using broken men. I'll have you know that much of the Bible was written by murdering men. Apostle Paul was a murderer and he turned the world upside down. King David was a murderer and he wrote much of Psalms. The Lord gave him the vision of storing up to build the temple. Moreover, he killed an inno-cent man, not a Peeping Tom." Her palm ran gently across my back as she talked about Moses and an Egyptian. But I didn't understand it all as I had my hands full, covering my eyes to stop the flow of tears.

*   *   *

It was good to get that off my chest; it was better to see all the possibilities Priscilla had for murdering men. Strange, with that seventy thing going, she didn't say a word about the law. Still, I was unmoved about feeding seventy people for five years. What stuck in my craw was her statement about having all the money I thought I was saving, taken away. That made me ill-at-ease, boxed-in and angry.

That night I had a terrible time with what little sleep I got. The morning finally came. I found myself at bitter odds with the thought of providing for seventy people for five years. Maybe it would have been different if I'd had a job and wasn't counting every penny. Those inherited funds would certainly fill a big void and provide a cushion for the future. This wasn't the case for Priscilla. She didn't consider these inherited funds hers, but the Lord's. Oh, how I wished she wasn't fixed on this!

What's more, I had a foreboding sense that her words about losing the funds in the end were somehow going to come to pass if I didn't give in. This wasn't hard to imagine, espe-cially with the continued curiosity of our Deputy Sheriff and the government's case against us on the rabbits. Regardless, there was no way I was going to stockpile for seventy for free. The thought sanded me.

That following morning, I expected to hear the noise of the shofar. It didn't come. It's ironic, though I wasn't a Christian, I sure found myself praying a lot; more often I was praying

Priscilla would give up her mission. When the shofar didn't sound off, I actually wondered if God had heard my prayer.

But it was no victory. I felt badly, as if I was ruining everything she hoped and prayed for. Furthermore, her words of losing everything I thought I was saving were still hovering. When I saw her downstairs, I almost ducked.

"Good morning," her voice chirped, as cheerful as the mountain bluebirds.

"Good morning."

She stood in front of our old-fashioned stove. "Would you like an egg?"

Sometimes I wished she carried a chip on her shoulder, it would be easier to deal with.

I got right to the point. "I've been thinking about that seventy … thing. My problem is with giving food and shelter away for free. Even a staunch liberal knows enough to spend the government's money … not their own."

"So you're concerned that you won't get paid back?"

"Of course. I'm not doing it for nothing." I shrugged. "I got to get paid. If I was in this, I'd be in it for the money. That's it."

"Don't you think God will pay us back?"

I rolled my eyes. Sometimes she just doesn't get it. "Maybe … maybe not, but before your inheritance check, our financial situation was pretty skinny. And like I said, those funds would shore up our beleaguered retirement money. Regardless, how could we do that buildup of food for the seventy if we're not paid back?"

"God always pays back. He's good like that. He can pay us back in so many ways, with good health …"

During a long pause, the fantasy of a payback, in the form of our Sheriff's curiosity dissipating, and our government's case over the rabbits dissipating, entertained me.

My wife looked thoughtful. "Remember the famine in Egypt? Joseph made Pharaoh quite the landowner."

"That's what I'm talking about. If the seventy have silver and gold or something to trade, fine. Otherwise, let their lack of preparation fall on their own heads."

I watched her take the egg carton out of the fridge.

"Would you like an egg?"

"Sure." I opened the kitchen window blind and looked across the valley at the Sapphire Mountains. The green of spring was showing vividly. My eyes held on the popcorn flowers of the serviceberry. "If we stored up for the seventy, it won't be good if some vagabonds point at our place and say, 'The begging is good over there.'" I looked her directly in the eyes. "The seventy are either in with us, in our compound, or they are not part of us. In other words, I'm not running a local store here, where if the neighbors run out of food, they come over to barter; forget that! If times are desperate, we'll have every Night Rider trying to blast their way in."

"I think your dream shows that God wants us to have oil in our lamps for five years. Jesus instructs us about the wise and foolish virgins as they await the bridegroom." She clenched her fist. "I'm not about to sell my oil to the foolish ones."

"Good, yes, sure. Considering these shaky times, I think non-perishable food might not be a bad investment."

She cracked open the egg and tipped it into the frying pan.

I continued, "I'll be honest, I'm not crossing the Rubicon to save seventy folk from dire peril; I'm not here to save the world, or a bunch of virgins, either. I'm in this for the money." I wanted to be clear on this, repeating, "I want the money. If you agree to getting paid back for our buildup with profit and good profit, then I agree to go ahead with it." I felt a strange release.

"Okay." She turned down the gas flame.

I expected her to be more excited about my change.

At last she raised her hand toward the ceiling and sent some thankful words to her Maker.

# The Buildup

From that day on, I was into stockpiling for the seventy, dead serious about profiting from the adventure. At times I felt more like a grocery store clerk, calculating how much profit margin I needed to make. Two hundred percent didn't seem unreasonable, and I planned on charging a few people, if they ended up with us, much more. If they were raving liberals, like one of my brothers, who believes the government should supply all his needs, then they were going to have to pay 500 percent.

The same applied to extreme conservatives, who were just as much an anchor on our nation's deficit. My uncle was an extreme war hawk who believed the U.S. should get into every foreign conflict possible, and be the world's police force. Well, wars aren't cheap; he was going to have to pay 500 percent as well. And, I wasn't going to give kids a break; they were going to have to pay the standard 200 percent. I surmised I'd give discounts to any sharpshooters who had their guns in order, could reload, came with at least 2,000 rounds of ammo and were able to have an impressive grouping at 600 yards.

Priscilla calculated that we needed over 160,000 pounds of food for seventy folk for five years. I told her 120,000 pounds of food was my max. If the Chinese could live on a bowl of rice a day, then Yankees could get two meals a day instead of three. Anyway, it would do them good to starve a bit. So she had to rework her food estimate to 120,000 pounds, mostly rice, beans, peas, barley, wheat and flax seeds. She pointed out that flax seeds make a good choice for oil, as they don't break down or go rancid if they are kept cool and dry. We also planned for a pallet of salt and sugar, and pounds and pounds of spices.

The trick in this plan was to hide it. One thing we learned from previously stockpiling was that there are too many loose lips in a small community. It's worse than Big Brother listening in on your conversations, reading your e-mails and spying on you from drones and satellites.

Three years ago I'd found this out the hard way. After I had a dream about the economic ship rolling, I ordered pails of grains, beans and various dry goods from an outfit out of Salt Lake. The problem occurred when the truck driver stopped at our neighbor Dewey's and asked for directions. Dewey noticed that the truck and forty-foot trailer were too big to turn around in my driveway. So he called and offered to offload it at his place. Without much thought, I took up his kind offer.

When I got to Dewey's, he was already helping the trucker unload. But when he saw how many pails there were and what was in them, I noticed an excitement come over him.

He happily said, "Boy, with all this food, you could just about look after the entire church."

What I found interesting is that he had told me years earlier that I needed to get saved because there was a Rapture coming. If I wasn't saved, then I'd miss the Rapture. So I'd asked, "Why would your church need any extra food for survival's sake; won't they be Raptured-up?"

He didn't answer and this was rare for him—he was always quick. Finally, a broad grin broke across his face. "It'd be nice to have something to eat if I didn't make the Rapture."

I chuckled. "Try to be a man and get your own darn food."

Months later I found out during a barbecue that Dewey had told the entire men's breakfast club at his church that we were stockpiling. One of them, my neighbor, looked up toward our place and said, "I know where to go when the stuff hits the fan."

"Where?"

"Your place; I hear you got all the grub."

"Where'd you hear that?"

"Dewey."

I knew right then that I'd have to move all the goodies out of our storage space and come up with some cockamamie story that we had donated everything to the food bank and were no longer survivalists, had found religion and believed that we are going to be Raptured-up. I also realized that when the big bata-boom struck, I was going to have to put on junky clothes and go around begging for food so the locals really understood that my storage space was empty.

This all sounds odd for someone who was gearing up for seventy people, but if everybody knows you've got food and they're all starving, wouldn't 500 folks show up to clean you out?

I figured the easiest and fastest way to hide buckets of food was to purchase two six-foot-round, three-foot-tall concrete culverts and a lid from the concrete plant, then get a backhoe in. Within hours, a seven-foot hole would be dug, the culverts set one atop the other, the concrete lid placed and hole back-filled. And if the backhoe operator asked, "What's it for?" I'd say it was for a well.

But the problem was, we'd need to bury about forty or more culverts to hold the fifty-plus pallets of dry goods, and the well story would have long dried-up. Additionally, if we went that route, we'd need hundreds, if not thousands, of five-gallon plastic buckets, as you couldn't put a fifty-pound bag of wheat down in a concrete culvert unprotected. Besides, there'd be the never-ending and expensive job of filling these plastic buckets. Furthermore, our landscape would be dug up like a darn prairie dog town before the grass grew back.

Our other option was to build an underground concrete unit. I knew this would draw questions from workers and concrete truckers. The best answer would be, it was a basement for a log cabin we were going to build.

The problem with stashing all the food in one spot was, if we got overrun, we could lose the entire cache. Whereas, if we had a number of those culverts and got overrun, we'd lose just one ... hopefully.

While contemplating how we'd proceed, we continued stocking up for the seventy, adding pallets of grains, rice, beans and wheat in our garage.

Priscilla, always a gamer, wanted to help move the bags from the flatbed of the truck, but I told her to not even think about lifting those fifty-pounders. Still, she found a way to push the bags off the pallets atop the flatbed into my waiting arms. I heard her talking to herself about leverage, while pushing the bags off the pallet using her leg muscles.

*   *   *

When we started on this adventure, my back hadn't completely healed from burying Wartal and I still walked with a limp. This didn't inspire a good attitude, and somewhere after dumping the 200th fifty-pound bag of Hagai rice on a pallet inside the garage, I'd gotten whiny about the escapade.

"I'll tell you what, those seventy better have a lot of money. And don't think for a moment that I'm taking some weepy-wompies in just because they're starving. Not when food's cheap right now. They can get their own stash." The weight of another bag of Hagai rice met my shoulder. I turned around to hump the bag to the garage.

Upon entering, I tripped on a corner of a wheat pallet and stumbled, then hit the concrete and rice shot everywhere. Struggling to rise, I unleashed a series of angry expletives that a deaf man could hear on the other side of the planet.

Priscilla monkeyed off the truck and came to help clean up. She didn't say a word, but I could see that she was disturbed by my outburst; there was no doubt that her knight in shining armor was tarnished.

Regardless of how tarnished I was, one thing about a project that requires secrecy—it doesn't stop because someone gets injured. We had to get those four pallets off the truck and into the garage before morning. In great pain, I carried on. Somewhere in this, Priscilla suggested we get more people involved in the food buildup.

Even though I thought her statement was wild, my back and elbow hurt terribly, and the possibility of another man with younger, stronger arms started to take root.

That evening I dragged myself toward the couch and flopped onto it.

Priscilla came in from the kitchen and touched my shoulder. Whenever she touches me like that, I know she's up to something. "You know Vicki, from the underground church?"

"I know of her."

"Her husband is a younger man from Bulgaria and is quite strong, and so is Vicki."

"Okay," I yawned.

"I was wondering what you would think if we asked them to be part of the buildup for the seventy?"

"They got any money?"

"I believe they live paycheck to paycheck."

"Why would I want to pay for their share?" I gave her a perplexed look. "What do they bring to the table?"

"Their strength."

There was a long pause as I considered them being part of the plan. If it wasn't for my back pain, this horse wouldn't run. "Do you think they can keep a secret?"

She nodded. "I believe those Eastern Blocers can keep to themselves. Same with Vicki; she's the leader of our prayer group."

"Eastern Blocer?"

"He's a Bulgarian."

"Do you really think they can work hard enough to warrant five years of food?"

She nodded.

"What type of job does he have?"

"He does the physical work at a recycler."

"How old is he?"

"I think he's around thirty."

"I wouldn't consider them if my back was right."

She was cheerful as she exclaimed, "If they accept, it would make them the first of the seventy."

"I didn't say I was going to go for this. It'd be a waste of everything if they were blabbers. Furthermore, there has to be some money involved. Their help would be great, but they have to get skin in the game."

"If you like, you can come to the next Bible study group. Vicki will be giving the message. You can meet them."

\*   \*   \*

I found myself at the next neighborhood Bible study group, or as they called it, the Underground Church. I went into the meeting with kind of a poor attitude toward any others joining our stockpiling because of Dewey's telling everybody and their dog about our last food buildup. Dewey is a good neighbor, but people have a tendency to talk. So when I met Vicki and Alex, the two prospective partners in the food build-up, I smiled when I was supposed to but, deep down, I had my misgivings.

Even with my reservations, I was impressed with Alex, who was showing off a Russian AK-47 to another fellow. He looked around 30ish, solid and strong and she appeared older, perhaps 40s. Both were kind enough. The way Vicki carried herself, sat up straight and spoke with a twang reminded me of a country western singer. Their three little dogs animated the meeting, at least their happy tails did. I came to find out that Vicki was a dog groomer.

Five other couples brought food. They all seemed excited that I'd come. I suppose Priscilla told them about me. I always liked potluck; food and guns are fun, and these folks were good cooks.

The empty seats at the table were tempting, but I left them for the ladies and sat off to the side. Yet they insisted that I take a seat, so I moved over.

I ate my meal while I listened to Vicki's conversation with another woman. She was forthright. "In Matthew 24, Jesus forewarns that Christians will be hated and killed. He doesn't say they'll get Raptured-up. To paraphrase, he says, 'Get mentally ready for persecution.' That's Christ talking, not some silly theologian." She said it with finality.

Her statement cut into the beliefs of a short, stocky fellow who tightened and bristled. He spoke with affirmation. "There will be a pre-tribulation Rapture, because God wouldn't have his children suffering wrath." He went on to explain his position.

Before he was finished, a farmer type, just as passionate, said he disagreed and went on talking about the Saints that will be martyred in the Great Tribulation, then asked, "How can they be martyred if they're all beamed up?" He concluded, "What you're advocating are two returns of Christ. The Bible says he only comes back once." He thrust his forefinger in the air. "And there will to be nothing secret about that event."

I can't say I understood it all, but the way those two were going at it, I wondered if they'd be friends in the end.

Somewhere in this Vicki threw her two bits in, "It's all about the preaching on prosperity and comfort. Oh, those ear ticklers." She pumped her hands playfully upward. "Happy, happy." Her eyes saw her little poodle, prancing across the floor. "Anything to make those poodles happy."

I didn't know who was right or wrong on this Rapture thing, but I found it interesting how much passion the subject inspired. I liked this woman's style, voice and definition, and figured this would bode well in a time of struggle. As well, I found myself looking over at the forearms of her husband. I liked what I saw; he looked muscular enough to easily move endless bags of supplies.

Yet in the days that followed, I grew reluctant to invite anyone in on our quest of stockpiling for the seventy, mainly because loose lips sink ships. I told Priscilla of my misgivings about asking Vicki and Alex. She said they were stockpiling too, and she thought they could be trusted.

In the coming week, lifting more fifty-pound bags didn't help my painful back or elbow to heal. Then there was the thought of moving the entire stockpile, over 120,000 pounds, out of the garage and into the underground units, once they were built. My 175-pound frame was screaming for a different way.

It was around this time Priscilla mentioned the possibility of inviting Vicki and Alex over for dinner, "Just to explore their views."

Because the question of building a supply for seventy people for five years was such an eccentric adventure, I was very apprehensive. They might think we were a little on the crazy side. I told Priscilla about my misgivings.

She suggested, "If you don't feel right about them, then we don't need to go there, but we can at least have them over for dinner."

I certainly wasn't going to lay my cards on the table unless everything about their views came up in spades.

\* \* \*

They came over on a Saturday evening. The formalities went by in a blur. They were impressed with our overview of the valley and Alex mentioned that a high place like ours was good to see anyone coming. This told me he had the right instincts.

During supper I asked him, "So, Alex, what do you think about the future?"

"I'm not optimistic. The company I'm working for just laid off three more people. I hope I can keep my job."

"I think we're living in the Last Days," Vicki said.

"How so?"

"I think we are coming to the end of time."

"Why?"

She went on, talking about the birth of Israel and how this started some seventy-year generational clock. I really didn't get her conclusions, but basically she had the same mindset as Priscilla. Somewhere in this, she said our valley was going to be a safe place and that all we needed to make it through the Great Tribulation was food, lots of food. In the end, I could see they felt just as doom-and-gloom about the future as any survivalist. I still was reluctant to take them on.

It was then that I had one of those back spasms. It was so abrupt it jerked me forward.

"Are you okay?"

How awkward for this to happen while we had company. "It'll pass," I managed to say, angled sideways, hoping it would pass.

Priscilla asked, "Is there anything I can do?"

At that moment, in my condition, I concluded there was no way forward without the help of others. I gasped, "Tell them about the dream."

Priscilla told them about the blue underground chamber, the five sets of blue plates, the fourteen place settings that sat atop the five tables, everything, as well as her interpretation.

When Priscilla was finished, I asked the couple, "Hypothetically speaking, if someone was extreme enough to build a stash for seventy people for five years, would this be something you'd look at as nutty, or something you'd want to be part of?"

"What would it cost us if we were nutty?" Alex grinned.

"I suppose it's like anything where you put skin in the game … it comes down to money and muscle."

"We don't have money."

Priscilla gave me a quick eye. "That could be worked out."

"What's the advantage of being with seventy people, gathered up in one place?"

"Protection. How would two people be able to do a 24-hour watch?"

Alex gave Vicki a nod.

She couldn't help but smile. "The Lord showed me something new was coming. I believe Priscilla's interpretation is right." She flexed her bicep. "We have muscle."

"As long as we get to be part of the seventy," Alex said with another energetic grin.

After this, the chatter flowed like a high mountain stream. There was a gung-ho-ness about the couple. And we opened up, explaining our plans to bury food. None of this surprised them, as they were also stockpiling, but on a much smaller scale.

This was a moving moment for Priscilla. At one point, I thought I saw her eyes fill with tears.

When they left, Priscilla gave my hand a squeeze and said with much emotion, "They are the first of the seventy." She put her hand over her heart. "God is in this."

"It'd be good if He was, but I just wish you'd take guns more seriously. I can't see the need for seventy, if they were all gun people and had lots of ammo."

\*     \*     \*

That week I hired an excavator to dig the underground unit. I love construction, and as I looked over the shale he tore into, I realized it was sound enough to use as a sidewall. Though shale was difficult to dig, it really had a fine look. I started thinking of a way to utilize it.

I began the footing on the underground storage unit, fortunate to employ a carpenter who had worked for us, off and on, over the years. I always thought it was a privilege to work with Bert, as he had a good sense of humor and was a hard worker. Sometimes a bit of manly competition would flare up between us, which would result in getting the job done faster, though in those days he carried the heavy work, as my back and elbow were still not healed. One thing for sure, there was no competition when it came to looks. Bert had that handsdown. The only thing I had on him was age, five years.

Taking off my boots after work one evening, I looked over at Priscilla. She was setting the supper table and the fading western light made her look quite wholesome. "I don't know if I've ever told you, but you are one fine-looking woman."

"If you keep talking that way, my head will swell and you may think differently."

"Sometimes I wonder how you ever ended up with this toad instead of someone like Bert?" Perplexed, I rubbed my bald head.

"I was just fortunate."

"Bert should've been in the movies."

"Maybe he's not interested in all that fluff."

"I think he's already figured out that the concrete structure is more than just a basement."

"Has he said anything?"

"Yes, he's joked, 'What are you building here, a bomb shelter?'"

"I don't think Bert is the type that will talk."

"If we go for spanning that upper area with concrete to utilize the rock wall, he will know that it's a bunker."

"I can't see us building it without Bert's help." She placed two cups down and walked back to the kitchen. "I can't lift those plywood sheets; they're too heavy."

A fine smell rose from the garlic sizzling in the frying pan.

"If I was to pick one fellow for the seventy, Bert would be the one."

"He's not a Christian."

"Who's to say we're getting a bunch of Christians?"

"I think we have to trust God about who He'd bring."

"Bert's a good hunter. He's more optimistic than anyone I know. He's had some woman trouble, but he's always supported his kids." I gave a reassuring nod. "He really loves them. And most importantly, he's good with a gun, a real good shot."

"I pray that God will choose each one of the seventy."

"I think he's savvy enough to keep quiet …" I gazed blankly toward the window "… but who knows?"

\*   \*   \*

In the evenings, Alex and Vicki started helping unload the dry goods into our garage. Thank goodness we lived in the country; it was no small task to drive in with four pallets on the flatbed without some nosy–nosy wanting to see what we got. The key was covering them with a tarp.

Alex was good and strong with unloading. Vicki was fun as well. Sometimes while unloading, she entertained us with a country western song. I think she would've been the queen of country if she'd pursued it. She could really carry a tune and yodel. All in all, they appeared a great addition.

My only problem was keeping up with Alex. He was the young blood we needed. They were good and steady, and true for two truckloads.

But on the evening we finished the second load, Alex took a look at all the pallets, then asked, "How much more do we have to do?"

"We are a little over a third of the way. But after the rest is completed, we still have to move it all down to the underground storage unit, once that's done. So we got a long, long way to go."

His mouth hung open as he tiredly gazed over the pallets. His face displayed one of those worrisome, This is too much looks.

After that evening, it didn't matter how many times we called them, they weren't available. In the beginning their excuses sounded right, but after a while I knew they weren't into it. It was so disappointing to travel by their house, loaded with four pallets and see both their vehicles; yet ten minutes earlier, Vicki had said she had to go and groom a dog, and Alex was supposedly off at work.

After this, I told Priscilla not to call them anymore. I didn't understand these people. And here we had told them our secret, exposed our plans to them. This was so disturbing.

Strange that this gal spoke with such conviction—she was a real good talker. And here they were going to get five years of food and shelter out of it. After this, I had a lot of self-doubt about the whole escapade.

If they were the first of the seventy, what would the rest be like?

Priscilla saw I was in a funk over this and started blowing that shofar again. At the time, Bert and I were forming the walls for the underground units as well as the foundation for the solar panels and wind generator, not to mention running power and septic to the underground storage unit. These projects and the accumulation of goods got so costly, I was really having second thoughts, as money was going out like a flood. Were we going way, way, overboard, or was the world's economic ship really going to roll?

Somewhere in all this, I met Priscilla coming up the porch steps as I was exiting the front door. She said, "You know, it'd be pretty difficult to feed and shelter seventy people in our house. What do you think about another structure for them to sleep in?" She said this as calmly as if asking for a loaf of bread.

"Do you think money is for nothing?"

Her open palm angled toward our distant out-buildings. "The old barn isn't a place where they could sleep in the winter. Even if we had a stove in it, the siding is so worn, you can see right through it."

"Eli has slept there just fine."

"Eli's different. You know it wouldn't do for ladies. It should have a kitchen and a bathroom or two."

"It's not like we need another structure for the tax man to hit. What if the world doesn't fall apart?"

"Hershal, do you think our house will be sufficient to look after seventy people?"

"With the kids gone, we need an extra building around the place like a hole in the head."

"Can you imagine seventy in our house, all the time, for five years?"

"I'm spent." I sat down on the steps, my back hurting.

"Don't you think another building would take the pressure off our house?"

"I remember how, thirty-five years ago, my uncle took my cousins off to live in the woods because he thought the world was coming to an end. Ten years later, he moved them back to New York. That was a long, long time ago. Now, with all the money going out, sometimes it's like I hear someone whisper in my ear, 'You're going to look like a fool, building underground this, underground that, gathering tons of food, setting up water catches, solar, a wind generator; the way you're spending money, your economic ship is going to roll before the Fed's.'" I gazed up at her. "Then the voice says, 'Now it's your turn to look like your uncle.'"

"That's the Devil talking."

"We are going through a pile of money."

"I suppose Noah looked outlandish building the ark out in the middle of dry land. I bet they mocked him." She held an instructing finger up so stiff, it looked as though she was going to stick it in the Devil's ear. "God has shown me that there are few people anymore who stick with the vision."

Sometimes I wondered if she'd drunk more purple drink than anybody. After our dealings with the queen of country and the Bulgarian, to even consider spending our funds on a new barn for people like that was wild. She went on to talk about something, but I wasn't listening. And to think this entire adventure came about because of a dream! A dream! This was getting too strange; stranger still that I was part of it and not even a discipling man.

As she came to her conclusion, I fanned my hand, indicating that I'd had enough. I got up. "The world isn't coming to an end any time soon. We need to sell a couple of horses before they eat up the last of our funds."

I limped away.

\*   \*   \*

For some reason, Priscilla couldn't just sell her house in Canada without the approval of her brother, Jack. He didn't mind her selling it, as long as she sold it to him, but for half the market value. Running short of funds, we had to let Bert go. This was rough, as we needed to complete the projects and we'd just got the bill from our lawyer, who represented Bunnies Unlimited, for $3,600. Interesting, it was the same amount that Priscilla mentioned Bunnies Unlimited could've grossed per week.

Stunned at the lawyer's bill, I called him. He said this was just the beginning of our journey through the courts, as the nature of the crime had collided head-on with the Endangered Species Act, which prohibits the possession, sale, harassment, purchase, or transplantation of endangered species. He went on to say he was trying to ward off the penalty on the first offense, a $100,000. fine and a year in jail.

I was frightened. Furthermore, the coincidence of his $3,600. bill was so striking, I figured the Devil was running with us.

Even with all this, Priscilla was so gung-ho on these projects that she was ready to sell her Canadian property to her brother for half the price. This disturbed me, and I told her to forget it. Still, I said it with great apprehension, as we were in a fix; the underground units were not finished, and we were out of money.

A bank loan was out of the question, because I had no construction contracts. And here we were, stalled on some secret adventure and couldn't cover it up. I will say, bitterness came around and I was sour that I had been tricked by the supposed Canadian funds. Furthermore, if God was in on all this, where did He go?

Priscilla's countenance was solid as steel. "The Devil isn't just going to roll over because of our vision. I don't think we have a whole lot of time left before the Ark needs to float." She gave a foreboding glare. "If the Yellowstone Cauldron blows off, none of that Canadian property will be any good, anyway."

"For half the going rate?"

"It's a way." She said this as if God was providing an open door. "I can call my brother."

She ended up doing just that, and that was the unfortunate end of her Canadian property. She was thankful, but I thought it was a sad cash-out.

*    *    *

I desperately wanted to get this survival thing behind me and get on with finding a real job. But without Bert, things really slowed down. None of the projects were going fast enough. To stay sane, I constantly told myself not to freak out, lest I lose the ability to be flexible. One example of this was the shale on the sidewalls of the excavator dig, which was solid enough to use as a wall. This turned into a space big enough for a bathroom, a kitchen, and a place where I could put a water storage tank. That ended any talk of new structures. If the supposed seventy ever materialized and didn't have silver and gold, they could sleep in this underground facility while the rest of us slept in the big house. This didn't mean they didn't owe me. Somehow they were going to have to pay for the grub they ate and the warmth they received, underground or not!

# The Grind

In the midst of the construction projects, Priscilla kept bringing home pallets and pallets of rice, beans, wheat, etc., to get us over the 120,000-pound mark. So we worked on construction in the day and unloaded the truck in the evening. I wished I could've stopped this train and stepped off to let my back heal. I also wished I was a better man who could forget about Alex and Vicki and their lack of commitment, but the thought of them was like salt on an open wound.

Priscilla was more optimistic and hoped they'd show up when we finally moved all the pallets out of the garage to the underground storage area. I didn't know what I'd do without another man's help once we moved the food down to the underground storage container, because immediately after that, I had to block in the door and entrance to keep the rodents out.

One of our biggest concerns was someone seeing what we were up to, airplanes especially, so we planned to load the unit at night. We were also concerned about bugs and mice; I'd read horror stories of their destruction of food storages. We were going to have to pay close attention to sealing around the door and powdering the perimeter floor with pesticide.

In spite of all our forethought, I still felt as if someone was watching. This premonition came about when we ordered 10,000 pounds of wheat from a wholesaler out in Billings. Sometimes I wondered if the FBI requires them to call if they get big orders like that. In hindsight, my advice is to drive a grain truck out to a farmer, pay cash for the product and make sure your license plate is covered with mud.

Regardless, after receiving that huge order, I felt as if we were on Big Brother's radar, so much so that whenever we left our place, I wondered if they did a little sneak-and-peek to see how we were progressing. These premonitions grew after finding odd things moved about, like the specialized battery of my camera inside my shoe, or another camera missing. Another time I noticed that the metal surface of the back door lock had been worked over, and that the electronics in the two motion detectors were fried. I could go on, but there was no doubt that something was amiss. In looking back, though suspicions were numerous, it's odd how my mind drifted back to fields of complacency. Then again, maybe my mind was stretched enough.

To top it all off, I got another call from Deputy Justin.

It wasn't long after the greetings that his questioning began. "I just wanted to go over that night's timeline with you. Can you tell me, what you did after you shot the porcupine?"

"Goodness, it was such a long time ago, I probably just went home, took a shower and went to bed."

"Do you always take a shower before you go to bed?"

*    *    *

Sometime in September, the concrete storage units were completed. Before loading them, we took a break to clean up our garden. Winterizing the garden was good medicine for my head, as I was tired of all that preparation stuff. It had been a good year for planting. We'd filled up all our sauerkraut crocks, mixing beets, turnips, parsnips, cabbage, carrots, onions, parsley, colored greens and garlic. What a harmony of flavors!

Frost had arrived and that is the signal to plant garlic. Priscilla considers garlic the most important plant we have, but I think lavender could be the best; either way, they both fight infection.

As I buried the garlic bulbs, a slight breeze touched my cheek. It spoke of winter's approach and hunting season. I thought of Eli. We hadn't seen him but a few times since he'd started as a sheep man, and I sure missed him. While I wondered how he was doing, I heard a vehicle. Looking up, I saw a truck coming down our dirt road. I didn't recognize it. It pulled in beside the garden's wire fence, dust rolling off its tires.

I grinned. Sometimes life is mysterious; you think or dream of someone, then suddenly they appear. Eli stepped out and came our way.

I waved at him and said to Priscilla, "Doesn't he look confident?"

Holding a spade in her hand, she was aglow. "He does have a job."

Behind him, the truck backed away. Eli had a bounce in his step as he entered the garden and closed in on his mother. With a wholesome smile, he gave her a long hug.

I patted his shoulder, loudly saying, "Did I ever tell you that I miss you?"

His cheerful look made me feel it was good and right to raise kids.

"Pinch him to see if he's put on any weight."

Priscilla felt his arm. "Oh, yes."

"Is everything fine at your work?"

He nodded and half-watched the truck drive away.

"Do you have those sheep behaving?"

He grinned and pulled out a wad of checks from his pocket, half ripping one in the process.

"You work all that time and you come home with paper?"

Again, he grinned, looking well-tanned.

"What you gonna buy with all them checks?"

He lifted his hands as if shooting a rifle. The light breeze touched his glossy shoulder-length hair.

"Guns are fun," I said, grinning.

*     *     *

I ended up taking him down to the bank to cash his checks, then off to the sporting goods store. During this time I was very conscious of being out in public, as my face had been so publicized on the front page of newspapers for the sins of Bunnies Unlimited. But that day I fought off those insecure thoughts, as I wanted to be with Eli when he purchased a gun, his first rifle.

He had to have a lever action 30-30. It didn't matter what I said about how a bolt action was more accurate. I found out later from the sheep man that Eli shot his first coyote with a lever action 30-30. I was happy for him, proud he'd earned it with the sweat of his brow.

*     *     *

We were going to need some help to load all the pallets into the underground storage. I really wished Eli was part of it. He was the only one I knew who could keep quiet about the buildup, but the very next day, the gal who'd dropped him off was faithful to pick him up.

Priscilla called Vicki to tell her that we really, really needed their help. It was quite a relief to hear that they would be there that weekend. This truly surprised me, and my hope in mankind was somewhat restored.

The weekend came and we were geared up with the 8 x 16 concrete blocks, two metal doorways, masonry mix, wet saw and tools, but Alex and Vicki didn't show. Priscilla called her cell phone to see if they were running late. Vicki never picked up. Why we went with them in the first place was beyond me, especially after being ratted out by our other neighbor on our first stash.

In the end, I reasoned you can't trust anyone when it comes to survival goods. And there was no way I was going to look after their survival needs for five years. No way! They weren't steadfast, so why should I be? For the few times they showed up to unload the truck, we would give them the equivalent in food, but that was it. They were on their own.

Without their help, it dawned on me to rent a forklift. The reason I hadn't rented one in the past was the way we gathered the food supply, spread over months. We could ill afford one then. But now my back shouted, "Rent it!"

After renting the machine, we locked our gate and when the sun dropped over the mountain, I had that forklift roaring. With Priscilla driving the truck, we kept the momentum going.

The forklift did a marvelous job. The only things that slowed us were loading the upper area by hand and placing cardboard sheets between the concrete walls and the bags of dry goods to prevent possible spoilage.

We were about halfway done loading the underground unit when the sun rose. Was I ever punchy! But the marathon had just begun, and it took another night to get all those pallets moved. If my arms weren't feeling rubbery when I slung the last bag up on the stack, they were when we started blocking in the entrance.

The third night found me filling a wheelbarrow with mortar before shutting the mortar mixer off. The night's quiet encompassed. I could've melted into the peacefulness and fallen asleep atop the cold ground, but cement doesn't wait on the exhausted. I pushed the wheelbarrow toward the block wall.

A distant coyote howled and was answered by another. Maybe they had a kill. I parked the wheelbarrow, rubbed my sweaty face, and glanced up at the quarter-moon. My tired eyes found my bride. "Can't you feel fall in the air?"

She nodded.

"Twenty years ago, did you ever think of burying food?"

She looked reflective under the construction light. "No. It's surprising just how fast this country has shifted in the last couple of years."

"Hasn't it happened fast?"

"This sure isn't my mother's generation where right was right and wrong was wrong." She looked thoughtful. "It's all gray now … the only thing that is clear now is the Devil is stepping out of the closet, and Christians are going into the closet."

My tired gaze stayed on her. Sometimes she had a subtle, tender look that melted me. "It's good to be with you tonight."

"I like you, too, Mr. Beecher."

"I bet we're the only folks out tonight burying over 120,000 pounds of food in this country."

She chuckled. "We have so much trust in this government, we should be doing another entire unit."

"I'm curious, why do you still go to that underground church when Vicki and Alex have such little backbone?"

Her tired eyes dropped. "I was hoping they'd come through."

*   *   *

Come morning, those 8 x16 cement blocks weren't getting any lighter. I was about tapped out, Priscilla too. Our beds were never so welcoming.

It took another night to get the entrances blocked off. I was really dragging when we went to set the doors. The meadowlark's morning song usually gives me comfort, but not that morning. I felt like I was on the last mile of two marathons and my biological clock was off-kilter.

We'd just come out of the underground unit for a cup of tea. I felt a slight breeze and glanced up the hill toward the windmill. It was nice to see it spinning. On the road, movement caught my eye. My heart skipped three beats as I realized it was a person. "Didn't we lock the gate?"

"Of course."

"Strange that someone would sneak in here in broad daylight."

"Who is it?" Priscilla started toward the road.

"Hold up. Let's get these locksets on."

The trespasser's presence kicked us into a higher gear; we couldn't get the locksets on the doors fast enough. In no time we were in the truck, in pursuit. By then, the intruder had gone up to our house and now was coming back down the road.

Hot under the collar, I powered the truck around the garden, heading up the road. My jaw dropped upon seeing who it was. I braked to a stop.

The door creaked open. I hopped out, forcing my body forward. "Aunt Jessica!" With arms wide, my exhausted body closed in on her. "What a surprise!"

As we hugged, her fine perfume wafted and my mind raced to come up with a story regarding the underground concrete unit, which was now sealed with steel doors but not covered with dirt. "How'd you get here?"

She pressed away, looking perplexed. "How do you think I got here?" She gave me a funny look. "Didn't I fly into Missoula?" Her New York accent branded her, as well as her stylish hair and clothes. "Think about it."

"You don't look a day older since I saw you last." I wasn't just saying this to impress her; she always carried herself well, her good height was well-supported, her back straight.

She looked me over and her lips moved, but she was somehow able to withhold what she was going to say. Finally, she looked up the slope from where we'd come. "Were you working this morning?"

"We were just getting rid of some old pesticides. They are nasty."

She took a cautious step back, as she is very conscious of her health. "Those are poisonous." Her voice trailed with anxiety. "No wonder you look so dreadful."

"I don't believe I got any on me." I looked over my pants. "But who knows?"

Priscilla was ready to give her a hug, but Auntie stopped her. "Priscilla, are you okay?"

My wife appeared conscious of her looks, putting her hand to her cheek.

I thumbed toward the gate. "We can give you a ride back to your rental car."

"Hershal, don't you know those pesticides will kill you?" She gave me a scolding gaze. "You should've taken that poison to the recyclers." Her hand pointed toward the area as if it were plagued, then she gave me a telling nod, her finger pointed at my pants. "And wash those."

"Yes, Auntie," I said half-jokingly. "Can we take you back to your car?"

She gave me an exasperated look. "Fuhgeddaboutit …" She started for the gate. "… and take a shower."

"Hold up." I went after her to give her the gate key.

As I turned back, I thought that, outside of my mother, Aunt Jessica is the only woman I know who can show up and lay her opinion down without me feeling her bossy. I'd probably wonder what was wrong with her if she was any different.

I was so tired when I caught up with Priscilla that I felt rode hard and disconnected.

She asked, "Do I look that dreadful?"

We trudged toward the truck. "For a woman who's worked four nights in a row, you look great." After starting the truck, I gazed in the rearview mirror to see Auntie striding away. "She is one independent woman."

"I suppose her success on the stock market has something to do with it."

The truck rambled up the hill, past the row of Russian olives, which were beginning to lose their leaves.

"She is no fool when it comes to trading futures. Even still, she and all my family are as dull as oxen as far as getting ready for the big bata-boom." I glanced over at Priscilla. She yawned. I rambled on, "And it's not like they're short on money for stocking up. I bet they don't have one 25-pound bag of rice or beans between them."

Priscilla looked half-comatose, placidly staring at the dashboard. The truck drove around the windmill.

"Remember at the family reunion, when I told Clara that she needed stuff to trade with, like silver and bullets? She looked at me like I was a kook. I remember her so-called joke, 'Do you still get around by dogsled in Montana?'" I was upset just remembering it. "Then when I pulled my sister, Marilyn, aside and mentioned, if she was concerned about surviving after the financial ship rolls, to either stock up or send some money out to us so I could make a stockpile for her. Remember that? Boy, did she give me a condescending laugh. I can hear her words, 'I'm sure there are no shortages of outhouses in Montana.'"

I shook my head; these people just didn't get it. "That hurt. I'll tell you what, after the big bata-boom, if she's lucky enough to make it out here, she's not getting her bowl of rice and beans 'til she digs a hole for an outhouse. And if she thinks she'll be getting any dessert ..." The truck neared the garage. "... and don't you give her any dessert, either." I looked over at Priscilla. Her head was tilted down; she was fast asleep.

*   *   *

Somehow I found the energy to get Auntie settled in, and I grinned when I was supposed to, but it was all an act; my body craved sleep. I supposed the telltale sign was, when listening to Auntie's latest trip, I leaned on the doorpost and nodded as if I were somehow paying attention, then nodded off while standing.

Thank goodness it didn't offend her. She shooed me off to get some rest, insisting it must be the pesticide. "And take a shower!"

# That Crazy Dream

Late that evening, the ringing of the front door's electronic motion sensor woke me. I didn't know what time it was, or, for a moment, where I was. It rang so many times, I was sure the intruder was back. This drove me out of the warm covers. I felt sluggish as I pulled a sawed-off shotgun out from under the bed and headed down the hallway in my underwear.

As I staggered toward the second-story deck that overlooks the porch, fatigue lay so heavy on my being that my legs felt separate from my body. While dumbly gazing at the gun, I banged into the glass door that opened onto the deck. Lucky I didn't break it. I blankly stared out the glass door, wondering why I was even there. Outside, darkness was thick. Finally, I recalled the front door motion detector alarm that had announced an intruder.

I opened the door and eased out onto the deck. A fall breeze met me. I heard a sound below and hurriedly fumbled for the dangling wire of the light switch on the weapon.

"Halt!" I called. The button end of the light switch wasn't leaping into my fingers fast enough, and I felt more threatened by the second.

Aiming the gun toward a distant field, I squeezed the trigger. The shotgun barked, flaming, and the slide of the shotgun resounded with a mean click.

Without my glasses, I couldn't see much but I feigned, "I can see you there!" Leaning over, my belly pressed into the iron railing. "Put your hands up and step into the open."

At last, my shaky fingers found the light button, illuminating the stairway below. I nervously jerked when I saw a figure. His hands appeared up, but I wasn't sure.

"There's buckshot here." A real fear swept me when he moved. "If you don't …"

A hint of perfume drifted up.

"Oh, my gosh …" I mumbled, stunned—it was my Auntie.

"Hershal Ward Beecher … Fuhgeddaboutit!"

"I'm so sorry, Auntie, so sorry. Ohhhh … I thought you were an intruder."

"Is this a Montana welcome?" She lowered her arms.

"I was sleeping, and the sounder went off." I quickly headed for the door.

Inside the house, I wasted no time ditching the shotgun, grabbing my glasses, pulling on my pants and shirt and hustling down the stairway.

Heatedly, I burst onto the main floor. "I am soooo sorry."

Near the hutch, Aunt Jessica held a wine glass and she looked as serious as an earthquake, formulating her bright-eyed attack—the underground tremors were on the move.

"When I heard the sounder, I just came out of this deep sleep."

Her hard eyes pierced me. "I think you've been living in the woods one day too long." She swirled her hand. "I can get you employment if you move back to the East Coast, don't you worry."

"I thank you, Auntie, but we're not ready to move."

She gave me the most exasperated look. "I am concerned about you, Hershal. The whole family is concerned about you. Your mom would have rolled over in her grave."

"Sure, sure, the thing is, we've had some trespassers. I just thought it was them."

"Trespassers? Did you contact the Sheriff?"

"Yes." I glanced at Priscilla. "I mean, no."

"What?"

"I-eee … just haven't got around to it."

"Good grief, Hershal! Can't you see something's amiss here?" She looked solemn as she stepped toward me. "How is it that you're sleeping all day?"

"It must be those darn pesticides."

"And why didn't you take them to the recycler?" Her stare was as piercing as a crow's. "They can kill you."

"I don't know." I played the part and stumbled toward the kitchen, rubbing my tired face, my thoughts drifting to what we were really doing, working on our food storage. It seemed such a long time ago.

\*　\*　\*

After supper, a soft pillowy tune drifted from the stereo. It spoke of happier times. Auntie cuddled her wine glass and wandered over the slate floor. I was reading an article and shifting around in front of the fireplace, trying to get in a good position for my sore back, when I glanced up to see a woman who looked as if she was on the prowl.

Auntie stopped in front of the antique buffet and viewed the AR-15 that leaned against it. Above was a head-mounted antelope, and to its side, a long window reached for the ten-foot tall ceiling. She looked over a few family pictures, then adjusted a doily beneath them.

Finally, she spoke, "I can see your black gun matches nicely with your blackout curtains."

"Isn't it a beautiful thing?"

Her searching eyes found Priscilla, who was pouring hot water into a teapot. "Priscilla, did you know, when Hershal was a boy, he always slept with some form of protection?"

I defended, "Only to keep the rambunctious at bay."

"He'd drag clubs or rocks into bed."

When you're found out, it's tough not to grin.

"One night he was kind enough to hit my Steven with a rock."

"It wasn't my fault; he shouldn't have leaped on me. I was sleeping."

"Tell me he doesn't still sleep with sticks and rocks?"

"No, he's graduated to a .45 caliber." Priscilla smiled. "And I've graduated to a .38 Special."

Auntie glanced my way. "I'm fortunate I wasn't shot."

I scrunched down, wanting to hide in my magazine.

"What are you reading, Hershal?"

"It's kind of you to change the subject." I lifted the magazine. "An article that explains the normalcy bias."

"What's that?"

"They say the normalcy bias is where smart people underestimate the possibility of a disaster and its effects. People believe, since something never happened … it never will happen."

"No need to worry about it, then."

"I suppose."

"What's his point?"

"Inflation, wars, that type of thing."

"Maybe a little inflation, but we'll be fine. This is the good old USA." She looked back with a questioning look. "Is that all?"

"He suggests there's something pretty big going on under the surface."

"Like what?"

"Inflation … wars."

"Good grief, Hershal, what's new about inflation and wars? Aren't we all going to die?"

Her question made me feel ill-at-ease over the construction of the two underground chambers, let alone our stash of 120,000 pounds of food.

Auntie finished with a belittling, "That whole thing is a survivalist's mentality." She walked toward me. The room's light displayed a face that looked as if it had just returned from some tropical island. "Hershal, maybe you need to live a little." She lifted her glass of wine.

"I suppose," I said, downcast.

"I'm just wondering if the economic ship will roll before the big bata-boom or after the big bata-boom?" Priscilla said.

"Good grief, Priscilla, how do you live like that?" Auntie's eyes were piercing. "This kind of talk is so gloomy."

I stared at the fire; yellow orange flames danced about bluish tinges. This hibiscus blue was the same as the walls in that vision of the underground room. I shook my head at that dream of the stacked blue plates atop the five blue tables. Considering it, disappointment covered me. What a nutty dream! And how did Priscilla ever come up with such a cockamamie interpretation? And here we'd been swept into storing food for seventy for five years!

Auntie swirled her wine glass, took a sip and carried it into the sunroom, then spoke in the most confident manner. "There is too much good in the world … This is a gorgeous view … the house lights in the distance … Priscilla, think of the good things and they will come."

Priscilla casually replied, "I hope it all works out for you."

Coming back from the sunroom, she responded, "As long as they don't shut down the sitcoms, chocolate and …" she lifted her glass of wine, "… I'll do fine." Smiling, she gazed at Priscilla. "I'm looking for a new outfit, Priscilla. Shall we go shopping tomorrow?"

\* \* \*

Later that night, Priscilla and I snuck out of the house and went down to the underground units. We ended up spending a few hours, covering the area with a number of large tarps. I placed some wood atop them and hoped we wouldn't get a strong wind.

A few days later Auntie left us, blowing away like she'd come. She never did go near the underground units as she was so conscious of her health, and the thought of pesticides gave her the willies.

Though we have totally different views on this world, I knew she loved me enough to fly out to bring me back to the land of peachy. Sometimes I wished the world was all rosy and we could play together in happy sandboxes, but she trusted in paper and I trusted in guns and gunpowder. Priscilla was the odd one out, as she trusted in the Lord.

# A New Season

The following week, I put a little kitchen and bathroom in our underground storage unit. They were nothing fancy, as I bought all the stuff secondhand. After this, I rented a backhoe and covered the storage facility, burying the concrete under a few feet of dirt. This was something I'd been anxious to do for a long, long time.

That evening, while walking under the spinning windmill and past the row of solar panels, I felt a wave of accomplishment. No doubt, it was expensive, eccentric and zapped our retirement; still, I am a builder who enjoys the completed project. I was actually standing under a windmill that was producing electricity. Just to listen to its sound was something. I stared across the valley at the way the sun's rays were falling on the mountains. With these projects complete, a part of me felt ready for something as big as the Yellowstone Cauldron blowing off. But that evening, no earth trembled or meteors resounded; quite the opposite. A peaceful sunset fell across the Yokino Mountains. It spoke of order, a new season, hope.

\* \* \*

Money from the sale of our horses provided a deposit on a fifth-wheel trailer for my journey to the oil country. I hauled that thing over 750 miles to the Balkin oil fields in North Dakota.

I'd imagined it would take a while to find work, but not in that country. It took about twenty minutes. No doubt there was a shortage of skilled workers. The trick was room and board.

In our framing crew, I was the oldest by far. The day I started, looking over those young bucks, I felt like a detached generation. If anything, I envied their power and the spring in their step. Few things slowed them down, not even the weather or that nasty wind.

During those wintry days, that wind could get to you. The day after I started, I picked up a sheet of plywood when a gust hit. The boys dug me out some 15 feet from where I'd been. I heard no end of it from them young bucks.

One called me, "Papa." What a smarty he was. "Don't pick up the plywood, Papa, you'll end up in another zip code."

It was quite something to be going against the wind when we raised a frame wall atop a sub-floor. In doing so, that same young buck pointed at me and said, "We're going to have to secure a rope to Papa. We don't want him disappearing."

That kid made me feel my age. And that cold country made me feel my bones. It didn't matter how many layers of clothes I was bundled in, I still felt cold. Our windmill would do well in that country.

It would've been nice to have Priscilla there, but we figured she'd better stay in Charby till after hunting season, as the poachers are quick to invade a vacant place. I missed her and often thought of her. It was especially lonely when I got back to the trailer at night.

I logged a lot of overtime and rightfully so, as it cost a small fortune to rent a pad for my fifth wheel. The remains of my pay went to taxes and my attorney. I worked four weeks on and one week off.

On those cold mornings, that smarty kid was ever a smarty. "Papa, did you eat your Wheaties?" And when I got to thinking about the world not coming to an end and DC swiping such a big portion of my paycheck, and having to deal with that smart-mouth kid, "Papa, do you feel like a man today?"

boy, I tell you, my attitude wasn't the greatest. That kid was lucky I didn't nail him with my framing hammer.

My time off found me back in Charby. It was so good to give Priscilla a hug. She was anxious to go to North Dakota and earn some funds to help pay for our attorney. We ended up giving Clyde, our outdoor cat, to Dewey, who always admired Clyde's mousing abilities, and Priscilla joined me, traveling the 750-plus miles to Williston. It was good to have her. Right off, she got a job at a restaurant as a waitress, and in no time they put her in charge of a shift.

Those days, and weeks, all we did was work, work, work. Priscilla was better than I at looking at how much the Feds took from her pay, often saying, "At least we have jobs."

*   *   *

Late March we got back to Charby. Passing the frost-covered garden, I looked up the hill to where we had buried the goods and shook my head at how costly that adventure was. It would've been different if the poles had shifted, or California had fallen off the map. But it was no different than the end of the Aztec calendar—a bunch of hullabaloo.

On the home front, there was a phone message from Eli's boss, the sheep man. I was a bit curious when I called him back. He was an easy-going fellow, always quite cheerful.

After we got past the courtesies, he said, "I want you to know that my daughter is expecting."

"Good, good," I responded, without much thought.

"You'd never guess who the father is?"

"Ummm." I could sense a groundswell, but I hadn't quite seen the wave.

"It's exciting to be a grandfather."

Finally, I got it! It came like a blast from Old Faithful. "Eli?"

"Oh, yes."

I had to grin at his excited voice. "Wow."

"Yes, I'm quite excited about it."

"Maybe they should get married?"

"That's what I was thinking."

"I should take Eli out to get a suit."

"That won't be necessary, we already took him and got all that. He's good to go."

"I'd like to meet the bride and talk to Eli."

"Sure, sure, come on over. Do you want to do it today?"

\*      \*      \*

Priscilla and I wasted no time in heading for the sheep ranch. Traveling there, I thought of the gung-ho-ness of the sheep man. I was a bit concerned, as this train was rolling down the track at quite a clip. Even still, there have been no end of well-thought-out marriages that ended in train wrecks.

The trip was a 25-minute drive that I enjoyed, as the sheep man's 320 acres were like traveling through a park that edged the river, with irrigated fields, stands of lodge pole pines and a few creeks running through.

The last time I'd come, Eli was with his sheep, so I figured if I spotted the herd, he'd be there. The sheep were spread out, but other than a sheep dog or two, I didn't see anyone.

I spotted the sheep wagon under some cottonwoods. It looked like it belonged, with its canvas top half-covered in leaves, a wisp of smoke rising from the smokestack. An old quad was parked outside. I pulled the truck to a spot not far from it.

Priscilla waited in the cab while I approached the wagon. Dried leaves crunched under my boots. The wagon wheels with their wooden spokes drew my attention. Above them, the sideboards looked freshly painted green.

I knocked. The wagon shifted here and there. I waited, listening to the gurgle of the creek just beyond the wagon.

The door opened and there was Eli. Something about him looked older, at least more confident.

"Hey, Eli ..."

The sheep man's daughter came up behind him. She was a hefty gal who gave me a look, then glanced out at the truck, then back to me.

"... Nancy?"

She nodded and pushed Eli, as he was in the way. He touched my shoulder as he hopped down, strode past, heading to see his mother.

"It's nice to meet you." I said.

"You, too."

I put out my hand. "I'm Hershal." Nancy took my hand while stepping down. She wasn't what one calls pretty, but a solid, healthy farm gal. "You've got a good handshake."

She glanced toward the pasture. "Those sheep don't just lay down when you shear them."

"I suppose they don't."

Shoving her hands into her jeans, she gazed toward Priscilla, who was being lifted off her feet by a big hug from Eli. "I've got to keep Eli in line, too." She gave me a teasing smile that I really liked.

"No doubt." I grinned. "So what do you think of all this marriage stuff?"

"It will be good." Her hand went to her midsection. "Eli's going to be a good dad." I sensed she was as plain as her old flannel shirt, as wholesome as a spring breeze. "I've been learning sign language."

"It's kind of fun to communicate."

"I wanted to ask, what's with him and houses?" She displayed a questioning look. "He gets nervous around rooms, and he doesn't like going inside our house. What's with that?"

"He's pretty much an outdoor fella."

"That's for sure." She glanced back at the wagon. "Even in the sheep wagon, he feels more comfortable with the door open."

"Can we take you out to lunch?"

"I'm sure you have a lot of things to talk to him about. Why don't you just take Eli?"

We drew closer to the truck and I could see from the way Priscilla was drawn toward Nancy like a magnet, that I didn't have time to fully explain Eli's fear of confinement.

"Oh, Nancy …" Priscilla hugged her as if she was her own child. "… How do you feel?"

"I'm fine." Nancy looked a bit uncomfortable, not used to all this emotion.

"Since I heard the news, I've been praying for you."

"I'm fine."

"How's your appetite? Are you keeping it all down?"

"I'm fine." She shyly gazed at the dried grass.

After the welcome, we ended up in the truck with Eli, backing away, leaving behind his future bride. She looked like a postcard with her hands in her jeans, the sheep wagon and creek in the background.

I said to Eli, "So, you're getting married," and emphasized, "like husband and wife." He was all grins, and waved at her as if she was the Queen of Sheba, the finest fiancée in the world.

She gave what I call a Montana wave, which looks like a push-away wave, as if saying, "You're too much."

I braked the truck right there, as I thought it wrong to go to lunch without her; it was silly of me to think he had to have some counsel in the first place. He was a big boy now.

Stepping out, I called, "Nancy, please come with us."

To our delight, she came.

*   *   *

One month later Jerold, Bethany and Raela came up from California to witness their brother tie the knot. Though it was short notice, I was impressed that they had gotten time off work. They were all sporting the energy of 20-year-olds. It was good to have them stay with us. We had the family again.

The marriage between Nancy Edith Green and Eli Benjamin Beecher was held at a country church just south of Charby. What stood out for me were Eli's words to his bride at the altar. He was dressed in a Western suit, his hair down to his shoulders, handsome as ever. After the preacher asked, "As far as your vows, do you have anything to say?"

Eli let Nancy's hand go to sign-out five words, "I will look after you."

That's all he said, and I'm sure that was a done deal. Impressed, Priscilla gave my hand a tender squeeze. That was a boy-howdy moment.

The dance and potato salad were good too. I liked the sheep man, such a cheerful fellow, and I liked his family too. What a robust bunch on the dance floor.

Somewhere in all this celebration, Priscilla and I ended up in each other's arms, swaying to the music.

"It's been far too long since we've been dancing," I said, holding her close.

She gave an innocent nod and tucked her head into my shoulder. Sometimes I feel quite fortunate to be married to her.

When we stood for the pictures, I suppose anyone could see Eli wasn't from my genes, as he was so much better-looking. It was good that he didn't know it, and wasn't in the least interested in his hair or what he was wearing. But when he stood in the midst of us, the picture's centerpiece, there was no doubt, no mystery that he wasn't from my loins.

It was amazing how well his farm bride looked, all spruced up in a creamy satin dress. There was something about her big arms pressing out of that delicate dress that I liked, found humor in, as their strength possessed the power to move men.

Interesting, I noticed him talking to her in sign language quite often. I was happy that he finally had someone he could really communicate with. Still, when I noticed this, it came with a hint of sadness. I wished I'd been able to use that skill more with him in his younger years. Strange, I'd always talked to him loud, moving my big mouth about like some eccentric donkey, thinking my drama would get through. Goodness, the things we do.

Eli's siblings were just as huggy as they'd always been, hugging their brother any chance they got. When I saw Raela holding him, I wondered if she was sad that he was marrying someone else. Regardless, they showed they loved their brother and I was surprised at their wedding gift for him, a sheep dog puppy. I'm sure it wasn't cheap, as it came from a California breeder. And I was pleased to see Jerold, now taller than Eli, just as teary-eyed as the rest of us.

Though it was cold outside the hall, the anticipation of Nancy and Eli appearing was worth the wait. They stepped out the double door amid a wave of cheers and scurried for their get-away vehicle. All the young people were after them, tossing rice.

Priscilla just held my elbow, leaned into my ear and said, "We're blessed. We're so blessed."

When I looked back on Eli's life in the woods and my worries of him turning into a recluse hermit, I sure didn't foresee Nancy, their marriage and a baby on the way. And that was less than a year ago. Boy-howdy, you get a woman involved and things can happen fast.

# The Yoke

The joy of our son's wedding was short-lived. The day before heading back to oil country, I got another bill from our attorney. His bill on the rabbit business was so substantial that I again called him. He told me that part of it was trying to fight off the EPA, who wanted to conduct an environmental impact assessment of the property. He went on to talk about dates that I'd be available for a deposition. The stress of this roiled my stomach.

*   *   *

Back in oil country, all we did was work, six days a week, and fourteen hours a day. I suppose I wouldn't have felt like I was in prison if we had been getting ahead, but darn near everything I earned was going to my attorney or Uncle Sam. Under the yoke, I became quite the bitter man.

Not Priscilla; she somehow believed that God was in the entire deal. I wondered if she'd sing the Kumbayah song if the government ended up taking our property. Furthermore, it didn't take much imagination to see this EPA study might unearth our stash for the seventy … or Wartal.

Around that time I had dark thoughts that the entire EPA was after me. I'd never had thoughts like that in the past, but the attorney's bills and the possibility of losing everything gave me migraines. I went through aspirin like candy. It came to the point where they didn't help and couldn't stop the continual throbbing. I awoke to a pounding head; it didn't stop till I fell asleep. More than once, Priscilla anointed my head with oil and prayed, rebuking the Devil and the sickness, but nothing helped. The migraines went on, day after day, week after week. Maybe the world wasn't coming to an end, but mine was.

Seeing that I had drawn in, Priscilla mentioned she'd be willing to learn square dancing. But I was in no mood for dance. It wasn't long after this that she went to the pound and brought back a Dalmatian/heeler cross. He was three years old and had a mind that would hop all over the place, but he was tender. We named him Sparky, as he had lots of energy.

When I drove down the road, he'd always sit right next to me, sometimes resting his head on my lap. I liked Sparky a lot, and my boss at work didn't mind me bringing him.

\*    \*    \*

For some reason, the time between spring and fall sped by fast. In the midst of this, we got a call from the sheep man, announcing that baby Kelsey had arrived. What joy! We couldn't wait to get back to Charby to see her. Three weeks later, in mid-November, we headed for home.

The sun was setting when we encountered a major snowstorm going over Rodgers Pass. I suppose I had a distant look on my face, as I was mulling over the cost of the 120,000 pounds of food we'd buried, that dream of providing for seventy people for five years. The fact that it had cost us our retirement funds and Priscilla's house in Canada was disturbing. To say this sat uneasily in my gut was a massive understatement.

Priscilla asked, "How you doing, hon?"

"Sometimes I wonder if I'm lost."

"No." She looked out into the falling snow. "We're on Highway 200 … going home."

"I don't know of too many unemployed men who did what we did."

"What'd we do?"

"Build that underground storage unit and threw all that food into it … all because of that crazy dream."

"We know God works in mysterious ways," she said, serious as the icy road.

Time and falling snow passed under the tires before she spoke again. "We know He fed the five thousand. And Jesus always shows up at church when we have potluck … This tells us God is in the food." She leaned my way and touched my arm in an appreciative manner. "God was with us in storing for the seventy. When you think of the coming Horseman, the Third Seal, there will be scarcity." She said this with assurance. "Jesus wants us ready … These plagues aren't coming from the backs of turtles, but horses, and they'll have speed."

Funny, she actually believed the whole … nine … yards.

\*    \*    \*

Truck lights illuminated Priscilla as she unlocked and opened our iron gate, pushing it through half a foot of snow. Sparky watched her hop back in the cab. I wondered what he was thinking, as he'd never been to our house. When we passed the snow-covered garden, I looked up the hill toward the underground storage area. I had to grin; otherwise I would have cried.

As we came around the leafless Russian olives, Priscilla said, "I think we need to get gas masks for the seventy. If things get bad, they're going to need gas masks."

My mouth fell open.

"And we need toilet paper for them as well. How are they going to get by for five years without toilet paper?"

"I want to tell you something." My voice was stern. "I've had enough of this seventy thing. There won't be any more of my wages or your wages going there, period."

"What do you think of our overtime wages going to it?" she asked, as calmly as a kid asking a teacher for a pencil. "They could die without gas masks."

"Good, we're all going to die." Tired of this continual doom-and-gloom, I shook my head. "One thing for sure, you drank more purple drink than anybody."

"Night is coming on when no man can work."

"Is that a proverb or something?"

"A verse."

"Goodness, Priscilla, preparing for the doom-and-gloom has cost us near everything and you just won't give it up."

She looked downcast, but I didn't care. I'd had enough.

*　*　*

Whenever I got back to Charby, I dreaded looking at the mail, as more often than not there was a bill from our attorney. Sure enough, my ever-faithful attorney sent one, and again it was substantial. I mumbled some words that don't need repeating and went straight to the medicine cabinet to get some aspirin.

Priscilla looked over the bill and watched me down the pills. "Why do you carry this court case around with you?"

"Maybe it's because that attorney and the tax man have taken just about everything we earned." I blankly stared out the kitchen window. "Then again, maybe it's because I've been cursed."

"Cursed?"

"I told you I murdered that man."

"It was an accident."

"Before he died, he laid a curse on me."

She abruptly stretched her palm my way. "I rebuke that curse in Jesus' name." She said this with determination, authority. "Get out of here, Devil!" She approached with steely eyes, pointing at me. "You are blessed."

Strange, I felt a release. It happened so fast, I did a double-take about that aspirin manufacturer.

# Favor

The next day we high-tailed it over to the sheep ranch. We were grandparents now and I had a lead foot, wanting to see little Kelsey. Without new tires I may have ended up in a ditch, as the roads were icy.

When we finally got there, it was really something to watch Eli, proud as proud could be, bring the baby to us and tenderly place her in Priscilla's arms. And to hold her; what a darling!

Nancy locked onto motherhood like a champ, her big arms wrapping about the little cutie. And to see Eli rubbing Nancy's shoulders as if she were something precious, then slipping his hand over Kelsey's bald head.

These were some fine, fine memories.

*　*　*

Later that day I called our attorney and told him that my migraines didn't warrant fighting the full might of the U.S. government over this rabbit business. I asked if there was anything that I could do to get it over with.

"In the deposition, I found something in our favor."

"Yes?"

"They euthanized the bunnies."

"What? How many?"

"All of them."

"Why?"

"I have a hunch they found the rabbits weren't purebred. That only enhances our chances of a strong suit."

"Suit? Who would we sue?"

"The government."

"I don't understand. Who sues the government?"

"That's the new norm."

"Goodness, do you think we'd win? And what would it cost?"

"Our chances of a victory are good … I need a $5,000. retainer."

"How much would we sue them for?"

"If we can prove that those rabbits weren't pure Rare Pygmies but a cross-breed, then they've shut down a viable business. I would say at least $500,000."

I was stunned. "Ya think?"

"They shouldn't have destroyed those rabbits. I can assure you they'll come to the table long before the case goes full-blown."

"How can you be so sure?"

"It's all Monopoly money to those DC boys. They don't care."

When I got off the phone, I wasn't sure if this was going to be one of those send-me-more-money things or not. Regardless, the next few days were the best days I'd had in a long, long time.

*    *    *

It was during that time we got a message from Aunt Jessica on the recorder. I figured she was doing just peachy, as the stock market was roaring. It was as if the entire world was jumping into our stock market. Interesting, though it was roaring, the economy was floundering. When I thought of her good fortune on the market, I often felt like a dinosaur. If we had any extra, which was rare, we purchased a silver coin or two.

Aunt Jessica wanted to know if we'd consider having the next family reunion at our place, on Labor Day weekend, the coming year, and even offered to foot the bill.

When I told Priscilla about Auntie's offer, she put her hands over her heart, glowing, looking as if it was an opportunity of a lifetime.

# Trespassers

However, that trip to Charby wasn't all fine memories. On a walk to our gate, I noticed a trail camera up in a tree that I had completely forgotten about. After recovering its memory chip, I viewed the photos; a number of elk, deer, coyote and even a black wolf had triggered the device at night, and then I saw the picture of two men. To see their images in broad daylight made my neck hairs rise, my territorial instincts flare.

One appeared to be about thirty, the other late forties. The older man was taller and had a ponytail. They could've been mushroom or antler pickers, but all my suspicions pointed toward the Wartals.

The game trail camera displayed the date, four months back, on a Sunday when we were in North Dakota. They came again, on another Sunday when we were in town, about the time I dropped Priscilla off for church and motored on to the sporting goods store in Middleton, some thirty miles away. Obviously, they knew we were gone. And who knows how many times they'd been on the property since the camera's batteries had died?

There was also one other picture of a man in an officer's uniform. He, too, came in broad daylight, although his profile shot wasn't that clear. After viewing him under a magnifying glass, Priscilla and I thought he looked a lot like Deputy Justin. This was disturbing. Here I thought officials needed a warrant to enter a property. That date was May 5, when we were back in oil country.

What dread.

I went on a search, looking for any disturbances around the dirt where I buried Wartal. Nothing was disturbed. In fact, new sage and bunch grass had covered that area. But this wasn't the case with our house. Downstairs, I noticed a metal storage rack just below a basement window; its top shelf was bent, as if someone had stepped on it. Above, the wood around the window clasp had been whittled out. Seeing this, a strong sense of vulnerability flowed over me.

After a long search of the house, we found a rifle, three 500 round boxes of .223 ammo and some jewelry missing. The rifle was the only one not in a steel lockup, as I had been in the process of remounting a scope on it. This angered me, as it was a shooter, and I'd hoped it would get me back on target. Also disturbing was the loss of a pennant necklace and a delicate gold watch from Priscilla's grandmother.

That night sleep escaped me. I was fighting a mind battle with the Wartals. I found myself listening to every sound. If the electronic motion detector went off, it could've been a rabbit, but I was sure it was those thieving Wartals. Soon I was creeping out on the deck, shotgun in hand, gazing over the rail at the lattice work where they'd accessed the basement window.

When I got back in bed, I felt their presence in the house and couldn't shake it. I don't know why, but the place felt dirty, and Priscilla was a good housekeeper. For sanity's sake I tried to tell myself that those men may not have been related to the Wartals. Yet in no time my suspicions returned to those men. They wormed around in my skull like that curse. If I could only get them out of my head.

Lying there, I considered my options. It would be good to report those two intruders to the Sheriff. But how could I, when so many fingers pointed straight at me? Furthermore, why was his Deputy on our property? I reasoned I had to see if Wartal's roommates resembled the trail cam pictures. I had to confront them.

Priscilla had an entirely different approach to this theft. The next day she took her small vial of oil, her shofar and headed off to anoint the property posts for who-knows-what. I was in the basement working on a window when I heard the long forlorn sound of that shofar. Perplexing, that she considered the theft on a spiritual level. This didn't make sense to me. She wouldn't need that hope if she took guns more seriously.

In my few remaining days in Charby, I put in a louder speaker on our security system and thought long and hard about going to the Wartals. I concluded if something got out of hand at their place, it would be best to go in the evening. Furthermore, it would be best to go the night before we headed back to North Dakota.

No doubt there was a measure of premeditation in my planning and to say I wasn't looking for trouble may sound odd, as I had a snub-nose .38 in each pocket of my coat when I drove toward their place.

It was just after 6 p.m. when I turned onto their road. Though their acreage was part of our subdivision, I'd not been down that way.

I'd made up this cockamamie story about a missing dog to tell them. Drawing near, I pressed on the brakes. My window was down a tad and it was one of those evenings in November where you could feel the definite cold of winter. With my hand on my .38, in my coat pocket, I stared at the Wartals' place. There had to be over thirty vehicles around their house, making me wonder if there was a birthday party going on.

This was no time for a confrontation. I drove away.

That evening, my only comfort came from a sign Priscilla made that we placed down by the gate: SMILE—YOU'RE BEING RECORDED. I hoped it would ward off intruders.

*    *    *

Back in Williston, though Priscilla had a sparkle in her eye over Kelsey and the hope of a new generation, it didn't curb her gathering for the seventy. I can still see her in the fifth-wheel, counting out seventy new toothbrushes before wrapping them each in cellophane and putting them in a cookie box.

And then there were the winter boots. At first, I noticed a few in a fifth-wheel cabinet. Later I came back from work unexpectedly, and found her unloading a big garbage bag from the trunk of her car. Noticing another bag, I went to help her, but she quickly said, "I'm fine. I've got this."

I grabbed the bag anyway; it was pretty heavy. "What ya got?"

She looked somewhat trapped and slowly replied, "Boots."

"Boots? For what?"

"They're winter boots."

"Okay … Don't we have enough winter boots?" I opened the bag. "Where'd you get them?"

"Thrift stores."

"Okay … Who are they for?"

"They're for the seventy."

I was stunned. "Goodness, hon." I gave her an admonishing glare. "Is it our job to provide boots as well?"

"If they are from the West Coast, they might show up with tennis shoes or sandals." Dragging her stash, she weaseled toward the fifth wheel.

"I'm not for this," I said irritatedly, then called after her, "What's next? Socks? Underwear?"

She wrestled the bag up the fifth-wheel's steps, half-muttering, "I don't think this End Time business, the Day of the Lord, is going to be just another rainy day. Just this morning there was news that said every military out there is gearing up for the Big One. They know it's coming."

Sometimes I found this woman unbelievable. She was single-minded, convinced disaster was before us.

*    *    *

That winter sped past in a blur. We kept our noses pretty much to the grindstone. I didn't think I'd ever get used to the cold winds of North Dakota. That smart-mouth carpenter kid who I used to work with, thankfully went on to another builder—good riddance. News on the Priscilla front was her starting a little prayer group with some ladies at work and a few from the trailer park.

One night it was my turn to cook and Priscilla was clearing the table, removing a newspaper, when she began, "Have you been following the war in the Middle East?"

"Somewhat," I said, without looking up from chopping an onion.

"The shameful press isn't saying a word about the Christians getting slaughtered over there. Not a word about those radical Moslems' butchery in Africa, either."

I knew her comment was about spooking me into more stockpiling. "It's unfortunate. But why they'd be hanging around those Moslems," I shook my head, "I don't know."

"Surely you can see this one's a whole lot bigger than any others?"

"Big or small," I shrugged, "I don't care, as long as our nation doesn't get involved … again."

Her frown said that she wasn't making any headway with me. She took some plates and placemats over to the table and tried another angle. "Have you noticed Europe's financial mess is spreading? The worst indebted nations will likely start heading for the exit, leaving their debt behind."

I turned on the stove burner, and moved venison to the cutting board. "Those Europeans are good at printing money and spending it." The onions slid nicely into the frying pan. "But that's their problem."

"I don't think you'd be so cavalier if you truly grasped who was holding those countries' debt. If they go belly-up it will certainly have a deep impact on our banking system."

I looked at her directly. "Priscilla, they say there's lots of troop movement in Russia and here lately it's not hard to hear the press talking about some new Neo-Nazi party rising in Europe, but I can't see the end of the world coming. On the contrary, people are getting married, the wild spring flowers are popping and I heard a meadowlark today." I could see she wasn't happy with my response, but I continued, "He was chirping away, speaking of no end of hope."

Downcast, she said, "Well, it's good you have no worries."

I began cutting up the venison. "I didn't say that. If I have worries, it's over those intruders who came on our property." I shrugged. "But being over 750 miles away, what can I do?"

Finished with the table setting, she flopped down on the booth's bench.

I set the steak on the frying pan and a long pause ensued.

Her voice was downcast. "There was an older gal at the store today who had to leave a number of items at the cash register because she didn't budget for them." She stared blankly at the dark window. "She looked embarrassed and kept saying, 'Prices keep going up and up.'"

"I bet you bought her those items." I gave her a questioning eye.

She didn't answer, but leaned sideways and scratched her head.

"You shouldn't be giving away our hard-earned money. How are we ever going to retire if you keep doing that?"

# Family Reunion

That spring, all I remember is working in the Balkins and on our time off, visiting Kelsey, Eli and Nancy, and getting ready for the family reunion. It was mainly the barn we were clearing out, as we planned on having a barn dance at the end of the get-together. Speaking of dance, Priscilla and I had started square dance lessons and I found it quite enjoyable.

On the world front there was a new IMF currency. I didn't know what it was all about, perhaps caused by the wobbly Euro or the falling Yen. Some said the dollar was about to lose its reserve status as China was now the world's number one economy. The Middle East was ongoing; Saudi Arabia was clever enough to try to get us more involved in their undeclared war against Iran but this was an election year and our politicians had to put on a show and war wasn't cool right now, least not as cool as lipstick and promises. Like any election year things were plugging away. Real-estate in Charby was finally going up as there seemed to be a wave of city folk wanting to move to the country.

That summer the weather took an interesting turn, blowing one storm after another across the Dakotas. It rained and rained and rained, setting a record. I just hoped for good weather, come the reunion.

I found this time interesting, because our investment in silver had suddenly spiked. This was strange for the summertime. Usually precious metal prices save their spikes for the overcast days of winter. No doubt inflation was on the rise, everything had gone up, but the way silver just took off was foreboding. Another oddity was some chatter about higher interest rates causing some failure in the derivative market. This came from our preparation group via e-mails. None of this news was mainstream, but behind the scenes, and I didn't pay much attention as we weren't in paper investments and I didn't understand the derivative markets. Regardless, a week before Labor Day, before our family reunion, I reached into my pocket, touched a Walking Lady Liberty silver coin and felt a whole lot richer.

I wasn't sure how many would show up at the reunion. But our hope rose when our kids, Raela and Jerold, arrived from California a few days early to give us a hand. Unfortunately, Bethany couldn't be there.

A few months earlier, I'd called Nancy to see if she and Eli could get the three days off for the reunion. I was tickled to see Eli, Nancy and Kelsey drive up to the house the day before the event.

That was a family reunion in itself. Priscilla was in her element, as she is quite the Nana. Kelsey was going to be one spoiled grandchild.

Come Thursday, the rising sun enhanced our excitement. Family was flying or driving in from back East, British Columbia, Saskatchewan, Kentucky, Washington and California. It was one of those enjoyable summer days with temperatures in the 80s.

That night's talk was thick with memories as more and more people arrived. What a joy to see Aunt Jessica! She looked sparkling in her designer wares, and had arrived with Uncle Bob.

I hadn't seen my uncle in quite some time and would've liked to have a long visit with him, but he seemed preoccupied with dropped calls from his cell phone service. I found out later that his concerns had something to do with the derivative collapse. Aunt Jessica hid her concerns over the market better, nothing that a glass of wine couldn't smooth away, nothing that her pleasant perfume couldn't cover.

It was nice to receive a tender hug from Aunt Jessica, but I wasn't too thrilled with her comments, "Oh Hersh, this house should only be used for reunions. Look how everyone wants to come to Montana." She smiled as she pressed away from me. "You just need to lock it up after, and make your way back to the city."

It was great to visit with a cousin I hadn't seen for thirty years. Before I knew it, our five outside decks and all the rooms in the house were filled with sleeping bags and suitcases.

Sleep finally found me, but it wasn't long before I awoke, hearing the deck's screen door creak. My 10-year-old nephew Micah whispered, "Sorry, sorry." I assumed he'd stepped on somebody as he headed for the bathroom.

I tried to go back to sleep, but wondered how it would be to have seventy in our house for five years. The thought of that strange dream that got us into stockpiling made me chuckled. It was a warm evening, the kind where, as a younger man, I enjoyed walking through the sage. Now I stared at the quarter-moon which shone softly through a window and wondered about the future.

A strange apprehension crept over me; I sensed something bad had happened, or was about to happen, somewhere on our planet. Was it in the banking sector, had a war got out of hand somewhere? I tried to dismiss this, but dark shadows of some ill event or events kept resurfacing. To counter, I tried to think of something other than the big world and reminisce about that evening. I recalled Aunt Jessica, just after dark, coming in from the sunroom, half-chewing a chocolate, casually saying, "I don't see any of your neighbors' lights out there. Does everyone go to bed early?"

I told her it was probably a power outage. With our alternate power, we didn't notice outages. I reassured her that Yokino's Electric Company was good at getting downed systems back in a hurry. Lying there, my mind drifted, and with it came the worry that our Electric Company would not be able to bring the power back. Finally, I admonished myself, why should I worry over such a basic thing? What could I do about it, anyway? Furthermore, how often do worries ever come to pass? I gave my sleeping wife an eye; were her worries rubbing off on me?

Trying to relax, I stretched my legs and arms. The heck with worries; this was our reunion, I needed to be happy. I needed to rediscover the kid in me. I forced myself to think about the pleasant memories that day, of shooting the bull with my relatives.

*   *   *

When the sun rose, my doomy gloomy thoughts were behind me, and I was ready to party with my relatives. This was our reunion! They were all as cheerful as the meadowlark chirping away. We separated into teams to compete in various games from throwing water balloons at each other to sack races. As we lined up for tug-a-wars, we were clueless about the Europeans lining up at banks. As we laughed and delighted in getting pulled into the mud, we were clueless about our President having an emergency meeting with the Chairman of the Fed, and military generals.

At lunch, as we indulged in barbecued elk burgers, we had no clue how the chess moves of the outside world would change our lives. Our reunion partied on; a bunch of us piled into the military truck for a trip to the river.

As we floated downstream on our inner tubes, taking in the sunshine, admiring the mountains and fish, much of the country was discovering that the ATM machines weren't working.

In the barn after supper, we watched performances on our makeshift stage of plywood atop hay bales. Nieces, nephews, our kids, plus a bunch of the older generation, sang, danced and performed crazy skits, the cornier the better. Outside our barn, the world's stage was hopping, missiles were flying.

That evening I fell asleep right off. The river had snatched my energy. A few hours later, I awoke to someone stepping on someone else. "Sorry, sorry." They came in from an out-door deck. Moonlight angled through a window and I was reminded of that day's fun. I grinned at the memory of Aunt Jessica falling out of her inner tube and Jerold rescuing her from a logjam.

The morning sun rose on the second day of the reunion, sending its rays over the sleeping bags spread across the decks. That day, we men entertained ourselves with a competition gun shoot, while the ladies had a tea party, fashion show and photo shoot.

My cousin Mark shone in the gun event with his long-range rifle. It wasn't surprising, as he was a Kentuckian and his passion was the outdoors. He had even brought some night-vision goggles. I envied some of his stuff. He was by far my favorite cousin.

After a noon barbecue, we hiked into a wilderness creek. It was one of the few areas that offered shade, as the trees there had been spared by a fire a decade ago. I told them our local joke about Charby getting charred by the Charbarians. We got into a thick patch of huckleberries. I never saw so many contented relatives, just happily picking away. Mouths and fingers stained bluish purple spoke of a free harvest.

After breakfast the next morning, family pictures, hugs, tears and good-byes played out. Priscilla's eyes were moist. I was amazed that forty-seven people had come from across the country and down from Canada for this reunion. Priscilla and I expressed our humble appreciation to them all.

I heard a few kids say, "Can't we just stay here? Why do we have to leave?"

In the midst of this, Aunt Jessica's rental car wouldn't start, or even turn over. We ended up cramming her, her brother, Uncle Bob, and my sister Marilyn into my car and heading for the airport.

Low on gas, I cruised through Charby, figuring I had enough gas to make it to Middleton, a much bigger town, where prices were cheaper.

We were about five miles from Middleton when Uncle Bob said, "This is quite the seventh heaven you live in. You shouldn't have a care in the world."

"Oh, he worries about everything," said Aunt Jessica, jokingly. "I know he's getting ready for the end of the world."

My uncle gave me a serious look. "You aren't one of those who worry about Yellowstone blowing off?"

Found out, I grinned. Sometimes I wish my front teeth weren't so big.

"Fuhgeddaboutit. You don't need to worry about a thing."

Uncle Bob was a big man who rumbled when he laughed. "I'll tell you why Yellowstone's not going to blow off ... It's that herd of buffalo." He chuckled some more. "If Yellowstone blew off, it would send that herd throughout the farm belt. That's not going to happen because they wouldn't be wild anymore." He laughed and laughed. "Buffalos aren't supposed to be hanging from trees." Tickled with himself, he tried to go on. "Buffalo wings ..." He laughed and laughed. "... There should be a country western song about how it's not right to see flying buffaloes." He laughed like a schoolboy telling a joke, and finally remarked, "One of you hillbillies should come up with the lyrics."

I could hear him snorting as he tried to stop laughing; his hilarity continued for a while. But I felt put down, and couldn't wait for Yellowstone to blow off and send all those buffalo his way.

Hardly anyone was on the road, which was strange for a Monday morning. Just outside of Middleton, I pulled into a gas station and found that the pump didn't work. The fact that there were no lights glowing on any of the neon signs should've told me something, but September's sun was bright and made it difficult to see the Closed sign.

Driving on, I glanced at my gas gauge. It was near-empty. "I wonder what's going on with that gas station?"

Rounding the next corner, I began to get apprehensive about my near-empty gas tank when I noticed the street lights were out. The next gas station was vacant as well. "Looks like we got a little power problem."

Aunt Jessica leaned over the seat to see how much fuel I had. Her breath was next to my ear, "Uh-oh."

I didn't see any life at the stores or restaurants; it was peculiar.

My uncle snapped, "Why didn't you fill up in Charby?"

"There are better prices in Middleton. Anyway, it isn't like we see these power outages very often."

"Safeway's open." Aunt Jessica said, still leaning over the seat, and pointed with rising hope at a vehicle turning into Safeway. She eased back into her seat as if it were all going to work out.

As we approached the full parking lot, I sensed something bigger might be going on. I'd never seen it that packed. Turning on the car radio, I fiddled with the tuner. The airwaves were silent. We motored on. I hoped one of the gas stations would be running on back-up power, but the next one was closed as well.

"Look." Aunt Jessica's voice was optimistic. "Bi-lo is open." The parking lot was full and vehicles were backed up to get into the entrance.

"Strange. The big grocers are open, but nothing else."

I drove on. "There's one more gas station, at the end of town. Cross your fingers."

But soon I could see that the last gas station was closed as well. "I'm not going to make it to the Missoula airport on the fuel I've got; in fact, I'd be lucky to make it back to Charby."

My uncle's heavy finger pointed to a spot by the bank. "Park right there … right there!" I could feel his determination as he looked toward my Auntie in the back seat. "We're going to hitchhike."

"Hitchhike?" My aunt's voice pitched.

My uncle gave me a prideful look. "Piece of cake for us city folk."

The car rolled to a stop. His gung-ho-ness swept the New Yorkers into getting-it-done with their thumbs.

I felt like a country hick who just couldn't get-r-done. They all looked so uptown in their Goochie this and Poochie that. I told them I was going back to the Bi-lo to find out what was going on and would return soon. After awkward good-byes and hugs, I was off.

Halfway down the block, I looked in my rearview mirror and saw a car pulling over for the hitchhikers. I was proud of my fellow Montanans, as they are charitable with their time and fuel. Maybe the New Yorkers would make their flight after all.

When I got to Bi-lo, it was so packed I ended up parking at K-mart, which was closed. A farmers' market was set up in that parking lot and they had a robust business. I headed toward the grocery store. Everybody coming out was pushing a full cart. Kids were following, struggling to push full carts as well.

On entering Bi-lo, I was stunned at all the activity. The shoppers had a snap-to-it-ness, a get-it-before-the-next-guy attitude. And the shelves were half-empty.

I glanced over at two gals who were standing by an ATM machine with an OUT OF ORDER sign on it. One woman's face showed stress. "This isn't supposed to happen, not ..." she hastily looked about, "... not here."

The other complained, "To think how fast it spread."

I could feel their anxiety and knew something bad had happened. Grabbing a cart, I looked over the crowd and wondered what in the world had put such a fire under these shoppers.

As I considered this, one of my neighbors, Dee, pushed her full cart near. "Aren't you getting anything?"

"I was thinking about getting dog food."

"You're not getting any frozen foods; they're all gone, sold off in an emergency sale."

"I've been out of the news for the last four days. What's going on?"

She was wide-eyed. "Haven't you heard?"

"No."

"Last Friday something happened to the credit markets. Then on Saturday a skirmish broke out between Japan and China. It got bigger. It got real big." She shook her head in dismay. "They knocked out our power." She gave me a questioning look. "Don't you know the power is out nationwide?"

"No. I got alternate energy and batteries." I glanced at the lights in the store. "Power outage?"

"They're on generators here." She swirled her hand around. "They're blaming the power outage on the Chinese."

"The Chinese?"

"That's what they say. Russia is in on it too. They say we're at war."

"War?" I must've looked detached.

"The world has gone crazy." Uneasy, she continued, "Chinese missiles are hitting satellites and lots of bases in Japan, hitting everything. It's the Chinese that knocked our grid down."

I gazed again at the lights. "Chinese? … How?"

"It's a cyber attack." She waved her hand. "Can't you sense fear in the air?"

"Something. Who's saying all this stuff?"

"Our government."

She was so stressed, she disjointedly asked, "Did you hear what Darrel did to my dog?"

"No." Half-listening, I tried to get my head around all this. It was so different than what I had envisioned with New York getting hit by the big bata-boom … now this whole thing starts over some little skirmish?

Dee went on to tell me about a neighbor who'd killed her dog. I was sad to hear it, but my mind was still struggling with the world's news. When she finished talking, the building, on cue, shook, whiplashing as if hit by an unseen wave. Shrieks filled the air. I gripped her cart for support and watched the store shelves ripple back and forth.

Dee asked, wide-eyed, "What was that?"

"It has to be an earthquake."

That kicked me into high gear. I said goodbye to Dee and loaded up, ending at the produce section to see if they had any lemons, as I usually have one every morning. There were four lemons left. I greedily snatched them, having a sense that I might not see a lemon in a grocery store for a long, long time.

Outside the store the excitement didn't stop; a vehicle had run out of gas right at the main entrance. I left my full cart and joined four other men to push the vehicle out of the parking lot, since there were no empty spots at Bi-lo.

I felt good about helping, part of the glue that holds America together. On the way back to the store I thought, whatever problems this nation faced, we were going to get through it. I carried this high attitude up to where I had left my cart. It wasn't there. I searched and searched but someone had stolen it, along with my feel-good, fine, American, get-through-it bunk.

# Brandishing a Weapon

Charby was just as powerless as the rest of the valley, the People's Market and their gas station were closed. This really put me on edge, as my gas warning light was aglow.

If I wasn't already sporting a poor attitude, another incident cemented it; at the far end of town, an older Chevy Impala swerved out from a side road and cut me off. From his curtness, I expected him to speed away. But not him. Even though the speed limit was 65 mph, he was dragging at 50 mph, so I passed him. Being low on gas, I wasn't going over 60 mph. Strange that he sped up and stayed right on my bumper. I thought he'd pass, as the road was clear. But not him. His aggressive behavior sent threatening sensations down my spine.

I viewed him in the rearview mirror. He looked in his twenties, and his clenched teeth and dark hair only added to his extreme look. If I'd possessed better judgment, I'd have pulled over and let him pass. But I felt so vulnerable; I reached into the side door pocket and pulled out my .38 Special.

Ahead, the road curved in and out, following the river. Through all this, he stayed right on my rump. At a straight stretch, where he could easily pass, I slowed to 55, but still he wouldn't go by. What was with this nut?

Finally, I grew so threatened that I lifted my shooter. I wasn't aiming the gun, yet I clearly displayed it, so if this was brandishing a weapon, then I was guilty.

In an instant, the Impala swung into the other lane. I glanced over at him as it roared past. He wouldn't make eye contact. My grip on the steering wheel relaxed; it was good to see that car speed away. What a belligerent fellow! In no time, he was way down the road. Eventually, he disappeared around a blind corner and this, I thought, was the end of it.

As the miles passed, I thought of Priscilla. As far as I was concerned, her kumbayah days were over. She really needed to know how to shoot at a nut like that guy. I needed to get her out to target practice. Furthermore, if this thing continued, we had to start thinking of round-the-clock watches so we didn't get overrun. They say, when society breaks down, the first three months are critical. She worried me, in that she saw too much of the good in people. What about the evil?

My concerns went from her to my low gas tank gauge. I steered around another blind corner. Up ahead, sitting in a pullout, was the Impala. Dread came over me as my car closed. The driver was outside the car, trying to get something from the backseat.

I passed by, continuing to watch in the rearview mirror. Just before I rounded the next corner, I was relieved to see the Impala was still parked.

As far as the gas gauge, I was breathing lightly, hoping … hoping that my light breath would get me the fumes to get me home. Time passed ever so slowly. I was a quarter of the way down a long open stretch in the road when I noticed a car in the rearview mirror. I didn't think much of it.

A half minute later, I looked in the mirror again. The car had closed the distance; it had to be flying. When I realized it was the Impala, fear took hold. I grabbed my .38.

He had to be going over 100 miles an hour. In no time, he was upon me, cutting into the other lane to pass. I moved my foot in front of the brake, readying to slam it. Then I shifted my weapon onto my lap, pointing the gun at the door. I was so threatened, my hand shook when I jammed my finger into the window switch, missing it a number of times before it finally opened.

Though I was not a committed Christian, I sure wasn't shy about sending up another one of those prayers that ends with, "If you get me out of this, I'll be a missionary in the jungles of Africa."

In the left lane the Impala slowed and was just about side by side with my car, when I glimpsed the driver's wild hair, open passenger window and an assault rifle muzzle that flashed, blasting right at me. I braked sharply, and saw a bullet hole through my passenger side window.

My car ended up behind him. To counter, I swung my gun out my window, aimed at the back of the Impala and let it bark, once, twice. I wasn't going to shoot anymore for fear of running out of bullets. Goodness, to think I was a prepper and the only bullets I possessed were in my weapon. The Impala sped away.

About a quarter-mile ahead, I saw the brake lights of the Impala. It swerved to the side of the road, then did a smoking U turn. My eyes darted about for a place to pull over, somewhere to hide. I was coming up on some Department of Forestry buildings. They sat in the open, surrounded by pasture. I only hoped there'd be someone behind those walls who could help. Slowing down, I turned in and drove to the back of the compound. That's when the engine stalled, then died. I was out of fuel. There were a few Forestry trucks about, which led me to believe there was someone around.

Seeing the Impala coming, I hastily hopped out and ran to a garage door, shouting "Hey? Hey?" I pounded on it, frantically searching for the best place to defend myself. But a handgun isn't any competition against an assault rifle. And here I only had three bullets left. I rapped on a metal door, yelled, "Hey?" then scrambled behind the protection of a pick-up. Trembling, I extended my weapon toward the closing Impala.

While I waited, I admonished myself for ever brandishing my weapon. I should have just pulled over and let him pass. My heart was pounding, my hand shaking.

The Impala slowed. Just short of the Forestry buildings, it made a U-turn and headed back the way it had come.

I took a deep breath to try to calm my nerves. It was so good to see that car going away! I thanked the good Lord and stared at my pea shooter, then chided myself for not having enough ammo—from now on I had to have my assault rifle. But there was no further consideration of being some missionary in Africa; the threat had passed.

On wobbly legs, I walked about to relieve my nerves, then stretched my arms in the air to relieve tension. After gathering my wits, I pulled a siphon out of the car and searched for a bucket to catch fuel. I snagged an old five-gallon pail at the side of a building and siphoned some gas out of a truck. I knew this was theft, but was determined to return the gas when things got back to normal.

On the way home, I was on the watch for the Impala. Strange how fast things can take a turn for the worse. Here I thought I was ready for the big bata-boom, but I hadn't even put up barbed wire on the west hill.

# A Different World

When I got home, I didn't have to bring Priscilla up on the news. Some of our American and Canadian relatives had returned to the house and filled her in on what they knew of the war. An anxious buzz rose, as they weren't sure about what to do. We told them they could just stay with us until the situation stabilized.

I think Priscilla thought this was the beginning of the end, because she headed off on a walk, out to the corner fencepost, and whenever she goes there, she prays.

I wanted to get my guns out and place one at each window, but the Canadians looked at our proliferation of guns as extreme. Also, they had kids, Micah, Jordan and Jumper, and I didn't feel right about placing guns about. So I just wore a holster, slung a bandolier over my shoulder and hoped I could rebuff the first attack alone.

I thought of securing rolls and rolls of barbed wire on the west hill. The Canadians' help would be appreciated. The problem with the Canucks is, they aren't near as spooky and paranoid as Americans. But this was a different world now. If this continued, they were going to have to look differently at my guns and bandoliers.

That afternoon about a dozen of us were gathered in the attic around the ham radio. I always liked this attic space, as it had two dormers, a skylight and five-foot-tall walls that angled up to the thirteen-foot ceiling. The radio sat atop a makeshift desk that also held our computer. Certain news in life is so striking that you have to hear it several times before it sinks in.

What we heard was: "Every military base in Japan and Okinawa was struck by Chinese missiles ... The CIA confirmed that the Chinese were behind the cyber attack, and have gotten into one of our most sensitive databases, the National Inventory of Dams. They opened floodgates, locked them open. There's extensive property damage, and death out there ... Over."

"Any good news on the grid? Over."

"With a number of the interconnection substations destroyed, it could be a long time before it's fixed. Over."

I was still stunned by how fast this came about and had to ask, "What set this all off? Over."

"Israel. Over."

"I thought it was China and Japan? Over."

"There's no mystery about it, war is in the air. It doesn't matter where you go, there's a real neurotic fear. This weekend, Israel put it to Iran and retook a bunch of land. On the other side, Pakistan lit it up with India. In Asia, U.S. and Japanese bases are getting hammered by the dragon. Good luck. And Russia took the opportunity to expand their borders. One way or another, everybody is getting sucked in. If they got missiles, they got targets. Over."

"The whole thing started last week with the derivative fiasco. Default, default, default. The ship rolled then. Over."

Finally a playful voice came over the ham radio. "No more money, no more honey."

"My bet is they'll be no election this fall. How convenient for this president, he stays."

After the ham operator checked out, nobody in our upstairs office said a word. Quiet hung in the air for some time.

In the background, we heard radio operators asking to trade stuff but all that sounded like clutter compared to the world news.

Finally, my cousin, Mitch, broke the silence. "Has the whole world gone bonkers?"

I commented, "I sure don't want to get sucked into another war, especially with China and Russia. And why should we be siding with Japan?"

Mitch spoke with fervor, his New York accent heavy, "But look what the Chinese did to the grid."

"That's not proven." Mark, my other cousin, was skeptical. "That's the CIA's claim, and we know how many wars those guys started."

"Yes," Julie, Priscilla's Canadian cousin, replied in a huff. "You Yankees have a way of getting into every conflict you can stick your noses into."

Julie's husband, Gordy, tried to subdue his wife's stern opinion. "With cyber stuff, anyone can point the finger at anyone else, claiming this or that, and it's not like you can find peace if you can't even identify the enemy."

Julie continued, "With your nation's financial situation, how do you have any business meddling in everybody else's business?" Her voice held a hint of sarcasm. "Oh, but you Americans know so much."

"There's no way like the American way." Mark's Kentucky accent twanged out "waaay." He added sardonically, "And there's no way like the CIA."

"Oh, come on. Is it all a conspiracy now?"

Gordy pressed his point. "That cyber attack stuff is an interesting ploy. It isn't like a bomb hits a big city; instead, a mole sits in a software system, undetected, till on a certain day, it comes out to play." He scratched his head.

"Who's to say our President isn't in bed with the Russians and Chinese and has worked with them on the grid deal?"

"I can't see that."

Mark mused. "It makes you wonder why the Wizard of Oz needs our lights out? What's really going on behind the scene?"

In the background, the ham operators put in their requests. "Do you have any gas or diesel you want to sell? Do you have any silver you want to trade? We've got vegetables … fresh vegetables. Do you have any .223 bullets. .308, .7mm.?" Considering the magnitude of the war news, I wasn't interested in parting with anything. "Do you have any chain saw oil you want to trade? Over." … "Our freezer has thawed out; does anyone have salt? Over."

Another voice came over the radio. "Has anyone seen Tex or Joan? I haven't been able to contact them for a few days. Over."

I was perplexed at why Tex and Joan weren't answering their radio, as they were the leaders of our preparation group.

"Has anyone been in touch with Marlene Jones? Over."

"Who's Marlene? Over."

"She's the leader of that Back to the Constitution group. Over."

Just above us, a sudden splatter of hail hit the roof. It was hardly a warning before all hell broke loose, pounding like nothing I'd ever heard. It became so intense, I wondered if it would shatter the skylight.

Panic drove us downstairs. We filed onto the main floor. The violent storm captured our attention, none of us got too close to the windows. I was in awe at the size of the hail. When the wind picked up, the hail started to hit the windows in the sunroom. It pelted down with a deafening din. I thought the windows would break for sure, and wasn't surprised to hear a crash from upstairs. Had the roof given in?

In fear, Micah, Jordan and Jumper drew near their parents. Jumper started to cry. I heard Priscilla praying in the kitchen.

Then, as suddenly as the storm came, it rolled over us, heading north.

Outside, the ground was covered with golfball-size hail. Upstairs, the skylight window was in pieces under a pile of ice. On the decks, all the bedding that wasn't under an overhang was soaked. In the driveway, every vehicle was damaged; the hoods, cabs and trunks looked as if they had been beaten by thousands of hammers. This was the first time I'd ever witnessed such a heavy barrage of hail.

*   *   *

While many of our relatives hung their sleeping bags over railings to dry them out, I covered the skylight window with plywood. Then I fueled up the diesel truck from a storage tank. I wished I had purchased a fuel tank to store gas; now it was too late.

A trip to Missoula to find my aunt, uncle and sister was warranted. After the incident with the Impala, I didn't look at this journey casually. I left my cousin Mark in charge and armed Gordy with an AR to ride shotgun. Though he was a Canadian, I figured he would be a decent backup shooter. He knew firsthand the power of guns, since he'd lost an eye from a BB gun incident in his youth.

A few of the ladies wanted to go help out on groceries. I didn't let on that we had plenty of food; my act was sure. "Come along, it'd be no good if we all starved to death."

Our trip up the highway was uneventful. In Missoula, I was surprised how packed one big grocery store was.

Julie looked over the full parking lot. "Maybe we'd be better off at Costco?" Her Canadian accent was precise.

But Costco was closed. So was Wal-Mart. I drove on to the airport. It too was closed. So where were my relatives? We could only assume they'd caught a ride back to Charby.

*   *   *

When we got back home, I wasn't yet out of the truck when Carl, one of Priscilla's Canadian cousins, walked toward me. "Did you hear about the West Coast?"

"No."

"Big, big, earthquake, ripped right up through the entire coast into British Columbia."

My eyes caught Priscilla's.

She quietly said, "It has begun."

I hoped she was wrong; I was worried enough about our daughter, Bethany, out on the West Coast. She sure didn't need an earthquake. And where were Raela and Jerold? Had they made it back to California, or were they somewhere in-between? Why hadn't they turned around?

That evening a windstorm kicked up. It was so sudden that few people were able to get their bedding, which was hanging off the railing, before it was swept away. Our windmill was screaming; the wind had to be over 60 miles an hour. The pine trees were bent, looking like they were barely hanging on to their needles. It lasted no more than ten minutes in its frantic journey north, and then dissipated. It left bedding strewn over the countryside.

We all went out to gather it up. Much of it wasn't dry from the earlier hailstorm, so we had relatives sleeping everywhere. Priscilla handed out every bit of extra bedding we had. Most did their best, finding a spot on a carpeted area in the living room or one of the bedrooms.

That night it was strange to walk into the sunroom and not see my neighbors' house lights. All was dark. Staring out that sunroom window, I felt a weightiness, a sadness—this old world was sinking in some heavy water, some dark, heavy water.

\* \* \*

The next day, our neighbor Dewey drove up to see if he could borrow some salt. His freezer was thawing and he needed to preserve his meat. I gave him three pounds.

Interesting, that same day he came back and said he needed more, calling me "neighbor," with pats on the back to prove it. This was somewhat strange for Dewey, as he's usually never pushy. Previously, we always borrowed whatever we needed from each other. It was totally new and awkward to have to tell him we had a bunch of folk who needed our remaining salt. He gave me one of those long, concerned, I-just-don't-understand-you looks.

Perhaps his look was spawned by the fact that he'd helped unload about 30 five-gallon pails of grub off that forty-foot truck back in the day, and so he knew how much we had. Then again, he would give his goods away to anyone who asked. I'm sure some folks were begging from him. I noticed two vehicles down at his place, and people wouldn't just drive around visiting, as gas was so precious.

It was obvious Dewey was put-out when he left. This was the first crack in our long relationship. Part of me had no trouble shrugging it off; one of those vehicles at his house was probably from his church, which was all about getting beamed-up before things got hot. Good luck to that ill-prepared crowd.

At that time we had over forty people at the house, including Priscilla's brother, Jack, who'd gouged her inheritance. So far I'd been pleasant toward him, but the accountant in me was already ringing up the tally sheet. If this situation went the distance, five years, I had visions of owning his entire spread. Even still, I had the same hope everyone else did, that the electric companies would get the grid working and all the family safely back home.

*    *    *

Just after supper, Priscilla and I started down the hill on a walk. I was looking for privacy. All these people around were starting to bug me, and here we weren't even into it a week. Above us, clouds were on the move, darkening the sky, and though I didn't notice a wind, I could hear a storm brewing, the definite rumble of thunder. We weren't a hundred yards from the house when flashes of lightning were seen on the perimeters. Their number gave us pause. We came to a stop and took in the fearsome sky.

"Have you ever heard such rumbling in September?"

"No."

"Can you feel humidity?"

"Oh, yes." She ran her fingers down her arm. "It's warm ... charged ... look, someone's out in the state land."

"He must be one of the bucket carriers, coming back with his load of water."

The rumblings grew and grew, until the fear of getting struck by lightning was greater than my search for privacy. We turned and headed for the protection of the house. Not far off I could see rain. This hazy midst was rapidly coming toward us. We picked up our pace.

Before we got to the front porch steps, the rain hit. In an instant, a cold wind swept downward. We were just inside the protection of the porch when hail fell. Bizarre; hail again? It was the second time in so many days. In the distance I saw the bucket carrier running for cover.

The man's plight was frightening. Hail pounded the ground, harder and harder. This barrage dropped the temperature. A cold chill blanketed. It was dreadful how large the hail were getting, heavy thumps violently striking the ground.

I could barely hear Priscilla praying, "Please Lord, please protect him."

I didn't think the bucket carrier stood a chance, as there were no trees in that area, and where he was running didn't make any sense. Finally, he put his bucket over his head and braced himself against the onslaught. I hoped he could keep it over his head, as this hail was large enough to damage his skull.

Above us, I could hear the hail pounding the deck, and I wondered if it was pummeling sleeping bags that had earlier been placed back outside. Then, as quick as the storm came, it dissolved and continued north. Priscilla came up from her prayers.

"Thank goodness we made it to the porch!"

In the distance I could see the bucket carrier heading back toward the spring. I was glad that wasn't part of our daily routine, and very happy that he'd survived. Above us, I heard someone going through the storm door, out on the deck. I assumed they were retrieving their bedding.

*　　*　　*

The next morning I took the same gang as before, in another run down the valley, in hopes of finding Aunt Jessica, Uncle Bob and my sister, Marilyn. It was just after 11 a.m. when we drove through Charby. People's Market and gas station were still closed, along with everything else, which wasn't much, as there were only a few restaurants, a few bars, a couple of gift shops and another gas station in our little town.

Middleton was a much bigger concern, about five times the population of Charby. Even still, Safeway was closed, along with all the gas stations. Surprisingly, Bi-lo was open. Its parking lot was half-full.

When I pulled in, I thought it curious to see a farmer who was set up in the K-mart parking lot already sold out and packing up. I wanted to see what Bi-lo had left.

Julie and her sister were adamant about saving us all from starving. Again, I didn't let on that we had tons of food, but went along with their fear, saying, "Forty-plus eaters can go through food in a hurry."

The two hopped out and strode toward the store.

Our gung-ho ladies were pushing carts into Bi-lo before we got to the entrance. But it was a wasted effort, as all the food was gone. It was haunting to see shelving that was entirely empty. They were down to cleaning supplies. If the dishwasher soap was dishwater soup, I'm sure it would be gone too.

We headed to Missoula, but the same scenario played out with all the closed shops and stores. What I found out of the ordinary was seeing security personnel in front of Wal-Mart and Costco, and these men were well-armed. Interesting, a tractor-trailer, a forty-foot hauler, pulled out of their loading area and another pulled in. Were they dropping off supplies or taking them away?

There was no sign of our relatives. The entire trip turned out to be a waste of fuel. The only value to that trip was informing our radio group of all the closed stores, to save them a trip to town, to save their fuel.

Back home, most went about tired. It was like the day after a festive event. There was a lot of shifting of bedding, as some sleeping bags still weren't dry from the day before.

If there was any excitement or anticipation, it came after sunset when Micah and Jordan came rushing in. The boys looked flushed.

"There are people down at the garden," Micah said, his boyish voice peeling off to the point of tears. "They're taking our food."

I wanted to get a look at whoever these thieves were from the upstairs window and bumped into Mark who was onto this situation as well. We plowed up the stairway, heading for the attic window.

My brother Freddy and his girlfriend Ellen were sleeping in the attic, but the wang-bang of our boots coming up the stairs woke them.

Freddy tiredly complained, "Do you have to be pounding up those stairs?" and stretched.

"We got some thieves down at the garden."

Mark snagged a set of binoculars from a shelf and knelt before the dormer window. More pounding of feet reverberated up the stairs as the Canadians filed into the room.

"Is there anything I can do?" Gordy asked.

My brother, Stan, asked as he came up behind Gordy, "How many are there?"

Mark declared, "They're back."

"Who?"

"Aunt Jessica, your sister Marilyn and Uncle Bob." His statement knocked the air out of our anxiety balloon.

Freddy tiredly asked, "Can everybody get out of here?" He yawned, staring at the ceiling.

Everybody funneled out of the room. I was the last to the stairs, glancing up at the plywood that covered the skylight, then turned to address Freddy, "Don't get to thinking you own this room, dear brother; this is the radio room."

"Move it," he said, rather demandingly.

Strange to hear that from someone who was eating my grub. I shoved the comment aside, assuming he was joking.

\*     \*     \*

Priscilla, Mark and I drove down to the garden. Aunt Jessica, Marilyn and Uncle Bob were tiredly leaning against fenceposts, gnawing on carrots, downcast, roughed-up and weary. We helped them to the truck.

Aunt Jessica told us they'd ended up at St. Patrick's Hospital, as Uncle wasn't feeling well. There, they waited and waited, only to find out that he could just get a shot of blood thinner. The hospital was running on emergency power, and that's all they could do. She thought he'd had a stroke. Because of his condition, they stayed that night at the hospital, sleeping as best they could in chairs. The next day, they weren't sure whether to hitchhike back to Charby or stay put. The deciding factor was that the hospital had no food or running water, so they left Uncle Bob's luggage and hitchhiked. Their second night was spent sleeping in the bush on the other side of Middleton.

Starved and exhausted, they ended up leaving the remaining luggage down at a crossroads, four miles back. We went to retrieve the luggage but it, too, had suffered the same fate as my grocery cart.

On the drive back to the house, I looked at my three relatives. Aunt Jessica's hand wouldn't stop trembling and her white stylish dress shirt wasn't so white; Uncle Bob's mouth hung open, his eyes so lifeless, it was surprising he was alive; Marilyn was so spent that her head was tilted as she slept. I thought how different they were from the prideful, rich, business-minded New Yorkers I'd left at the side of the road a few days earlier. It was hard not to feel sorry for them; now they didn't even have a change of clothes.

Even after we got them fed, Uncle Bob moved like he'd lost a gear, like he'd aged. We gave up our beds to the three; they needed a good sleep.

That night I lay with Priscilla on a piece of foam on the floor at the foot of the bed. My lack of sleep probably had something to do with seeing Uncle Bob, so famished, so wobbling that we had to help him up the stairs. His condition was a real eye-opener. For the longest time I lay awake, thinking about the plight of city folk in a society without power, without water.

They say water is more important than food; I truly realized it when I saw neighbors heading for a spring a half-mile away. That day, more than once, Micah and Jordan come running in to point out someone walking across the state land. Through our spotting scope in the sunroom, I could see they were neighbors carrying 5-gallon buckets. I suppose this image would be nothing new to Africans, but Americans?

One neighbor made that trek a few times, as he had horses, sheep, birds, goats, dogs, cats and who knows what else. Considering their struggle, I was finally content with what we'd spent on alternative energy.

My concerns drifted to my kids, Raela, Bethany and Jerold. With the West Coast earthquake, I hoped Bethany was okay. Why didn't she just leave California and get out here? And why hadn't Raela and Jerold returned?

Unable to sleep, I whispered to Priscilla, "Are you awake?"

"Yes."

"I'm worried about our kids."

"Jesus will look after them."

"I sure hope Bethany is okay. There are just so many people out there on the Coast."

"I pray for her every morning."

"I don't know why Jerold and Raela just don't turn around and come back."

"God will look after them."

I lay there for the longest time, unable to go to sleep. I found it perplexing that Priscilla put all her hope in Jesus. My only hope for my kids were in the handguns I'd gotten them for graduation gifts. Hopefully, they were packing them.

\*　　\*　　\*

Our evenings were spent by the radio to catch any news. Most disturbing were the reports from the West Coast earthquakes—tens of thousands of casualties, thousands of downed buildings and fires that had swept complete areas. My worries of Bethany rose with every poor report. And where were Jerold and Raela? Why didn't they just get out here?

For me, the war news was a relief compared to the news from the West Coast. All that news came through our military. As far as our grid returning, they kept saying, "Any day now."

It wasn't long before some of our company started letting their hair down; with it came complaints. Petty complaints like one from Jack, Priscilla's brother, who about had a bird when we started watering down the coffee, sending more water through the grounds, a number of times. We had done this to prolong our depleting supply, but Jack thought this sacrilegious.

My brother Freddy wasn't shy about voicing his complaints. If he wasn't frustrated over who kept opening the windows downstairs, which caused a breeze in the attic, then he'd be whining about us coming into his bedroom. Yet, here that room was the radio room now, our only portal to the outside world. Uncle Bob was no slouch at complaining either, the house was either too cold or too hot, and why hadn't the government gotten everything back together yet? As sure as the morning, he'd be prodding me to go back to the hospital to get his luggage.

If complaining was in order, a wooden dining room chair and the living room rocking chair were busted because of someone's carelessness, and the 25-year-old porcelain sink handle and the glass doorknob to the main floor bathroom were also broken. And what happened to my fine hunting knife and all my socks and underwear?

Here we were, hardly into this, and I felt as if I didn't have a life and was mashed into looking after everybody. I wasn't a happy camper. I had gotten into this for money, for profit, and here the wealthiest of the bunch, Aunt Jessica and Uncle Bob, no longer had a second set of clothes.

On the other hand, Priscilla had no problem with the servant mindset; she served everybody as if she was serving Jesus. This is an area in Christianity I didn't care for; was God just a God of love? Was love just about giving? Where was the balance, the other guy's responsibility? Before, when I considered getting right with God, I thought it was my inability to place Him above my guns, but now, with the shape the world was in, I wondered if my wife's Christianity was unfavorable for surviving. Doesn't this kind of love lead to enabling?

# Work for Your Food

I determined to get those relatives who were sitting around, up and working, helping to pay for their keep. I had no desire to be the sheepherder, but to stay sane and not have my wife work her fingers to the bone, I had to distribute responsibilities.

The gems were the ones you didn't have to ask; some willingly did bathroom patrol every day. These were jewels, and I mean jewels, whereas my brother Freddy wanted to know what day I was doing bathroom patrol. Priscilla's brother, Jack, and Freddy's girlfriend, Ellen, had no trouble sitting on their rumps all day, reading books and whining about the most ridiculous issues. Uncle Bob, for some strange reason, thought I should pick up a newspaper when I went to pick up his luggage. I had no intention of going after his luggage, and why there would be any newspapers running in this powerless country was beyond me.

Their laziness drove me to what I called the "work for your food program." When I announced this right after supper in front of everybody, it was met by an outright laugh from Freddy.

As quiet fell over the supper table, I gazed at him, advising, "Tomorrow morning, the work meter starts." I gave him a friendly point. "And you will have an opportunity to pay us back for all the grub you've been consuming."

"I think I'll just sleep in."

Although his statement wasn't loud, it was like a blast over the bow, putting an edge on the end of our fine supper.

I shrugged. "If you don't work, then don't show up for breakfast, lunch or supper."

Silence blanketed the room.

The next day, bright and early, I fired up a chainsaw and gave a rumble, a wake-up call. After breakfast, most responded to the noise of my diesel truck and caught a ride down the hill. There were a few stragglers, my brother, Ellen, Priscilla's brother in particular, but all and all, we put a major dent in the pile of logs.

Two days into this we had our entire winter supply cut, chopped and stacked. I was pleased, as usually it takes over a week for me to do the same.

The women weren't outdone, as they went at the garden to harvest, clean, mulch, and mow. They even rounded up the old horse chips and roto-tilled them in, as well as planted a new winter crop of garlic. I don't think that garden ever looked so good. And from the garden produce, they filled every fermentation pot for sauerkraut.

*   *   *

Before the end of the day I got a visit from a neighbor, Al. Micah had spotted him walking up our road and gave me warning. My other neighbors called Al the animal guy, as he had no end of pets; they didn't speak well of him because of how rundown his place was. Though it looked like a castle compared to the Wartals' place. I'd only talked to Al a few times at our road maintenance meetings, and I liked him.

With Micah standing near, Al and I talked about the woes of the world. This was the first time he'd ever visited our place, and I figured he needed something. Eventually he asked me if he could borrow some food. I knew he had three teens and a wife, and part of me just wanted to give him what he wanted, no questions asked—but then there was that five-year, seventy thing that said, You might be needing that food for the long run, don't give him a thing.

I told him about how challenged we were, with all the folks we were looking after. He could see vehicles filling our parking lot.

I ended this poor-us talk by giving him a studied eye. "Considering all your animals, you should have it made."

"What do you mean?"

"Aren't you a meat-eating man?"

He frowned, stepping back. "Those are my pets."

"Okay, what do you have to trade for food?"

"Can't I just borrow?"

"Borrow?" I thought it selfish that he should not offer to trade anything; here he had all that livestock. I felt he was trying to take advantage of me. Minutes earlier, I'd planned on giving him twenty pounds of rice and beans and sending him on his way, but now, that number dropped.

I leaned toward Micah and said, "Go get a pound of rice and a pound of beans."

That was all Al got. He wanted to play games? Then I could play games.

*     *     *

I am a believer that idleness leads to poor thoughts and whining, so I was determined to keep the momentum rolling. With the woodpile done, the other option was the barbed wire buffer. The following morning a group of us men and the two boys, Micah and Jordan, started work on the west hill. There was an assortment of shovels, picks, sledgehammers, four-foot metal stakes and two rolls of barbed wire. I was measuring, and spraying the ground with fluorescent paint to show where I wanted each stake slammed in.

My older brother, Stan, silently got after the task, setting up a roll of barbed wire so he could unroll it. This wasn't the case for Freddy, who had hardly started working the fencepost slammer when he delivered a list of complaints. "This will never work … It's too rocky … This is stupid … You got to call this off."

"Just keep at it," I encouraged. "With your strength, you'll get it."

He abruptly dumped the slammer. "This is nuts!" A crazy scowl portrayed his disgust. "What? Putting in barbed wire to ward off zombies?"

"I don't believe there are any zombies, just desperate people."

His face furrowed into a mocking grin. "Once the power comes back on, this place is going to look goofy."

I couldn't disagree with him, as it was the first time I had built a barbed wire fence that ribboned in and out with wire every six inches; but regardless of how weird and eccentric the project looked, I had to act as if I'd built thousands. I pointed. "These fences are the new rage."

"What, to protect you from Martians?" His grin had splashes of sarcasm.

One of the boys, Micah, innocently said, "My dad says it stops the werewolf."

His brother Jordan asked, "Werewolf?" and suspiciously looked about.

I caught the eye of Jordan and Micah's dad, Travis, who sheepishly looked away.

At that, I wanted to get rid of my brother, but beat the hell out of him first. I gave Freddy a steely glare. "If you don't like it, you can check out."

"What?" he said, aggressively. "Everything around here is your way or the highway?"

"Isn't it my house?"

"You're taking advantage of us."

"How?"

"By making us slave away for food."

"I'm not asking anyone to do a job that I'm not doing."

"You're just trying to be the big dog, making us do all the slave boy stuff."

I felt cornered. "This barbed wire is to help protect all of us if things get out of hand, if society really starts breaking down."

"If! You said, 'If!' If asteroids hit the planet, if mountains melt away, if zombies come knocking."

"I won't be complacent about it!" I angrily looked toward my car. "Excuse me! Aren't the bigs going on? Didn't the biggest earthquake ever just happen on the West Coast? Isn't the whole grid down? Aren't they out of food at the grocer's? Isn't thievery the new order? Didn't my car get shot?" I glared at him. "You are eating off my table, and if you don't like the rules here, you can go. Nothing's stopping you!"

"Well," he gave me a disdainful look, "I don't need this." He started to back up.

"Like I said, you can always check out."

"That's your answer to everything." He walked away, half-calling back, "You might as well shout, 'If you don't like it, then get out of here!'"

The foulness he left behind was thick.

Micah watched him stomp away, then glanced at our barbed wire. "I think it's fun. We're building."

I wasn't going to stop work. I didn't care how hot the day was, how eccentric the task was, how rocky the ground was, how mentally out of it most of the Canadians were, how sweaty we were, or how stiff-necked those steel posts were to get pounded into the rock, my manhood was bruised.

Grabbing that slammer, I took my frustration out on the iron fencepost, driving it downward. But those rocks were as stubborn as my brother.

Come the lunch bell, one hungry, tired group dragged itself toward the house. Despite my weary limbs, I was hell-bent on having a clash with my brother, if he was lined up for lunch.

Fate didn't let me down. When I came into the kitchen, sure enough, he was standing right up near the head of the line, chatting away to the women, happy as a lark. Sometimes I'm amazed at the gall of certain people. Most of the men who worked on the barbed wire looked over at Freddy with an air of What's he doing here?

I tried to be calm as I stepped toward him. "Hey Freddy, can I talk to you for a minute?" I nodded toward the front door.

"How about after lunch?" he said with a sly grin.

Annoyed, I thumbed toward the door.

He shook his head. "You can wait."

His comment stuck in my throat like a fist. I closed in on him. "How is it you are bellying up to the bar when you didn't work?"

Freddy's girlfriend Ellen quietly said, "I was going to give him my portion."

I gazed at her. "That don't fly here."

Freddy turned emotional. "When I pounded those posts, my arms were …" He drew in his breath heavily, and tears came to his eyes. "… It was so hard pounding into that rock, my wrists were literally about to crack."

His theatrics were so much like a sissy that the others were frowning, and a few ladies stepped back. Even my sister Marilyn looked as if she wasn't sure how to deal with him. I thought it appalling how low his antics had fallen; this was a 54-year-old man, not an embarrassing little boy. "Like I said, if you don't work …"

"You don't expect me to hurt myself, do you?"

"If your arms were hurting, you could've always slung the barbed wire."

"Of course, you want me to work, and for me to have energy I need food, so after lunch I'll get with it."

I nodded and stepped away, but when I glanced back at the hard-working men and kids who were with me on that hill, including my older brother, Stan, something bit at my gut, angering me. "Look." My gaze seared into Freddy's back. "This isn't going to work. Your presence here is not fair to the others. You didn't work."

He gave me a look that could kill, then headed for the front door. I watched him walk away and loathed the thought of being with him for five years.

After lunch, Priscilla coaxed me outside. She suggested that we were too cooped up and maybe we should all take a break and go to the river. Indian summer was still in the air, hot enough to fantasize about a swim. I'd lost a lot of my punch on that darn hillside, but I still wanted to keep working on it just to outsmart my brother.

Conversely, I knew that the rest of the group would be elated to take a break and swim, as there wasn't much wind to generate the power needed to heat water. Our solar was challenged just to deliver enough power to our well for drinking water, let alone bathroom needs. Five-gallon buckets had been set in each bathroom, replacing the toilets.

We ended up heading for the river in the four-door diesel truck, with three people in the front, four in the back seat and fifteen in the box. Gordy rode shotgun. When you're going for a swim, it's amazing how fast conflict can fall away. The atmosphere was jolly. Even the adults had a childlike expectancy. Some of the older folks, along with Carl, had volunteered to look after the place. I didn't feel comfortable leaving Freddy behind, so I took him.

The trip took an odd turn when I spotted a dead deer on the side of the road. My dad had been the road kill king, understandably, with seven of us. I hit the brakes and turned the truck around to take a closer look.

Except for Priscilla, the women stayed put. So did the Canadians, though their frowns and sneers were aimed at the dead creature, as if it were plagued.

The boys, Micah and Jordan, and my brother curiously looked over the swollen midsection. Priscilla quietly suggested that we should leave the deer for now and pick it up on the way back. She headed back to the cab as if her words were final. I was trying to figure out just how long it had been lying there.

"It's too far gone. Dad wouldn't even take it," Freddy said and took a number of steps toward the truck as if his words were final.

"The heck he wouldn't; goodness, how many raccoons did he haul in? And no end of deer and elk. Remember that dead bear?"

Freddy didn't answer.

About that time, Mark dug himself out of the back of the truck.

When I heard a vehicle, I thought of getting the deer before the next guy. "Hey, Freddy, give a hand here."

"What are we doing?" Micah asked.

"You ever get tired of rice and beans?"

"I do." Concern was written all over Jordan's face. "Why doesn't anybody go to the store?"

Freddy gave me a mean look. "I thought we were going swimming?"

"As soon as we get this doe dressed."

"Dressed?" Micah looked quite perplexed.

I winked at Jordan. "This deer is going to be good eating."

I was reaching for the doe's leg when Mark came past and grabbed the opposite leg, muscling it toward the back of the truck.

"This will be good." Mark's Kentuckian accent laid out, "gooood."

I returned my brother's hard look. "Give us a hand here."

"This is nuts!" snapped Freddy.

His disdain was so clearly displayed, I thought him humorous. From then on, it was difficult for me to keep my pressing teeth from coming out to play.

Inside the truck bed, it was odd to see a bunch of city folk in their cut-offs and bathing suits watching us as we readied to toss in the white-tail doe. If any of them hadn't considered us hillbillies before, they sure did now.

Mark called to them, "Scoot away from the back in there or I'm going to treat you to some dead meat."

There was a mad shuffle away from the tailgate area. With a heave and a ho we tossed her in.

Staring at the scramblers, Mark joked, "It's not my fault, you've been going through food faster than a pack of teenagers."

I looked them over and advised, "If we can get this doe dressed fast enough, we can get back to the river." I sensed their disappointment in not going swimming and rightfully so, as it was hot and sweaty.

Freddy scowled. "It will never happen. You should drop us off and gut out this stinking doe yourself."

I headed for the cab and heard him carrying on, spilling out his guts.

On the way home, I continued to chuckle at my brother's sourness. I suppose I could've dressed this doe myself, but I wasn't willing to just leave the relatives without extra protection, down at the river, with hoodlums running around.

After picking up some knives, I drove to a field to gut it out. Some of the city folk just couldn't handle the sight of us working, and waited upwind, looking troubled.

When we got back to the barn and hung the carcass up, I was more encouraged, as Carl and Ivan, Priscilla's cousins from Canada, had no problem ripping the hide off that doe, nor were Micah and Jordan disturbed by any of it. The meat didn't look bad and the barn was fairly cool. I concluded there was hope for some of these city folk.

*    *    *

At the river, the whole gang wasn't shy about plowing into the cool water. I stood watch, feeling like the Sheriff of our group, carrying a .38 in each of my pant pockets. Occasionally I felt a sense of foreboding and gazed suspiciously toward the trees. Other times, that water looked so refreshing, so tempting, that the boy inside of me wanted to come out and play. And when I drew near Micah or Jordan, they were eager to splash me. I ended up giving my guns and Sheriff duties to my cousin Mark, then took off to splash them boys.

It was rare for me to stay out in the sun, frolicking around for more than an hour, but those boys needed my attention. I sure did enjoy that refreshing river; its whirling back eddies possessed a melody. I found myself looking down on the swirling flow around my pants, and thought, Nothing here feels like the end of the world; my cares were floating downstream.

On the way home we saw a number of vehicles coming over the pass into our valley; most had California plates. There was no shortage of long faces. I was surprised they had made it this far, since somewhere along the way, they had to refuel. How could they get gas at a station if the power was down nationwide? I concluded they must've hauled some gas cans.

# Wars, Earthquakes, and Tsunami

That evening after supper, we gathered in the attic around the ham radio to listen for news. As I tuned in the radio I could feel apprehension amongst them, their chatter was agitated, it was as if everyone was on an intense caffeine high.

Everyone quieted when the radio crackled. "China is claiming they had nothing to do with the grid going down. They're also claiming their ships were attacked first. Over."

Concerned about my daughter, Bethany, I lifted the mic. to my lips. "Does anyone know anymore about those West Coast quakes? Over."

The voice of another radio operator questioned, "Has anyone heard from Tex and Joan? Over."

There was a series of "Negative" replies.

Another voice crackled, "They say it was a tectonic shift, right up and down the entire Coast. That kicked off the tsunami. Over."

There were immediate murmurings from the Canadians in the room who were from the West Coast.

Julie moaned, "Tsunami?"

The voice of another radio operator crackled, "I'm worried about Tex and Joan. Can somebody go over and check on them? And how bad was the damage from those West Coast quakes? Over."

The voice of another radio operator crackled, "It's bad; they say it's the worst ever. News of downed bridges is trickling in, eight feet of glass from high-rises in San Francisco, LA, Seattle, Portland, Vancouver and all the way up to Fairbanks.

The worst of the tsunamis hit Seattle and Vancouver. Portions of those cities are gone."

After the news, requests for bullets, silver, food, gunpowder came over the airwaves but I only half-listened, as my thoughts and worries were on Bethany.

Julie looked somber; she was from a suburb of Vancouver, British Columbia.

My brother, Stan, from Tacoma, Washington, gravely commented, "I just hope my neighbor keeps feeding our cat and dog." This was the first thing I'd heard him say in some time, as he'd been unusually quiet.

Julie's husband Gordy said, "I wonder if our house is still standing."

It was somewhat bizarre to hear my cousin Mark's words, "What if this whole thing was set up by the CIA?" He glanced at all the cheerless faces.

"You Americans are so suspicious." Jack frowned. "How do you come up with this stuff?"

Mark countered, "It'd be easy for them to set a series of nuclear bombs underwater, along the Coast."

Jack tiredly questioned, "Why would they do that to their own people?"

If I hadn't had enough bad news that night, Priscilla rolled toward me in bed and quietly said, "The Lord spoke to me."

"Yes?"

"He told me that He was going to burn America not once, but twice."

"Okay, hon." After all the doom of that day, this was the last thing I wanted to hear. Goodness, none of the headlines from either heaven or earth were good. Events up to now were so abrupt, so pressing, the consequences were hard to mentally stand against. I was beginning to think that I didn't have enough guns and ammo to ward off what was coming. This rushed heat to my face. I felt quite inept at looking after our little group, let alone seventy. In this whirl of worry, I thought again about getting right with God.

Finally, I asked Priscilla, "Could you tell me why a God of love would burn America twice?"

"I don't know."

"Maybe that wasn't God who spoke to you."

"Do you think God is just the god of love?"

"Isn't that what you said?"

"Don't you think there's a mystery to God that we don't understand?"

"I suppose."

"Certainly love is one of His stronger points, but the Bible says He hates as well. Read about Esau, read about Saul, read what He says about certain sinners."

"Who is this Esau and who is this Saul?"

"They're both in the Old Testament."

"Aren't we in the New Testament? Isn't it all love there?"

"Even in the New Testament it says He is so disgusted with certain sinners that He turns them over to reprobate minds."

"What is that?"

"A mind that doesn't know right from wrong."

Her comments gave me more of a reverential fear of God, so much so, I desired to get right with Him. But He was sure making it hard; with Uncle Bob snoring away in the bed above us, I could barely think.

Wanting to be alone, I arose and stumbled toward the screen door that led onto a deck. The door slid open. I walked to the rail, touched it and gazed toward the Yokino Mountain Range. It was darker than dark out, no moon, and I could feel the cool of autumn.

Holding the rail, I shuffled along, careful not to step on the foam bedding of those sleeping there. I hoped to get to a chair that sat in the middle of the deck, a place where I thought I'd find solitude. This was difficult, as bedding was laid out right down the forty-foot length of the deck.

No sooner had I sat down than I heard Micah whisper, "Hershal, is that you?"

He was in the closest bed. I bent toward him and whispered, "Yes."

"I hear someone coming up the hill."

Jordan leaned into Micah and pointed. "They're coming up right over there."

Micah added, "Do you hear that?"

"What?"

"Down the hill, the rocks keep moving. ... They're coming."

"Shhh, shhhh," cautioned Jordan.

I listened. Finally, I heard a faint clatter of rocks.

"It's over there, down the hill." Micah rapidly pointed.

"Shhh, shhhh."

"They're coming."

"You boys give me a hand."

They started to get up and Micah asked, "Where're we going?"

"Micah, you go get my cousin Mark." My hand found Jordan's. "Jordan, you come with me."

I crept along, with the boys in tow. When we got inside, I pulled Micah toward me and whispered, "Tell Mark not to turn on any lights and be quiet." My fingers released Micah.

"Where are you going to be?"

"In the closet."

Micah headed for the hallway. Jordan and I wove around the various beds and into the closet. I shut the closet door, flicked on the light and turned toward the gun safe. My nervous fingers struggled to spin the dial clockwise, counterclockwise, then back twice. Not getting it right the first time, I had to start over. Again the safe refused to open. In my struggle, I could imagine the approaching enemy; there had to be a bunch of them, all armed to the teeth, but the faster my fingers moved, the more I screwed up. There was a tap on the door. I switched the light off, opened the door to let Micah and Mark in, then shut the door and flipped the light back on.

"Mark, this is the combination ..."

I was in a panic as I watched him fool with the gun safe's dial, spinning it one way, then the other. He was unable to get it the first time. On his second attempt it finally opened.

We talked in whispers as we loaded the 556s.

"From the deck, you can cover the area up to the rock wall around the fuel tanks. I'll cover the north side."

"Where you gonna be?" Mark tested the light switch on the 556. It glowed against the wall.

"I'm going down to the driveway and cut them off at the quad garage. So you'll have this side," I motioned my hand, "and I'll have the other."

He nodded.

"I'm not interested in killing anybody, but if they shoot, we shoot."

"What if it's the government boys? They know you're part of that prep group."

"Government or not, nobody should be sneaking in on us at night."

I glanced at Micah and Jordan. "You two take these guns. Micah, you give yours to Gordy. Jordan, you give yours to Ivan." I gave them bullets as well. "Tell them to come to the upper deck, and be quiet about it."

I turned off the light and we all exited the walk-in closet. Mark headed for the deck, while the boys and I stole past my snoring uncle, out the bedroom door and down the hallway.

Micah tapped on the door where Gordy and Julie slept, while
Jordan and I went down the stairway. On the first floor, I quietly let myself out the front door while Jordan headed across
the dark living room, banging into a chair while looking for
Ivan.

In no time, I was down the outside steps and hurrying
over the driveway. I felt the power of the gun and had this
crazy thought of being an invincible patriot who was about to
defend my property.

At the edge of the concrete driveway I slowed, as there was
gravel that could announce my presence. At the end of the
driveway the ground dropped twenty-five feet, fairly steeply.
I bent and listened. I heard movement. It was quite close to
the barbed wire that we'd put up. Silence. I waited and waited.
Minutes passed. At last, I heard the crack of branches.

Though the hillside below consisted of jumbled fallen
trees from a previous fire, it also had outcrops of rocks that
nobody could walk across without a lot of clatter. There were
a few patches of pines that had made it through the fire and
areas of dried pine needles where a person could move without being heard. The only consistent feature was its steepness.

Feeling I was in the wrong place, I crept to my right, stumbled, sending a clatter of rocks across the gravel. This killed
any surprise. Having been found out, I swiftly strode toward
the edge. I was so focused on taking hold of the dangling light
switch on my weapon that I completely forgot about the strobe
feature on the light. So when I finally snagged the switch,
aimed the shotgun downhill and squeezed, the light strobed
in surreal flashes.

A strange silhouette appeared; the intruder looked as if he
was trying to get up a steep point. But it was either too difficult
or he didn't possess the strength, as his shoes kept slipping
backward. The strobe light flashed and flashed. This sight was

so striking, and made me so nervy, that I fired a shot over him and moved quickly to my right.

Did I mention that Priscilla had built a two-foot-tall rock wall that snaked along part of the edge? I was so intent on the intruder that when I hit this wall, my momentum carried me straight over it. Unable to cushion my fall, because the rocky ground abruptly sloped downhill, I hit chest-first, then flipped, head over heels. Who knows where my weapon ended up.

Disoriented, I saw Mark's light flash then I glimpsed someone. A gun barked, then barked again.

My world quietly slipped into darkness. When I awoke, the sensation in my chest was so different, I figured I was dealing with the shock of a bullet. My head began to clear, then came intense pain in my back and chest. I tried to lift my hand to see where I'd been shot. My ears rang, and in my peripheral vision, tiny stars faded into darkness.

\*   \*   \*

"Is he breathing?"

I saw shafts of light waver as several hands dragged me up the slope.

"That's an ugly gash on his forehead."

Priscilla's voice, "Oh dear Lord, please, please."

Someone's hand slipped, and my head hit the ground.

Freddy chuckled, "Slippery as a greased pig."

"Leave him be, leave him right there."

Light blazed directly on my face.

"Maybe he just got the wind knocked out of him."

"Hershal, are you okay?"

"That's an ugly gash."

There was a hovering of humanity about me, a flashlight in my eye. Hands probed my chest.

"Hershal, are you okay?"

Freddy's voice said, "He's sure no Rambo."

"Jerold, what did you come in at night for? You scared us all half to death."

Freddy joked, "The problem with his big teeth is, he looks happy."

Staring woozily at that blazing flashlight, I managed to whisper, "Who were they?"

"That was Jerold and Raela. They ran out of gas in Nevada, then came all the way back."

Again, Freddy, "I can step up and guide this ship. I know that's what he'd want."

Just the thought of Freddy running the roost made me want to find my muscle. I tried to sit up. Pain stabbed at me like a knife. Part way up, I felt so dizzy all I could do was pant. Thankfully, a hand grabbed my shoulder to steady me.

"Easy, Hersh." It was Mark's voice.

Then Freddy's voice, "This is a lot of work. He's heavy. Let's go get something to eat."

*　　*　　*

The next day, I lay in bed. My aching ribs wouldn't allow me to do otherwise. Just breathing or trying to find a comfortable position was a real challenge. I had a lot of time to think, and wished the others would see the importance of continuing the barbed-wire fence, but I didn't hear anyone pounding on those steel stakes. Interesting, without my pushing to get the fence done, it didn't happen. But I wasn't upset, as sometime last night I recalled someone saying that Raela and Jerold were back. I hoped that wasn't a dream. At last, I fell back to sleep.

A touch on my forehead, and I opened my eyes to see Priscilla.

"How do you feel?"

"There's something wrong with my chest."

She nodded, "Your ribs are black and blue."

"Was I shot?"

"No. I'd like to put a cold washcloth on your forehead."

That's all I remember of that conversation.

Somewhere in the middle of phasing in and out of sleep, my eyes opened and there was Micah. He was faithfully clearing his throat, looking directly down at me.

"I heard your brother tell how we don't need any more one-man decision making."

"He did ... did he?"

He nodded, quick as a chipmunk.

My palm came up to pat him.

"He took my toilet paper, too."

"When I get my wheels back, I'll ..." With those darn aching ribs, it was quite a struggle to speak. It didn't matter which way I shifted, pain followed, stabbing me like a knife.

The next time I opened my eyes, Micah was gone. Lying there, I considered my brother; I had to deal with his rebellion, but that would have to wait.

The next time I awoke, Priscilla was touching me. "I have soup for you."

"I'm afraid to eat."

"You need energy. You need to stay hydrated."

I gave a small nod.

"With the overcast, the solar's not powering the well. I was thinking of going to the river and taking some buckets with us."

I tiredly gazed at her, half-wondering if her presence was a dream.

"There are a number of ladies who weren't able to make the trip the other day and want to wash up, too."

"Who's riding shotgun?" My ribs hurt just to speak. "And who's going to protect this place when you're gone?"

"Freddy volunteered. He and Mark can keep an eye on things at the river, and Gordy, Ivan and Travis can stay with you."

I blinked and she was gone. I was about to drift off again when I heard the diesel start. Lying there, I thought of my brother; a whisper here and a whisper there, and suddenly he was swinging a gun, protecting those at the river. I clenched my teeth; he'd better not have helped himself to that open safe.

The truck was hardly down the road when a wind kicked up from the south, and what a blow. A door slammed. In pain, I struggled to sit up, as I knew the bedding on the west deck was going to be blown away. I gazed out the window, and psyched myself up to rise.

I watched the wind peel dust off the dirt road and flame it upwards. Another door slammed and I felt the house sway. The bathroom window was open—the windmill just a-buzzing. Out of the corner of my eye, I saw bedding being swept off the deck.

My son Jerold rushed through the room and out the door to the deck. My daughter Raela hurriedly followed. What joy to see them! The wind accelerated, howling so hard I wondered if the house would stand. How Raela wasn't just swept off the deck with her armful of bedding was a wonder. She staggered through the door.

Jerold followed, looking all windblown, dragging a pile of bedding. He dumped that in a growing pile and loudly declared, "That was half of it." He shut the deck door. "The wind got the rest." After shutting the bathroom window, he came toward me. "Your windmill's roaring."

I gave a nod. "It's so good to see you two." My weak voice may have been lost, but I forced myself onto my feet as I had no desire to be the last one out of Dodge if the house blew away.

No sooner had I risen when the pain in my ribs took me. I flopped into a cushioned chair. For the next ten minutes, we listened to the storm. I don't think I'd ever heard wind hit the house so abruptly and with such force. The house shifted and creaked.

Jerold was drawn toward the bathroom to view the windmill. Raela leaned against our bed, across from me, not talking, as it was better not to compete against the wind's howl.

Returning, Jerold raised his voice. "The water in the toilet bowl is swaying back and forth, back and forth."

I nodded, trying to mute my fears.

As abruptly as the storm arrived, it dissipated.

"I'm so glad you two are safe." My eyes went from Jerold to Raela. Jerold was unshaven, and looked a bit scruffy; Raela looked tired and thinner. "Please tell me about your trip."

Jerold began, "We ended up in Elko, out of gas. You know that Nevada is without power?"

"I heard it was nationwide."

"We hung around there three days, trying to get gas, but no luck. So we left the vehicle and hitchhiked." He moved toward Raela, who was leaning against our bed. "We caught a ride with a family heading for Utah. They were real good folk and gave us some food."

Raela joined in, "We saw lots and lots of military equipment heading west."

"Where?"

"Some were on trains, some on the highway."

"And they were setting up military roadblocks."

"Roadblocks?"

"Right out in the middle of Highway 80 … desert."

Raela explained, "And they had piles of buses."

"Buses?"

"Military buses." Jerold shrugged. "Empty. I've never seen anything like it."

"Maybe that's to help keep order. I just hope Bethany is okay."

"We saw this one train that had tanks, tanks and more tanks."

"Our ride dropped us off at Wells."

"What's Wells like without power?"

"Like a casino without power … pretty lifeless. We were stranded there for a few days, and without food."

"We couldn't buy anything, nothing was open. We couldn't even get water." Raela gazed out the window where raindrops were starting to hit the glass.

"Finally, we caught a ride. We ended up just short of Jackpot, and that's where we camped for the night," Jerold went on, "down by a small river."

"I was so thirsty. That water never tasted so good."

"The next morning we caught a ride to Twin Falls. There was a local farmer who'd set up a vegetable stand. We were lucky to get there before he sold out."

"We only got a few tomatoes and a cucumber."

Raela interjected. "And we had to pay a fortune for them."

"Rides were pretty skinny when we got north of Arco. A gal there had us in and gave us some food."

"Her bean soup was so good. We were so starved. That was the first honest meal we'd had in a long time."

"We finally got picked up by this …" Jerold looked as if he was searching for adjectives, "… real creep in a pickup. He kept looking at Raela. Then somewhere along some windy area he pulled over, saying he was going to relieve himself. We didn't feel right about him, so when he headed for the bushes," Jerold thumbed toward his sister, "she took her handgun from her purse and put it under her sweater. When the guy returned, he came back on my side of the cab, opened the door and pointed his gun right in my face. It happened that fast. I thought I was a goner." Jerold touched his sister's shoulder. "She said, 'Don't shoot him. I'll do whatever you want, whatever you want.' Sure enough, his gun came down. That's when she let him have it." He wrapped his arm around her. "She's my hero."

Raela took a deep breath as tears appeared in her eyes.

With much emotion, Jerold really hugged her. "She saved my life."

"I suggest you don't tell another soul about that man." I gave Raela a look. "Are you okay?"

"I'll ..." she pressed her hand over her eyes to cover a flood of tears.

"I'm sorry, Raela." I struggled to get up. It's odd, you don't think of your own pain when someone else has deeper pain. I ended up on the other side of her, taking her hand. "Honey, you did what you had to do. Thank goodness you had that gun."

Her wet eyes focused on her brother, admiringly. "Jerold's going to live to be a hundred."

*   *   *

Sometime past noon, I noticed the windmill wasn't turning, which was a concern, as there was still enough wind to spin it. Further east, I saw movement and figured it was one of the neighbors going for water. In pain, I made it to the dresser, snagged some binoculars and shuffled back. Peering through them, I picked out a Palomino and a few other horses. I wondered if the animal guy, Al, had run out of hay. I had never seen horses freely roving around that chunk of state land.

My eyes returned to the windmill. It was tough to see the wounded machine. Had the high winds damaged it? This

# My Guns

Things were getting too uncertain. What could I count on anymore, except my guns? As I lay in bed considering this, I half-recalled Priscilla saying something about my brother, Freddy, being good with a gun. That sucker better not have helped himself to my guns.

The rest of that day sleep pulled me down. At some point I awoke because I thought I heard a door squeak. The room was dark and I thought I glimpsed the back of someone going into the gun closet.

"Freddy?" My voice was weak.

I listened but there were no sounds from that room to add to my suspicions, so I shucked it off as a bad dream.

Later that evening, while lying in bed, Priscilla told me about her trip. She spoke quietly, as Uncle Bob snored away in the bed above us. Because of the storm, she didn't initially go to the river but on to Charby to see if there was any commerce. Nothing was open. By the time they got back to the river, the storm had passed and they indulged themselves, washing their bodies and clothes. She also mentioned there were a lot of vehicles coming over the pass into the valley and a number of street people in Charby. I found her comment odd, as Charby wasn't a town of destination but only a point of passing, and I'd never seen street people in our town.

I impatiently waited for her to finish before asking, "Could you tell me who gave Freddy a gun?"

"I thought you did."

When I heard that, the hair on the back of my neck rose. "Noooo." I painfully sat up. "Could you tell him to get in here?"

"Can't we leave that till tomorrow?" she pleaded, adding in the most exasperated tone, "People are asleep."

I arose and was growling as I entered the safe closet. Shutting the door, I turned on the light to see what else he'd helped himself to. But I had too many guns to instantly know which ones were missing. The gall of someone to simply help themselves to my guns. This wasn't right. I wanted to beat him up, then beat him up again, but I was in no shape to do any beating.

I stared meanly at the open safe. It presented a quandary; how to protect the place, when last night, in the heat of battle, it took over five minutes to unlock. That wouldn't cut it in this precarious world. And how could I keep the safe open with someone like my brother running around, helping himself to who-knows-what?

The rest of that night I slept uneasy, and yes, I ached, but more so I was itching for morning to confront my thieving brother. Uncle Bob's snoring didn't help. By morning, I wanted to put a muzzle on him.

First thing the next morning, I told Priscilla that I needed to see Freddy. Despite the pain in my ribs, I went into the gun safe closet, got down on my knees and went through the safe's shelves. It took a while to organize everything to find out what was missing. About forty minutes into this, I was so intent in searching for missing guns, I didn't notice Freddy until he cleared his throat. Startled, I banged my head on one of the shelves before I popped up, madder than mad. With steely eyes, I viewed him. He looked as if he was trying to contain a grin.

I'm not sure if I mentioned he was four years my junior, had a full head of hair, was taller, better-looking, and in my condition, no doubt stronger. I didn't care, I wanted to club him, then club him again.

"Who gave you permission to help yourself to my guns?" I said as I stiffly rose. My palm opened, motioning, instructing him to give me back my gun.

"We had to have protection at the river." He had a pleasant look as he pulled my 10mm out of the back of his pants and extended it my way. "I figured you'd approve."

"So you just took it?" I gave a rapid affirmative motion and snagged my gun. "Without asking?"

"You were sleeping. What was I supposed to do?"

"Don't ever help yourself to my guns again."

Micah abruptly poked his head in. "There's a car coming up the road!"

"That boy's going to make a good lookout," Freddy said admiringly.

"Micah, could you run and tell Mark and Gordy that we've got company?"

Micah disappeared.

Freddy offered, "With all this stuff going on, I should be packing a gun."

"If you ever take something from me again, you'll be on your own and I don't give a hoot where you end up." I grabbed my .38, my holster, and waved to him to go.

Freddy didn't appear to be hurt by the reprimand, and backed up just enough for me to shut the closet door. Smarting from him taking my gun, I went into the bathroom to view the approaching vehicle. I didn't recognize the car and thought we should either lock the gate or put someone down there to stop vehicles from driving up—there were too many outsiders coming into our valley.

It was strange to react like this over an approaching vehicle, but with all the stuff happening, I was getting paranoid. Snagging another .38, I determined to get down on the driveway before the vehicle came round the curve. I swallowed my pain and headed for the stairway.

Somewhere in my haste I realized I didn't have a backup. Who would protect our family if I went down? And here I'd just taken a gun away from my brother.

What a struggle to finally get to the curve in the road, an area shielded by a six- foot-tall rock outcrop. I was breathing heavily and the pain in my ribs drew sweat. I heard the car coming around the blind bend. If there was any relief in all this, both my handguns were out and in plain view.

My mouth dropped open when I saw who it was.

"Hi, Hershal!" Vicki elatedly exclaimed from her car's open window.

Stunned at seeing the gal who was the first of the seventy, a gal that flaked-out on her part back in the day, I stepped back.

"How have you been?" she asked, as if nothing had ever happened.

Feelings of betrayal and distrust washed over me. "Vicki." It was difficult to appear welcoming. I gave a small nod and only averted looking like a Rare Pygmy Rabbit caught in the headlights by putting my guns in their holsters.

Behind me, Priscilla's energized voice came down the steps. "Well, look who's here." She happily descended. "Isn't God good!"

Sometimes I wished this gal of mine had more of a mean streak.

Vicki sprang from her car and joyfully cried, "Sister!" The queen's possessiveness of this word cut me deeply; here she'd hardly done a thing in the food build-up, yet now she was calling Priscilla "Sister."

I froze and witnessed Priscilla hurry toward her; Vicki's three dogs joined in, merrily leaping from the car. Before them, the two fluttering angels melted into each other's arms. Vicki's smile was so creamy, it was tough to view. The two staggered in lush giggles till the whole thing finished with the queen breaking out in a soft-shoe shuffle. I wanted to puke.

The boys, Jordan and Micah, came into this mash, with Jordan mimicking Vicki's jig and Micah petting her dogs. One dog, a fat poodle, came straight toward me. I was struggling to hide my cold look and show some hospitality, so I painfully bent a knee to give the poodle some rubs.

Planted there, I half-listened to the two excited sisters while I considered the audacity of this individual to ever return to our house. And here we'd told them our secret. It didn't help matters when I heard her say her husband had worked in oil country, "Making good money, too."

I continued petting her poodle while thinking of words to erase our former invitation of being part of the seventy. As I formulated my plan, this dog suddenly turned and straightened, seeing something, evidently disturbing. I arose; there was Sparky. He was standing as stiff as I felt, and gave her dogs a stern look. It didn't matter if there were fifty dogs; this was his turf. Baring his teeth, he growled every few steps.

One of Vicki's whinier dogs came toward Sparky. They must've done some dog talk because her dog suddenly spun around and Spark was sniffing his or her rump. That was all it took. Amazingly, Sparky was won over.

I walked across the driveway, continued to search for the right words and acted like I was looking toward our gate.

Behind me, the happy gab was chronic.

I made it to the edge of the road and stood there for a minute as I considered how to tell Vicki, without being cruel, that she was no longer part of the seventy. Nothing came to mind, so I headed for the house.

As I walked past them, Vicki swung her hand toward me. "Hershal, did you hear about the aircraft carrier that was hit by Chinese missiles?"

This news halted me. "No."

"I'm sure glad you invited us to be part of that vision you had of the seventy and all." There was a glee about her. "Did I tell you I know this couple that would be real good in your communal situation?"

The gall of this woman was striking. It sanded me like coarse sandpaper.

"They're real hard workers."

"Well, I wanted to talk to you about that." I pulled out my wallet. "You know, after the first couple of shipments, you and your husband didn't seem interested in the project anymore so, well … in the end, we lost interest, too." I made good contact with her blue eyes. "It was kind of a wild adventure at any rate." I faked a grin. "So we ended up giving all that food to the food bank." I took three $100. bills out, crinkling them into my palm. "Anyway, how much do I owe you for your help on those two shipments?"

"Ohhh …" she moaned, looking as if a sad cloud had floated down upon her.

"Yeah, we were sorry we got rid of it all. If we'd kept just a quarter of it, we would've been worth a fortune." The bills were extended her way. "Would this make it even?"

"I don't want your money." She looked grave. "Lately, I was thinking how important seventy people would be against the wave that is coming. Everything is just happening so fast."

Priscilla gave me a pleading look.

I countered, "I think this whole thing will blow over, and who knows, maybe you can stock up then." I again extended the money toward her. "This will get you started."

She raised her hand in protest. "If there was a way to start it again," she said with a questioning appeal, "what would one do?"

I could've said a lot of things, but she was trying to worm her way in. I shrugged, "Don't you think everything will work out in this old world? It always does."

"My dad said that he detected nuclear fallout on his dosimeter yesterday."

Priscilla's eyes widened. "We have fallout now?" She gazed up at the darkening sky.

On cue, drops of rain sprinkled the driveway. They helped my exit and I headed for the open garage door.

The two women weren't far behind. I suppose this had more to do with the hope of revitalizing the seventy than drops of rain. Regardless, I was glad Vicki could witness that the pallets of rice, beans, wheat, etc. were all gone. Even so, her comment on the radiation worried me. Was my daughter Bethany okay?

Mounting the stairs, I entered the kitchen, where the ladies were busy making split pea soup and wheat bread. There was always excitement in the kitchen in the morning, as they were abuzz with breakfast as well as preparing lunch.

I was lucky to get a cup of coffee that had only been hobo'd, run through the filter three times. It had little of the smell or taste of real coffee, but its dark color spoke of better times. Holding the cup, I was drawn toward the sunroom, where Mark was peering through the spotting scope. What was he viewing? The door creaked as I entered the room.

Without looking up, Mark said, "There's some horses out there."

"I saw them yesterday. I bet Al ran out of food for them."

"I hear horse meat's good." Mark's head rose from the spotting scope.

"Sometimes you worry me." I took an uneasy sip of the watered-down liquid.

"I'm thinking of an open gate, say …" He pitched his chin east. "… the one over there." His eyes widened as his fantasy unfolded. "Them horses entering your property are going to steal some of your good grass." He shrugged. "Don't them horses have to pay rent?"

"I don't want to hear it."

He gave me an annoyed look. "Cousin, aren't we living in weird times?" When it came to his beloved meat, he had a smooth way of speaking. "It'd be nice to have some meat in that soup." His gaze went to the large pot on the stove. "Can't you just taste it?"

"They used to hang horse thieves in this country."

He gave me a carefree grin. "If we don't get them horses … somebody else will."

*　　*　　*

My thoughts were on my cousin as I struggled up the stairs. Here a Kentuckian thought nothing of eating a Montanan's horse. I say, times had changed.

In the purple room, I shuffled over to the bay window to see if Vicki was gone. Unfortunately, I saw rain bouncing off her car. That bugged me.

The rain turned into a downpour. It was something to watch it cut loose. But that didn't stop Micah and Jordan from dashing out of the garage with outspread arms, happily taking a rain shower. In no time, they were playfully hopping about.

I thought of what Vicki said, about her father detecting radiation, and wondered if those boys were taking a nuclear shower. Concerned, I opened the window and called out, "You boys get inside." But either my call was weak, as my ribs wouldn't allow me to yell, or they had a bit of the devil in them, as their frolic was unremitting. I had to go tell them to get inside.

My ribs hurt as I made it back down those steps. When I got to the bottom of the stairs, just before the garage, I heard a resounding crack, a noise as loud as a gun's blast. In front of me, the walls appeared to move.

Around the corner I heard Vicki. "What was that?"

It sounded as if the stairway had collapsed, but I could still hear the clatter of shoes thundering down the steps. Ellen rushed down the stairs, shocked. "What was that?"

In front of us, Carl shared our alarm, his eyes warily looking about. "It could be another earthquake."

I glanced at our nine-foot foundation wall and was surprised to see a quarter-inch-wide vertical fracture.

"God is shaking the earth!" blared Vicki, wide-eyed and frantic."God is shaking us!"

Her comment made Jordan groan. He fearfully looked at Micah. "God's coming." His arms hopelessly fell. "What do we do now?" His voice trailed off as nervous tears welled up.

That woman! The dread she cast; how I wished she'd leave. And here, she knew our secret.

* * *

Somewhere around noon I got a visit from Paul, a neighbor. We were on the front doorstep, out of earshot of everyone, which was always difficult in our place. I had to raise my voice because of the wind and rain, "What brings you out in the rain?"

"Food."

Paul was raising two kids by himself and had his challenges, though you'd never know it, as he was always pleasant. Another thing I liked about him was his shooting ability. He was a real good shot and the only neighbor I'd let hunt on our place. A while back, he'd downed a nice elk and had given us a quarter of it. These qualities were worth a lot to me. Still, there was an accountant in me that had nothing to do with the love of a neighbor.

"I can't just let you walk away with what little we have. It might come back to haunt us. Who knows how long this thing will last? If you want to work for it, fine. Or if you got silver or gold or something to trade."

"What kind of work you got in mind?"

"Security; it would be no good to get overrun."

The wind picked up, and the wounded windmill, which had been barely turning, suddenly spun with an eerie grinding. IRRRREEERRRERYY! I was afraid that any second the thing could fly apart. Paul's poncho flapped as he leaned into the wind. IRRREERRRY; the grinding whine was like a weird harbinger of the future.

"If this thing goes on, you're going to have to start thinking about moving over here."

He grinned. "Don't you have enough folks already?"

"Someone said there's safety in numbers. I hope they're right. Anyway, why don't you come for lunch?"

I was glad that Paul joined us for lunch. There was no end of gab from my family about the earthquakes, and Vicki's news of the detected nuclear fallout and the ruined U.S. aircraft carrier. I'd had enough of dread and wanted to enjoy a pleasant meal with our neighbor, so I blurted out, "The secrets behind these delicious breads and the soup are so very important now."

The talk quieted down and people gave me peculiar looks. I said to our fine cooks in the kitchen, "You gals make me feel like a man of means. Please tell us where you got your recipes."

"Well …" started Julie, Priscilla's Canadian cousin, quite matter-of-factly, when a shot rang out from our room above us. Silence.

Mark scrambled up and had his handgun out before he got to the stairs. He bounded up them.

The men clambered up behind him. I trailed, as my sore chest was smarting. Oh, the anticipation, as I went up those stairs. When I got to the top of the stairwell, I heard Jumper crying.

Mark called out, "It's okay."

We found Jumper, crying away in my gun safe closet. Below him was one of my handguns. His crying motor accelerated as others looked in on him. What a scream!

It wasn't long before everyone heard about the mishap. No end of advice came my way over the open safe; mother hens do advise, and sometimes with a peck. Feeling admonished, I wanted to shout louder than Jumper, "Isn't it your responsibility to look after your own kids? Why should they be crawling in and out of my closet? And how in the world am I supposed to protect the place with the gun safe locked?"

I ended up giving a handgun to Jerold, another to Gordy, and placed a rifle in a high spot, out of reach of kids. That was the unfortunate end of the open safe.

That afternoon I got another visit from our neighbor, Al, the fellow who owned no end of animals. He wanted to know if he could borrow some more food, yet said he had nothing to trade. I wondered if he'd spotted Paul coming back from our place. I wasn't in the best of moods, but since he was married and had three kids, I gave him a pound of rice and beans.

# The Extractions

Every evening we got news from the ham radio and Meshnet. Meshnet wasn't the Internet, but an interesting local communication system, five times faster than the Internet and now, like ham radio, very active.

After supper, we talked about getting the news out to the neighborhood, as we thought it selfish to just sit on it. We decided to send 8 x11 sheets out with Micah and Jordan, who'd pedal them down to telephone poles, some of which were up to three miles away. Since they would only be in our local area and not near a highway, we figured they'd be safe enough. If nothing else, this activity would keep our minds, and the boys, exercised.

Julie, Gordy, Natasha, the Canadians, plus my sister Marilyn and my cousins Mark and Josh volunteered to be the news crew. We gathered upstairs in the attic after supper around the computer to catch the news and ready our one-page report.

I stood in the stairwell, leaning against the stair rail and had a good view of the group of six. Josh worked the keyboard, sitting in front of the computer monitor. The rest sat in a semi-circle around him. They were engaging to listen to as they hashed out what would be tomorrow's headlines.

I always liked that attic space; it had the feel of a tree fort. During that time, Freddy and Ellen cleared out. With the windmill fried, our solar was barely keeping up with our water needs, so we only ran the computer and a milk bottle light. To make it worse, there was this greenish design of a mermaid that swirled about the milk bottle light so it barely gave enough glow for the keyboard.

I could just make out the faces, all leaning forward, nervously frowning at the ham radio or the computer monitor, in anticipation of the next report.

Over the ham radio, a member of our preparation group said, "There's been an explosion at Tex and Joan's place. With the fire, it was hard to tell what happened. Over."

Another ham operator interjected, "A neighbor said they saw a black helicopter that night. Over."

The radio crackled, "Marlene Jones is gone as well. Over."

Another caller asked, "What happened to Monica?"

The radio crackled, "Her house is pretty much shot up, but her body wasn't found. A neighbor heard a helicopter there. Over."

Another caller, "John MacDonald is gone as well."

Mark gave me a questioning look. "Who are these people?"

"John MacDonald is a preacher in Middleton. Monica used to lead a Back to the Constitution group. Tex and Joan are leaders in our preparation group. I don't know Marlene Jones."

"Why is the government zeroing in on them? What did they do wrong?"

Marilyn abruptly pointed at the computer monitor, exclaiming, "What???? Ash and lava spewing from Mt. Baker, Mt. Rainier, Mt. Shasta, Mt. …"

Josh complained, "I can't see how we can get all this gloom onto one page."

"Just start with the bad stuff and end with the good stuff."

"Where's the good stuff?" Josh groaned, reading the monitor. "There's nothing good here." He looked at the monitor. "They say a plague is sweeping the globe."

"We better start cooking with garlic, lots of garlic."

Gordy noted, "Those volcanic eruptions had to be caused by the earthquake; tectonic plates shifting."

Josh tapped the keyboard. "So what do we say about the volcanoes?"

Mark was emphatic. "I still say they must've put a series of nuclear bombs underwater, all along our Coast."

Julie gazed at him in wonder. "Who?"

"Our government boys."

"How do figure that?"

"It's obvious you don't know our government. They're a bunch of parasites that are going after their own citizens."

"Can't we just get the news out?"

"We need to tell everybody about the nuclear fallout. That should be on the first line. Next should be that plague."

"Just say that West Coast volcanoes are active."

Josh rapidly typed in the headlines. "I'm trying to figure out how much detail to put down on that earthquake."

"Keep it tight. It's only a one-page report."

"Should we say," Josh pointed at the monitor, "San Francisco's under eight feet of glass? Or do we write about the downed bridges? Or do we talk about the split in Hoover Dam? Or do I mention what the tsunami did to the coastal towns? Do I mention the rip in the earth was over 300 feet? Or just talk about all the aftershocks?"

Again my heart was heavy for my daughter Bethany. Was she still alive?

Out of the corner of my eye I noticed Jumper coming up the stairs. He was in his pajamas, carrying his teddy bear, looking much more innocent than in his earlier handgun incident.

"Just say it's bad on the West Coast," Gordy said, rather seriously.

"I have to be more detailed than that."

"Tell them the CIA started the whole thing," Mark said with finality.

Julie countered, "Would you give it up about the CIA?"

Mark was unmoved. "I'm not giving nothing up on them control freaks. Didn't we just hear about their helicopters extracting good rednecks?"

"I'm sorry," Julie replied, "I just can't see them doing that to their own people."

Jumper gave me a tentative look as he came around me. Generally, I'd shoo him back to bed, but he was a welcome contrast to this gloomy crew, so I acted as if I didn't see him.

"The extraction news should be at the top."

"That kind of news can get us in trouble."

"This is no different than the Gulag. We need to get people ready when them CIA boys come a-knocking."

"Mark, is it always the CIA?"

"CIA, FBI, the United Nation troops, the President, DC ..." Mark said in the most exasperated manner, "... they're all the saaaaaame!"

Natasha pointed at the monitor. "Here's another emergency measure. "Curfew after 9 p.m."

"That's indirectly saying ..." Mark's Kentucky accent was strong, "... the government's men will be sneaking around at night, and they don't want you seeing them snatching our upright citizens."

"It wouldn't be good to print that, either."

"People need to know about the curfew."

"I bet this whole thing was started by our good President to consolidate power. And, what do you know—we can't have an election without the grid working."

"It wouldn't be good to print that, either."

Jumper ended up behind Mark, his eyes captured by that little mermaid on the glowing milk bottle lamp.

Mark was adamant. "Why are we doing this?"

"To tell people to wash their vegetables because of the nuclear fallout, maybe talk about the benefits of iodine," Gordy said. "As far as that plague goes, maybe talk about the benefits of garlic, colloidal silver and oil of oregano."

"Sure," Josh said, somewhat sarcastic. "How are we going to get all that on one page?"

Natasha was apprehensive. "I don't like this. If we start getting the news out, everybody will know that it comes from us. If there is a real military crackdown, then they'll be coming for us."

Mark was obstinate. "We've got to print that extraction business. People need to rise up against these punks. Tyranny can't reign if people are informed; we've got to print that."

"I agree with Natasha," Josh said uneasily. "If we print that stuff, they can come after us."

Outside, the wind started to blow, sudden and strong. Inside, our group was quiet; the consequences of being under Big Brother gave us pause. I could sense an invading fear. The howling wind intensified, rattling the roof's slate.

Jumper was the only one who didn't feel the uneasiness. He was drawn toward that green mermaid on the lamp like a diver to a sunken treasure. He couldn't get through the opening between Mark and Natasha's chairs, so he crawled underneath.

Outside, the wind awakened the wounded windmill. HMMMERRIEEE; it sounded like a B-52 bomber with a blown engine, IEEEEEERRRIEEEE!

Mark's hands unfolded in a questioning manner. "So … we are supposed to live in fear?"

There was a long pause. The wind continued to assault the roof.

At last, Natasha moaned, "How'd we get into this newspaper thing in the first place?"

Jumper came alongside Josh's chair, his little hand reaching toward the glowing milk bottle lamp. He touched the mermaid.

After Natasha got Jumper back to bed, they had a vote on whether we should announce the extractions or not; three were for it and three against, so they turned to me for the deciding vote.

I told them I'd sleep on it.

*   *   *

Lying in bed, I felt as if I was in a fix between looking after the seventy by keeping the news and our opinions to ourselves, or blowing liberty's horn and warning our neighbors. It wasn't Uncle Bob's snoring that kept me awake; I was disturbed over the disappearance of people we knew, good people. Those helicopters had to be government. If we didn't awaken the community to rise up and fight, then who would fight?

Somewhere in all this calculating, I heard a distant shot. It came from the east. I waited, listening for another. My worries went from broadcasting news of the extractions to setting up 24/7 security on the property.

On the floor beside me, Priscilla whispered, "Are you awake?"

"Yes."

"Did you hear that shot?"

"Yes."

"Maybe we should have all-night security?"

"I've been thinking about that for a while."

"Paul and his family would be good to have as part of the seventy."

"I think so, too."

"Maybe we should see if there are any out-of-staters down at the Bolo Dance Center that got stuck here."

"Maybe."

"Vicki and Alex would be good to have."

"Please don't start."

"She told me that Alex had a drinking problem back then."

"They dropped out, so that's that."

"I like Vicki."

"Please, I don't want to revisit it." I heard the distinct thump, thump, thump of a helicopter.

"I wonder if a friend of ours is on that helicopter?"

A flash of light illuminated the bedroom walls, then another flash. I sat up and gazed through our window. In the distance, I saw lightning, its bright arch driving into the ground. This was followed by thunder, cracklings, rumblings. An interesting purple/black mist drifted over the dark gray horizon. It hovered around a white glow that vibrated outward as several bolts of lightning drove into the mountains. Rumblings of thunder followed, marching toward us like the heavy beat of drums. The wind joined and grew stronger until I could feel the house sway.

From the bed above us, Uncle Bob asked, "What is it?"

"It's a lightning storm, Uncle. You have a front-row seat."

"Do you have storms like this often?"

"I've never seen one this intense." The eerie sound of the wounded windmill broke upon us like a rolling bucket of bolts. IRREERIEEIRIEE. It howled as if it would blow apart. IREEERIEEEIRIEEIRRRRIE!

The door to the deck swung open and in came Jordan, pulling his bedding behind him.

Micah was on his heels, dragging his bedding as well. "Is God going to blow this house down?"

# Volcanic Ash and Nuclear Fallout

The following morning while brushing my teeth, I casually glanced out the bathroom window. What a shock to see everything covered with what looked like dirty snow; its gray color was as eerie as a moonscape.

I couldn't get outside fast enough and ended up on the front porch, where I ran my curious hand across the slate. This was my first experience touching volcanic ash. I left a trail of footprints in it as I walked down the steps, and along the stone walkway.

On the road, pedaling around the windmill came Micah. He called out, "Do you see it?"

"Yes."

"It's everywhere, no matter where you go."

I noticed Jordan pedaling behind Micah. He didn't have the lung power that Micah had but I doubt that this fine dust was good for anybody.

I coughed a bit and felt my ribs, but continued toward the road.

I met up with Micah, who braked and stuck out his foot, then pointed behind him. "That animal guy is coming up here."

"Where?"

He thumbed back toward the hill.

"Thanks." I ruffled his dusty hair before heading toward an overlook to see if I could spot Al.

"We heard turkeys." Micah called.

"Can we eat them?" Jordan pedaled up.

"I'll tell Mark." I looked over the countryside for Mark. It would be good to know what he remembered of the shot last night and to talk to him about security plans.

Al was not far away. This was the fourth time he'd come up to our place since the world took a spin, and I was getting tired of his constant borrowing. "Do you have any yeast? Baking soda? Flour? That rice and beans went in a hurry; how about if I borrow a bag this time?"

I assumed his teens had something to do with him running out of food so fast. Regardless, I'd had enough, especially when he got bold enough to ask for coffee. People shouldn't ask for coffee. Furthermore, Al said he had no money to pay for what I gave him and never offered anything to trade.

Previously, I had a talk with Priscilla about Al's excessive borrowing. She thought maybe he and his family should be part of the seventy and come to our place to camp. The problem was, I'd never seen his three teens help on bucket patrol or do any work around his place. Additionally, you couldn't walk up to their house without stepping in sheep or goat or duck or horse waste, guinea hen or peacock or dog droppings. What a mine field! Inside the house were ferrets, a raccoon, rats and cats. I'd been there once and came away itching, with no desire of ever returning.

I walked past the woodpile and looked over the west hill in search of Mark. The morning was cool and I wondered if it was from this drifting ash. Then again, it could just be fall.

Fall was no doubt Mark's time of year, as he was all about hunting. In the days since the grid went down, he had knocked off two deer and some of our Pygmy Rabbits. I asked him to leave the Pygmies alone, as there's hardly any meat on them and they were just starting to make a comeback. We hadn't eaten much of the meat as most was still hanging.

Al found me by the woodpile. After griping about world events and coughing from the drifting volcanic ash, he asked if he could borrow some food, anything to eat.

I was prepared for this, retorting, "Look, Al, you can see from how many folks we have here, I can't just be giving our goods away without a trade. I just can't."

Al looked overworked and concerned. "Okay." His hand pointed toward the state land. "I've a few horses that I'll trade for their weight in rice or beans."

"I think you're asking a fortune for them horses. I used to have a few horses, but they ate too much." I shrugged. "How do you even feed a horse with all that drifting ash?"

He cleverly avoided my question. "I've got a variety of birds. I'll even put that peacock on the line."

"What good's a peacock?"

"They are very good look-outs. If a coyote comes, they'll be yapping and chattering. They're good like that."

I heard the quad coming up the hill.

"I've also got some sheep and goats."

"Are they good eating?"

He gave me an admonishing glare. "No, you can't eat my sheep; they're pets." He frowned. "They're pets."

The quad came around the corner, with Mark at the controls. Right off I noticed something peculiar; the front end was higher than usual. I watched its approach, curious to see what was on the rack.

Al was oblivious, as his back was to the quad.

"Do you have any chickens?"

"I can't part with my chickens, but I do have guinea hens."

My cousin, clueless about who I was talking to, motored the quad directly toward us. He sported a showy grin.

My eyes went from the Kentuckian to Al, then my mouth dropped open when I saw a massive hind quarter on the back of the quad. I'm not so sure if my face turned a reddish hue, but I know my heart sank.

About ten feet from us, Mark's face displayed the pride of a hunter, Nimrod in all his glory. But when Al turned to see who it was, Mark became apprehensive; his eyebrow rose.

Al gave the meat a casual glance. "I didn't know hunting season had started."

Mark didn't miss a beat; his voice was strong, firm, manly. "In times like these, I don't think Fish and Wildlife would mind us starting a few days early." He glanced up to the house. "We've a lot of mouths to feed."

If anything, I was thankful Mark had skinned the Palomino and sawed off its hooves. Even still, I was surprised Al didn't realize it was a horse. I had never seen such a red slab, and had to suppress my rising anger at my cousin. He was a monster for meat. While he circled the quad, I had to tell myself that he was the type that couldn't help hunting. Thank goodness, he motored back down the road.

"How much do you want for that peacock?"

"Its weight in rice or beans."

"You should be paying us for taking that peacock off your hands."

I went on to trade Al a ten-pound bag of rice for his peacock. No doubt, we did need more security; maybe this squawking bird would spare us from stumbling over rock walls in the middle of the night.

# Our Security

With the drift of volcanic ash came alarm. Maybe these escalating wars, this nuclear fallout, the earth-quakes, the plague and those volcanoes spoke of something bigger. Regardless, everybody pitched in to construct two Hugelkulturs near the barn. These vegetable-producing gardens would come in handy if water became scarcer, as they'd be fed by rain from the barn's roof.

Julie, a bandana covering her nose and mouth, led the charge, instructing us in how to shape the gardens. That Canadian had us all working, digging or foraging for rotting wood. With my sore ribs I wasn't the greatest help, but wariness about the future drove the others.

In mid-afternoon, I heard our new peacock. Its alarming cry made me think we had a coyote on the prowl. I broke away from those Hugelkulturs and walked about fifty yards to look over the bluff toward the garden. We had placed the large bird there because it had a six-foot wire fence for protection and some garden leftovers it could glean.

An older car had just passed the garden and was heading toward the house. Not recognizing it, I turned and called, "Mark, we got company!"

My brother Freddy walked toward me, then stopped. I thought he wanted to come along but I couldn't tell as half his face was covered by a bandana. Unconcerned, he stepped toward his girlfriend Ellen, and flapped his arms like a bird. She lifted her shovel and gave him a don't-come-any-closer look. I thought, as goofy and unreliable as he was, sometimes it was still good to have him—he cut through the seriousness of the times.

When I called to Mark, he had been sitting against the barn, resting, half-dozing from his night's work. The urgency in my voice woke him. He loped past the beehive of activity around the Hugelkultur toward me. Though he looked a bit dopey, he had sense enough to bring his rifle.

In no time we were in the diesel, driving up the road. I looked over at him. Mark had a calm demeanor; nothing ever seemed to surprise or bother him. I don't know if it was because he was a night person or because he simply minded his own business.

As intact as my territorial instincts were in speeding after this car, you'd think I'd have implemented a full-time security plan a long time ago. But that had somehow been shifted to the back burner.

We caught up to the puttering car near the windmill. It came to a stop at the entrance of our driveway and I pulled up right behind it.

Mark hopped out, rifle in hand, and positioned himself ten feet behind their passenger door. I wasted no time in getting around the back of their car, positioning myself to the side of my cousin, my handgun out.

In the meantime, a young man stepped from the car and grinned. "Hey, brother."

I had one eye on him, the other on the passenger, who held an assault rifle. Their visit spelled trouble, but you'd never know it from the driver's casual manner.

"How's it going?" This good-looking kid displayed no end of confidence as he slowly came toward us.

"How do you know me?" I asked suspiciously, then looked at the passenger to see if the direction of the AR's muzzle had changed. I realized that if Mark and I were killed in this encounter, there'd be only my son Jerold and one-eyed Gordy to protect our group. Strange to think this way when someone comes up your driveway.

"Aren't you Hershal?"

It would be difficult to tell, as half my face was covered with a bandana to filter out the dust. "Who are you?"

"Egan." He had a real smooth way about him. "What's going on?" Approaching, he extended his hand to shake.

I motioned with a flick of my handgun not to come any closer. "How do you know me?"

"Through Alex and Vicki."

This comment struck me like a fist. Vicki and Alex were telling everybody and their dog about us.

He stepped back, and sent an admiring thumb toward the windmill. "I approve."

I fingered the trigger, as I wasn't buying any feigned praises.

"Did you hear about the war in the Middle East?"

I shrugged, not wanting to continue this conversation, only wanting them off the property.

"It's gone nuclear."

"What brings you here?"

"I was wondering if you had any extra food you can trade us? ... brother." And there was that grin again.

Feeling gooped by all this "brother" talk, I shook my head. "Isn't Bi-lo still running?"

"They're out of everything."

"How many people are you looking after?"

"I'm hanging out with a few buddies."

"We've got more than a houseful here." I angled the gun at all our parked vehicles. "We've got hungry people here."

"Well, Vicki and Alex just want you to know ..." He stepped toward me to shake hands.

I aimed right at his hip. "I think you better leave."

Stepping back, he hastily nodded as he headed for the car, his voice trailing "… that they love you with the love of the Lord."

His statement sat sourly in my gut. Vicki and Alex's lack of commitment was clear, and here they'd told these fellows about our stash. What was a secret amongst them religious folk?

The presence of the two men troubled me even more as they drove down the hill, puttering along slowly. I was sure they were taking in our entire landscape, mapping it out for the future.

\* \* \*

On our way to the barn, I had a conversation with Mark regarding security. He had a good eye for that kind of thing, and suggested we put lookouts on this hill and the east hill. It all sounded real good, but before I knew it, I was helping him prepare the horsemeat, as no one else would touch it with a ten-foot pole, and then supper was on.

After that, I had to deal with our water supply, which wasn't working, thanks to drifting ash blanketing our solar panels. I checked on our solar batteries, only to find the voltage was too low for the 220-volt pump to work. I had to shut that breaker off and tell our group that it was going to be a dry night. Furthermore, I had to cut off all electricity, so no news went out. Still, by nightfall, no security had been instigated.

\* \* \*

That next morning we set up half-hour shifts to sweep off the solar panels, as the volcanic ash wasn't waning. Then came our first bucket patrol to the spring.

I left Jerold in charge of security. Gordy, Travis, Carl, Mitch and I swung our 5-gallon buckets about and, despite bandanas, still chatted away as we trekked through bunch-grass and sage. The topic was what they were going to do when they got back home. Two were concerned about their pets. My thoughts went to my daughter Bethany in California. I only hoped she'd get out here, and soon.

Interesting, here we were on a trek to the spring, yet no one mentioned nuclear fallout. In considering this, I said, "We might be walking through nuclear fallout."

Gordy replied, "I sure feel that ash. It dries you out."

"Hershal, do you have any iodine?"

I nodded. "Some." Then I felt the earth tremble. "Whoa, Nelly!"

We all stopped and braced against the sway.

Carl looked suspiciously at the ground. "These earthquakes are something."

"Look how long they go on."

I broke out in a sweat. "It's like the earth is shaking apart."

"It's phenomenal."

I apprehensively stared at a nearby pine. Its bark was trembling, its needles moving up and down.

The earthquake passed—we could breathe again. We strode on toward the spring. Despite my bandana, I found myself clearing my throat quite a bit. I kept an eye out for Mark. Who knew what time he'd gone out hunting? No doubt O-dark hundred. The spring we headed for was used by wildlife, so I thought we might see Mark.

I liked that spring. It was a little Garden of Eden, with welcoming knee-high grass. The lushness was quite an odd-ity in our dry country. Back in the day, someone had laid a large tractor tire there; water constantly flowed over its rim. Impressive trees surrounded that area. But now, everything was covered with that microscopic dust.

With one dip of the bucket, it was easy to capture all the water I could lift. I had to pour some back, as my sore ribs wouldn't allow me to carry more than two gallons. This was frustrating.

On the way home, I constantly found myself shifting the bucket from side to side. This arduous journey was more up-hill than downhill. Somewhere along the path, I thought, if this was going to last five years I was going to end up with some pretty strong arms. And when I thought of the expense of that wind turbine, its twelve-foot-deep foundation, all the electrical stuff, what a waste of money that turned out to be. Furthermore, the crazy sound the thing made when it came alive during real high winds was downright frightening. A hand pump at our shallower well down by the barn would've been a better idea, and far cheaper.

Ascending a steep hill, we constantly stopped for breathers. While resting, I found myself looking up toward the saddleback timbered area of Eli's old camp. I wondered if that was where we'd all end up.

I knew water hauling was no small deal. Besides our drinking and cooking needs, how does one clean dishes, clothes, kitchen, bathrooms, not to mention their body, without water? Not to mention the thirst of our house plants.

A gunshot jolted me out of my reflections. Other shots resounded—they came from the house.

Leaving our buckets, we hurried up the hill to see what was going on. I was huffing and puffing, holding my sore ribs, when I came over the rise. In the distance, I saw a car on the curve just this side of the driveway, facing downhill, ready to take off.

A figure was on our deck above the sunroom. I hoped it was one of our group. He appeared to be aiming or shooting, but at over 600 yards away, I couldn't tell. Fear came over me when I saw someone standing behind the windmill's steel tower, the perfect shield. He was shooting toward the house. Another person was crouched behind the five foot cut-in of the driveway, also shooting at the house.

Gordy, Travis and Carl were chomping at the bit to help, but what good was my handgun from this distance? Mitch was a big man and hadn't come over the rise yet.

"Come on," I urged, while trotting in a different direction. "I've got a rifle buried somewhere ... over here. Maybe it's still good."

The area we crossed was open terrain, a bad spot to be in. But the biggest target was the person on that sunroom deck. I hoped it wasn't Jerold, as he had no business being there. As I hurried toward my stash, I constantly looked toward the battle. Gunshots continued. It was frightening to see someone running around that deck before taking cover. I was perplexed at this action.

I found the rocks where, years earlier, I had buried a bug-out rifle. "It's here." I knelt and couldn't dig fast enough. Carl, Gordy and Travis joined in. I pointed to another spot. "Dig there. The ammo is there." A number of gunshots drove our digging.

It took longer than I liked to find the plastic beneath the soil. Finally I pulled the caps off the two six-inch-wide PVC tubes. In one tube was an assault rifle, in the other, ammo clips. "Who's a shooter?"

"I can shoot," Travis said.

I liked the fact that he was gung-ho and extended the weapon toward him. "Slap the magazines in hard."

Then he was off, bounding across the landscape. Carl ran to keep up.

With all this shooting going on, Gordy pointed toward the east hill. "I bet that's Mark shooting across."

"There's hope in Mark's lead." But my hope vanished when I again saw Jerold scurry across the sunroom's deck. Was he out of ammo and trying to draw their fire; was that his plan? Was it selfless or idiotic? He needed to stop doing that. I chided myself, as I hadn't left enough ammo, or access to the gun safe.

In front of us, a bullet drove into a log with a heavy thud. We hurried for cover. Gordy rushed for a tree up the hill.

I had just taken shelter near a pine tree when I heard a motor. A truck appeared down by the gate, speeding over a rise, a trail of dust in its wake. In seconds, the truck flew past the garden. Surprisingly, it curved off the road, veered through the sage and charged straight toward me.

I lifted my handgun and took aim. I was about to pull the trigger when I realized it was Paul's truck. When it braked and came to a halt, there was dust and dust and more dust. What a relief to see him pull his rifle out and hustle toward us.

I pointed up the hill, saying, "We got intruders."

"Do you know their positions?"

From above, Gordy called, "One's right behind the windmill."

Paul gained the protection of a tree and carefully looked over the hillside; there was about a 150-foot elevation before one could be in a position to counterattack. But Paul had good legs and powered up that hill like Travis had.

Rocks tumbled behind him and he went up and up. It was encouraging to see him gain a good position near the ridge. But my hopes were put on hold when I saw Jerold again pop out on the deck. Another shot rang, and something weird about the way Jerold moved made me feel ill. It was as if a wave had hit him.

"No, no," I moaned, mournfully shaking my head. "Please, God." My words became more desperate. "Ohhh, God, please, please."

It wasn't long afterward that Travis, Paul and Mark brought this battle to an end. I don't know if I was good for much; my battle now was to stay sane. As I headed up the hill, I said to myself, Jerold couldn't have been shot. I had to dismiss what my eyes had witnessed. I had to believe that he'd be all right. But my mind was careening and I kept repeating, Jerold couldn't have been shot … No, no, not my son, he couldn't have been shot…

When I entered the house, I knew something was terribly wrong. Everyone was silent. I went straight upstairs. Gordy, Travis, Paul, Carl and Mark followed. The sound of their rumbling boots competed with the blood pounding in my ears. Upstairs, I was drawn down the hall like a magnet. I curved into the master bedroom that adjoined the outside deck. To my left were a number of bullet holes that had pierced the sheetrock, spraying dust across the carpet.

Freddy came through the deck's doorway. He held a metal mixing bowl; inside were blood-soaked rags. My sorrow was deep at the sight of all that crimson.

Freddy said, "He ran out of bullets. If I had a gun, it'd be …"

I heard no more, but began to tremble when I looked out the storm glass door. My breath caught at the sight of Jerold's shoes and pants, laid out on the deck. Halting a few feet before the open door, I stared at my son. He was laying face up, his blood all over the slate.

Priscilla was down on her knees, with one hand on Jerold's chest, praying. Julie held a sheet, and waited behind Priscilla. Someone had placed a pillow under his head; the white covering stood out amongst the smears of red. Raela was leaning against the iron railing, weeping.

A hand rested on my shoulder. This touch, this love, our loss, my failure, made my knees crumple.

I sobbed.

# The Funerals

Every ounce of misstep and confusion that I was under, Priscilla was above. Several of us were south of the house, just over our pets' graveyard.

Priscilla held Raela with one hand and pointed at some bunch grass with the other. "This is the spot. Gordy, can you round up the men and take charge of the digging?"

"Yes." He coughed from the drifting ash and adjusted his bandana.

It was then that I heard that voice again, that accuser's voice. "This is how it works with murdering men."

Priscilla looked my way, her lips moving, sound coming out. "Hershal, can you go get Eli?" I don't know if it was dealing with that other voice, but her question hardly registered.

As I stared upon my son's future grave, the accuser's voice was clear. "The fruit of your killing." It even had a rhyming rhythm. "One by one, your children will go. That's how it works, you know."

Priscilla asked, "Mark, would you be kind enough to build a coffin?"

"You bet."

"We have some plywood. I'm sure you can find 2 by 4s."

Mark went off.

She turned her attention back to me. "Hershal? Can you go get Eli?"

I viewed Raela's wet eyes.

With a thud, Gordy placed a large rock on the proposed spot. "Is this where you want it?"

"Yes," Priscilla answered, then called out, "Mark, do you think it's possible to have a funeral this afternoon?"

Mark looked at his watch. "I'm going to need some electrical power."

She pointed toward the underground culverts that housed the solar inverter. "You can bring the lumber up the hill here. There's a plug in our underground room."

Again, Mark went off. Behind us, the grave was already being dug with shovels and picks.

Sometimes I wonder what Priscilla does with her feelings. This was our son, but it was as if she had put her feelings in a steel box and slammed the door.

Freddy cursed the rocks.

Again, I heard the accuser's voice. "Dig one grave and then another." I was frightened when I looked at Raela. She never had the strongest heart. When she was younger she'd had some fainting spells. Now, with Jerold gone, her tears hadn't stopped flowing. The accuser's voice nagged, "You might as well dig her grave too."

Priscilla let go of Raela and came toward me. Before I knew it, I was within her grasp. Her voice echoed. "Hershal, it'd be good to bring closure to this as soon as possible. Can you go get Eli?" All this was said so matter-of-factly, almost like a coach giving a player instruction before sending him into the game. At the middle of my back, she gave me a small push, then turned to Raela. "Raela? Come on, honey. Let's go up to the house. Jesus will help us get through this. He's good like that."

*   *   *

There was no burial for the intruders. These weren't the two men from the previous day. I've no idea who three of them were, but the fourth had driven the concrete truck that poured the underground unit. We piled their corpses into their vehicle and I drove it while Gordy followed in the diesel.

Somewhere along the Yokino River I found a turnoff and left it behind a clump of trees. When I walked away and looked back at that car, how weighed down its trunk was, I thought what a waste of life.

I climbed into the diesel and Gordy rode shotgun as we continued on toward Eli's. On the way, I glanced at the short-barreled shotgun that rested across his lap and thought of my awful failure not to provide enough ammo for Jerold and the others. Guilt descended on me like a vulture. My son was dead! And here I was a gun man!

When we drove through Charby, I noticed a Hispanic kid standing on a street corner. I'd never seen street people in Charby, never once, and now there were at least thirty. One of Priscilla's songs came to mind, "Count your blessings, count them one by one." A real bad mood rose up in me against that song, and blame for Jerold's death and the locked safe. I aimed my accusations toward the heavens. What blessing was there in Jerold's death?

That song triggered a real battle within me; the clash was filled with sarcasm. I tried to fight against this onslaught by saying God was good, over and over. Jerold's death came down to my poor planning, to my lack of getting him enough ammo. It was stupid of me to lock that safe. Why did I do that, in such a heated rush? It was the result of getting pecked upon by everyone, plus Jumper's high-pitched scream within the gun closet.

In this swirl of blame, my failures crawled about my orb like worms. My head ached. Sometimes I wondered if demons had me. For sure God didn't like me.

By the time I got to the sheep ranch, I felt as if I'd been beaten up and run over. The gate was chained with a large padlock. I wasn't sure if it was a wasted trip. Gordy had nodded off. I left him sleeping and strode onto the sheepman's place.

There was no sign of anyone at the sheep wagon. Behind it, the creek was just a trickle, grayish from the volcanic ash.

I continued down the road, coughing at times, patting the dust off my bandana. After rounding a corner, I spotted a distant herd of sheep. A dog barked, announcing my presence. I pressed on, blinking, clearing my throat, and holding my bruised ribs.

Nearing the herd, I saw someone. I figured it was Eli, but I couldn't tell, as half his face was covered in a bandana. He approached through the middle of the herd, holding his rifle. The sight of his weapon told me there was more to this locked gate than just coyotes. I wasn't 100 percent sure it was Eli until I noticed his worn, torn overalls and his familiar walk. Then a real rush of emotions swept over me. Now Eli was my only son.

When I reached him, I wanted to hug him, but I just stood there, thinking about how to use sign language again. I couldn't tell if he was smiling as his mouth was covered. I put out my hand. Behind him, his sheep were just a-baaaing up a storm.

I was pretty slow in spelling out the words in sign language. "Your ... brother ... is ... gone. We ... are ... having ... the ... funeral ... Can ... you ... come?"

I don't think the message sunk in until he saw my eyes water. Then he teared up and came at me with a big hug. We hung there for a while. His sheep looked heavy, covered by the drifting ash. It was good to have Eli. I ran my fingers over his shirt and squeezed his arm, wanting to hold onto him forever.

*   *   *

Nancy was her good, wholesome self. My granddaughter Kelsey wasn't shy about toddling into my arms. She was so tender. For the rest of that day, I was constantly blinking back tears.

Nancy's dad would've liked to come to the funeral, but they'd been losing sheep to poachers, so he had to stay. Nancy and Eli brought bedding to sleep over. We dumped it in the truck box and they piled into the four-door.

In Charby, that same kid I'd seen earlier on the street corner was still there. I didn't know of too many Hispanic kids in this neck of the woods. While I considered what he might be selling or doing there, that song played again in my head, "Count your blessings, count them one by one." As soon as that tune kicked in, Jekyll and Hyde stepped in, blew out the fire of counting any blessings and replaced it with scorn and blame. I battled these dark thoughts and reasoned that if I understood why Jerold had died, then I could walk away from this sorrow. Not long after, my head started pounding, the-thump, the-thump, the-thump.

The pictures of the rest of that day had a watery view; volcanic ash drifting over Jerold's casket, people coughing as we bowed to pray, men shoveling dirt and rocks atop the casket, everybody coming inside for a bite to eat, looking out the sunroom window at the wind in the trees above his grave.

While Aunt Jessica told a funny story about Jerold fishing her out of the river, the wind increased its speed so much, it ignited the wounded windmill, IRRREEEIRRRE. What a fearful sound those windmill blades made! Ash dust bellowed up the landscape, seemingly shooting straight at the sunroom window. IRREEEIRRRIERRRIE.

\*   \*   \*

As I lay in bed with Priscilla, my battered mind mulled over all that had happened, from the first shots up at the house, to Jerold laid out on the deck, to the Hispanic kid on the corner, then back to Jerold laid out on the deck, to us setting his coffin down, to him laid out on the deck.

"Eli told me they're losing sheep to poachers."

"We have to pray for them."

"I don't think God listens to me."

"How come?"

"I don't think He likes me."

"Don't say that, He loves you."

"It was my fault Jerold died."

She touched my hand. "You can't blame yourself for Jerold's death. It was his time."

My stupid emotions swept, and it took a while to get them under control. Finally I said, "It's my fault, I should've had security up. Those intruders shouldn't have gotten past our gate."

"Why? Because you buried him, instead of him burying you?" I could feel her fingers rolling about my wrist. "You can't dwell on this. We need to move on. We need to pull up our bootstraps and bring more people in. There are families and neighbors out there that God wants to bring in." She lifted my hand to her chest. "We need to do what the Lord wants and bring it up to seventy."

*　*　*

The next morning I heard some news out of California that stressed me. Sadly, the death of my son had turned me fatalistic. Would Bethany be next? Mark saw what a bad state I was in and started work on security plans without me. To stay sane, I got busy loading up the bedding for Eli and his family, to get them back to their ranch.

Priscilla was usually up and rolling by 7 a.m., but not that morning. Downstairs, a number of ladies had asked about her. Around 8:30, I came into the bedroom and was surprised to see Priscilla still in bed.

Bending on one knee, I leaned over her. "Are you okay?"

It was good to see her eyes open. She gave a small nod, but there was sadness in her eyes. It was unusual to see her so downcast, she had been so strong for so long.

I took her hand and gave it a squeeze. She has such small wrists, it's a wonder she does everything she does. "Everybody's asking about you." I pulled the covers over her shoulders. "It's good to have you here, hon."

She mumbled, "Why don't you go to the Bolo Dance Center and see if any out-of-state people got stuck?"

"Okay. I'm taking Eli and Nancy back anyway." Leaning over, I tried to encourage her by mumbling some lovies in her ear. I wasn't about to tell her the bad news out of California.

She gave me a tired look. "It'd be good if you could take a bag of rice and beans to the sheriff's department. We can ill afford to lose those men. I don't want to think what this county would be like without them."

I nodded, and kissed her forehead, before rising, heading for the door. At the doorway I looked back at my wife. Here she was concerned about the Sherriff's department but as far as I was concerned, she was the glue that bound us all together; we could ill afford to lose her.

*   *   *

Gordy rode shotgun and Micah and Jordan begged to come along, so we had a full truck, with Kelsey, Eli and Nancy in the backseat and Sparky at their feet. That morning there was a real nip in the air; winter was definitely calling.

On the way to Charby, I drove by a friend's place. Earl Hall was an old-timer, in his 90s. When I drove past, I looked up at his two apple trees, great trees, over 100 years old and real good producers. In the fall you could hardly drive by his place at night without seeing deer in his yard. They loved his apples. Priscilla loved apples, so I pulled over to see if Earl would mind if we picked some. Maybe this would help cheer us all up.

I parked in his driveway and everyone piled out. We all stood there, staring up at the trees, coveting those apples. Evidently we weren't the first people drawn to them, as there wasn't any fruit on the lower branches.

I walked toward Earl's entrance door, knocked and looked through the door's window. The small vestibule had a few plastic pails of old coffee grounds, eggshells and rotting vegetables. I waited and knocked and waited some more. Finally, I went around the side of the house to look in the dining room window. Sparky followed.

With the grid being down, I wondered if Earl's family had picked him up, so I was a bit taken aback when I saw him sitting at the kitchen table. I could only see part of him, as the table blocked my view. I rapped on the glass, but he didn't move. This scared me and I went back to the entrance door.

"Earl?" To my surprise, the doorknob rolled. I pushed the door open, entered quickly and went into the kitchen. Sparky didn't follow, but whimpered. "Earl?" Every kitchen cabinet door was open. Earl was slumped over the kitchen table, looking as if he'd fallen asleep. I couldn't see his face, but there was that unmistakable smell of death.

As I passed him, I gave him a wary glance. The side of his face that you could see was gray and sunken. I moved into the living room, then spun around. The stench was too much. I rushed for the door.

Stumbling down the steps, I saw Gordy approaching. "It's not good." I looked beyond him to Micah and Jordan, and raised my voice. "You boys can pick as many apples as you want. Monkey on up." I pointed to the back of the truck. "There's a bucket back there." My attention came back to Gordy. "Old Earl's gone."

"Dead?"

I nodded.

"You think we should bury him?"

"It would be right."

Eli, Gordy and I dug his grave in his garden, a place he'd always cherished, tending it even in his later years. I found it disturbing, rude, that someone had helped themselves to everything, had cleaned the house out, and I mean gone through every cabinet, dresser drawers, everything, but didn't have the civility to bury Earl.

When we buried Earl, thoughts of Jerold were before me. His death was so raw and surreal, there was a part of me that didn't believe he was gone, but he died some more when we buried Earl. Dirt is dirt, and Earl's body going into dirt was real.

By the time we put the last shovelful of dirt on his grave, the apple-pickers—Nancy, Micah and Jordan, had dumped four buckets of apples into the back of the truck.

As we drove away, I thought of Earl and the fact that we had no ceremony or prayers over his grave. I don't know why people pray for dead people, and I wasn't going to ask Gordy or Nancy if they knew. Earl lived a good long life and as far as I knew, he was good to his neighbors. What was there to pray about? But I'm sure if Priscilla was there, she'd have prayed about something.

There was something about dying and the afterlife that I wanted to dodge around, sneak past. I'm sure, if I really had

# The Round-up

We motored on and drove into Charby. Odd, that Hispanic kid still stood on the corner, in the same spot I'd seen him the previous day.

"Every time I pass by, that kid's been on the corner and he's not even wearing a scarf to filter out the ash."

"Why don't you find out what he's doing?" Micah said in the most matter-of-fact manner.

What made me brake was the sight of Bert, my carpenter, walking straight across the street. I swerved to the side of the road, just short of the Sheriff's office.

"Can you give me a minute? I haven't seen Bert in a while … I want to hear what he knows." Nobody minded. Jordan and Micah leaped out and made a beeline across the street for the Hispanic kid. Gordy, Eli, Nancy and Kelsey stayed put.

I opened the door and called out, "Hey, Bert."

Bert turned and came my way. We did our boy-howdies in the street before drifting to the sidewalk. Just beyond was a closed gas station where a number of street people were congregated under its porch.

I found out that Bert was waiting for a ride, as he had just been in to see the Sheriff.

He rattled on. "Did you hear what happened to Mary Brighton?"

I shook my head.

"Mary took in one of these street people." He thumbed toward that group in a sour way. "And it ended with the gal robbing her blind."

"Is Mary all right?" I looked over those street people. One stood out. He was as big as a lumberjack and, if a downcast face added to honesty, he possessed both.

Bert nodded. "You got to watch 'em. It's crazy. They're flooding into the valley." He pitched his chin toward some fresh graffiti that was sprayed on a building.

It read I'm Dead … You're Dead.

"That's rude. When was the last time you ever saw graffiti in our town?" Again he thumbed toward the group of street people. "Them people shouldn't be here."

Now I looked on the lumberjack with suspicion.

"Did you hear about that epidemic?"

"There's been word of it on the Meshnet."

Bert woefully continued, "They say it's knocking off near 50 percent, and near 100 percent of the aged and the fats." He turned and warily eyed the street people. "It'd be good if somebody would blow up the passes." Frowning, he glanced across the street at the Sheriff's office. "The Sheriff should do this valley a service by running these people right out, then blow up the passes."

It was strange to hear Bert talk like this, as he was generally optimistic. It was also odd to see him unshaven, his face not so clean-cut, not so handsome.

"Did you know the U.S. has got the patient on that plague virus?"

I shook my head, not wanting to believe our own government was behind it.

"They GMO'd it. They let it loose in Africa as a population control. Now look out." His eyes found me. "Someone said colloidal silver will fight it. You got any?"

"No." I lied.

"I know people who'll pay big bucks."

I shook my head.

"Anyway, you got any fuel you want to sell?"

"No."

"Come on, I know you've got those big tanks."

"They're all empty."

"You've heard the new emergency mandate?"

I shook my head.

"No hoarding. And big fines if you're caught, confiscation of everything … prison."

His statement disturbed me. "So the government can legally steal everything?"

"Pretty much. They're as desperate as the rest of us." His grin was cheerless.

I mumbled some words that don't need repeating.

"Did you hear what's behind the volcanoes?"

"No."

"They say some subs fired ballistic missiles at every one of our volcanoes along the West Coast."

I shook my head in dismay.

"That's what set off all them earthquakes."

"Whose subs?"

"They are either Chinese or Russians. But think about it, by hitting the West Coast volcanoes, they are indirectly saying, 'If the US keeps shooting their hot stuff at them, then they're going to put the next one down Old Faithful."

"We are smoked if they hit Yellowstone."

He gave me a nudge. "What's going on up in your neck of the woods that you need to hog all that fuel?"

I must've looked distant as I considered telling him about Jerold. "We have a lot of people there."

"At your place?"

"Yes."

"How many?"

"Over forty."

"That's a handful." He leaned away, giving me a doubtful look. "You haven't been picking up these street people?"

"No."

"Well, if it's going that good, you should sell me some fuel."

"I didn't say it was going good ... We were attacked."

"What?" He frowned. In the meantime his ride appeared, pulling to the curb beside us. "Anyone hurt? Is everybody okay?"

"Jerold ..." I teared.

"Is he okay?"

I shook my head.

What?" He looked stunned. "I'm sorry, Hershal. Are you okay?"

Jerold died a bit more when I shook my head.

Somewhere in this, his ride honked, then shot out a line of swear words about the scarcity of gasoline, finishing his rant with, "Are you going to stay there all day or what?" His words were barely out of his mouth when the earth shook.

I braced myself and stared at Bert.

Swaying, his hand came up to his heart. "Gosh ... The way it's happening will make a believer out of you."

I gave him a sad nod. A half-minute passed before the shaking receded.

"Hersh ..." Bert folded into me with a hug. "... I'm sorry about Jerold." It was different being held by him.

We said our goodbyes and as I watched the car drive away, I felt like such a failure. My lapse on security stuck in my throat.

I headed toward the boys, who were still talking to the Hispanic kid. To my left, the well-framed fellow I'd noticed earlier came toward me; his plaid shirt and suspenders spoke of a lumberjack. Fearing I'd be begged upon, I halted, as I could see our paths would cross. This didn't stop him.

Nearing, he brushed volcanic ash off his arm. "Do you have anything I can help you with?"

I tried not to stare, but his presence was quite powerful. "What can you do?"

"I'm good with wood. I've been in the lumber industry most of my life. I can prune as well as drop trees, chop firewood, anything like that ... I can do whatever you need, and I'm not too proud to clean toilets."

I liked his manly voice; actually, he had possibilities. "What about security?"

"I'm a good shot. I've hunted since I was a kid. And I don't mind the night shift. What do you got?"

"It's pretty much a communal situation, with six ten-hour days. I'm in charge. You get two-and-a-half squares and a roof over your head. You have any weapons?"

"Yes."

"Much ammo?"

"Over a thousand rounds."

Up to this point this man was well-suited for the task. Even still, we had been fooled by Vicki and Alex. If this was truly a five-year deal, I could ill afford to make the wrong choice. How does one get rid of a person if they don't work out?

It's too bad I couldn't take him to a scanning machine that would scan his mind and see what was really inside; who's to say he wasn't a murderer? I tentatively looked over his powerful arms and asked, "What are you looking for?"

"I don't mind working twelve-hour days. I like to work." He looked thoughtful. "Generally, I charge a couple hundred a day, but in this situation, I'll give you a break, say, $100 a day. But it has to be in cash."

"Heh!" I exclaimed, astonished that this man would be asking for money when our group would look after him. His value dropped to dirt. My eyes seared him. I would've liked to shout, "How about you paying me $200. a day to look after your sorry hide?" But I didn't have to; he heard my reaction and was backing away.

This was wild. Was I supposed to supply his food, shelter and protection, and pay him? And here my son gave his life in protecting others. This whole thing was crazy—and to think I got into this for the money!

The only thing that made sense was Priscilla's request to supply the Sherriff's Department with food. Reminded of it, I went back to the truck to retrieve the bag of rice and beans then proceeded to their office. Holding those commodities, walking along the sidewalk, I was quite conscious of the stares of the street people, even from across the street.

Someone called out, "Hey, you got any more of that?"

I felt like I was carrying something quite precious when I made it inside the Sherriff's office. To the right was his office, its door closed, to the left a counter and behind it stood a secretary. She smiled when she saw what I was carrying. I headed for her and rested my load on the counter, shoving it to her.

"This is for your department."

"There is a God." She looked cheerful, half looking back at Deputy Justin whose chair slid back as he rose from his desk.

"Hershal." He gave me a friendly nod.

"Deputy." I held eye contact with him, feeling like I had to stand up to the skills of this investigator who had haunted me over Wartal. I thumbed back toward the Sherrif's office. "Please say hello to Sheriff Dave for me."

"Will do . . . and thank you."

I headed for the door, half turning back, "Thank you for all you do." When I got out of there I thought it strange to be feeding the team that had been on my trail. Regardless, these were strange times.

Back at the truck, I saw Micah approaching, his disappointment obvious, his arm angled toward the Hispanic kid. "He's waiting for his mom to come back. She told him to wait there."

Jordan trotted up behind Micah, thumbing back to the street corner. "He's been waiting there for three days."

While I weighed Jordan's statement, I glanced again at the retreating man; we'll see how he fares when his belly starts aching.

Worry was written all over Jordan's face. "Do you think his mom will ever come back?"

"I've no idea," I said, my eyes returning to the Hispanic kid faithfully waiting on the corner. "Why don't you give him an apple?"

The boys were quick to grab some apples from the back of the truck and ran toward him.

I headed for the diesel, having no idea how that one act would trigger the next. In no time, one of these street people was coming my way. Seeing her out of the corner of my eye, I swiftly rounded the front of the truck, did a fast shuffle into the protection of my cab, and shut the door. But that didn't stop her. Neither did the rang-bang of the diesel starting.

She came right up to the window and loudly asked, "Do you have any food? I've got kids." There was desperation in her voice.

Eli was ahead of the situation. He had opened the window between the cab and camper shell, grabbed some apples and handed them to me. I passed them on to her.

Her eyes pierced mine. "If you need anything, and I mean anything, I can do it for you."

I knew she meant business, because she causally dropped her shawl down her shoulder, and it was cold out. I sadly nodded and wondered what this world had come to. Eli handed me another apple. I gave it to her.

She couldn't thank me enough. I didn't know how to deal with this woman so I drove forward, leaving her standing there. Thankfully, the boys got the hint and dashed back to the truck.

Micah had barely opened the door before calling out, "Can we take him with us?"

"Get in."

"I don't think his mom will come back."

"Get in."

Micah whined, "He's going to die waiting for her."

Before he was in, I powered the diesel forward, as there were other women coming my way. Eli pulled Micah in and shut the door. With an eye on the Hispanic kid, I drove in his direction. "Where does he go at night?"

Micah pointed to the corner. "He just waits there, on the corner. That's where his mom told him to wait."

Jordan pleaded, "Can we take him home with us?"

"You don't just take kids home."

As we passed him, Jordan and Micah waved. The kid was eating an apple with one hand and waving with the other.

"Some folks call that kidnapping."

Micah replied, "I call it saving his life."

As the truck drove on, both Micah and Jordan were looking back at him. Jordan moaned, "Maybe his mom's not coming."

No doubt this kid's plight was distressing, as fall was upon us and getting cold. I figured, on our way back through Charby I'd have a talk with him.

\* \* \*

I dropped off Eli, Nancy and Kelsey at the sheep ranch before motoring on to Bolo.

Volcanic ash drifted off the tall pines as I turned into the Bolo Square Dance Center and Campground. Its beautiful park-like setting was lost in the dull gray covering. I ended up taking one couple from Arizona, and a single man from Texas. He was hauling a fifth wheel; the others were in a mobile home. Both units were newer models and spoke of affluence, but I wasn't that excited about the people, mainly because of their age. I could've taken a bunch, but we could ill afford additional older folks. I sure hoped this wasn't going to be a five-year affair. Who's to say they'd last that long? Furthermore, how would they do night watch when winter hit? We really needed younger, stronger, more enduring folks.

On our way back to Charby, I considered the plight of the Hispanic kid and that same "Count your Blessings" song came up in my head. And again, that same foul mood rose against that song, and blame for Jerold's death.

A block before the Hispanic kid, Jordan's arm came straight over the back of my seat. "There he is!" he exclaimed, right in my ear.

I rubbed my ear. "You need to turn your volume down."

"You can pull over, up there," Micah instructed.

"I don't need to be told how to drive," I snapped, frustrated over hearing everybody's two cents on everything. Annoyed, I didn't park where Micah suggested, but fifty feet beyond the kid.

I had previously told the Bolo group that I might pull in at Charby on our way home, so the caravan did the same, pulling in behind us.

Jordan had his door open before I had mine open.

"You boys wait in the truck."

"Can't we go with you?"

"Wait here." I snagged a red construction crayon before stepping out.

"Just tell him to come with us. He'll come, I know he'll come."

"Get back in there, will you?"

Finally, Jordan obliged.

As I came around the front of the truck, I noticed one of the street people correcting her little girl with a hard slap across her cheek. The girl put her hand to her dirty face but didn't have the energy to cry.

Her mother scowled and pointed toward the wall. "Now get over there and sit down!"

It was sad to see this girl start to whimper as she walked away. Not far from her, the lumberjack sat on the concrete, leaning against a building, looking not so big and strong. I headed for the Hispanic kid on the corner.

Sometimes in life I run across the most interesting views; generally, I see them in the wild, but this one came from down the sidewalk. Out of the misting ash, like a vaporous silhouette, this 60ish-looking gal appeared in a flowery spring dress. She moved ever so cautiously, still trying to find a lady's step in heels and this classy, classy dress.

I angled my head to see if my vision was true. This peculiar bird looked as if she'd flown up from, who knows where, Miami? Certainly the white fabric, designed with long parrot-green stems bouqueting into tropical flowers, spoke of better weather. I concluded she had no business in that light dress and, as fragile as she appeared, it could be her burial gown.

After hearing what had happened to Mary Brighton, I had to harden myself to these street people. But she was such an oddity, I questioned, "How's it going?"

She halted, and swayed so much, I thought she would tumble. My hand shot out to stop her from falling. She grasped it and held my thumb, looking as if she wanted to say something, then just gave a nod. Human touch holds a strange mystery.

"Have you been in town long?" I asked.

She appeared confused, and though she was holding my thumb, she still swayed. "I don't know." Her lips and mouth were dry, her voice raspy as a bar room. "Do you know the date?"

"I'm not sure. Do you have relatives here?"

She shook her head. "No, I just …" Her voice dropped off. A small breeze swept strands of her hair toward me. I could smell her; it wasn't good. "No." She seemed conscious of how she looked, and weakly drew back her dyed reddish hair. I imagined a stronger breeze would've blown her over. "I just …" She half-looked behind her for something.

Concerned that she would fall, my other hand cupped her elbow.

Micah came from behind me. "Do you want me to take you to him?"

I suppressed my impatience by directing him, "Can you take this lady to the truck and give her an apple?" I offered her hand to him while catching her eye. "Do you not have a coat?"

"Today I was going to see my mother."

"Where's she live?"

Again she looked thoughtful.

"Maybe I can drive you there. What's your name?"

"Alice."

"I'm Hershal, and this is Micah."

Chomping at the bit, Micah thumbed toward his buddy on the corner. "He's right there." He took her elbow. Glancing back at me, Micah guided her toward the truck like one would guide their feeble grandmother.

I could see why the boys liked the Hispanic kid. He was a fine representation of his bloodline: black eyes, black hair and nicely roasted-coffee-color skin. But he looked so tired. My heart went out to him.

"I hear you're waiting for your mom?"

"She told me to wait here." He looked confused, then glanced beyond me, checking a passing vehicle, studying it. The car passed before his attention returned to me. "She going to come."

"My name is Hershal; what's yours?"

"Maximo."

"I've got two kids who are chomping at the bit to take you home, if you like."

"I don't know what my mom will do if I'm not here."

"I don't know, either." I put my hand out, feeling the cool air. "Can you feel winter coming?"

"It's getting cold."

"I don't think your mom wants you out here, with winter coming."

"But how will I find her?"

"I can write your name on the concrete and my name and phone number. And when we come back through, we can see if she's around. Do you want to do that?"

He paused to think, "Can you put it here?" He pointed to a spot on the concrete. "She told me to wait here."

I ended up clearing the volcanic ash off the spot and writing—Maximo—Hershal Beecher—Charby—and my phone number. I wondered how long it would take for ash to cover it.

When Maximo grabbed his pack, Jordan excitedly came our way, exclaiming, "You can sit in the back with us," then relieved Maximo of his backpack.

Ahead, I gasped at the sight of the entire group of street people, who were at the back of our truck, getting apples from

Micah. He was straddling the tailgate, handing apples out like there was no tomorrow. Gordy had gotten out, as he'd wanted to do something about this, but looked unsure. Even the lumberjack wasn't too proud to get an apple.

I called out, "Let's go, Micah." Pacing forward, I realized the parrot lady was near the back of the truck, eating an apple. I hurriedly addressed her. "You said you were going to visit your mom? So where's she live?"

She took a long look down the street, then flicked her finger a few times in that direction.

Again I called out, "Let's go, Micah," and then looked at the parrot lady, "Do you want a ride?"

"Sure … sure." She nodded and offered her free hand. I took it and guided her toward the back door of the cab.

It was then I noticed Jordan was not just leading Maximo toward the other side of the truck, but also a little girl. I'd no idea where she'd come from, but her coloring and the fact that she was holding Maximo's hand, said that she was his little sister. She was such a little novelty, wavy dark hair, a dirty Cinderella t-shirt, that it was hard to pull my focus off her and back to Micah.

"Let's go, Micah." I was conscious of our dwindling apple catch, and called with urgency, "Let's go!"

The challenge in getting this parrot into the high cab was that she wouldn't let go of her apple. In the midst of this, I kept calling back, "Let's go, Micah."

In the back seat, Jordan hurriedly reached across his two guests, grabbed onto the parrot lady and struggled to pull her.

Seeing how rough his boyish enthusiasm was, I chided, "That's enough, Jordan."

I was so frustrated with Micah giving the world away, I determined to take off, even with him straddling the tailgate.

I paced around the front of the truck and wasted no time in hopping into the cab and firing up the diesel.

One of the street people, a short-haired, equally determined gal, came toward Gordy's window and barked, "It's illegal to hoard!" I think she thought us daft because she aggressively said, "If you leave, I'll get the Sheriff after you!" She pointed at the back of the truck. "Those are the community's property ... the community's!"

Seeing Micah in the rearview mirror, stepping down from the tailgate, I powered the truck forward. It didn't matter to me that he wasn't in the cab. I was mad at him.

This circus expanded, as Micah ended up running down the street to catch us. I let him run.

With his hand raised, he yelled, "Wait for me! ... Wait for me!"

I hated to think what the folks who we'd picked up from the Bolo Dance Center were wondering when they viewed Micah chasing after the truck. Who knows, maybe they thought I was taking them to a cannibal's lair.

I drove a bit farther before pulling over.

When Micah got in, I addressed the parrot lady. "Alice, where's your mom live?"

Looking perplexed, she took the apple out of her mouth. "Mom? Why she's dead and gone."

As I weighed the situation, my eyes met Gordy's. "Where do you want to go, then?"

"Today I was going to go see her."

Micah had barely caught his breath. "You can come with us."

I gave him a hard eye.

She asked, "Where're you going?"

Micah didn't get my look at all and answered, "Up to the house."

A long, labored pause ensued, then her raspy voice said, "Okay."

I drove on, ticked off at myself for picking up this gal. Looking in the rearview mirror, I saw the mobile home and fifth wheel trailing.

Just out of town, I glanced back at her," How'd you end up in Montana, Alice?"

She looked up from the apple. "I don't know."

"What did you do for a living?"

"I'm a blues singer ... traveled the world."

I took her news with a grain of salt as I was feeling like I was the butt of a con.

Gordy had turned toward the kids. "What's your name, little girl?"

She didn't respond.

Gordy extended his hand toward Maximo. "What's your name?"

"Maximo."

"What's your sister's name?"

"Rosita."

*   *   *

God only knows how I ended up with this menagerie of characters; perhaps it was His sense of humor. This only got more bizarre when we motored up the hill. Alice must've seen something she didn't like, perhaps the house rising above the butte or the windmill rising even higher, because she worriedly pointed, "I've been here ..." then gasped, "... take me back!" She wailed like a frightened child. "Take me back!"

I eyed Gordy; it was wild. How did we end up with this blues singer instead of that lumberjack? Still, her comment allowed an out, and I was content to take her back, as she was breathing heavily, obviously frightened. The kids were jammed into each other on the opposite side of the cab, looking across at her as if she were plagued.

"As soon as we get those other two rigs parked, I'll take you back; no problem."

The truck came around the windmill.

Her heavy breathing turned into a mournful raspy sound that was so woeful, I was sure she was going to be the next funeral. I parked, honked and looked back at her. "Not a problem. I'll take you back."

Before I opened my door, Micah sprang out, turned to Alice and exclaimed, "You're going to like Priscilla," then bolted for the house.

"Micah!" I called, wanting to catch him.

But he was too light-footed, bounding up the steps, hollering, "Priscilla!"

Sometimes I wanted to pound that kid.

I knew that if Priscilla was up and rolling, she'd capture that blues singer, so I hastened up the driveway, waving the Texas rig into the parking area.

"Priscilla!" Micah disappeared into the house.

The wind and ash swept around, curtailing anything other than my instructions to the man from Texas. His fifth wheel pulled to the spot where I was pointing. Looking toward the entrance, I saw Jordan taking Maximo and Rosita up the stairs. I waved the Arizona rig in, as I wanted to get underway. But this Arizona man was a poke at moving his rig around.

I gave up on him and paced toward my truck. Halfway there, I noticed movement up near the porch. It was Micah and Priscilla. He held her hand as they came down the steps. I knew right then, we were stuck with the mixed-up parrot lady.

# Military Time

Sergio, the man from Texas, had hardly parked his fifth wheel before he was at the business of surveying the property, looking over the west hill; next, I saw him by the main water catch, looking down toward the gate, studying the east hill.

I desired to give Micah what-for and reprimand him over all his charity, but I ended up talking to Sergio about our water situation. He had a small bulldog that Sparky was sniffing and growling with, telling him who was boss, but the bulldog wasn't buying. It was a good thing Sergio held Bullet on a short leash.

"I'd like to give you a hose and an electrical hookup, but we are down to bucket runs to a spring." I pointed. "It's over half-mile that way."

His eyes covered the area like a hawk. "What plans have you made for security?"

A rush of guilt covered me. "That's one area I've been pretty slack on."

"You've got a great overview. It's quite commanding." He confidently stepped forward, pointing to our east hill. "Do you own that?"

I nodded.

"Those two hills make that entrance point defendable, that's for sure." He moved about like a dog on point. "Impressive." He must've been an intense character in his time.

"If you have any thoughts on security, I certainly welcome them." I thumbed toward the second story, where bullets had pierced windows and stucco. "Yesterday we were attacked."

"Any hurt?"

"My son is no longer with us."

"I'm soooo sorry." He looked as if he really meant it, and touched my elbow.

I wished he hadn't done that; my emotions flowed during those days after Jerold's demise. I bent down to pet Sparky. "No doubt we can use some help on security."

"I'll draw up a plan. But I warn you, the only way it will be successful is for your people to change. They'll have to have a military mindset."

I arose, and took a few steps away from him, as I didn't know how to deal with those darn emotions. "What was your trade, what did you do before you retired?"

"Retired Marine, retired auto store manager."

He was a block of a man that looked Marine, and for that matter, so did his bulldog.

"Good, good. I'm glad you're here."

The Arizona couple was interesting as well; Gloria was a retired nurse who wanted to help at whatever she could; her husband Ernie was a retired insurance salesman and square dance caller. I knew her nursing skills would be invaluable to our group, but I wasn't sure if we could use his skills at all. Still, he wasn't shy about helping out.

\*    \*    \*

I would've liked to have an afternoon nap, but with the buzz of humanity, it was difficult to find any privacy. Their needs were taxing. Priscilla had set Alice up in the purple room on the floor between two beds.

I was coming out of my bedroom when I noticed Alice standing next to the door of the purple room, staring directly at the door, moving it back and forth.

As I passed by, she said, "This door squeaks."

I stopped to listen, and there was the faintest of squeaks coming from it. "Sure enough."

She didn't say, You should oil it, but it was implied.

I walked away, assuming she was used to higher-end places.

I went on to the green bedroom to shut a window because the wind started to blow and I had to dodge around a bunch of bedding and clothes just to get to the glass. After shutting the window, I took a long look at the fifth wheel and motor home. I was tired, and envied the Texas and Arizona folk, as they had a private place to sleep undisturbed.

*   *   *

Every morning I awoke, I was mindful of my daughter Bethany and her safety. Here she was in a state that had no power, no running water, had no end of earthquakes, with millions of people. Who's to say they weren't all a bunch of cannibals now?

She was going to have to use that gun. She needed to have lots of ammo. She needed to get out here. Maybe she was already gone. I wished I could block out my dark thoughts, but they were as present as the drifting volcanic ash.

That day, the ladies made a number of apple pies. Their sweet cinnamon smell drew me momentarily out of the doldrums. In those days, when I got a moment to stick a fork into a good time, I tried to enjoy it to the fullest. But with Jerold's death still raw, it was challenging.

In the midst of sipping on my watered-down coffee, and drawing that warm pie toward my mouth, in came Micah. "I don't know if you know it, but somebody went potty right on the trail," his arm pointed, "just above the gate."

Why he had to tell me that while I was trying to enjoy a bite of apple pie was perplexing. I will say that this head honcho thing is not for the faint-hearted, as there was no end of complaints. Maybe they thought I was their dumping ground. I really wanted my house back. I knew this was self-centered, it might've been different if Jerold was around, but I wanted to kick everybody out, then crawl into bed and lick my wounds.

Later that night while lying in bed, I grumbled about this to Priscilla.

She quietly said, "God has brought these fine people here for His purpose. We're not here for ourselves, we're not here for a popularity contest, we're here to look after them."

"I told you before and I'll say it again, I'm in this for the money, and if and when it goes past forty days, then we are going to have to do a business meeting with each and every one of these folks to find out how they are going to pay us back for all the good grub and hospitality they've been getting."

She moaned, "Oh, honey, can't we let Jesus pay us back?" She asked this in the most simplistic manner. "He can give us good health, bless us, protect us …"

Rising anger caught me and I cut her off, "Oh, like He did with Jerold? … Sometimes I wonder if you married the wrong man."

She touched my hand. "Certainly not; you are the one."

"With Bethany and Jerold gone, it shows that God doesn't find me favorable."

"Don't say that, Hershal. He loves you dearly, and He's looking after Bethany. He has her under His wing."

\* \* \*

The morning after Sergio showed up, he presented a security map and plan to me.

As I reviewed it, he said, "What you really need is someone in charge of security."

"What do you think about being that someone?" I don't know if I was looped into the question, but it was the beginning of his mission. He latched onto the task like a general, posting times and places for guard duty. It didn't matter how old someone was, if they had eyes, they were conscripted.

That night was the first time we had all-night security. This was done in three-hour shifts and was challenging, as the temperatures had just started freezing. I was surprised to see some of Priscilla's secondhand winter boots paying off. With the cold, I was quite conscious of Bethany's situation. If she was traveling toward us, coming through the mountains, would she be warm enough?

*     *     *

The next morning my eyes were barely open, when I thought of Bethany again, and my fatalistic worries started anew. Oh, how I wished she'd just show up on our doorstep, but that is not where my dark thoughts went. Surely she had perished. To stay sane, I got busy building outhouses.

That day, Sergio worked with all who needed to learn gun safety.

By afternoon they were shooting at targets in the field. I took a break from my outhouse building to see how Sergio was coming along. Though his safety training was serious business, some of it was entertaining, especially with Julie's moan after she shot the AR. The gun recoiled in a blast, and a shell ejected, flying by.

"Ohhhh." Her eyes had a pleading look, as if someone had just slugged her.

"Shoot again," commanded Sergio, half-looking back at the different gals who were next.

Kablam. "Ohhhh," Julie moaned, blinking from the shock.

"Shoot again," commanded Sergio, sure as a clock.

Julie warily looked down the sights. Kablam. "Ohhhhhh!" she moaned, her face filled with dread. Though she was in her 60s, she had a younger face that really showed the stress of the moment.

I noticed the next gal nervously scratching her neck, not looking forward to her turn.

Priscilla's eyes met mine. She quietly said, "It's a little hard."

*    *    *

Gloria, Ernie's wife, mentioned that we should have a schedule for chores and volunteered to draw one up. Priscilla agreed. That retired nurse reminded me of Sergio, as she really took to the task, getting together with a number of other ladies. This happened rather quickly.

It's ironic, previously I had looked at the two couples from the Bolo Dance Center as too old, real liabilities; but what did I know? They turned out to be real gems.

Alice, the gal I picked up from Charby the day we got Maximo and Rosita, was the only one I wished I hadn't stumbled upon. I never heard her volunteer for anything, and if something wasn't up to her standards, she wasn't shy about letting someone know. If she poured the last of our watered-down coffee into her cup, she'd lift the coffeepot and look at whoever was closest, saying, "We're out of coffee," implying that they should make some.

What I found comical was my brother Freddy's attraction toward her. Not long after she got her legs back, I came in for supper and saw his shoes under the table, tapping hers. She sat across from him and this could've easily gone unnoticed, as there wasn't an empty spot at the table. Furthermore, Freddy's girlfriend was sitting right next to him.

Seeing this, I curved in to throw a log on the fire and, bending down, I stole a glance at their shoes. Alice didn't look as if she minded playing footsie with another woman's man. Though dismayed at Freddy, I had to grin, I don't know why, but I had to grin. He was such a smoothie, carrying on a conversation with both her and Ellen, happily grinning away and playing footsie with Alice.

\*    \*    \*

Little by little, our group came under a military mindset, a regimented way; if you weren't sure where you were going, just look at the schedule. It told everyone when they were to haul water, do bathroom patrol, guard duty, honey pot hauling, kitchen duties, cleaning, dig out lookouts, bring in firewood, etc.

I thought the schedule would knock the wind out of complaining, but not so with Freddy. He openly voiced his anger about putting so many on round-the-clock surveillance when one person could watch the main road, which was easily visible three-quarters of a mile away. It was pointless to argue with him over it. The only job he liked was running interference at the gate. We called that job the talker's post, as one had to convince any incoming beggars that we needed food more than they did. If the schedule wasn't set up to accommodate him, Freddy would try to exchange his shift to get that job.

There were a few people who were just naturals at the talker's post. Mitch and his son Jerome were probably the best we had. They were Easterners who owned a fish market and had persuasive voices. I think they actually believed what they were saying. Anyone coming up the road looking for handouts who thought they had a poor-me story had another thing coming when they ran across those two. But this talker's post was what Freddy liked. I didn't think much of it, even when a fellow who I didn't know asked for my brother to come and talk to him at the gate.

*     *     *

Sergio put us on military time, and I should've been happy with the way things were shaping up, as Priscilla and I had less and less responsibilities with Sergio and Gloria in charge. But deep down I couldn't shake the doldrums over the loss of Jerold, and every passing day I became more certain of Bethany's fate. I tried to fight against this by staying busy, by telling myself that she had a gun, but I couldn't shake it. Sometimes when I looked at Raela, I wondered if she was next. This was quite threatening, as she was always weepy, mourning over Jerold, and didn't have the strongest heart. This constant worry raised my blood pressure.

# Murderers

I could've drowned in despondency, but more often than not, life proves that someone is worse off. Our neighbor Al, the animal man, came to tell us what had happened to another neighbor, Patty. But when he started to speak, he became so emotional, so teary and choked-up that all he squeaked out was, "Patty's dead."

A number of us men piled into the diesel and ended up at Patty's. Her house, nothing fancy, just a quaint two-story affair, sat on twenty acres on the outskirts of our subdivision.

Before entering her place, I saw my neighbors, Ernie, Toby and Lynn, all with bandanas around their faces, digging into a spot at the back of her house. I assumed they were digging her grave.

Toby loudly called out, "I wouldn't go in there if I were you."

Despite his warning we headed for the house. I followed Sergio through the entrance to the kitchen. Right off, I smelled death. All the cabinet doors were open and ransacked; I doubted there was a bottle of spice that remained. Passing through Patty's kitchen, the sound of our boots echoed over the wood floor. The living room carpet helped mute our noise. I found myself peering around Sergio. Ahead, to the side of the stairs, lay the corpse covered in a sheet. To the right were her plants, cactus mostly. To her left lay a crumpled pile of clothes. I noticed a torn blouse.

It was then I realized I didn't want to witness any more, but there were others behind me and like it or not, I was going to view this dead widowed nurse.

The way Sergio bent on one knee, placed his fingers on the sheet and half-looked back at us told me this wasn't his first time examining a dead person. Mark, Gordy, Carl and Freddy were present as Sergio drew back the sheet.

There was a gasp. With a curse, Freddy bolted.

I stepped back; I should've heeded Toby's warning.

Poor Patty's naked body had been tortured. Some freak, or freaks, had used her cactus. The gruesome intrusions upon her feet, legs, torso and face proved there were maniacs on the loose. I thought, if the same madmen were torturing me, looking for my treasure, they would've gotten that information long before they came up my leg. The grayish/reddish carpet underneath Patty had done its best to soak up her blood.

\*    \*    \*

This brutal scene sent such fear into the neighbors that a meeting was called that afternoon. It was as if our subdivision had been raided by savages. We gathered in the usual spot where we had our road maintenance meetings, down where our two roads intersect.

Twenty-four people showed up, everyone in our subdivision except for the Wartals, who never showed up for anything. I sensed a real anxiousness, with people pacing out their nervousness. In previous years, we'd been able to come up with an equitable solution as far as looking after the gravel road, so I was confident we'd come up with a Neighborhood Watch or something.

Because of the drifting ash, we were all wearing hats, bandanas, scarves or face masks, looking very much like a group of train robbers.

Ernie, our young neighbor, his wife, and their three little kids were present. Generally, he's pretty quiet, but he was the one who lowered his bandana and started, "After seeing what they did to Patty, I am appalled that such," he paused as he searched for the right word, "animals exist around here." He looked toward her house. "They got in and out of there without anyone noticing." He flicked a finger toward the Wartals' house. "Patty's place does border the Wartals'."

"Those guys are in and out of prison all the time."

"I thought I saw a moving truck in there this summer."

"Well, that's why we're here," Sergio said, rather calmly, "to come up with some boundaries ... security."

Toby, his wife and their two kids were there. He was a wiry fellow in his thirties and both of them hunted. "Speaking of boundaries, whose truck is this?" He pointed at a newer 4 x 4 diesel, Dodge, the only vehicle sitting on the side of the road, thirty feet or so from us.

"I saw it here this morning."

"Is it from your group, Hershal?"

"No."

"I would've said something earlier, but I thought it was one of your group."

"This is not right." Toby frowned. "Here we don't even know whose truck this is."

"It's probably a poacher."

"He's got no business parking here. Not in our subdivision," Lynn adamantly said.

"That's an understatement." From Toby's aggression, I thought he was going to use his handgun on that truck. He searched our faces while pulling out a knife and folded the blade open. "Nobody owns it?" He inquisitively glanced about. "Why don't we drop our face coverings and see who's here?"

We all obliged, pulling down our face coverings. I noticed everybody looking about, studying each other's faces.

"I bet it's some poacher trying to get to that state land back there." Lynn pointed up the ridge.

Toby strode toward the truck's front tire. "After Patty and that shootout up at Hershal's ..." he shook his head in dismay, "... nobody's got any business here."

"We should adopt a shoot-first policy."

Feeding off this, Toby raised his knife to the sidewall of the truck's tire. "Going once, going twice ..." He glanced back at us, then pointed at a gal I'd never seen.

"It's not mine," she exclaimed.

"Stick it!"

Toby stabbed the tire. Air whooshed out. His brash action surprised me, especially right out in the open, with so many witnesses. What's more, it appeared everybody was in agreement with it.

Toby pointed at the unfamiliar woman and candidly said, "I haven't seen you before."

This middle-aged gal reminded me of a chipmunk when she blurted out, "This is my dad." She grabbed Dewey's arm. "I came down from Bolo because of gangs from Missoula." She gave a nervous nod. "They were attacking houses at night."

"Anybody doing anything about it?" another woman asked.

"Not at night. You'd hear shots, but nobody was doing anything."

Lynn sarcastically frowned. "As long as it happens to the other guy."

The gal continued talking about ransacking and killings and a house outside of Bolo that the government took over.

"That's our government for you." There was venom in this retired farmer. "You don't know who's good or bad anymore."

Our neighbor, a postal worker, looked at him with concern. "I haven't had any trouble with the government."

This gabby Bolo woman jerked a long finger at my house. "I think they'd like a place like that, because it offers a good overview."

Al, the animal guy, broke in, "After seeing Patty, I'm having a tough time sleeping."

Sergio replied, "We've no trouble sleeping."

"Don't you worry about this stuff?"

Sergio stated, "We've twenty-four/seven guard duty."

Ernie's wife gave me a hopeful eye. "Hershal, I heard Elaine's moving over to your place. Do you need any more people?"

I found it surprising how fast this news of Elaine had traveled, as it was just yesterday that Priscilla and I talked to Elaine about her predicament. Tongue-tied, I didn't answer.

Sergio looked at me. "It's possible, depending on your work ethic in our communal situation. We expect six days a week, ten hours a day, shifts on chores and guard duties." His grin sported a challenge. "With that, you get twenty-four-hour security, two-and-a-half squares a day and a roof over your head." He raised an instructive finger. "In addition, I imagine Hershal and Priscilla have to be compensated for looking after your sorry hides."

"The king's portion," Bob, a new neighbor, said in a condescending manner.

Sergio gave him a hard eye. "It's not for everybody."

"I was just joking," Bob said.

Sergio shrugged. "Our setup is not for everyone."

"It was just a joke."

Ignoring Bob, Sergio turned away from him while writing something on a sheet of paper.

"Hershal?" Al spoke with urgency. "Do you have room for my family?"

I felt the eyes of everyone looking at me. Though I didn't care for how disordered Al's place was with all his animals, I was on the spot.

"How many?" With pen in hand, Sergio looked my way.

"There's five of us."

I gave Sergio a small nod. It would be too cruel to reject Al.

"We just have room for you." Sergio's comment drove the rest to press in.

"We'd like to come in, too," said another neighbor.

"Can I come, Hershal?" Bob asked.

I sensed his desperation, everyone's desperation.

"We can only take so many." I pointed to Sergio. "He's the man."

They pressed around Sergio as if he was selling the last tickets out of Siberia.

He raised an instructive, commanding finger. "There's one other caveat, and that is church on Sunday. If you don't make church, you don't eat." Sergio was a believing man, as bad as Priscilla and forthright about it.

I stepped back, bent down and petted Sparky. With this drifting ash, I wished he'd stay home, but he always got out. Glancing up at the group, I was taken aback at how Patty's hideous murder had galvanized our neighborhood.

I didn't know much about one retired couple, as they kept to themselves. After the meeting, they made it clear to Sergio that they would rather just stay in their own place and ward off the bad boys with their own shooting abilities. He was a military contractor and had two sons in their 30s. He asked, "Why don't you just let us borrow some food and we'll protect this sector?"

Sergio wasn't about to part with a breadcrumb unless they did their ten hours. His response was, "It's not for everybody."

I suppose they must've had enough food, as they didn't press the point.

Before arriving at our meeting, I had had a brief conversation with Sergio about the possibility of other neighbors joining us. I had no idea how many would be interested and reasoned that, even if we went over the seventy, it wouldn't be long before the grid returned, and everything back to normal.

Bob called out, "Hershal?" and came toward me, "Hershal?"

Sergio quietly said, "Don't you dare take this guy in." His gritty eyes made his point. "He's a taker."

Lynn's voice interrupted. "Here comes the truck guys." He looked up the hill. Two men appeared from a jagged rock area, both sporting rifles. Coming down the high ground, they looked quite intimidating. "Looks like the meeting's really over."

With the Dodge angled sideways, its tire flat, everybody except Bob and Toby headed for their houses. Strange, minutes earlier we were all in agreement over Toby's brazen action, but with consequences coming toward us, retreat was now just as brazen.

"Hershal?" Bob called.

I glanced back to see Bob and Toby standing by the truck.

"Just leave him," Sergio said with disdain. He looked back and called out to Toby, "No time for macho, my friend. You'd be better suited with a long rifle. That's what we need now."

I was relieved Toby took his advice, taking off after his wife and kids, who were heading up the road.

"Hershal?" Bob asked, pleadingly.

Sergio pressed me forward. "Let's go."

With Sparky at my side, I walked quickly, trying to keep up with Sergio. Though he was in his late 60s, he strode as if he'd carried a backpack in years past over no end of mountains.

We weren't fifty yards from the truck when I heard swearing, coming from its owner. "… Who killed my tire?"

Sergio's pace quickened. I wasn't about to turn back.

There was more swearing from the truck's owner, "… Kill my tire, will you!"

The shot from his rifle made me jump.

The swearing intensified, "… Get back here and fix this!"

Trembling, I hurried along.

Sergio glanced my way. "If we make it to that corner," his eyes went to the bend in the road, "you go up the hill and see if you can get Carl."

"Okay."

"Get him situated in the cover of those rocks." He sent a quick instructive look up to an outcrop of rocks that had a commanding overview.

I nodded.

Mockingly, he said, "Ironic, a number of us had handguns, but none of us had a rifle." He shook his head in disbelief and seethed, "And this was our first security meeting." His face was red, and I could tell that he was mentally engaged in a war.

"Strange how fast it happened."

"From now on, we carry rifles."

"You can take the military truck. The key is under the seat."

Another shot rang out. The road exploded to the right of me. Sparky bolted, running up the road in fright.

The truck guy yelled, "You two get back here."

I could hear the distinct bolt action of the rifle, locking in another round.

"Don't stop," Sergio instructed.

I felt the crosshairs of a scope comb my back. Ever-conscious and fearful, I looked ahead to the corner. If only we could get around it. Though we were moving at a good clip, it was as if time had slowed.

I imagined a spray of red on the road and looked over at Sergio. "I just want you to know, from the little time I've known you, you are a real game-changer." As soon as the words were out of my mouth, I wished I hadn't said them, as a superstitious air came. Did the crosshairs shift to Sergio's back? We were within twenty yards of that protective corner.

Sergio looked over at me. "It's been good knowing you. I think you have a good thing going."

"Do I ever want to run!"

He gave an encouraging look. "Don't."

I was counting the seconds when another shot rang. I jumped.

The truck man yelled, "The next shot's for you!" Again, the gun's action played.

A cold sweat broke out on my brow. My life flashed before me. Was I right with God? I sent up a hasty prayer for protection and held my breath. It was as if I was walking on thin ice, heading for that corner.

The earth seemed to sway. I missed a step, felt off-balance, sure I was hit by his bullet. Bizarre. I was still able to walk. This vibration went right up and into my heart. In shock, I gazed at Sergio. He was just as wide-eyed, but earthquake or not, we kept on. What relief to gain the protection of that corner! What blessed relief!

That was where we split. Sergio continued down the road and I headed up the hillside. It was steep and I was huffing and puffing when I made it to a tree. My heart was beating so fast, I thought it would explode. The ash didn't help. If I wasn't sucking it down, I was constantly blinking. Trying to catch my breath, I stared down the hill at Sergio. He was pacing up the road, heading toward our military truck.

Still gasping for air, I bent and blankly gazed at the ash-covered ground. I'd never felt like an old man until then. And this wasn't a game for old men or, for that matter, any man. Finally, I lifted my head and called out, "Carl?" but it was a weak call.

As I slowly headed up the hill, I continued to call his name.

Somewhere in this, I thought of Toby's action with that knife. Though it seemed justified at the time, it sure held consequences. His action was too brash. I just hoped everybody had gotten out of harm's way.

"Carl!" I struggled up the hill. "We need help!"

It was good to hear the military truck start.

Out of nowhere, young Maximo appeared, bounding across the hillside. His energy, the spring in his legs was encouraging. In no time he had drawn near.

Breathing heavily, he asked, "What … what do you want?"

"Don't come near this edge." I thumbed. "There's bad men down there."

He curiously looked toward the edge.

"I need Carl. Can you round up Carl?"

"He's coming." His arm swung up the hill. "He's coming up there."

I crouched down and approached the edge of the jagged rocks to view the shooters. Seeing one aim straight at me, I threw myself on the ground.

The rifle resounded. Rock exploded, sending debris over me, dusting the back of my neck.

I turned to Maximo. "Get out of here!"

A shot rang farther up our hill. Scooting back I angled my head up the hill, searching the area above, wondering who the shooter was. To my great relief, it was Carl. He was lying prone, his rifle hanging over the rocky edge, aiming toward the Dodge. I hadn't seen where his bullet hit, but it must've been respectable, as the men took cover behind their truck.

The same loudmouth swung his arm and yelled, "Why don't we call it even?"

Another shot rang out farther east, from near Toby's house. One of the truck men staggered back, then dropped. It was strange to see a human go down, but to be honest I was thrilled.

Toby yelled, "That's for Patty!"

The other man hastened to the driver's door. As he opened it, a bullet burst through the windshield. The man dropped his weapon, threw his hands in the air, yelling, "I give!" and scurried to the back of the vehicle. "I give!"

Another shot ripped through his tailgate.

"Hold up!" I called and rose with a wave of the hand. "Let him go. We don't need to bury him."

At the truck, the man yelled, "I give."

Up the hill, Carl was taking aim. There was such a vengeful spirit that I again called, "Let him go. We don't want to bury him."

At the rear of the truck, the one man helped his wounded buddy up. The wounded man flopped into the back of the truck. The other, with his hands up, walked tentatively toward the cab. In no time the truck was off. Flat tire or not, it rolled, bumping, thumping down our dirt road.

In the distance Toby cheered, "Ohoe!" I don't know if he had Native blood, but he was shaking his rifle, giving a triumphant cry. "Ohoe!"

This was the first time our subdivision had come together to stop a force. I carried that exhilaration until I turned and saw Maximo. He had witnessed this, and disappointment came over me, as I could see he approved.

# Our Neighborhood

They'd been saying for weeks that the grid was returning, and this news was getting chirpier. With the possibility of it happening, Sergio decided against bringing everyone into our house. There wasn't enough room anyway. Instead, he used Dewey's house as an outpost. This made sense, because Dewey had a good-sized house, a good woodpile and a propane supply for cooking, so why heat up more houses in his area? Additionally, the house had a good overview of the road.

With us providing the grub, it looked as if it would work, but Dewey's hospitality didn't extend toward one neighbor. That just happened to be his closest neighbor, Al's clan.

This put Sergio in a fix. I told him he should go over to Al's and see first-hand what the matter was, as I already knew that Dewey was concerned about bugs. There was no mystery about this; everybody knew that Al had animals inundating his place.

Sergio returned from Al's place, walking up the driveway. Though his face was half-covered with a bandana, he still looked concerned. "I think we're going to have to leave them there."

"I can't just be giving food away to Al and his clan without some form of payback."

Sergio scratched his chest. "It's one thing to itch when you have the possibility of a shower, it's an entirely different sport when there is no possibility of a shower … We'll have to make Al's house an outpost."

"Nobody's going to want to do guard duty in that house."

He sadly nodded, while scratching his scalp. "I know ... they got ferrets, rats, guinea pigs and who-knows-what in there. I'll just have to post times for Al's clan to do guard shifts at their house, and get them on other projects about your place. What else can we do?" He shrugged, fingering his ear. "Anyway, we've lots of forces now."

Except for moving various neighbors' bedding down to Dewey's, and cleaning out the air filter on my diesel, there wasn't much to mention about the days that followed. If there were battles, they were over small stuff, various neighbors saying this or that about the others, nitpicky stuff. Strange how touchy people are.

*   *   *

With our extra forces, Sergio wanted to post a watch at Patty's. He assumed whoever attacked her would return. It was around noon on the 35th day that Sergio, Paul, Lynn, Gordy, Carl, Toby, and I ended up looking over her property. Within thirty yards of her house was the dry creek area, a depression that funneled toward the Wartals.

Suspicions played, and we followed a path down that dry creek that we figured the murderers used. This creek had been worn down from centuries of run-off, low enough so that our heads couldn't be seen by the Wartals. We followed a game trail. It was a pleasant walk, in and out of burnt areas, and I felt comfortable, as we were gunned up with rifles.

Charcoal stumps pressed upward and someone had done a good job at sawing away, clearing the dead falls off the trail. We came to a split, a Y in the dry creek where one leg went up toward Al's place and the main channel angled toward the Wartals.

Sergio halted and pointed to the side where water had previously carved out a back eddy that was somewhat hidden.

"That's a good spot to set up a watch. One could hide amongst the fallen trees and cover anyone coming down the trail."

Gordy concurred. "We could build a little covering with that scrub. It's a good spot to intercept anyone going up toward Al's or Patty's."

Carl joked, "Maybe hook up a phone service first."

I wondered if his goofy comment was spawned by nerves, as there was something creepy about that area. I don't know if it was the memory of Patty's tortured body, but the place gave me the spooks. A crow perched in a nearby pine gave us its ominous opinion with an odd garbled caw. I noticed he was on the lower branches, trying to get away from the drifting ash. I didn't like that place.

From the Y, we could see Al's place, but a bend in the dry creek bed prevented us from seeing the Wartals' house. I was quite curious to see the back of their place and was glad Sergio went down that path.

Rounding the bend, a barbed wire fence cut straight across the dry creek. Farther, up a knoll, was an old single-story house. There was nothing notable about it except the huge junkyard around the house, filled with old wrecks, junk, engines, junk, buses, junk, vans, cars, trucks and more junk.

Carl pointed at the ground. "Look at that."

To the side of the path, right below the barbed wire, was a small bottle. I couldn't tell what it was as it had a covering of volcanic ash.

Carl picked it up. "It's rosemary."

"I bet it came from Patty's."

"Probably fell out of their booty."

"Don't get your fingerprints all over it." Sergio was firm. "Just put it in your pocket. It could be used as evidence."

Condemning stares went towards the Wartals' house. If there were any doubts about the killers before, they were driven out by that bottle of rosemary.

My dad once said, "No good comes out of certain houses." I used to think that was extreme, until I looked at that junkyard, that house. The sight of it rubbed me deep.

Carl's gaze was fixed on it. "So that's where the bad boys live."

"Maybe we should just shoot the hell out of it right now." Gordy lifted his rifle, taking aim. "That would save all this sneaking around."

Sergio stepped to Gordy's side. "With the grid coming back, I think restraint is in order."

"Hold me back." Gordy still aimed his rifle. "Too bad I don't have a bazooka."

"I'd rather spend my time somewhere other than a courtroom." Sergio's eyes caught Gordy's before he headed back down the path.

We followed, some reluctantly.

When we got to the Y, we looked over the spot in the dry creek that was set back, chewed away by former run-off. Everyone concurred that it had good possibilities of intercepting someone coming down the trail. If there would be a problem, it would be from above; someone traveling the rim might see us. And there was a hunter's moon rising.

# The Plague

The news from our Meshnet and ham radio had no end of doom-and-gloom. It was the speed of the events that was so gripping. It was one event stacked on top of another that made these times so pressing, so much so, the mind wouldn't venture into fields of hope, but was seized by fear of what was next.

It was becoming hard to mentally stand against these dark thoughts. Moreover, with Priscilla's doom-and-gloom interpretation of the book of Revelation—wars, scarcity, calamity, and the Devil—I became quite conscious that this wasn't just another time in history, that this really might be the End Times.

One would hope the government would do something but, more often than not, their decision making was so poor it was scary to have them intervene. What really drove suspicions was when we heard stories of DC confiscating people's property. There was even talk that they caused the derivative failure, and there was no end of conspiracy chatter that they let the plague loose. I didn't want to believe that, since this Sudden Death was so nasty. But sure as a new day, we'd hear something about that plague.

I don't like to be callous, but when I hear of something bad happening elsewhere, my first thought is that it should stay there. Evidently I wasn't the only one with this view, because the next day we got news that all four passes into the Yokino Valley had been cut off, blown away.

Homeland Security put the blame squarely on a militant religious group. I didn't know how they came up with a religious group, but I only wished God would bless the men and mules that humped the dynamite up those passes to trigger the explosions. I didn't mind being cut off, not one bit, anything to stop that angel of death from coming into our valley. Furthermore, with the valley cut off, I thought the extractions might end.

But the downside of this action was that the plague was already in the Yokino. I found this out two days later, when I was summoned down to our gate to see my daughter-in-law.

As I drove the diesel toward the gate, I wondered why Nancy didn't just come in. Then again, my brother Freddy was the talker on duty, and he's just a bit different.

When I stepped from the truck, I was puzzled why Nancy was on the other side of the gate, sitting by the road. Why hadn't Freddy let her in? This bugged me, and as I neared him, I said rather tersely, "What's up?"

He pointed toward her. "She says she might be infected."

This news made me halt at the gate. "Hi, Nancy. Are you okay?"

She looked ten pounds lighter when she stood up. Off-balance, she swayed.

"What happened?" I shot a glance toward her car to see if Kelsey was in her car seat, but shade from the pines made it difficult to see inside.

Nancy took a couple steps toward us, her voice cracking. "A while back my dad sold some sheep in Charby." She talked slowly, tiredly. Though I couldn't see her mouth, as she was wearing a bandana, I knew she was grief-stricken. "When he came back, Kelsey came down with that sickness." She pressed her hands to her eyes and cried.

"Oh, Nancy …" She looked so pitiful. "… I'm so sorry."

In-between her tears she got out, "My dad's no more … Kelsey worsened, so we headed to Missoula to see if we could get some medicine." Her voice pitched higher and she choked up so much, she couldn't speak. It was difficult to watch her. As she sobbed, I chanced another look toward her car. But the way the tree shadows played over the windshield, I couldn't see if Kelsey was inside.

She struggled on. "We got to the roadblock a few miles before Missoula, where they blew the pass. They told us to go back, but Eli took off from there."

"Hiking?"

"Yes."

"How long ago was that?"

"Four days," she sobbed.

"Nancy, I'm so sorry about your dad …" I was tentative, afraid to ask, and looked again to see the baby's car seat. "… Is Kelsey okay?"

She shook her head and looked so wretched, weeping there, I wanted to go give her a hug, bring her in, hold her, something, anything, to comfort her. Here was my daughter-in-law, without her father, without her husband, without her daughter, infected, alone.

Seeing her like that, thirty feet in front of our gate, was perhaps the saddest moment of my life. "Nancy, we can set up a place, an empty house, not far from here. We will provide for you. After a quarantine period, you can come in. You can be part of us."

Between her sobs, I barely heard her say, "… Eli."

"I'll go check on him. But don't worry about Eli, that boy's a survivor. He'll outlive us all."

"… My sheep."

"Do the sheep have water?"

She nodded.

"That's all they need. Don't worry about them sheep. And we can go look in on them."

She started to walk toward her vehicle.

I exclaimed, "Goodness, Nancy, you are all alone out there. You can't go back." I glanced at Freddy, hoping he'd concur.

Wiping his eyes, he called out, "Nancy, you need to stay here." He pointed east. "We can get a house for you."

Her tears muddled with the drifting ash, smearing her face as she took a step back.

"Hold on, Nancy," I urgently called. "I've got something for you." I raced to my truck.

I retrieved bottled water from the truck and was contemplating going with her, but a war broke out within me over crossing that line. That plague was nothing to fool with, that killer wasn't picky. When I returned, my eyes met Freddy's.

He quietly mumbled, "Be careful. You know how contagious that thing is."

Passing the gate, I extended the bottle toward Nancy. "Nancy, I can look after the sheep, and I'll drive out to Missoula and see about Eli. That's not a problem. It won't take long to set up a house for you." I slowed down and extended the bottle. "It's good water from our well."

Behind me, Freddy desperately called out, "Hershal, just put the water bottle on the ground. Twenty feet is never too far for that plague. Come on, Hershal, right there!" His fear was infectious. I halted.

I set the bottle on the road, advising her, "I'll go get you some lunch. We've got warm soup."

Freddy added, "The ladies make some real nice bread. It'll be warm, for sure."

"We'll get you set up."

She looked as if she was trying to decide whether to live or die.

"Did I ever tell you that I'm happy you're my daughter-in-law?" A part of me wanted to just sweep her off her feet and wipe away every tear, but dread froze me.

Freddy abruptly said, "I'm going to get you some food, stay there. I'll be right back." Clearly on a mission, he headed for my truck.

I called to him, "Tell Sergio we're going to need a house set up." Turning toward Nancy, I encouraged her, "Eli will be back. Don't worry about him. He's the ultimate survivor." But, after the death of Kelsey and her dad, these words were just words.

Behind me the diesel started. I glanced up the hill and fought the grief of my granddaughter's passing then looked back at Nancy. "There's a vacant house up there that has good views."

*   *   *

Thankfully, Nancy accepted our offer, but it wasn't an easy matter, securing her a vacant house. I didn't want to put her at Patty's. The memory of her tortured body was just too vivid, and I didn't want to worry about Nancy's safety out there near the Wartals. I had my hands full with my sorrow over Kelsey, Jerold's death and my fear for Bethany, not to mention Eli's disappearance.

There were three other vacant houses—Ernie's, Toby's, and Lynn's. All of them were living at Dewey's. Ernie's place was closer to ours, so I went to talk to him about Nancy's predicament.

I had hardly finished when he pointed out. "Patty's place is open."

"If she were your daughter, would you put her in Patty's house?"

He looked confronted. "We're moving back to our place."

"How come?"

"I can't stand living with Toby." He shook his head. "It's just not working out."

"Can't you just put aside your differences?"

He shook his head. "I'm sorry to hear about your daughter-in-law. But we got a problem with the Keoghs, and it's not getting better."

I wasted no time talking to Toby about Nancy having his house for a bit. But he also mentioned Patty's. He said it wouldn't work as they were always in and out of their place. Disappointed, I went on to Lynn. He too was moving back to his place as soon as the power came back.

Their excuses disturbed me. It was terribly disheartening. Here we were, providing food for these people, but they wouldn't make any concessions for our infected daughter-in-law.

I suppose, if I was to be fair, the fear of that plague was huge, and each person assured me that if we put Nancy in Patty's house, we'd be able to guard it. Sergio said the same. Sadly, that's where Nancy ended up.

This worried me a lot. That day, every time I walked toward Patty's house to drop something off for Nancy, in my mind's eye I saw Patty's tortured body. Was that the way Nancy would end up? To counter this, I gave Nancy a .44 revolver and lots of ammo.

That evening, Gordy and I drove over to the sheep ranch, but found no sign of Eli. We went all the way up the highway to where the road was cut off, covered by rubble from the hillside above; there was a well-worn path to Missoula, but there was no sign of him.

The next morning we drove that road again. Driving sixty-odd miles to the outskirts of Missoula was no small adventure, as we constantly had to stop and shake out the air filter on the diesel. Gordy was on his guard, sitting up tall. On the way back, we were shot at just this side of Middleton. With three bullet holes in the truck box, we made it to the sheep ranch, but again, there were no fresh tracks in the volcanic ash, no sign of Eli.

I was a ball of worry. Priscilla, though grief-stricken about Kelsey, was much more optimistic about Eli. She held out that any second he'd just walk right back into our lives, "Like he did that Christmas!" The upbeat way she said it, I could see him tapping on the kitchen window. What a precious jewel that kid was! I tried to reassure myself that his strength would get him through. The last time I saw him and squeezed his arm, it was stronger, married life had been good for him. For sure, his strength would get him through. But again, when I considered Jerold, Kelsey and Bethany's fate, I slid into the doldrums. That despair was as encompassing as the drifting ash.

In my despair, I wondered where God was. Was He going to take all my kids? Was it because of that curse? He had to have something against me.

# Like He Did That Christmas

That night, lying in bed, it wasn't Uncle Bob's snoring that kept me awake, it was my worries over my daughter-in-law. It was easy to imagine the Wartals after her. Would they poke her to death, like they did Patty? This was terribly worrisome. Lying there, I admonished myself for putting her in Patty's house. What an idiot! She would've been better off back at her sheep ranch instead of being the sacrificial lamb in our subdivision. The devil had to be in that decision.

Priscilla rolled my way, her fingers touching. She whispered, "Hershal, are you awake?"

"Yes."

"Do you know how many we have now?" Her voice held optimism.

"No."

"With Nancy, we have exactly sixty-nine." She squeezed my arm with affirmation. "And just in time, as tomorrow will be forty days."

A windstorm abruptly hit the house. I didn't know if I'd ever get used to the way storms suddenly appeared now, so jarring.

"Why is forty days so important to you?"

"The Bible tells us that in Noah's time, it rained for forty days and forty nights. It says the last days will be like that of Lot and Noah. Can't you see how God is putting it all together? Don't you see, the seventieth, our last one will be Eli?"

"And what if Eli doesn't show?"

"He will. God is good. Eli will come."

"I'm worried about Nancy. I think she's next."

"Next?"

"The Wartals are going to get her."

"I rebuke that in Jesus' name."

"I should've never put her over there."

"God will look after her."

"Priscilla …" I tried to halt my rising resentment. "… instead of living off all that hope, maybe you should take a look at reality. Isn't Jerold gone? Isn't Bethany gone? Isn't Kelsey gone? Isn't Eli gone? Can't you see?"

"Bethany is not dead; you don't know that. And Eli will be the seventieth, you'll see. Why would God take all our kids?"

"I don't know, maybe that curse never came off, maybe God doesn't like me. I don't know."

"Don't say such a thing. He loves you. God loves you unconditionally."

"Nancy's next."

"I rebuke that thought in Jesus' mighty name."

"It was crazy to put her in that house."

"You need to speak words of faith toward her. God will prevail."

"Do you think God would mind if I gun down the Wartals?"

"Why do you talk like that? If you knew Jesus …" she said this, quite exasperated, "… you'd know He's for you."

"Anyway …" I said, with a measure of indifference toward God, "… goodnight, Priscilla."

It was quiet for about twenty seconds before she said, "God didn't take Jerold."

"If God didn't take Jerold, then I can't blame the Devil, either … it was my fault, I should've had security up."

"It is not our job to figure it out. Can't you say it was his time?"

"It was his time because of my mistake."

"No … no."

I heard a distinct hum. It was different yet sounded quite familiar. I listened. Unable to distinguish the sound, I pushed up on my elbow, but it was difficult to hear anything except the howl of the windstorm. "There's been more news of the power returning."

"What is it?"

"I wonder if that's the fridge." On the nightstand, I saw the blinking red glow of a digital clock. Fearing Nancy might be exposed by the house lights, I arose.

"Where are you going?"

I grabbed my pants and quickly dressed. "It's time to visit the Wartals."

She moaned, "Please don't go there," and struggled to sit up.

"I can't do that lackadaisical thing again." Leaning over, I found a pair of dirty socks and my boots.

"You know that Sergio has security down there. God will look after Nancy."

"Sergio's a good man. You two are of the same mindset." I grabbed my guns. "If things don't work out …"

She interrupted, "Please, Hershal, don't go."

I bent on one knee. My lips clumsily bumped into her forehead. I gave her a kiss and mumbled, "You're a fine wife, Priscilla."

She spoke with haste. "With the power back, things will be better; you'll see, the sun will be bright tomorrow. God will look after Nancy, you'll see."

"Maybe I'm part of that." I pulled away from her and rose. Carrying my guns and boots, I quickly headed for the door.

"Hershal? … Hershal?"

I had to get out of there before she got up. In my haste, I bumped into the door frame, exiting the room.

Going down the hallway, I could see the effectiveness of Sergio's military clock; Jack, Priscilla's brother, was coming out of a bedroom, on his way to guard duty.

He looked back at me. "Are you also on guard duty?"

"Yes," I quietly mumbled. Every time I saw Jack, I saw the man who stole some of my wife's inheritance.

"At least it's a full moon." He entered the stairwell. I followed. His surprise came when I flicked the stairway light switch.

"Hey, hey!" he exclaimed. Grinning, he nodded toward the light. "That's an Oh Canada, if I ever saw an Oh Canada."

"Maybe you'll be able to go home, after all," I said, trying to be civil, as there was always a part of me that wanted to set Jack right.

"I sure hope so. If they can get those passes open, and if they can get the gas stations and the stores open." He stopped on the stairwell landing and caught my eye. "If I can harvest those potatoes before it gets too freezy, I bet I can sell them for three times the money."

I thought he had a lot of ifs going. "Great, great." It was easier to act civil, as my game face was coming on. I went past him on the stair landing.

"Will you be going back to the oil fields?"

"We'll see." I went through the stairwell door.

The lights on the main floor were aglow. I could hear Julie and Gordy in the kitchen, excitingly chatting, their Canadian accents quite chipper. I grabbed my coat off a couch, felt for my flashlight in a pocket and made a beeline for the back door, quite aware that Priscilla might come after me.

Off to my side, Julie ran her hands through flowing tap water. "Look, Hershal." She lifted dripping fingers. "Real water!" Her smile was ever so happy.

Gordy pointed at the tap. "Hope is flowing, Hershal, it's really flowing."

"Isn't it great?" I forced another grin and then, just before going through the door, I thumbed back. "Priscilla says, 'The sun will be bright tomorrow.'" Those were my last words before going out that door.

Sparky met me in the mudroom. "Hey, Spark," I said as I cut across the floor, determined not to let him out. He whimpered and licked my hand, but I held him back. "You're a good dog, Spark." I slipped out the outside door, shutting it.

Outside, I felt the cool of fall and wasted no time in putting on my boots. With my coat half-on, I hastened down the steps and pulled my bandana from a pocket.

My actions were pretty much premeditated; earlier that day I had reviewed the photos of the two intruders, caught, back in the day, on the game trail camera. The Wartals' place was calling.

The full moon allowed me to walk quickly down the same hill where I'd pursued Richard Wartal three years prior. Everything about that experience seemed surreal, the memories of the chase, the cumbersome logs, the tree where I shot the porcupine, the military truck whose presence hadn't stopped any intruders. The only thing different was, I didn't need my flashlight, since the glow from the moon was so bold.

Knowing where our guards were, I used the dry creek area and crawled under our barbed wire fence. Staying low, I followed the dry creek bed. At a certain point, I was in amongst some trees. Using them as cover, I looked back at the spot where I'd shot Wartal.

I stood there for a moment and considered him entering someone else's property, the criminal mindset it takes to cross a boundary, a property line, without due regard for ownership. I concluded that I now possessed the same illegal thoughts toward the Wartals, and I had much more in mind than just peeking in their window.

I hit a dirt road. The moon with its weird hues was exposing me. My pace quickened. In the distance, I could see house lights—more importantly, Wartals' house lights. I cut across an open dry grassy area.

When I got into another stand of trees, I stopped and looked over the valley. It was strange, here I was on a murderous journey, yet something spoke of hope. Maybe it was the glow of house lights or the cool of winter, a new season, the yellowish-orange of the deciduous trees, or a change in the wind that helped clear some of the volcanic ash.

It was as if Creation itself was speaking, which made me wonder if God talked to man. Looking up, I searched the dim stars, and realized how important light was. Scanning the heavens, I felt insignificant and wondered why God would ever talk to men, let alone this man.

My view came back to earth, the smoke rising from a distant cabin's chimney. It spoke of warmth, a homey comfort. My mind drifted back to the seventy and how our place would be emptying out soon. It was eccentric that I had gotten into all that preparing, all that food storage, because I thought money was in it. In considering this, I started to grin. It may have been a sad grin, but nonetheless, it was good to grin. Some of this odd humor had to do with my peculiar wife, who thought God was speaking to us.

This was more smoke; it couldn't have been God. An extraordinary dream, yes, and the interpretation was even more outlandish. But wasn't God perfect in His abilities, His counts, His measures, His choices? And to think He'd talk to me through a dream? That was wild. God wouldn't choose a murderer, a fellow who was only doing it for the money, and wasn't even right with Him.

A bout of coughing brought me out of my contemplations. I cleared my throat, over and over. Just then, I noticed a green light emerge from the sky, seemingly out of nowhere. This green, the dancing glow of Northern Lights, was quite perplexing; I'd never seen an aurora here before, certainly not this far south. Its greenish light rose like an ocean wave with many streams of light that swirled in and out, in and out, burning through the night sky. My mouth hung as I watched this light curve into an S shape. Another burst from the side looked as if the legs of a massive game bird were touching down, the greenish smoke defusing. And just as it came to its crescendo, cresting and curling over, a meteor streaked straight through it.

My eyes widened. The meteor was as big as an office tower, its white flaming tail clearly distinguishing itself against the greenish background. It streaked west—straight across the valley, disappearing beyond the mountains.

I found myself pinching my arm. Maybe we weren't out of the woods yet. The sight of the meteor was like a slap in the face to the idea that the world would somehow get back to normal. Its appearance was so weighty, I sensed the arm of the Devil who knew his time was short. This drove a wedge into my emotions, which were down one minute and hopeful the next, only to be awed by the view of a disappearing who-knows-what—an asteroid?

On cue, the earth shook. I squatted down, trying to keep from falling over. Stepping back, my boot slid into a good-size critter hole. I ended up on my back, atop dirt that was still trembling. When it stopped, I sat up and felt something move under the sole of my boot. A snake? I ripped my leg right out of that hole and scrambled up. I hurriedly limped on, acutely aware of all my shortcomings.

How do you get away from God? I could try to justify myself, but in reality the events that had unfolded upon the earth were so fantastic, they cut through any insincerity, any phoniness. Their magnitude and speed were awe-inspiring. Their reality made me very aware of God's judgment, His all-seeing eye, and I was aware of the way I'd treated Him. I had treated Him poorly, had even set my guns above Him.

I wanted to get right with Him, I wanted to ask forgiveness but before I knew it, the Wartals' driveway stretched and I was drawn toward their porch light. One minute, I felt as if this journey was like the cycle of life, imminent and certain, the next minute, I wondered what I was doing there. The thought of Nancy ending up like Patty reset my course.

The porch light illuminated the small house and reluctantly cast some of its glow toward the clutter that encircled the place—old appliances, a broken-down hen house, old vehicles, junkers, junkers and more junkers. I bet there were over thirty vehicles, all parked haphazardly.

Halfway into this clutter, I felt intimidated. My hands slid into my coat pockets, feeling the grips of my .38 Specials. They gave me some courage. As I walked toward that door, I was more and more convicted about my attitude toward God over the loss of my kids and granddaughter. Here He'd given me life, and I had become bitter toward Him. Strange to think I'd come this far in life without walking with Him, and now was bitter toward Him. The closer I came to the Wartals' front door, the more I wanted get right with Him. Thoughts and words of how to present myself to Him were coursing through my mind when I stepped under the Wartals' porch light.

I stared at the glass storm door, and my thoughts shifted from God to what story I'd tell the Wartals. "I'm looking for my lost dog. Have you seen …" Hearing someone inside, I jerked, then quickly gave the storm door a rap. I promptly slipped my hand back into my coat pocket to grip the .38. My breathing and my legs were heavy.

Through a window to the left of the door, I saw movement of light in the dark room. Those flashes started a pounding in my skull. I waited, anticipating the Wartals were gunning up. It was then I realized that my bandana was still positioned over my face. I pulled it down.

Out of the corner of my eye, I thought I saw the edge of the curtain move. I surmised I was being watched, and acted as if I didn't notice, rapping again on the storm door. Again, my right hand felt the security of my weapon – my left hand nervously palmed the other gun. I was sure that I'd see the face of someone any second, and blankly stared at the door, wondering if it would be the tall man or the short man from the game trail camera images.

After a long wait I stepped back, and became conscious of someone sneaking toward me from the outside. I half-glanced back, then turned and stepped away from the porch to view the far corner of the house. My suspicions played amongst all that junk, vehicles and clutter. I nervously backed up, glancing again at the door, then the house corner. Those were some sadistic animals that worked Patty over. There was an ominous presence of evil and my backward pace quickened.

Dread pushed me down the driveway. Fear of my life evaporating caused me to take a quick, reverent glance toward the heavens. The thought of ending up on the wrong side of eternity made my eyes sharp, my legs strong. With huge breaths I limped on, considering how I'd present myself to Him.

A voice countered, "What kind of God would take Jerold, Eli, Bethany and Kelsey?" While heading toward the protection of an old Plymouth, I tried to block the question, squirrel it away in my pounding skull.

I glanced again at the Wartals' window and noted sporadic lights. Reaching the Plymouth, I looked inside its open window. Its front seat was empty, looking as if it were waiting for me. It was then I did something that was against everything I stood for—I pulled out my guns and tossed them on the seat.

Seeing them lying there, I was fully aware I was entertaining fate, but fought the urge to retrieve them. I felt naked without my guns and was so stiff when I stepped back, that when my boot hit some junk, I stumbled and went down.

Part of me wanted to call off this meeting with the Lord and retrieve my guns. The mental battle ensued, with the voice returning. "What is God's reward for you in looking after the seventy? Was it your kids' deaths? Was that the booby prize?"

These piercing questions killed my meeting with God; now, if anything, I was indifferent toward Him. Getting up, I headed for my guns. Their steel, their power, was something I could trust.

Standing at the Plymouth's door, I glanced at the night sky and hopelessly asked the Lord, "Do You like guns?" It would be something to hear a resounding lightning strike. But there were no words, no wind, no sound, nothing. I mumbled, "I like guns." There was sadness to my comments, but even more to my expectations of God.

I stared through the Plymouth's door at my weapons which lay within reach of the steering wheel, then at the Wartals' lights. I reached down and took my Smith and Wesson. When I lifted it I thought of Jerold, Bethany, Kelsey and Eli. Their faces were before me. It would be good to see them. I lowered my .38, placing it back on the seat then pushed away from the car's window. A few steps toward the Wartals' house, I felt under their rifle scopes. The fear of eternity without my Maker was halting.

The Devil drove, "What kind of God would take your kids and let the Wartals live?"

I pressed on toward their door, and yes, I headed toward their guns without my guns.

At the entrance, I turned my back on the Wartals and my eyes to the heavens. Behind me, light flashed. I wanted to say something to God, but heard that voice again, "He doesn't like you … It's what you did."

Staring at a bright star, I fought the desire to whisper, but clearly spoke, "I don't get You." Disappointment covered me. I was quite aware of my past, of not trusting God, of something I did that had caused my kids' deaths. Flashing movements inside the house made me think someone was coming, so I turned, nervously grabbed the storm door, pulled it open and gave that entrance door a knock. Waiting, staring at the door-knob, how I wished I was right with God.

Heavy-hearted, I mumbled, "Please, Lord, please forgive me for my wrongs." I put my hands over my damp eyes, trying to stop a stream of tears, gasping out, "I really need you. Please come into me."

My blurry focus went back to that doorknob, anticipating any second it would spin. Who knows how much time passed before I realized that my anticipation of a person coming was just the TV's movement of light. I haphazardly wiped my eyes and looked about, saying to myself that I was supposed to be saved now. Maybe I could go see my kids. Lifting my head, I looked at the window. These Wartals weren't making this easy. Would they ever open the door?

That voice came again, "The sneaks. They just sneak."

Strange to hear that same voice after I had prayed. But it rang true, *sneaks* was a good word for that crowd. They had to be sneaking around, sneaking around our house, peeking in at Priscilla, and sneaking around Patty's and sneaking,

sneaking, sneaking. I looked toward the corner of the house. Were they there? Anger rose in me; what a bunch of cowardly sneaks.

"I'm hear!" I called, and aggressively walked toward the house's corner. Nearing a broken-down rabbit hutch, I looked into the darkened junkyard. They must've snuck back.

I'd had enough of these sneaks; more so, I'd had enough of my sneaking around life, or death. Additionally, I wasn't sure if I got saved. I didn't feel any tingles, or hear angels singing, or see the stars shine any brighter, or sense the throbbing in my head subside and I still heard voices. Maybe it didn't take.

I made it back to the front door and bowed my head again and closed my eyes this time, mumbling, "Jesus, please, please, I hope You take me." I stared at the front doorknob for a while and wondered if anything was different. Because I didn't feel anything different, I wondered if I'd always be cursed. At a loss, I hauled back and gave the door a good pound.

It flew open. A foul smell oozed out, the type that speaks of death or crazies.

This melted my anger. Apprehension gripped me, blood pounded in my head. "Have you seen my dog?" I sheepishly implored. To the side I could hear the news on TV. "He got loose ..." My voice faded.

With trembling hands, I warily stepped onto the worn carpet.

The TV news flashed, lighting up the dark living room. The announcer's words , "Tornadoes, hail, and rain ..."

The place stunk appallingly. I took another step inside and called, "His name's Sparky."

Dark paneling encompassed the room and I leaned toward the kitchen, half expecting to be targeted. There were two bedrooms, one lit and one dark, with a bathroom in the middle. I looked past the kitchen, taking a careful step toward the bedrooms. Maybe Wartal's brother was in the dark bedroom.

But it was too dark to see inside. Maybe he was in the bathroom. Its door was closed but there was no light coming from its edges.

I whispered, "He's a good dog."

Drawn toward the bedroom light, I proceeded around the kitchen table. A person lying on a bed came into view. Why didn't they hear me pound on the door? Was something wrong with him? And why were the cabinets open, barren, yet the sink's faucet running? I slowly moved toward the person in the bed—perhaps that's why I didn't see him.

I ended up at the doorway of the lit bedroom. Before me, the body of a woman lay atop the covers. From the color of her skin and her open eyes, she was past the point of sleep. A pill container on a nightstand spoke of suicide. Looking over her classy dress shoes and black slacks, I wondered if she was even related to the Wartals.

Saddened, I half angled my head to hear the evening news. "… A tidal wave has struck …"

Though repulsed by the smell of death, I entered her room to see if the pills she had taken were aspirin. My head pounded as I lifted the canister to read, Valium. I put the canister next to her pack of smokes.

Stepping back, I took a long look at her. She appeared to be in her 40s but could've been in her 30s, having one of those hard faces that showed worry, toil and life's stress more than most. The corpse was dressed in a red sweater, fluffed-out mohair that looked oddly festive, perhaps her best sweater.

I wondered what day she had taken her life. From her sunken face, she appeared to have been dead for a few days, but I was no expert. Distraught, I turned away, half-listening to the evening news. "Locusts are sweeping the Middle East …"

My head continued to pound and I wondered if there was aspirin elsewhere. I stepped toward the door.

That's when I spotted him.

A bare-chested, bony boy of around two or three years old stared at me from the far side of the kitchen table. He broke my gaze and his eyes locked onto a plastic baggy atop the table. He looked surreal as he reached for the baggy. It was just beyond his reach.

From the other bedroom, I heard something. It could've been bedsprings. I had a strong urge to look to see who was there. But I fought that urge, forced myself to act as if I was unaware and stepped toward the boy. "Hey there."

He pulled his hand down from his quest of the baggy as if caught.

The light from the TV continued to pulsate against the dark paneling and older dark furniture. The news announcer said, "A radical religious group has bombed ..."

The boy again reached and reached for the baggy, finally touching it. In a flash, he dragged it to the table's edge. It fell to the floor. I noticed something yellow inside. Pills?

He bent to snag them and up came the plastic baggy. In one motion, his hungry fingers scooped in, dug them out and delivered them to his mouth.

"Oh, no, you don't!" I rushed him, coming round the table, and swept him off his feet, lifted him up and worked my fingers into his mouth. Gravity helped me get the yellow pieces out.

He gave a weak, mournful cry. It was a cry of hunger.

I set him on the floor and flopped into a chair in front of him. I was puzzled at what had come out of his mouth, as the yellow wasn't hard, like pills, but soft, like corn. "I'm sorry." I noticed other empty baggies on the floor, but not one left on the table. "It's okay," I said as I reached to pat his shoulder. It was saddening to feel how bony he was.

I heard the floor creak and sensed someone coming up from behind. I couldn't move. Bizarre, I felt stuck in glue, as if I was under some spell. Breathless, I stared at the teary, brown-eyed boy. My thoughts were on eternity; what would God say if I came into His presence?

The boy's eyes widened as they focused on something behind me. My skull pounded, the-thump, the-thump.

I jerked when a cat ran its whiskers along my pant leg, its engine turned on, purrrrrrrr. The boy whimpered. I had startled him.

"It's okay," I managed to say.

The cat moved on toward a two gallon cooking pot that had a bit of water in it. "It's okay." I hadn't noticed the pot before as it sat right up against the wall, beside a table leg. There was a plastic cup next to the pot, and the sloppiness of the user in spilling water on the vinyl floor provided water for the cat. I bent to look under the table, and saw a bag of cat food.

"So that's what you've been living on?" I said to the boy. Curious, I found myself on my knees, reaching for the bag. "Momma left you something." I was surprised to see nothing in that bag, not even crumbs.

Rising off the floor, I caught a whiff of his soiled underwear. But I didn't care if he was a smelly creature or Wartal's son, or for that matter, how perilous the times were, he was coming with me.

"Hey, little buddy." I ran my hand over his oily hair. "We need you at our place." I knelt and touched his skinny arm, then dropped his underwear to the floor. He stood there, naked, dirty and vulnerable. "And I'm not charging you anything."

I lifted him toward the sink to wash him. "Not because you're strong, or have lots of silver, no, no ..." His little foot touched the counter. "... It's hope of the future you bring." Touching his chest, I looked into his brown eyes. "You're a gift."

My emotions flowed as I turned the water tap toward the hot side, hoping for warmth. He trembled, staring at my teeth. I'm sure he saw a big set of teeth, as I was grinning, then again, since he reminded me of Eli when he showed up from foster parents, maybe he was viewing my tears.

I worked the sink sprayer up his legs. Though the water was lukewarm, he whimpered. Turning him about, I sprayed his backside. "That's right, little buddy, you're a gift from God." There was a bottle of hand soap which I used to wash him.

His whimpers were tender, the type that didn't know if he was happy or sad.

I held his arm and worked the spray over him. "When Eli was a boy, he liked to dance about." These words were just out of my mouth when the power went out. The room was black as pitch, with no more noise coming from the TV. The boy's whimpers had tones of fear.

"It's okay, little buddy." I steadied him, while my free hand reached into my coat pocket to dig out the flashlight. He was so slight. "We'll get going in a minute."

The glow of the flashlight shot upward, across the ceiling. Holding the light in one hand, I lifted him out of the sink. He was shivering.

"We'll get you back to our place." I carried him. The flashlight's beam led to the bedroom opposite the dead woman's.

A bed there had an indentation where the cat slept. Holding the boy on my hip, I wasted no time in ripping off the bedcover and snagging a blanket. I laid him atop it.

He was trembling badly.

I began to wrap him. "Hey little buddy, there's some nice snuggly-wugglies here." Sweeping him upward next to my chest, I curled the velvety cloth back around him. "That's going to get you the fuzzy-wuzzies." I laid him back down and wrapped him some more. His little brown eyes gazed up at me.

We left the room, my flashlight bobbing about the floor, kitchen cabinet and the dark paneling as we crossed the living room.

"I know a woman who would love to meet you. She's been talking about the seventy, you know?" I pulled some of the blanket over his face and walked toward the front door. Without power, the house was quite lifeless, and with its sickening smell, death was its only voice.

I made it outside and was looking forward to shutting the door on that eerie house. My concern was the cat. Thankfully, it had followed me out. "Good, good."

I tucked the flashlight in my pocket and glanced down at the boy. His face and body were well-covered by the blanket. "You know, Priscilla will never guess who her seventieth is."

Peering through damp eyes, I pulled my bandana over my nose and headed toward the old Plymouth. The clutter of vehicles, though pressing, wasn't as formidable as before.

Trying to keep the little guy warm, I cuddled him, firmly. "Little buddy, did you know you're a gift from God?"

# Epilogue

That night's power from the grid turned out to be just a wishful blip. It could've been snuffed out by the ongoing earthquakes. With our passes closed, Yokino Power had their hands full trying to get spares of anything. And I don't suppose the shortage of transformers, which were produced in the countries we were at war with, was beneficial either.

We never did find the boy's real name. The following day someone torched Wartal's house. I've no idea if it was one of our seventy or one of the Wartal brothers, but it was burned to the ground. In any case the boy's real name remained a mystery. Yet there was no mystery to the love that was poured into him.

The ladies were like a flock of mother hens with that little fellow.

I could hear Priscilla saying, "We have to be careful not feed him too much, he has to get used to it."

Her cousin Julie responded with much concern, as if his very survival depended on it, "Oh, yes, we have to be very careful in the beginning." Her fussing went on.

It was my brother Stan who started calling him Sonny. The name stuck.

Sonny's presence really helped unite our seventy. Even the neighbors became family to him.

Priscilla hoped Nancy would take Sonny under her wing, maybe he'd be a bridge for her sorrow over the loss of Kelsy and Eli. But early flames of this didn't catch. It didn't matter to Sonny; he flowed amongst us like a family reunion at a theme park.

When I sat at the kitchen table and watched this little guy, it was quite easy to think of Eli when he was young. But sometimes when I'd hear about the wars, social breakdown, and feel the constant earthquakes these thoughts would drift to the dark side and I'd wonder if Sonny was a telegram from the heavens—WE REGRET TO INFORM YOU … Eli is dead. When that foreboding moment hit, the battle in my mind would begin. I would counter by looking toward the window, the same window Eli had tapped on the day after Christmas, way back in the day. And I would try to imagine him tapping again. TAP, TAP, TAP, then tell myself that God wouldn't take my last son, He wouldn't do that, He's got too many plans for him. Surely Eli and Nancy were going to have more sons and daughters. He was surely going to show up any day now. He was the ultimate survivor. Eli would outlast us all.

Sometimes during those mental battles for Eli, I viewed a kaleidoscope of visions; I saw him during the time he was pushing his boundaries, the time when he was young, the time when he fooled us into a game of hide and seek; I saw him in the distance, having that playful eye as we called for him, "Eli, Eli …" I saw him when he was older, in that ragtag, black Mohair coat, coming in from a storm; I saw him down at the barn, with his big grin, so big, so true; I saw him taking me to his camp, and his lean-to with all his furs; I saw him at the church altar with his new bride, his fingers working in his language, signing out to Nancy, 'I will look after you.'

"Eli, Eli …"

# ACKNOWLEDGMENTS

I'd like to thank my wife, Elaine, for her endless editing, critiquing, and her patience in bearing with me on this writing adventure. It has, no doubt, been a long row to hoe. But we wouldn't have it any other way, now would we?

Thank you to Linda Allen, Joseph Schmalenbach, and Thomas McLain for their kind critiquing. I'm so fortunate to have you as friends.

And I'd like to make a very special acknowledgment to Dave Sabosky, who has worked with me for over 20 years. Thank you, Dave!

This book wouldn't be what it is without all their efforts. As far as I'm concerned, you all are gifts from God. Thank you all so much.

31448991R00218

Made in the USA
San Bernardino, CA
09 March 2016